STAGES

K. R. DHROSO

Dhroso, Kalyn R., 1986—
Stages : a novel / by Kalyn R. Dhroso. – 1st ed.

Summary: When Roxanne Clarke meets a stranger, Luke, she is unaware of just how much of an impact he will have on her life. Through everlasting grief from the death of her father, turmoil with her twin sister Regan, jealousy from her best friend Tyler, and the anxiety of her first year away at college, Roxanne finds Luke to be more than just a friend or lover, but someone who will eventually save her from herself.

ISBN 978-0615707303

Printed in the United States of America

For my husband, Andi—
I've been so blessed to have you in my life. No one pushes me
harder and gives me the encouragement I need more than you.
I love you.

PREFACE
ROXANNE

It was my graduation day.

It should have been one of the many happy milestones in my life, but I couldn't force myself to smile. As I sat in my black cap and gown next to all my fellow seniors, including my evil twin sister Regan, I peered into the stands to find my mom, my best friend Tyler, and some extended family. I tried to smile as they caught my glance. For their sake, I needed to seem excited. But deep down inside, my stomach hurt with grief. There was one person that was not sitting with the masses of people. The one person I wanted to be there more than anyone else.

His death was four and a half years ago. I never stopped grieving his loss. I never fully reached that "acceptance" phase. My father was everything to me. He was my friend, my teacher, and my coach. I had absolutely no idea what I was going to do without him. He wasn't there for my high school graduation and he wouldn't be there for my college soccer games, my college graduation, the father-daughter dance, or the birth of his future grandchildren.

As my thoughts drifted back in time, I recalled our last family vacation together. My parents, my sister, and I were in New York City to celebrate the New Year in Times Square. My father was leaving the next day on a plane to Paris, France for a business trip. His position as the CEO of his own finance company occasionally took him away to different countries to make negotiations with international investors.

He loved traveling and his work but was always full of joy to return home. Without him, our family just never felt complete. That New Year's Eve was the best day I ever had, primarily because it was the last full day I would ever spend with my dad.

I remembered dropping him off with my family at his gate inside the John F. Kennedy International Airport. Of course we were sad to see him go, but we always had the comfort that we would be seeing him again soon. I couldn't help but notice the travelers around us as my family members said their individual goodbyes. As my eyes wandered, I found a young teenage boy watching us. He held a look of sadness, clearly missing his own family. I smiled faintly, letting him know I understood his loneliness. Kissing Dad goodbye, we had no idea that that would be the last time.

We had only begun to worry about his flight when my mother hadn't heard from him eight hours later, when he was scheduled to land in Paris. After calling his phone multiple times and leaving messages, Mom decided to call the airlines to check on his flight status. Sitting in our kitchen, I waited for her to tell me his flight had been longer than expected or had to land at another airport due to inclement weather. I never got that simple answer.

I watched as my mother crumpled to the floor, phone still attached to her ear, horror flashing across her face. I ran to her and called for my sister. Patiently, I waited for her to say something. Leaning in to hear the lady on the other end, I heard, "Mrs. Clarke, I am so sorry..." I couldn't listen any longer. I will never forget the look on my mother's face, coupled with those last words I heard over the phone.

Once the sobbing momentarily subsided, my mother calmly, slowly explained to us, "The plane your father was flying on began having trouble while flying over the ocean. They're unsure what exactly happened, because communication was disrupted. They believe there was a bad storm...and lightning..." She couldn't continue.

Her helpless expression spoke more than her words. We all sat on the floor, holding each other for what seemed like hours. Time was lost.

At that moment, my mother became one of my most prized role models. She desperately tried to manage our lives with the same gusto as before the accident. At first, I couldn't understand how she was able to move past the mourning, until one night I heard her crying behind her closed bedroom door. Picturing our family without him was difficult. Our mom was brave and strong and I admired these qualities, knowing I could never be like her. She held the family together as much as possible.

His bodiless funeral took place the day before school started back. Life as I knew it was changed forever. My faith became makeshift. I prayed to God every night that relief from my internal pain would come. Why my family? Why *me?* My father was a good man. He didn't deserve to be punished. We didn't deserve to be punished.

Relationships also changed. I couldn't manage to be social anymore, which led to cracked friendships at school. I was unable to be the same person I was on New Year's Eve. By contrast, my sister recovered much more quickly than I did. I would say I never really recovered. She was able to keep her life together, moving on swiftly. I was unforgiving at her ability to remain sane and normal. I was jealous.

After that January, my twin sister became just another girl who happened to live in our house. Our sisterhood would never be the same. In fact, I loathed her most of the time. She responded with similar feelings, though I didn't know why. Why did she have any reason to be upset with *me*? I wasn't the one that disregarded our trip to New York like it never happened. She lived in a fake world where pain didn't exist. I lived in a world where pain never ceased.

My thoughts shifted back to reality as I realized those around me were beginning to stand. It was time to graduate. I inched forward, the line in front of me growing shorter. The girl to my left stared at me as I erupted with a loud sigh. I didn't want to move forward in time. I wanted to go back to that snowy, cold night standing in a crowded Time Square, thousands of people huddled together, as the ball dropped on the New Year. How desperately I wanted to be there. Instead, I was in humid, sunny Florida, graduating with 223 girls my age. They were consumed with thoughts of the college life awaiting them in a few months, while I couldn't shake the picture of my father from my mind.

I stepped another foot closer to the aisle, only realizing that my sister was receiving her diploma and inevitably, my turn was next. I looked up at the Principal, surrounded by the School Board. "Roxanne Olivia Clarke," rang the voice of the valedictorian into the microphone. I inhaled deeply and made my feet move. I breathed evenly as I thought sarcastically to myself, *cheers to the rest of my life.*

STAGE ONE

DENIAL

1

ROXANNE

Crunch, crunch. Huff, huff.

It was five o'clock. It felt exactly like five o'clock, so early in the morning. I knew I had been running for at least an hour, though I didn't bring my watch this morning. Sometimes it was easier to run long distance without the constant reminder of time. The thought of time could slow you down. You just have to move your legs and pray your lungs can keep up.

The air was brisk and the trail smelled of wood, swamp, and horse. The smell was routine, a part of my life here. I was on the St. Francis Trail in Ocala, Florida in late May. Horse country. Swampy wetlands surrounded the trail, the outside world hidden behind the greenery. As the washed out gravel and hugging branches engulfed me, reality seemed far away.

Crunch, crunch. Huff, huff.

The sky was still dark, which I preferred. It never took long for my eyes to adjust to the darkness. My favorite part of running so early in the morning was always daybreak. I welcomed in the light. I felt like I was watching mother earth awake from a long sleep. The trees swept over the worn path on both sides, making a tunnel of infinite green. The ground was painted with twigs and fallen leaves, marked on each side with two lanes, for the coming and the going. It was easy to lose yourself.

Crunch, crunch. Huff, Huff.

I heard the crunching sound of bicycle tires against the ground. Another second later, a cyclist passed me quickly. I could feel the wind rush against my left side with the pass. I watched the bicycle's back reflector light flicker and eventually fade as the cyclist dashed into the tunnel of trees.

Crunch, crunch. Huff, huff.

Crunch, crunch, crunch, crunch...

In what seemed like a matter of seconds, I realized I was being passed again, though this time it was by another runner. *That's odd,* I thought. I had been running this trail every day for months and hadn't found human interaction on foot until at least six o'clock.

The runner was male. He swiftly moved beside me, like a gazelle. Our steps were in synch. Out of the corner of my eye, I could see he wasn't wearing a shirt. His body was fierce. I desperately tried to keep my eyes forward, willing myself to concentrate on my breathing. I figured he would pass me soon enough.

For a minute or so, we both raced forward, staring not at each other but straight ahead. It was as if we had planned this run together. I was confused. *Who was this guy?* But I couldn't keep my thoughts off his physique and the way he moved. He ran so gracefully. With every stride, his breath kept the beat. I wondered how long it would be before he spoke.

"So tell me," he started, a minute later. I glimpsed toward him. He was gorgeous, with a strong jaw and friendly face.

He continued, "What is a pretty young girl doing running this early in the morning? Aren't you afraid to run in the dark?"

I made a face. "What are you doing?" I asked, courageously.

He returned my look with curious eyes. "Running. What are you doing?"

I rolled my eyes. "This," I pointed back and forth between us, referring to the conversation that was taking place. I preferred to run alone. "What are you *doing*?"

"I already answered that question," he said. "Next question."

"Okay, then, why would I be afraid?" I shot back.

He recognized the defense in my voice. "Well, it's just that it's dark and you never know who you will come across on a public trail."

I smirked. "Someone like yourself?"

"Clearly, I'm not a threat." His dark eyes pierced me. Somehow, I knew he was right. Although he was definitely more built than I was, I was sure I could take him down. I pictured myself using all the self-defense moves I learned in karate many years ago. I almost laughed aloud at the thought.

I snapped out of my daydreaming. "And why is that?" I tried to sound tough. I hoped it worked.

His response was simple. "Because I'm harmless."

"How do *I* know that?" I asked him.

"You don't."

"Exactly."

"That's exactly why you should trust me."

"That makes no sense," I argued.

"What makes sense is that you shouldn't be out here by yourself." In that moment, I could picture my father giving me that same advice. I was not thrilled about that connection.

I was in no mood to continue talking. Although feeling slightly exhausted, I sped up. Who cared if I had already been running for miles and miles? No one would tell me what to do.

As I moved ahead of him, my mind wandered back to the image of his body and the way it was so mesmerizing. The urge to slow down was almost overwhelming. Despite the temptation, the memory of his annoying words kept me at a quick pace.

"Where are you going?" He sounded disappointed. "Aren't you worried something will happen to you and you won't have anyone around to help?"

Rolling my eyes, I didn't turn to look behind me. He was proof of why I didn't date. I didn't need someone to protect me.

It was almost six in the morning and still quite dim outside. Although I tried to push my thoughts as far away from the trail as possible, my mind focused on him.

I didn't understand it. I couldn't escape him. Something about his voice...and his body...I tried to force myself into distraction without success. I continued to increase my speed. The trail would be crossing the path that lead to my neighborhood soon. I was ready for the first chance to get away.

Crunch, crunch, crunch. Huff, huff, huff, huff.

My breathing came heavy now. My side cramped from the increase in pace. I concentrated on pushing through it. I was far ahead of him when I turned to see the distance I had put between us. To my surprise, he wasn't pushing his luck. It actually seemed he was slowing. I was glad, yet, disappointed.

I couldn't remember the last time I had received so much attention from a guy before. I had guy friends, sure—well, really just one—but this was different. Almost like *flirting*. I shuddered in my steps. Flirting was not my thing. Really, I had no idea *how* to flirt!

I could hear crunching twigs back in the distance. *Still there*, I muttered quietly to myself.

The sun was rising easily over the tunnel of trees now. The air was becoming thicker, sticky. I was certainly familiar with humidity. Loathing the air's thick moisture would never change.

It was quiet. I hesitantly turned my head to look over my shoulder. No sign of anyone. I breathed easier. Before I could turn to look forward again, I felt my foot catch something hard. Next thing I knew, my knees gave out beneath me and I was in the dirt.

Great, I thought as a rush of pain hit me, *twisted ankle*. And I was alone.

I sat flabbergasted on the stiff, graveled ground for a minute as I tried to concentrate on anything but the pain. Twisted ankles were an injury I was accustomed to after all my years of playing soccer, but the pain seemed intractable. It hurt *a lot*.

I pleaded with myself not to cry. I was almost eighteen years old and I could take care of myself. Scrunching my face together at the pain, I could feel the buds of tears in the corners of my eyes. *Stop being a baby!* I screamed at myself. *Just get up and go home.*

Fighting back the undeniable tears, I struggled to stand and balance on my good leg. I inhaled a deep breath, brushed off the dirt from my shorts, and prepared myself to walk the rest of the distance home. As I slowly put more weight on my twisted ankle, I realized that I was not going anywhere quickly. *I can get through this,* I reminded myself, *just slowly. Slow is good.*

With each limp step, incredible pain shot through my ankle. I bit my lip to focus and tasted blood. I bent over and put my hands on my knees, bargaining with myself. *You have had worse injuries. Keep walking!* I tried to remember the last time I saw a runner hurt on the trail. The memory never surfaced. No such memory existed because the average runner did not traumatically get hurt during a run.

My head was still lowered when I heard the sound of spitting gravel beneath tennis shoes coming toward me. I quickly blinked away my tears, relieved that I would have some help getting home. A sigh rang out under my breath and I braced myself for the humiliation I was going to face. At the same time I lifted my head to greet the on-comer, my jaw dropped.

All I could manage was, "Why you?" Unfortunately, he was still as beautiful as he was a few minutes ago.

He raced toward me, his face filled with worry, yelling, "Are you okay?"

Before I had a chance to express any sarcasm or frustration, my stranger was at my side, pulling my arm over his shoulder and bracing my weight to begin walking. I was aware that the trail became dangerously quiet. The only thing I could hear was the sound of his breath. Despite the heat, goosebumps prickled my arms and a cool sensation came over me. As an attempt to extinguish the unforgiving pain, I slowly inhaled through my nose with each step.

"Are you cold?" I asked, anxiety creeping up within my chest.

The guy looked at me oddly, sweat dripping from his forehead. "What are you talking about?"

"I don't know..." My head began to spin.

"Maybe you're in shock. Just calm down," he suggested.

Anger hit me before I could manage a second step. My anxiety dissipated, irritation sinking in. "I don't need your help." I couldn't help but recognize that it *was* easier to walk with him practically carrying me.

He laughed at me. He actually laughed! *What a jerk.*

"I would have to disagree."

In my stubbornness, I threw his arm away from me and attempted to walk by myself. I could be self-sufficient. I didn't need him or anyone else. I lifted my chin upward, managed a prideful smirk, and stepped forward. I nearly collapsed.

Before I could decide what to do next, he scooped me up in his arms like I was weightless and stalked forward. *Humph.* I folded my arms across my chest with a look of disgust on my face, though I was surprised at how enthralled I was by the feel of his arms around me.

After a minute of silence, he spoke in his soothing voice. "Didn't I tell you it wasn't safe to be running by yourself? Now look at you." He eyed my body swiftly and then held my gaze.

His sly comment and outright confidence was enough to make me forget my pain temporarily. "Stop! Put me down." He hesitantly listened and softly set me on the ground.

He stared at me at a distance of a few feet. He crossed his arms over his bare chest in an expectant way. I feebly glanced in his direction. As the blood rushed down into my foot from being upright, my ankle began throbbing. I winced. He didn't make a sound or move at all. He just stood there, his eyes piercing right through me.

"Who *are* you?" was all I could bare to say through my gritted teeth.

His mouth formed a half-smile. "Luke."

"Well, *Luke*, I should tell you that I don't normally accept help from strangers."

Those brown eyes of his brightened as he answered, "We're not strangers anymore."

I cackled. "We most definitely are strangers. You don't know anything about me. For all you know, I'm a serial killer." I raised my eyebrows as if to challenge him.

Luke uncrossed his arms and stepped toward me. "Your name is Roxanne and you are not a serial killer."

2

ROXANNE

I saw him there, sitting at a table in the corner near the front.

The café was very crowded, with the sounds of different tongues mixing together to form new languages. I was absentmindedly ignoring the conversation happening at my own table with my family. My head followed the movement of each person as they passed our table. I watched each facial expression and all the hand gestures to decipher the foreign words. The culture was entrancing. I did not speak Italian, but was able to pick up certain familiar words.

The older boy was laughing and chatting with another boy. The smile on his face was contagious—I could only smile watching him. He seemed carefree, the very characteristic I wish I possessed. His face lit up the room—that or the sun was intensely bright that day. Italian boys were handsome in their own distinct way. Their dark hair and olive skin was radiant. All the beautiful faces accented the more beautiful, romantic city of Venice. I secretly wondered how much my plain-looking American family stood out amongst the natives with their striking features. How would my simple look compare to the gorgeous Italian females here? I figured I would only be noticed for my stark contrasting differences.

In the background, I thought I heard my name. Breaking my gaze away from the boy in the corner, I turned my focus back to the table. When I looked back, the boy was staring at me. He wasn't smiling as he once had. The charismatic appearance he had carried was gone. Although he did not smile, his brown eyes were soft.

Blushing, I quickly averted my eyes. I wished I had more confidence and that I wasn't so embarrassed about everything that had ever happened to me. I shouldn't even have given myself credit for his attention—he was probably looking at someone behind me.

Pretending to pay attention to my dad drone on about his past trips to Italy and going into intricate detail about every attraction he saw, I caught my sister's eyes across the table from me. She mouthed, "What?" I shook my head. I would tell her later. She shrugged in response. My twin was not only my sister, she was my best friend.

A few minutes had passed and it was becoming too hard not to look back around the room. Maybe if I were innocently glancing around, my obvious staring wouldn't be so obvious. I worked my eyes from table to table, starting at the back of the small, traditional, hole-in-the-wall café and making my way to his table. I hoped I wasn't noticeable.

I took a courageous peek in his direction. Not only did he meet my gaze, but his smile had also returned, beautiful and infectious. I couldn't refrain from greeting his gesture with one of my own. My face radiated warmth, surely appearing flushed.

Suddenly, I heard my sister yelling at me.

I was aroused from sleep with a start, hearing my sister ramble loudly as she rummaged through my room.

Groggy, I tried to pull my thoughts together. Although I realized that I was dreaming, my dream was a very real memory. It was very old, involving every member of my family. And a handsome, Italian boy. A strange sense of déjà vu overwhelmed me. His face was a blurred vision as I tried to recall the details of my dream. Had I seen him before? Surely not.

"Where is it?" she yelled at me.

I pulled my blankets over my head. The sound of her voice was annoying me more than ever.

Jumping on my bed, she yanked the covers down. "Tell me!"

"What," I angrily asked, "Do you want?" I grabbed my blankets back.

"Where is my pink shirt?" she asked, forcing the blanket back into her hands.

I slapped my hand over my face. Sighing, I reminded her, "I don't wear *pink*!"

"You took my shirt, you little thief!" With ease, she whipped all of my blankets and sheets from my bed and threw them aside.

Laughing, I said, "Oh, was that the one I accidentally bleached?" I shrugged. "Whoops."

Stomping her feet loudly against the floor, my sister made a horrid sound and left the room. "I hate you!" she yelled back to me.

"Ditto," I mumbled to myself, pulling the covers from the floor and back over my head. The one morning I wanted to sleep in, I was disturbed.

I closed my eyes, hoping I was still tired enough to fall back asleep. The image in my head of the boy was fading. I had already forgotten his distinct features. Before the dream, I hadn't given one thought to the handsome boy in the café. It had been so many years ago. Under my eyelids, I tried to picture his glowing face, but it was very vague. I sucked in a deep breath, exhaling slowly.

I struggled to ignore the background sound of my sister ranting around the downstairs and my mother's efforts to calm her down. I wasn't sure how my mother survived life with two teenage twin girls. Soon, she would complain about graying hair and how we had been the reason for it.

Recognizing my sleep was extinguished, I rolled onto my stomach and stared at my wooden headboard. I wanted to see that face again. It felt so strangely familiar. I sighed another long sigh. I knew I couldn't live in this dream world for very long.

Sluggishly, I got up. I walked over to my dresser, pulling the top drawer open and peering down into it. My choice in apparel was very casual, not owning much of anything fancy. I grabbed and pulled on a pair of jeans and soccer t-shirt, then grabbed flip-flips from the closet. Tapping my chin, I pondered how I would spend the rest of the day.

"Roxanne!" I heard Mom call from below. She had a deliberate way of making her voice shrill in the morning.

"What?" I called back, hoping she heard.

Mom repeated, "Roxanne!"

"Coming!" I shouted, trying to hurry down the stairs. I was reminded of my healing ankle with every step. It had only been a few days since my embarrassing fall. Quickly, I tried to push the memory of the injury and the obnoxious boy from the trail from my mind.

As I made my way into our kitchen, I noticed Mom had a coy smile. I could only imagine what she was up to.

"You'll never guess who I just spoke to," she said, trying to catch my curiosity.

"Did the university call to take back Regan's letter of acceptance?" I asked, sarcastically.

"I heard that!" screamed my sister from another room on the main floor.

"Good!" I screamed back.

"No, of course not," Mom waved me off. "But still, guess!"

I rolled my eyes. "Mom, I have no idea."

"Elaine McAllister. You remember her. She and her husband coached the track team at your middle school. Such a sweet lady..."

I searched my brain for some wave of recognition. I would have run track in middle school, but I was preoccupied with soccer. "Didn't she have that geeky son that wore those huge glasses?" I started laughing at the memory of the pudgy boy, who clearly didn't look like he belonged in a family of runners.

Mom's face fell flat. Quietly, she said, "Yes, I believe that was him *five years ago.* Funny you should mention him. Elaine will be so elated to know you remembered him!"

I could sense what my mother was getting at. "What have you done?"

She pursed her lips and brought her fingers up to her mouth. "I, sort of, set you up with her son."

"What!" I shouted.

"Well, you won't date Tyler so..."

"No! Why would you do that to me?"

Mom's eyes brightened. She reached into her pocket and pulled out a photograph. Handing it to me, I hesitantly accepted it.

"Ben's so handsome now! Look, no glasses!"

I shook my head, sighing loudly through a clenched jaw. I held the picture loosely in my hand, not bothering to look at it. It didn't matter what he looked like; I wasn't going on a blind date.

"No way, Mom," I handed her back the picture.

"It's sort of a done deal."

I stared at her dumbly. "What?"

"You are meeting him tonight for dinner and a movie."

"What is wrong with you? I can't do that."

"He's cute, Roxanne!"

"I don't care. I'm not going on a date with him!"

Mom folded her arms across her chest. "Oh yes, you are."

My eyes widened. "You can't make me."

"Honey, just do it. For me? It would make me so happy to see you out with a nice boy."

A grunt escaped my throat.

"I don't care if you never see him again. Just this once?"

Covering my face with my hands, I thought about the consequences of saying yes to her proposal.

The sound of heels pierced the air, clicking obnoxiously against the tile floor. Snatching the picture from our mom's hand, Regan grinned. "You would pass this up? You're such a loser."

I stuck my tongue out at her.

"I'll date him if she doesn't," Regan informed Mom.

Mom pointed her finger at Regan. "You date *too many* boys. Can't you pass some along to your sister?"

Regan and I both laughed out loud simultaneously, a rare occurrence.

Regan spoke first, "None of them would *ever* date her."

I added, "And I would never date any of *them!*"

"I don't see how two people with matching DNA can be so different." She turned to me. "So, will you do it? For your momma?"

I sighed, nodding my head. "Just this once."

She grabbed my shoulders, beaming. "Thank you! You won't regret it, I promise." Mom followed her words with a wink.

Oh, great, I thought, *what have I gotten myself into?*

I arrived at the restaurant approximately five minutes early.

The picture Mom gave me was the only way I had of recognizing him. Unfortunately for me, I left the photo at home. If I had any luck, the guy wouldn't recognize me either and I could go home sooner rather than later.

It was almost seven o'clock. I was already beginning to count down the hours before I could go home. If all else failed, I would pretend to become violently ill and skip out on the movie.

I was dressed in jeans and a plain yellow shirt, accented with a pair of casual black flip-flops. It was clear I wasn't trying very hard, though I thought I at least looked presentable.

As I waited on a bench outside the restaurant for my blind date to come sweep me off of my feet, I watched the various people walking by. Against all hopes, I had to reasonably assume that my mother had given Mrs. McAllister a picture of myself for her son to use to identify me. At least I wouldn't have to approach him first. Suddenly, a lump swelled inside my stomach. I was starting to feel a nervous rumbling, making me sick with nausea. There was a good chance I wouldn't have to fake my illness.

Someone tapped me lightly on the shoulder, causing me to jump slightly. My time was apparently up; I would have to suffer through the date. When I turned to greet Ben, I was unpleasantly surprised.

"What do *you* want?" I asked the guy from the trail, who was staring at me expectantly.

He looked at me oddly.

I leaned in close, my voice barely over a whisper, "I'm waiting for someone, sorry. No time to chat." I shrugged my shoulders and turned away from him, again scanning the faces of the people passing by, pretending to search for my company.

I inherently knew he hadn't moved a step.

He abruptly cleared his throat.

I looked back at him, glaring. "Yes?"

"I have some bad news."

My mouth dropped slightly, my eyebrows raised. "Excuse me?"

"I don't think he's coming."

I folded my arms across my chest. "You can leave now."

"Wouldn't he already be here by now?"

I shouldn't have responded, but I couldn't stop myself. "He might be running late."

Luke shook his head. "Do you really want to date someone who is not punctual?"

I scowled at him. "I really don't want to date anyone!"

Chuckling at my honesty, he said, "Then, might I ask, why you are here, waiting patiently for someone, who is not only late, but also someone you aren't interested in?"

I didn't respond. He was obnoxiously right.

He continued to stare awkwardly at me, trying to read my expression.

"He'll come." My voice wasn't solid.

Quickly, Luke replied, "Sure, sure he will."

"I don't care what you say."

Suddenly, I sensed Luke's posture stiffen. He hastily turned to me and grinned. "Alright, then. Have a wonderful night." With his parting words, he turned on his heels and began walking away from the restaurant. I was filled with questions, even as ruffled as he made me. I assumed he was waiting for someone, waiting to eat at that restaurant, anything that would make sense. I definitely didn't expect him to walk away.

I waited.

I waited twenty minutes for Ben.

I sat quietly as the minutes ticked away. I was growing impatient and irritated at both Luke and Ben. Maybe Luke was right; maybe Ben wasn't coming.

Sighing, I rose from the bench and brushed off the back of my pants, deciding that it was time to leave. That was what I wanted anyway, right? Grabbing my purse, I turned to scan the area once more for any sign of my late blind date.

I rolled my eyes as I saw Luke in the distance, strolling casually back toward me, hands in his pockets. I was learning he was very unpredictable. I considered walking away but my feet wouldn't move.

As he approached, I heard him mumble, "So, no show?"

Looking briefly at the ground, I humbly smiled. "Why are you here?"

"Well, you must be hungry. Can I offer you my company?"

I had to admit he was right about Ben, and I considered his suggestion. What could it hurt to eat dinner with him? I was starved.

Lightly shrugging, I said, "Sure, I guess."

"Great," he grinned, ushering me toward the restaurant entrance. He pulled open the door for me.

"Roxanne?" I heard a male voice call out from behind us just as we entered the building.

Turning, I curiously searched for the owner of the voice.

"Roxanne?" the guy said once more. He was medium-height and build, with shaggy brown hair. He had fair skin with a glaze of tan, which wasn't uncommon for most guys residing in Florida.

"Yes?" I responded, quite confused.

Then it struck me. No, it couldn't be.

I muttered, "Ben?"

He nodded enthusiastically. In his hand, he held up a twenty-dollar bill and pointed to Luke. "I changed my mind. I don't want your money."

Turning briskly to face Luke, my face flushed red.

"Jerk!" I yelled, pushing him aside. I started walking away from the restaurant, so frustrated I wanted to scream. When I passed Ben, I sincerely apologized, "I'm sorry... I can only take so much humiliation in one night."

How could I be so easily fooled?

3

REGAN

There was nothing better than the beach, beer, and friends in the summer.

The sun was warm on my skin as I lay in my bikini on a beach towel next to my best friends, Stacy and Leah. Sporting our flashy sunglasses, we gossiped and tanned while the group of guys we came with set up for beach volleyball. The light breeze traveled at the perfect speed, gently brushing my skin and ruffling the loose strands of my hair. It was hard to keep from thinking about how much I would miss my friends once school started in a few months.

I turned my head to Stacy. "So, what's going on between you and Matt?"

She grinned widely. "Oh, nothing."

The three of us looked to the guys in the sand, fumbling with the net to make it straight. All of our guy friends were attractive and their charming personalities were hard not to fall for. We all had very casual relationships; never hurt feelings, just in it for fun. Although we would never admit it, none of us could resist any of those boys.

"We've heard *that* before," commented Leah.

Suddenly, a splash of cold water hit my body and I jumped. "Ah!"

"Wet swimsuit contest!" hollered Jared, Matt's brother, after pouring a bottle of water on the three of us.

"Pervert!" we cried in laughter, drying off with our towels.

I began to settle back down in the sand when I saw him.

He approached our friends, seemingly interested in joining the volleyball game. He was tan with the build of a swimmer, his swimming trunks riding low on his hips. I sat up on my elbows to get a better look. He wore a backwards hat with dark, curly hair sprouting from underneath. His upper body was sculpted to match a god.

"What are you looking at?" Stacy asked.

"Matt's off the market now," Leah joked.

They followed my lead and sat up, instantly appreciating my drawn attention.

After a moment of silent awe, Leah asked, "Wow, who's he?"

I shook my head. "I wish I knew."

We watched as he momentarily glanced in our direction. Synchronously we all waved at the gorgeous man. He laughed.

From behind, our friend Tim mumbled, "It's rude to stare, you know."

I turned around, smiling. "You're just jealous!"

He shrugged bashfully and joined the rest of the guys on the sandy court.

"Do you think they all feel threatened by him?" Leah questioned, watching their interactions with the newcomer.

"Oh yeah," Stacy and I responded simultaneously.

"Well, he's right, we probably shouldn't stare." Lying back down, I closed my eyes, letting the sun drain my energy, the image of the handsome guy sketched into my mind.

"To each her own, girl," Stacy said, continuing to gaze at the stranger.

Eventually she got bored watching the game and joined us in relaxing, letting the music from the speakers nearby drown out the slurs coming from the guys in their efforts to smash the volleyball.

Abruptly, I was awakened from my light sleep as the volleyball hit my leg. "Ow!" I blurted out, sitting up and rubbing the newly acquired sand off me. I could hear the guys laughing.

As I peered up, I saw him running toward me. I held my breath.

"Are you okay?" he called out, his voice filled with concern.

I smiled and nodded, "Yeah, I'm fine. It just surprised me."

He grinned, his perfect white teeth glistening in the sun. Picking up the ball, he tossed it back to the group, but didn't move. I removed my sunglasses, thankful that Leah and Stacy were still asleep next to me. I wanted all his attention to myself.

He cocked his head to the side. "You look just like someone I know."

I frowned instantly. "That's funny. I get that all the time."

He stuck out his hand. "I'm Luke."

I took it gently. "Regan."

"So, are you by any chance related to a certain girl named Roxanne, who happens to look *exactly* like you?"

I pursed my lips. "Do we really look that much a like?"

Luke nodded.

I grumbled as he sat down in the sand next to my towel.

Holding his knees with his muscular arms, he said, "Believe me, that's not a bad thing."

I eyed him suspiciously. How did he know my sister? She only had one guy friend and I didn't even understand why *he* stuck around.

Before I could ask him my dire question, Luke said, "So, I have a question for you."

Though unsure of why he was probing me, I nodded. "Go ahead."

"What's your advice to a poor guy who can't get the attention of a certain girl?"

Was he really asking me this? I thought. He should *not* have trouble getting attention.

"I'd say she's crazy," I barely muttered, drawing pictures in the sand.

"Thanks, but her sanity isn't up for debate. What do I do?"

I stared at him. "Are you referring to my sister?" The thought made me want to vomit.

"And if I was?" he asked, squinting at me with his chocolate brown eyes.

"I'd say that *you* were crazy."

Luke's smile shrunk. "You don't think I'm good enough, do you?"

"Ha!" I laughed out loud. "Are you kidding?"

He was obviously confused.

"Listen, my sister... she's a different breed."

"I'm not following," he admitted.

I shook my head. "Look, I don't know how I can help you."

"Maybe you could, oh, I don't know... tell me everything you know about her? Maybe then I could sweep her off her feet."

I paused, considering what he was suggesting. He was making me nauseous. It was clear this guy didn't know the *loving* relationship I shared with my sister.

"So?" he asked. "Can you help me out?"

I couldn't resist his innocent smile. "Sure, I'll see what I can do."

His face lit up, placing a hand on my forearm. His touch was soft and cool. "You're the best, Regan."

It was difficult not to return his gesture, so I smiled back. "So, now I have a question for you."

He looked wary but nodded, "Shoot."

"How do you know Roxanne? She's never mentioned you before." I didn't add that she never told me anything.

"Well, it's a long story..."

"You don't look like the guy in the picture," I said, remembering the blind date she was forced to go on.

Luke laughed. "What picture?"

Wrong guy, I thought. "Oh, never mind."

"Okay, I met her on the trail, running. Then I saw her the night of her blind date, which I presume is what you were referring to, and well... I sort of paid her date to not show up."

"How much?" I asked, curious.

"Twenty," he shyly admitted.

"That's pretty low."

He bobbed his head slowly. "Yeah, I guess I shouldn't have paid him off. That was desperate."

"No, I meant, you should have offered him more. Twenty was too low."

He chuckled, considering my suggestion. "Maybe you're right. If I had given him more, there would have been no possible second thoughts."

"Exactly," I agreed.

"No, but seriously, it was pretty desperate," Luke said, looking between his knees into the sand.

I shrugged. "Yeah, it was. But you had good intentions."

He peered up at me. "Did I?"

A cold shiver went through my body as I stared at him.

The silence was short. Luke stood, brushing off the sand from his trunks.

Too quickly, I asked, "So, when will I see you again?"

His mouth formed a brilliant grin. "Don't worry. I'll find you."

I must have looked puzzled as I watched him turn around and amble down the beach, away from the guys, the volleyball game, and me.

4

LUKE

This was going to be harder than I expected.

I didn't want to lie, but I had to. I didn't want to pretend I was obsessed with getting a girl's attention, but I had to. And I definitely didn't want to use her sister in the process, but of course, I had to.

Even with my pure intentions, I couldn't deny that one lie would inevitably lead to another. There was no way around it. Should I have just been honest? No, not really. That would have ruined the whole plan. I had a job to do. It should have been that simple but I was beginning to recognize that nothing was ever that simple.

This had to be the hardest thing I have ever had to do. Life was not about me anymore. This was my first assignment and I didn't want it to be my last. I had to be successful. I *could not* fail. Failure was not an option. I was so very afraid of failure.

It was going to be hard to keep my head straight through the entire course of action. I had to be strong.

But what if I couldn't be strong enough? I forced myself to never consider the possibility.

All in all, I *was* a mere human. But I *must* not feel like one.

5

ROXANNE

Tyler was absolutely my favorite person.

But I wasn't going to tell him about my horrendous blind date experience.

He was my best friend of fifteen years. You could say he was like my brother, even though others would disagree. The rumors about our "friendship" were numerous. Even though we didn't attend the same high school, the mockery didn't stop. The evidence against us was clear: we attended every school dance together, studied together, and spent most waking hours together. I could even recall back to our first day of kindergarten. That was when all the awful, childish teasing began. I imagined that the rumors wouldn't end with our graduation from high school.

I had to shamefully admit that Tyler was my only way into the male mind. Since he was the only male I had ever really spent time with, I was uncomfortable interacting with other guys. On the contrary, he never seemed to need help when it came to females. I wasn't sure what I would do if Tyler ever got a girlfriend. Thankfully for me, he never dated. I knew my luck would change eventually, especially once we entered a campus of thousands of students, half of which were female. I didn't care to imagine his arm around another.

Tyler was the reason for my staying in Florida. He had received a full-ride scholarship to the University of Florida because he was so smart. High school had been a breeze for him. He wanted to be an engineer. School was fairly easy for me also, but only because I had a built-in tutor as a best friend.

Unlike Tyler, I was attending college in search of something other than academia. I was going to rule the soccer field for the next four years. The ends of my lips curled upward into a smile at the thought. I had the grades to get in almost anywhere, so it didn't really matter where I went to school. My dream was to coach soccer and if I could achieve that at the University of Florida, then I was content.

Tyler was sitting on a barstool at the island in my kitchen staring at me. "Can't you just *pretend* to be excited? We're leaving Ocala and starting new lives! What's better than that?" He was glaring at me now. I was relaxing in the loveseat in the living room trying to find my happy place—away from thoughts of school.

I scrunched my face together. "Gainesville is only forty-five minutes away. I wouldn't exactly consider that *getting away*." Ocala and Gainesville were literally down the highway from each other. I continued, "Can't I just be happy for you? Or *pretend* to be?" He nagged me more than my mother.

I was excited about going to college, but not for the same reasons as Tyler. I was ready to start playing Division One soccer as a midfielder. Soccer was all I knew. I was anticipating an ultimate devotion to the sport so that I wouldn't have much time to think about other things. I worked better on a schedule. It was so much easier to be busy than to be bored.

Tyler had more sound reasons for his excitement. He was anticipating interacting with new people and starting classes. I had never met anyone more engulfed in learning than Tyler. He was very intelligent. He was lucky. At least I had my legs.

He tilted his head to the side like he does when he wants me to be serious. "Most kids can't wait to leave home and go to college. Why are you being so difficult?"

"The only thing I'm looking forward to is—" He didn't let me finish.

"Soccer. Is that all you care about?" I didn't see Tyler frustrated very often, though I was an expert at provoking him. "Soccer isn't everything. Don't you want to make new friends? Maybe meet a guy? Having a boyfriend wouldn't kill you, you know." Although he was trying to make a point, I recognized his jealousy. He was the last person who wanted me to have a boyfriend.

"I meet guys all the time..." My mind floated back to the trail. I hadn't thought about that morning in a few days. I had avoided the trail and the restaurant for fear of crossing his path.

Tyler's mouth fell open. "Don't kid yourself."

"Hey!" I gaped at him. He was right, I knew. "Alright, so maybe one guy, every now and then."

Tyler smirked. "That's what I thought." He looked smug.

I wasn't going to let him off the subject easily. "What about you? You aren't one to work any magic on the girls around here."

My best friend was not only intelligent but also motivated and driven. Additionally, Tyler was a very caring person. He was definitely the perfect guy for someone—not me, but someone. He would make a girl very happy someday. I hoped I would be dead before I saw that happen.

He shrugged slightly. "Not interested." That was his usual response to my few inquiries about dating. I knew Tyler well enough to know that he was indeed attracted to girls, though he never mentioned any in particular. We intentionally didn't broach the subject often.

With that, the topic was dropped, and Tyler went back to the more important conversation at hand. "So, what classes are you signing up for?"

I was tired of all this school talk. "Does it matter?" My irritation seeped into my voice.

His eyes didn't meet mine. "I guess not."

I waited patiently for him to speak again. His voice was slightly higher than the average 18-year-old boy. He also spoke fast, flashing his white teeth in a large smile throughout his speech. Tyler looked like an exact replica of a pop singer. His sandy short hair looked perfectly sculpted. His skin was soft and sun-kissed. His lean body sat hunched over a course catalogue, casually browsing his options for the fall semester. It did bother me a little that he never dated, as I knew I was the very reason. He was so attractive. He didn't need to spend all of his spare time with me. Some girl out there was waiting for him. I should feel lucky, but I felt guilty instead.

"Do you think you'll find a girl at school?" My curiosity was taking over.

Without looking up, he answered, "I don't want to talk about it."

I shot an annoyed glance his way. "Tyler."

"Okay, how's this? I'm not looking."

"You should look." I regretted the words as soon as I spoke them. All at once, I was speaking the truth but not wanting to acknowledge it.

Tyler continued to stare down at the catalogue, though whether he was actually reading I wasn't sure. I saw his eyes shift, but not in my direction.

I sighed loudly, so he would hear. "Okay, you're not looking."

With a slight glance, he noticed the worried look in my face. In a swift movement, he slipped off the barstool and sat beside me on the loveseat, placing an arm around my shoulders. "Hey, look, we haven't gone to the same school for four years. This will be a good change for us! I just want to have fun with my favorite girl and the rest will fall into place." His charm forced me to smile.

"There's that beautiful smile." He grinned. "Well, I've got to be off to help at the barn."

Ocala was known for horse racing and breeding. Many residents owned horses. Tyler's family, as well as mine, didn't invest in the horse business, but he earned money by working for a family friend. He absolutely loved it.

"You should stop by later, if you want. Call me, alright?" he called as he sprung off the couch and headed toward my front door.

"Sure thing." I wished he didn't have to leave me. I always enjoyed his company, even in silence. We understood each other. I would probably take him up on the offer to see him.

With the sound of the door shutting, I snuggled deeper into the loveseat. I debated about taking a shower—I hadn't changed since my run that morning. The debate didn't last long. I leaned my head back against the couch, folded my arms across my chest, and closed my eyes.

I woke a few hours later to the sound of my cell phone vibrating. I wearily slipped off the couch and staggered to the kitchen for my phone. After spotting it, I flipped it open. NEW TEXT MESSAGE. It was from Tyler.

WHERE ARE YOU? ARE YOU SLEEPING?

He knew me all too well. I responded: I WAS UNTIL YOU WOKE ME. SEE YOU SOON.

I hurried up the stairs into my bedroom to change into clean clothes. I replaced my running shorts with comfortable jeans and switched out my tank top for a t-shirt.

I opened my closet doors to throw in my running shoes and grabbed older tennis shoes to wear.

Racing out of the house, I made sure I had my cell phone, my wallet, and car keys. I auto-unlocked my car as I locked the house up. As much as I loved running, I also enjoyed driving my new, hefty, yellow Nissan Xterra. My Nissan was a gift from my mom for getting college paid for with soccer scholarships. Another reason I loved my Nissan was that it was the one thing I owned that I didn't have to *share*.

Jumping into the driver's seat, I shoved the key into the ignition. I robotically turned the music up and flung my seat belt around me. *Click.*

Windows down, wind through my hair. Oh, how I felt free!

The drive would take close to ten minutes. My family lived across town from the horse farms, but it was such a nice, peaceful drive. The trees were a brilliant green against the sky's blue background. White patches of cloud dotted the scene. The sun was warm on my arm as it rested on the door. Momentarily, I was thankful I was staying in Florida for school. I didn't want to leave the brilliant, sunny weather.

I turned right off my street heading toward a main road. Reflexively, I looked in my rearview mirror. My mouth dropped as I recognized who was behind me. The man looked an awful lot like my stranger and the one who sabotaged my blind date, recognizable by a backwards hat and warm smile. I blinked purposefully, hopeful I was imagining him.

He was driving a very plain, older, white Toyota Corolla. His face was relaxed, as if on a refreshing drive through the country. I gawked at him, hoping he would notice.

A stop sign was fast approaching. I slowed to a gentle stop at the four-way intersection, checking all directions for oncoming traffic. Taking my foot off the brake, I felt the car ease forward. And then—it died. I cursed under my breath and tried the ignition again. I heard nothing but a grinding sound and felt a sense of panic. *This car is new! This can't be happening...*

"Need some help?" a strangely familiar voice spoke, right outside my window. I turned toward the voice and almost fainted. It was *him*. I inhaled deeply in an attempt to slow my quickening heart rate. I felt the sweat beading on my forehead as I stared into those eyes. I wasn't sure what to feel at that very moment: anger or relief?

I finally managed to speak. "What are *you* doing here?" I had asked him that very question before.

He rested his arms on my windowsill, looking behind my SUV at his own car stopped behind mine feet away. "Well," he began, "It seems to me, but correct me if I'm wrong, that your car has died."

"Oh, really, I hadn't noticed," I said curtly. Trying the ignition again, I heard the grinding noise and sighed.

"Do you mind popping the hood?" Luke asked too politely.

"Yes, I do mind, actually." I folded my arms across my chest in protest and huffed.

"So you want to be stuck here until someone calls a tow truck to have your precious car hauled out of the middle of the road?"

"That actually sounds like a good idea. Thanks." I wasn't budging.

Without permission, Luke reached his long muscular arm through my open window and grabbed the knob that unlatched my hood. After the *pop*, he ducked over to the front of my Nissan and hitched the hood up on the metal stands. The sun reflected off the yellow hood and pierced my eyes. I blinked away the bright spots consequently left on my vision. As soon as I could see, I slipped off my seat belt and pulled my door latch to get out in objection. It wouldn't move. I hit the *unlock* button and tried again. Nothing. *What is going on?* I frantically tried to see around my hood to see what he was doing to my car. There was no getting around the massive hood to investigate. I jetted across the console and heaved my body into the passenger seat. I tugged the door latch on that side and shoved against the door. My weight was not enough to dislodge the door. Climbing back over to the driver's side, I called out the window, "What do you think you're doing? And why can't I get out?!"

He chuckled and peered around the hood to look at me. "I'm helping you. You could at least show some kindness. And if your doors are stuck, maybe you need to take this thing in for a check-up. It doesn't seem safe at all." After he spoke, he disappeared back into the engine. There was no sound coming from the front of the vehicle.

Settling back into my seat, I forcefully exhaled through my parted lips. I didn't understand why I couldn't get out. Was my car defective? Did Luke have something to do with my car malfunctioning? *But how?* I wondered. I tried not to fret. How did he tamper with my locks right in front of my face? Shaking my head at the possibility, I tried to dissolve the thought.

I stared unknowingly at the steering wheel. Not knowing what else to do, I tried the key again. Against all odds, the loud noise turned to a soft hum. *Yes!*

Suddenly, I heard the hood slam and Luke stalked to my window. "Are you trying to kill me? You could have at least told me you were trying the ignition again."

"Do you want to know the honest truth?" I asked, wanting nothing more but to leave.

"You really shouldn't lie," he advised.

"Neither should you," I defended.

Anxiously, I checked again for oncoming traffic. The coast was clear. Now was my chance.

Speaking quickly, I said, "I really have to go." And with that, I thrust my foot onto the accelerator and made a left turn out of the intersection. I sighed heavily in relief. Why couldn't I get away from this guy? I never had trouble getting rid of boys before. More often, I felt like I repelled them.

Glancing swiftly into my rearview mirror, I caught sight of the white Corolla turning left onto the same road. I was dumbfounded. *Why wouldn't he leave me alone?* I asked myself. I had to admit that his interest was a bit endearing, but only a bit.

The white car was approaching faster than I had expected. Cautiously, I decided to pick up the speed. Forty-five miles per hour...50...60...65. If I got stopped for driving 15 miles per hour over the speed limit, it would be saving me from having a stroke from frustration. I would take the ticket.

Against my better judgment, I peeked into the mirror again. He was still there, staring right at me. I could feel the heat flush through my face; I was annoyed. Half of me wanted to forget about it, the other half wanted to slam on my brakes.

I didn't understand why he followed me. I knew boys could be stubborn and annoying, but he was different. There was something about him, but I couldn't put words to the description. I wasn't used to this—the chase.

Arriving at Mr. Stockfield's barn was my top priority. Concentrating on clearing my mind, I turned up the music. I simultaneous felt my heavy foot against the gas pedal and watched the speedometer increase to 70 miles per hour...

I finally arrived to the gated entry to the farm and I could see Tyler's red Ford 250 truck parked outside the horse barn in the distance. Quickly, I reached outside my window to press the entry button. The gate swung open at my request and I lurched forward onto the property. Checking my mirror again, I was relieved to find myself alone. I barely sighed, still unnerved that I was being followed. The gravel flung up to hit the underside of my SUV as I traveled down the unpaved driveway. I parked my car next to Tyler's enormous truck and hopped out. Peering into the barn, I searched the numerous faces to find him. *Where was he?* I anxiously thought. I warily smiled at some familiar faces, not remembering any names, and trying not to draw any undue attention to myself. There were probably 25 workers in the 30-stall barn. Most of the workers didn't speak English, so I wasn't afraid of offending anyone when I didn't strike up conversation.

As I turned to head to the business office, I bumped right into someone. It was Tyler. "Oh!" I gasped.

"What's going on?" he asked, concerned.

"Do you have any repellant?"

His eyebrows furrowed in confusion. "For what?"

"For boys," I answered, folding my arms across my chest.

6

TYLER

W hy was I the one that had to endure this?

Didn't Roxanne have any girl friends to talk to? I already knew the answer to that question: not one. Sure, she had plenty of girl *acquaintances*, but no one worth spending time with. Roxanne spent most of her time with me. I wasn't going to complain about that.

I unwillingly listened to her talk about this guy like it was a funny joke. Although I couldn't read her mind, there was something obvious about the way she talked of him. She pretended to be annoyed, of course, but I knew deep down inside she was flattered. How was it fair that this guy comes along out of nowhere and grabs her interest but I have been after her for years and we're still only just friends? I must be doing something utterly wrong. I needed some advice.

We walked to my truck for some privacy. Part of me itched to figure out what this guy had that I didn't. I wanted to know what made her face light up. I wanted to be the one to make her look like that.

"He's weird," Roxanne commented. "I don't get it. He doesn't even know me." She jumped into my truck, shutting the door behind her.

I followed, asking, "Roxy, why is it so weird that a guy is interested in you?" Roxanne must be oblivious to her pretty face and flattering figure. She was beautiful in every sense of the word. Her freckles accented her tan face in a very cute way. Her cheeks were full, making her smile contagious. I wished she would let me run my fingers through her long thick hair, but she hated that. I recognized that if she had gone to a public high school, many guys would have pursued her. For this, I was glad she had gone to an all-girls Catholic school.

"I don't know. Paying off my blind date and following me around isn't exactly my vision of a perfect romance," she answered.

"He sounds desperate," I added, making sure it was clear I didn't approve.

"I know, right?" Roxanne agreed. I silently sighed in relief.

I listened to her recall her blind date experience and the morning on the trail after she sprained her ankle. I wished that I had been there with her. If only I had thought to surprise her on a blind date. And maybe I should start running with her. Granted, I would slow her down. I was not as athletic, especially in long distance running. Even more than that, I would have to lie to her about why I wanted to tag along. A bodyguard was not what she was looking for and I knew that. I couldn't help but be protective of her. She meant everything to me.

We sat facing each other in my truck as she continued. She recalled how annoying the guy was while running on the trail, how he knew her name. Then she told me about his offer to take her home, which sent a chill up my spine. Thankfully, she declined and made it home on her own. I always told her to keep a phone with her, but she never listened. Roxanne finished her recap, "I turned to see if he was following me. And then..."

"And then?" I questioned, curiosity undeniably leaking from my voice.

"Gone. He was gone. There was no sign of him anywhere," she finished. "I should have been relieved, but it was so weird! And then he shows up at my blind date, pretending like my date stood me up, offering me dinner."

"It was weird for good reason," I agreed. My eyebrows creased with worry and I pleaded, "Please don't go running in the dark anymore. And don't go on blind dates with guys! It's not safe. I don't care who your mother knows."

She shook her head from side to side. "Oh, don't worry, I won't. I learned my lesson. And just so you know, I went against my will."

"Yeah," I said, absentmindedly.

"And apparently it doesn't matter where I am! I have run into him three times in the last week. So weird."

I looked into her eyes, my face stone-like. "Are you afraid?"

"Of Luke?" she asked.

"No, the boogie man," I said sarcastically.

She shrugged her shoulders. "I don't know. Should I be?"

"Well, yeah!" I raised my voice.

Squinting in my direction, she questioned, "And why is that?"

"Roxy," I began, "Isn't it a little suspicious that he's found you three times now?"

Her eyes were soft. "What should I do?" she asked, turning her head to stare at me. I was instilling fear in her, as I had hoped.

"Do you want to know what I think?"

"Yes," Roxanne answered. Anxiety was creasing her smooth skin.

"Well," I smiled, and then continued, "I think you should stay at my house from now on. It'd probably be best if we slept in the same bed, so you're protected, of course. And for safety's sake, we should go everywhere together."

Punching my arm, a smile cracked across her lips. "You're an idiot."

I lifted my hands up in defense. "It's only to keep you safe."

"Right, I'm sure of it. I would also guess that you would have to stand guard in the bathroom while I showered, too?"

"Well, of course." I couldn't help but grin. Her expression mirrored mine.

"You're such a guy," she stated.

"Why, thank you," I responded.

We sat quietly for a few minutes. Different thoughts were rushing through our heads. I wanted so badly to be able to read her mind.

Roxanne's head was cocked to the side, concern moving across her dazzling face. "What are you thinking about?"

"I'm just worried. I don't want anything to happen to you." There were so many words I wanted to say, so many.

She managed another smile. I almost melted, but I had to keep my cool. "I'm glad I have you. To protect me, I mean." She rarely admitted her need for others; this was a promising step in the right direction.

Casually, I reached for her hand and interlocked our fingers. Just a friendly gesture we took part in occasionally. "You can count on me."

She was carefully rubbing the back of my hand with the tips of her fingers. Didn't she know how this shredded me on the inside? We had decided many years ago that we were only friends. Well, *we* didn't decide that; *she* decided that. We could only be friends, according to her. I had always wanted more than that, but I also wanted to please her, even at the expense of my own feelings. I woke up every day lying to myself that she would see me for what I was—the only one for her. I found myself fortunate that she never seemed interested in any guys, all except for this one, of course.

"I like you," she spoke gently, patting my hand. I could barely hear her speak over the pounding in my heart. *Get a grip*, I demanded of myself.

"And I like you," I responded. I didn't just *like* her, but I knew she wasn't admitting her undying feelings for me.

"Why don't we get out of here?" I suggested, trying to avoid an awkward situation, at least for myself.

"Don't you need to finish working?" Roxanne eyed my playfully.

"Nah, I will just tell Mr. S that you were having one of your girl mental breakdowns and that you desperately needed a shoulder to cry on. He's married; he'll understand." I grinned, praying that she would laugh.

Surprisingly, Roxanne pulled me into a hug, refusing to argue with me. "Okay, fair enough. Where are we going?"

"I can't believe you even have to ask," I answered, grinning widely, appreciative of her willingness to leave.

The corners of her lips turned upward, a thoughtful expression settling across her soft face. I instantly knew where her thoughts were.

Urgently, I hoped out of my truck and jogged to the main office. I pleaded my case with my boss, Mr. Stockfield, who graciously granted my leave without further questioning. I practically skipped back to the truck, jumping up into the driver's seat and slamming the door shut. I turned the keys in the ignition and listened as the engine roared to life. My eyes turned to my best friend, who was watching me. "Ready?" I asked anxiously.

She nodded, a beautiful smile accenting her already beautiful face. Where else would I rather be?

Clearwater Lake was one of the many lakes corralled within the limits of Ocala National Forest. With a one-mile perimeter, it was ideal for taking strolls and benefiting from the weather that central Florida had to offer its inhabitants year-round. Numerous trees lined the lake, and it was spotted with benches for resting. Geese populated the place and it took skill to avoid the evidence of their occupancy on the surrounding path. At the perfect angle, the sun would spread its light across the rippling waves of the lake, reflecting just enough to force passersby to shield their eyes from the brightness.

I brought Roxanne to the lake the first time I asked her to go out with me during our freshman year of high school. She said no, of course. Regardless, this has been our spot, per se, since that very day. I would never forget that afternoon, filled with memories of good and bad emotions.

Tyler, you know you mean the world to me.
I agreed. *But?*
But that's exactly why we can't be more than us...what we are now...
I was confused. *Why?*
I can't love you as more than a friend. If I lost you, I couldn't bear to live with myself.
Now I was dumbfounded. Who was talking about love here? And what's this about being lost?
Maybe it doesn't make sense to you...
You're right.
...But trust me, it's better that we love each other as friends.
There again with the love talk.
I know it doesn't make sense, but it will someday. Then you will understand.
I would never understand girls. Ugh.

I was fourteen years old then. I didn't comprehend her words; I had no idea what it meant to really love a girl. Furthermore, I had never lost someone that I loved and, ultimately, I couldn't relate to her. Not long after that conversation, I realized she was *afraid* of losing someone she loved again. The first time was enough for a lifetime. Even with that knowledge, I was still ignorant about the situation. She purposefully rejected me, believing that she was saving herself in the long run. I guessed I couldn't blame her, but it did hurt.

It hurt the first time I asked her and it would continue to hurt through the last time I asked her. I must have been a slow learner. All I knew was that she was worth the rejection.

Many days we spent at the lake, talking about our futures and mindlessly joking about the answers to life's fundamental questions. We enjoyed picnics, Frisbee, walks with our dogs Lucy and Max, "studying," reading, swimming, and occasionally running—very occasionally—on the outlying cement path. There was no other place like it and it would always be *our* lake.

I pulled into the nearly empty parking lot and shut down the engine. The parking lot overlooked the lake; it was a glorious view. We held so many memories here, I wondered if the lake meant as much to her as it did to me. Without turning my head, I shifted my gaze to her face. She sat quietly, staring into the water just as I had a second before. Aware of my eyes, Roxanne turned to smile at me. We were on the same page.

"You know, it's been awhile since we've come here," she asserted, hoping down from the truck cab. "Why is that?"

"Oh, I don't know," I started, shrugging as I followed her lead. "I guess we've been busy. I've been working and you... well, you... what *have* you been doing?" I questioned sarcastically, winking at her. Before I shut the door, I pulled a worn blanket out from behind the driver's seat.

"I've been busy!" she declared. "I've been training for soccer. That's hard work."

I tried to look smug. "Right. Hard work. I'm pretty sure a task that requires little effort does not qualify as *hard work*. Now, manual labor is a whole different ball game."

Ready to refute, Roxanne opened her mouth, "Hey now—" Suddenly she stopped, as if having an epiphany. "That reminds me! The Cardinals are playing the Reds tonight!"

I shook my head, refraining from laughing. "You are so easily distracted. How can you function day-to-day?"

"Oh, that's easy. Because you keep me straight." Roxanne began purposefully walking faster as she spoke, heading diagonally toward a wooden park bench planted twenty feet away.

My eyebrows furrowed as I reluctantly followed. "I hope you realize I will not always be around to take care of you. And where are you going?"

At my words, she abruptly stopped and spun around to face me. Concern flushed her already pink-tinted face. "Why would you say that?" Roxanne asked, ignoring my question.

I was confused. "Roxy, you don't *need* me. You can take care of yourself. What do you think will happen when we graduate college? I mean, eventually we will move away from each other." I stared into her reddening face, rapidly realizing that my words had made her eyes swell with tears. I quickly spoke, "Oh, now, c'mon Roxy... don't cry."

In a swift wipe from her palms, Roxanne cleared all evidence of hurt. Her voice slightly shook as she disagreed, "I'm not crying." She sniffed twice and hesitated before speaking again, probably making sure her voice was steady enough to speak clearly. Looking at her feet, she asked, "Why do you want to move away from me?"

I grabbed her by the shoulders and lifted her chin up toward my face, now only inches from her own. "Are you serious? If I could live next to you forever, I would. I don't *want* to move away, but the likeliness of it—"

Roxanne interjected before I could finish, distinct irritation in her voice. "What? The likeliness of it is what?"

I was sick of this game. Against my better judgment, I spoke words that had been on my mind for so very long. "Stop kidding yourself Roxanne. The reason you never want to talk about the future—a future involving other people—is because you don't want anyone else to be in your future. You want me! Why is it so hard to admit this to yourself? I try to convince myself that you only want to be friends, but I can't do it. I cannot *force* myself to believe that you don't want me the way I want you." I quietly inhaled a deep breath; my heart beat quick in my chest. As I calmed down, I sighed, thankful that I didn't unload the powerful words I promised myself I wouldn't say.

Without a sound, Roxanne turned her back to me and began walking toward the bench. I trailed her steps from a few feet behind. I only slowed when she reached the bench and ungracefully plopped down to face me, her face stern. She learned forward, propping her elbows on her legs and cradling her face between her hands. I decided to take my chances and sit down beside her. I distinctly put more distance between us than usual, as I knew what was coming. I was used to this routine.

After a minute, she changed her posture to look into my eyes. I patiently awaited my rejection. Maybe it wouldn't even hurt this time. Finally, she spoke, almost too apologetically, "You know we can't be more than friends." Oh, who was I kidding? It would always hurt to be rejected by the love of your life.

I wanted to scream at her. I wanted to force her to be honest with herself. At the same time, I wanted to hold her in my arms and kiss her. I could only imagine what that would feel like. Not one time did I muster up enough courage to steal a kiss. Fear entrapped me, I guessed, but fear of what?

Disappointed in my tolerance, I mumbled, "I know."

Roxanne rose from the bench, grabbed the blanket I was carrying beneath my arm, and stalked off in a familiar direction. I instinctively knew where she was headed—asking myself if this was really a good idea right now—and hesitantly stood to follow along.

Many trees, of all types and sizes, surrounded the lake. The biggest tree, a wide oak, sat adjacent to the water, swaying gracefully in the light breeze. Since we were kids, Roxanne and I had claimed this tree as our own personal playground. As we got older, instead of playing make-believe around the trunk and branches, we used the tree as shade to talk. In all the years we had come to the lake, there had never been another spot for us.

I watched Roxanne carefully as she spread the blanket out under the shade of the oak's leaves. As if in a routine, she laid down on her back, crossing her legs at the ankle and pulling her arms back to support her head. Shockingly, she looked peaceful, an uncommon occurrence.

The grass was a soft cushion beneath my body as I lay down next to her. I was trying to act as collected as she was, though I was not sure I was putting on a good act. I mimicked her actions by crossing my own legs and bringing my elbows up behind my head. I sighed loudly, and then immediately wished I had remained quiet. I was surprised when she didn't move an inch to react to my presence and audible frustration.

I decided to break the tension with one of our common questions, "What are you thinking about?"

Roxanne continued to stare straight ahead, into the masses of green leaves and thick, brown branches sprouting off the tree's trunk. "I don't feel like talking right now. Can we just enjoy the silence?"

Nodding to myself, I agreed, "Okay."

After a few minutes of silence, I maneuvered onto my side to face her, propping my elbow for support. I fiddled with a fallen leaf from the tree as I thought.

My eyes lifted from the leaf to her face. Her eyes were closed, her chest rising slightly with each breath.

Impulsively, I leaned over. Before she could sense my presence, I softly put my lips to her own. The moment lasted longer than I could have hoped for. I was elated by this small milestone I had achieved.

Sitting up, she gently removed me with a hand gripping my chin. Slightly shocked, but with a sense of wonder, Roxanne shook her head.

"Let's not do that again," she casually demanded, lying back down. Her eyes closed again, and with that, the silence recommenced.

Silence with Roxanne I could handle. Life without Roxanne, I could not.

7

REGAN

I loved shopping.

Shopping was my favorite pastime, as long as I didn't include talking on the phone or hanging out with boys. I may have seemed shallow, but I couldn't care less what people thought about me. As long as I was happy, that was what mattered.

As I pulled into the mall parking lot, I whipped my little silver BMW into a spot close to the entrance. The less walking outside I did, the better; I needed to conserve my energy for the indoor trek. After I shut my door, before taking another step, I appreciatively admired my precious car. It was a gift from my mom—well, a mandatory gift, really—because she gave my sister a new car for getting a scholarship to college or something like that. I was going to college too, but my mom would be forking the bill out for that one. I wasn't nerdy enough or talented enough to get a scholarship. I didn't need to waste my time on things like homework or after-school sports when I could instead be enjoying my friends before we all parted our ways in the fall. I couldn't stand the thought of being away from them. I was nothing without my friends.

I glided toward the mall doors, designer purse in hand, ready to take over the place. I normally had no desire to go anywhere by myself, but today was different. I needed some personal time, hoping to relax and enjoy being with me, myself, and I. I was rarely alone these days; I was constantly joined at the hip with Stacy and Leah.

Stacy was heading off to New York and Leah off to South Carolina for school in August. I didn't know who would replace them. We have been the three musketeers since freshman year of high school. College wouldn't be the same without them. I planned on joining a sorority to make up for the loss in close friendship.

From store to store I paraded, trying clothes on here and there. I was recently endowed with my allowance and the money was burning a hole in my checking account. There was one thing I was proud of when it came to spending money: I was no easy pushover. On a typical shopping trip at the mall, I would go to each store I fancied once, without buying. After I had rummaged through countless clothes, belts, purses, and other accessories, I would go back through each store and buy the items I desired most. There was a method to my madness; I would know what each store contained, and therefore, I would not be disappointed with the purchases I made. I rarely made returns.

After the fourth store, I realized I was hungry and it was close enough to lunchtime. I was so quick to get to the mall that I hadn't managed to grab any breakfast before I left the house. Being the mall rat I was, I knew exactly where I was in relation to the food court. As I moved across the intersection of mall wings, past the kiosks full of cell phone covers and sunglasses, I began to smell an all-too-familiar scent. The smell of heaven: fattening fast food.

I knew fast food was bad for my body, but I honestly didn't have to watch my figure. For this, I felt extremely lucky. Amongst my friends, I was the only one that ate pizza more than once a year. Pizza was a part of my weekly diet, along with soda, hamburgers, pasta, and ice cream. My sister was also thin, but unlike myself, she actually counted her food intake. She was practically a vegetarian, with all her organic foods and soy milk. I shook my head in disgust as I thought of all the nauseatingly healthy food that filled our kitchen cupboards.

Once I received my hamburger and cheesy fries from the cashier, I grabbed a handful of napkins, five ketchup packets, and picked a lone table. My mouth was watering before I could even take a seat. As I picked up my hamburger, before taking the first tempting bite, I was tapped on the shoulder.

"Excuse me, is this seat taken?"

His smile immediately lit up the large room and his bright eyes stared down into mine. He was sporting the familiar backwards baseball hat that I recognized from the beach, with a small "LA" emblem directly above his forehead. His striped long-sleeve shirt and blue jeans made him stand out from the rest of the mall inhabitants with short sleeves and shorts.

Luke was pointing at the seat next to me, awaiting my answer. I was slightly awestruck; hopefully it wasn't obvious. I was instantly grateful that I hadn't taken a bite yet because my mouth was hanging slightly open.

"S-sure," I barely mumbled. Could he even hear what I said?

He pulled the seat out and sat down, his seat forward but body facing me. "Great. How have you been, Regan?"

I tried to compose myself. Clearing my throat quietly, I responded, "Oh, good, thanks. What are you up to?"

"Well, this *is* a mall. I was actually thinking of buying something. If that's okay with you, of course." Luke grinned in his sarcasm. I wasn't a fan of sarcasm, but maybe this counted as flirting.

My girl instincts kicked into high gear. I casually replied, "Are you here with anyone?" I looked around him innocently.

"No, no. I'm here alone. I was actually hoping to run into you soon, so good thing I came." I began to blush as he nodded toward my plate, "Nice burger."

"Want some? I wasn't going to finish the whole thing anyway," I couldn't help being coy. It was my nature.

"Not hungry. Thanks, though. I'll wait until you're done." Luke folded his arms in front of his chest and sat quietly.

Pushing my plate away, I decided I wasn't hungry anymore. He frowned at my abstinence from food. "Why aren't you eating?" he inquired, seeming concerned.

"I lost my appetite," I quickly responded.

"And why is that?"

"You surprised me, that's all." I could feel the warmth in my cheeks rise again from embarrassment as I poorly explained myself.

"You need to eat," he declared as he pulled my tray back toward me. Nodding in the direction behind us, Luke offered, "Hey, I'm going to run into that bookstore for a bit while you finish. Meet me in there by the Travel section."

I dumbly bobbed my head up and down in agreement. Rising from his chair, he pushed it back under the table and released a parting smile. "See you soon," he beamed, waving slightly, striding off toward the large bookstore.

Once he was out of sight, I shoveled down my food faster than I ever had before. I wiped my face with the remaining unused napkins, used hand sanitizer on my hands, and checked my face in my hand-held mirror for any repairable flaws. *Good to go*, I confirmed. I slipped out of the food court and headed into the store. Shamefully, I realized I had never once been in this bookstore since our move to Ocala fifteen years ago. I wasn't a big fan of reading, textbook or leisure. I would choose television over a book in a heartbeat.

Absentmindedly, I struggled through the various aisles, surprised at how many books there were. Aisles, aisles, and more aisles of books! I examined each section heading as I passed by the lanes of books, wondering where Travel would be. I spotted a sales associate and politely asked him to point me in the right direction. He pointed me toward the opposite end of the store and I thanked him. *Goodness*, I thought, *more books?* Weaving through more shelves of books, I finally managed to spot the Travel sign.

I walked into an aisle filled with informational books on different countries from around the world. My finger glided from title to title: Albania...Australia...Brazil...China. As I lifted my head to search for Luke, I was stunned to see him leaning against the end of the bookshelf, staring at me. "There you are," he said, half-smiling.

"Oh, hey. Sorry, I've never been in here before and it's way easy to get lost." It was especially easy when every aisle of books looked the same.

"Well, there's a first time for everything. Come, follow me, I want to show you something," Luke grabbed my hand and pulled me into the next aisle of books, my heart momentarily jumping out of my chest. There, I noticed a book hanging off the edge of the top shelf. He reached and pulled it down. The title read *Italy: A Traveler's Guide*. I stared at him with a perplexed look. Luke himself had a funny, childlike look on his face, particularly through his eyes. He looked younger for a moment.

"You look excited," I laughed.

He grinned. "Here, let me show you." I watched his fingers as he flipped from the index to the specific page he wanted. Without a word, he showed me the contents of the page: *Venice, Italy*.

"Is this where you're from?" I asked, my eyes glancing over the beautiful photographs of the elegant city.

"It's my home town," he affirmed, reading my expression. "Venezia..." Luke sighed, pronouncing the city's name slowly, in a loving manner. "You wouldn't believe there was a more beautiful city in the entire world."

I returned his smile, agreeing, "Venice is beautiful."

"Have you been?"

Nodding, I said, "Yes, maybe four or five years ago. My dad loves that place." Well, *loved*.

"Great, great."

I cocked my head to the side. "What are you doing in Ocala?"

Luke's face went flat momentarily. I waited for him to speak.

After a few seconds, he responded in a lighter voice, "Everyone wants to come to America." Luke's eyes seemed to brighten as he spoke. "I have friends of the family here."

"Oh, I can't imagine Florida being better than Italy. It's awesome there."

"Oh, really?" he absentmindedly asked. Then Luke smiled, "It's funny...we always seem to want what we have don't have." As he stared off into the distance, his face looked much older than he seemed.

My eyebrows furrowed with curiosity. "Sorry to change the subject, but how old are you?"

Too quickly, he responded with a sigh, "Eighteen."

"You make it sound like you've been eighteen forever." I laughed at the thought.

"Sometimes it seems that way." His eyes were soft.

"Nah, I heard life goes pretty quickly once you get into college," I tried to meet his eyes as I spoke. "So, where are you going to school?"

Luke's shoulders hardly shrugged. "Gainesville. But enough about me, I want to hear about you. Where are you going to school? What are you going to major in?"

I enjoyed the attention, but I was getting tired of standing. "Oh, I'm going there too! Do you mind if we sit down? All these books are making me dizzy." I smiled playfully.

"Of course," he returned my gesture with a wide grin, "Here, let's go sit over there by the fictional books. They have some really comfy chairs." Grabbing my hand again, he pulled me in the right direction. I was thankful he was leading the way.

Once in the fiction section, we each plopped down in our own chair. Propping his right elbow on the armrest, he rested his chin in his hand and stared at me intently. "So you're attending the University of Florida also?"

I had temporarily forgotten what we were talking about. "Yeah! I think I'm going to major in Journalism."

Luke seemed interested, "What kind?"

"What kind of what?"

"What kind of Journalism? Newspaper, magazine, broadcast?"

"Oh, broadcast. The cameras will be rolling, letting me come into the home of every American. What could be better than that?"

"You would like being on camera, getting all the attention. I think you'd be good." He spoke without a hint of emotion. I wasn't sure if that was a compliment or an insult.

"Thanks?" was all I could say.

"Don't worry, that was a compliment. You are very easy to listen to and of course, you're very pretty. Who wouldn't want to watch you give the nightly news?" Luke winked, grinning at me, his white teeth gleaming brightly.

My heart began to race as my cheeks flushed red. "Well, thank you."

Luke didn't miss a thing. "Ah, you're blushing. I feel honored." I thought I saw him move a little closer to me. I had to keep breathing; I had to relax.

Unfortunately, my compliments didn't last long. "So where is Roxanne going to school? Same place?"

Unintentionally, I frowned. Of course, how did I not realize the conversation would turn to my perfect twin sister? It was never about me. I felt foolish. I made a disgusted face. "Roxanne? Yes, unfortunately. With my luck, she's bound to grace me with her wonderful presence on more than a monthly basis since we're both living on campus. I pray we end up on opposite sides."

Surprise briefly emerged on his face as he recognized my hostility. His expression smoothly cleared to nonchalance. Luke chuckled, "I'm guessing you two aren't close, then?"

"No, not close at all," I confirmed. "But, I do have some dirt on her."

His eyes brightened. "Oh?"

I nodded enthusiastically.

Luke leaned back in the chair. "Well, let's have it."

"She absolutely *hates* compliments. And competition. She loves people messing with her hair. And junk food. Oh, and she doesn't really like sports other than soccer."

I watched his face intently. He slowly nodded his head, narrowing his eyes at the ground. I began to continue with my lies when he interrupted.

"You're making all this up, aren't you?"

My face fell. He was definitely not as gullible as I'd hoped. "Yes..."

He continued, "You really mean the opposite of what you said."

Again, I admitted, "Yes..."

"Got it." Surprisingly, he loudly chuckled once, a lasting smile on his lips.

A minute seemed to pass. I changed the subject. "So, why doesn't Roxanne like you?"

He dropped his elbow from the armrest. Shyly, he said, "I guess I don't know how to approach girls. I thought she would think I was...I don't know...charming, or something." His eyes shifted downward and he started playing with his hands. "I guess I was wrong."

I shook my head. "Why would you think that?"

"Like I said," he pointed his thumb at his chest, "desperate."

"You're not desperate." How could any girl not respond to Luke with utter awe? He was perfect. I guess that was why he liked *her*.

He shrugged. "Desperate for her."

Casually, I disagreed, "I don't see how a girl couldn't like you." I tried not to come off as vulnerable.

Leaning across his chair and into mine, he touched the top of my hand. "You're sweet. I really admire that quality."

I wasn't sure why I hadn't melted from my chair onto the floor. Before I could pull myself together, we were interrupted. I only realized this when Luke turned his eyes away from mine.

The sound of her voice pierced through the quiet atmosphere of the bookstore. "Regan, what are you doing here?" My sister strolled toward me down the fiction aisle, sheer shock across her face. "A bookstore is the last place—" she trailed off, eyeing the handsome guy sitting next to me, hand on top of mine. Her expression was furious, absolute fiery.

"So you think you're pretty sly, don't you?" Roxanne almost yelled, clearly repulsed.

Luke turned to look at me, barely smiling. He leaned closer and whispered, "Am I being sly?"

Folding her arms across her chest, she glared at the both of us. Solemnly, she declared, "I need to talk with you in private. Right now."

Simultaneously, both Luke and I responded, "Me?"

Roxanne pointed at Luke. "You first."

Luke willingly ascended from his chair and stood in front of her. His face was expressionless. "After you," he opened his arms and swung them to the side, allowing her to lead the way. Roxanne stalked off toward the doors leading outside. I was thankful the conversation was being taken outside; bookstore customers and employees were beginning to show some irritation.

The silence in the bookstore was deafening. It was almost too much to withstand. I sat alone in my comfy bookstore chair, desperately wishing I were a fly on the wall outside.

8

ROXANNE

I couldn't believe my own eyes when I saw him sitting next to my sister.

Holding her hand! Was I jealous or furious? I couldn't decide, maybe both.

Luke followed me as I pushed past the endless aisles of books and out of the store, stopping alongside the building. I turned to glower at him. "What do you want?" I yelled.

His face was straight, not even a flicker of emotion. "What do you think I want?"

I shook my head angrily. "Oh, no. Don't make this into a game. Tell me why you keep showing up everywhere I go and why you are here with my sister."

He stared above my head as he thought quietly. Finally, he spoke. "Well, to answer your second question, I happen to think your sister is very nice and I enjoy spending time with her. And I figured the answer to your first question would be obvious."

My head started to throb. "As a matter of fact, it's not obvious. And how do you know my sister?" I couldn't care less about my sister, but I had to know the answer.

Infuriating me, he smiled. "Well, you see, I happened to run into her here at the mall and she strikingly reminded me of you. I asked her if you two were related, and low-and-behold, she's your twin! Crazy how things work themselves out." Luke's smile grew wider.

"I don't believe you."

"Alright. You could always ask your sister, but you won't do that, will you?"

I stiffly frowned. "I don't need to ask her."

"Why is that?" he replied swiftly.

"I don't need her to tell me what she thinks about you. I'm sure you bewitched her like you tried to bewitch me on the trail and on my blind date. I can tell your type."

Luke laughed, too loudly. Taking a breath, he said, "You think I was trying to bewitch you? I don't even know what that would look like!" The cackling continued.

I didn't believe this was a laughing matter. "Then why are you following me?" There, I said it.

His eyes brightened. "So, you think I'm following you? Can't you give a guy a break?"

"Give you a break?" I asked, glaring at him.

"What does a guy have to do to get a date around here?" Luke rhetorically asked.

I shook my head. "Whatever it is, it's obviously *not* what you're doing."

"What do I have to do? I asked you outright, I offered to help you when you fell, and I tried to help you when you're car died. What else can I do?" His eyes were pleading now, the most vulnerable I had ever seen him.

I stood there, staring at his pathetic face.

Before I could answer, he continued, "And, by the way, I have yet to be thanked for my kindness."

My mouth dropped. I wanted to wake up from this nightmare. I knew guys could be jerks, but this was becoming ridiculous. I closed my eyes, hoping for answers to miraculously fill my head.

Understanding was all I wanted. Trying to calm myself, I opened my eyes. He was still there.

Against my better judgment, I lashed out. "Kindness? You have got to be kidding me! You have been following me ever since that day at the trail—maybe even before then—and I want you to know that I am *not* afraid of you!"

Luke's lips curled down into a mope. I could tell my reaction was unexpected. "You have no reason to be afraid of me. I really am harmless. Mere coincidences, that's all. Maybe a sign?" Even though his mouth remained still, his eyes brightened again.

Hatefully, I replied, "What do you mean *a sign*? Like, a sign from God? I seriously doubt that."

"Why are you so closed-minded? Sometimes things happen that are out of our control. Don't you know that everything happens for a reason?"

I concentrated on the meaning of his words. Although he was clearly referring to our nonrandom meetings, it was impossible for him to know how hard his words hit me for a different reason. Unsuccessfully, I tried to focus on Luke. But how many times had I heard that very sentence since the death of my father? A flood of bad memories rushed into my head.

I was unable to speak. Of course, I tried. But silence was all I had to offer.

A look of concern flashed across Luke's face when I didn't respond. "Are you okay? You look kind of sick." He stepped toward me. I tried to step back but found myself unable to move. I tried to nod my head, but that didn't work either.

"Roxanne? Please say something." He took me by the shoulders as I struggled to stay in the present. I felt nauseous. My yearning to stay pleasant to the people around me disappeared as I fought back tears. I thought I had finally conquered my grief. Wondering how I tricked myself into thinking I was strong like my mother, I realized I was lying to myself. My life was a big lie.

Suddenly, I felt extremely light-headed.

My head hurt as I slowly woke from unconsciousness. Opening my eyes, I quickly closed them in response to the bright light of the day. "What happened...?" I spoke to whoever happened to be around. Surely I wasn't alone. Wiggling my fingers, I recognized the texture underneath them: concrete. Why was I on the ground?

The voice that responded did not make me feel at ease. "You passed out. I guess my good looks were too much for you to handle." Even though I couldn't see his face behind my closed eyelids, I could sense a smirk. *Ha ha*, I thought.

I resisted the urge to go back to sleep and instead opened my eyes to look at the guy that stood kneeling on the ground next to me. I looked around. The bookstore's giant sign stood twenty feet above me. I struggled to get up, using my arms to brace my weight. Recognizing my difficulty, Luke lifted most of my body up without my help. "Do you want me to get your sister?" He asked, peering inside the store.

I refused, "Oh, no. I don't need her."

"Too bad I'm going to call her anyway." Luke snatched my purse off the ground and searched for my phone. I felt too weak to stop him. After retrieving it, he slid it open and pressed a couple of buttons. Pressing the phone to his ear, he waited. Then, he answered, "Hey, it's Luke...I'm outside with your sister. She passed out...Yeah, I don't know why...I know, I know...Do you want to take her home?....You want me to?....Are you sure?....Okay." He hung up and grinned at me. "Looks like your sister left you in my hands."

I could sense people were staring at me. I waved them off, trying to smile. "My sister would leave me with a mass murderer," I informed him.

"Lucky for you, I am not a mass murderer," he commented. Biting his lip, Luke began skimming the rows of parking spaces outside the store. "Did you want to take your car or mine?" I couldn't comprehend the look of distress on his perfect face.

"You are *not* driving my car. I can drive myself, thank you." I didn't need a chauffeur.

"Stay here, I will go get my car. You don't need to drive yourself anywhere after losing consciousness, *thank you*." He enjoyed mocking me and I was not fond of that.

I sighed and folded my arms across my chest as I watched him head into the parking lot. My eyes followed his position as he moved from row to row, apparently lost. Eventually, he disappeared from my line of vision. I gazed into the store window to see if I could find my sister so I could curse her out in sign language. Maybe she trusted this guy, but I didn't.

Hearing an engine pull closer, I turned my head back toward the parking lot. It happened to be a black Dodge Charger. Remembering Luke's car to be a white Toyota, I returned my attention to the window.

"Hey!" Luke's voice rang. I turned back around, where I caught sight of him in the driver's seat of a Dodge Charger, leaning his head toward the open passenger window.

My jaw fell slightly. I slowly walked forward, still hesitant to jump in the car with this stranger. Opening the passenger door, I asked, "So, what's this?"

He didn't understand, evident by the puzzled look on his face. "What do you mean?"

I sat down into the soft leather. Pulling the seatbelt around me, I clicked it into place. "The car. What are you, a larcenist? Do you steal cars for a living?"

He rubbed his chin. "Something like that. Does that bother you?" The car moved forward.

"Oh, no. I actually sell cocaine as my night job. We're practically one in the same," I joked, rather irritated.

"I didn't realize you even had a day job," he nervously laughed. "I would never have taken you for a drug dealer, though." Luke sped forward, pulling onto the main road in town. He seemed uncomfortable behind the steering wheel.

I leaned my head back against the sweet leather headrest. I silently prayed I would make it home in one piece.

Breaking the silence, Luke asked, "So, why did you faint back there?"

My head continued to pound between my temples. I kept my eyes shut to cover the pain. "I don't know. Hyperthermia?"

"Hyperthermia?" he responded, wary.

I opened my eyes and turned to face him. "Yeah, you know...having a high body temperature," I established.

His eyes rolled in annoyance. "Duh, I knew that. I meant, why hyperthermia?"

I shrugged. "Just a guess."

"That's not a very good guess," he pointed out.

"Does it matter?" I asked him, wishing for silence.

"Uh, yeah, it does. I would like to know if I need to take you to the hospital," Luke told me, with a hint of irritation.

"Don't worry, I don't need a hospital." I hoped he would stop questioning me.

Another minute of silence passed as we both stared straight ahead at the road.

"Why don't you sleep? You look tired," he commented.

"Are you kidding? I shouldn't even be here with you right now. And you think I should sleep while you drive me off to God-knows-where?"

"You ask too many questions. Just close your eyes."

To be fair, I was tired. I forced my eyes to stay open during the next few minutes of the drive. Against my will, my eyelids slowly drifted shut as the gentle vibration of the car against the road rocked me to sleep.

When I woke, we were at my house. "How did you know how to get here?" I questioned. As the car slowed to a stop, I pulled the door latch open and stepped out.

He mimicked my actions, shutting the door behind him. "Again with all the questions."

Luke was working hard to annoy me, I could tell. "It's really creepy."

"Your sister gave me directions. How else?"

That was a possibility. I decided I didn't have the strength to refute him.

I lead the way to the door. When I realized Luke was following me, I stopped. "Thanks for the ride. You can leave now." Turning my back on him, I stepped forward to try the doorknob. It was unlocked. "Hello?" I called into the house. Mom was probably parked in the garage. I crossed the threshold and paused inside the doorway.

The voice that returned my call was not expected. "Roxanne, is that you?" Tyler responded from the kitchen, his voice was growing closer. I heard his footsteps against the hardwood floor. He was quickening his pace to reach the door. As he hurried through the house, he informed me, "Your sister called me, which you know doesn't happen very often. I was worried when I saw her name on my phone. I figured it was an emergency. She said that I would be upset—" He met me at the door, stopping abruptly and staring past me. Confused at the sight of Luke, he asked, "Who's this?"

Luke came forward and held out his hand politely. "I'm Luke. Just a friend of Roxanne's." He turned his face toward mine with a smile. *Right*, I thought, *friend*.

Tyler's face was stout. He was not pleased at this revelation. "Tyler," he unwillingly accepted Luke's hand stiffly. "If you're her friend, why have I not met you before?"

Surprised, Luke responded, "Oh, I didn't know I had to ask permission to be friends with someone." *Uh oh*, I panicked.

Tyler barely moved his lips as he spoke, "Who said anything about permission? She's her own person. I've just never met you before." I could see he was trying to stay calm for my sake and I appreciated that.

Feeling a little nauseous again with all the bickering, I walked forward passed Tyler and sulked to the couch in the living room. I closed my eyes, resting my feet on the opposite end.

Tyler and Luke followed me into the living room. Barely opening my eyes, I noticed Luke pointing his finger between Tyler and I. "Is this your boyfriend?" he asked me, in an accusatory tone.

I stalled my answer. Part of me wanted to lie. That would have been the safe thing to do. Then again, I didn't want to confirm everything Tyler had been hoping for. I couldn't be anyone's girlfriend. Not now, not ever. I was damaged beyond repair. Trying to decide what to say, I looked knowingly at Tyler.

Sadly, Tyler sighed, "No. Just friends."

"Good thing," Luke grinned.

Silence filled the air. The situation was quickly becoming awkward. Feeling dehydrated and yearning to grab water from the kitchen, I swung my legs over the front of the couch and stood. As soon as I was in the upright position, I felt dizzy. "Oh..." I moaned.

In a split-second, both Tyler and Luke were at my side. Synchronously, they asked, "Are you okay?" I silently sat back down, trying to ignore the blackened vision and the question. Shaking my head, the spots began to dissipate and my vision was clear again. Both boys stood above me, concern etching their faces. After recognizing that I was fine, they turned to look at each other. They looked like two opposing football players after a bad referee call, the point right before a fight breaks out.

Anxiously, I cried, "Hey, I'm fine now." Their staring wasn't interrupted. I was beginning to get worried.

Being the first to break stance, Luke turned to face me. His eyes were filled with gentleness. How did he do that? Turn anger off and on like that? "I think I'll be going now." With a last glare at Tyler, Luke began walking out of the living room toward the front door. I could feel my heartbeat pick up.

Without thinking, I called after him, "Where are you going?"

He slowly turned his head and gazed at me. "Don't worry. I'll be back." He managed a parting smirk, then turned back around to leave. My breathing slowed.

Tyler stared at me as I watched the empty entrance to the living room. Dropping his body down next to mine on the couch, he asked, "Luke?" Irritation filled his words.

I wasn't sure what to say. I grimaced at his reaction.

"That," he stood, pointing outside, "is the guy?" Tyler sprang off the couch and began pacing the living room, running his hands through his short hair. He looked a bit frantic.

Stopping midstride, Tyler turned toward me. His face was an awful shade of red. I didn't like it.

He boomed, "Are you crazy? That guy is creepy!"

I was pretty sure I had dismissed that possibility. "No, he's not exactly creepy."

"How do you know that?" Tyler screamed at me. He had never once screamed at me in our fifteen years of friendship.

I weakly shrugged my shoulders. "I don't have a good answer for that. I just know."

Shaking his head, I heard him slightly laugh. "You're dumber than I thought, getting in a car with that punk."

"What did you say?" I asked, hoping I had heard him wrong.

"You heard me, Roxanne." His voice and face were unchanging. He meant what he said.

Quickly standing, and praying for no dizziness, I stalked out of the room.

Realization dawned on me. Where was I going? This was my house!

I headed back into the living room and stood in front of Tyler, arms across my chest. "Get out. Now!"

Without another word or look, Tyler stepped behind me and walked out of my house.

As soon as I heard the heavy door slam, I ran upstairs and threw myself onto my bed. How did this happen? I wasn't even sure I had experienced the last thirty minutes at all. My best friend was against me and I was sticking up for a stranger. This felt completely wrong. But against all rational thoughts, I couldn't deny the sweet voice ringing inside my head: sometimes, things happen that are out of our control.

STAGE TWO

ANGER

9

TYLER

I sat in my truck down the street from her house. She told me to leave, but she didn't say how far I needed to go.

My head in my hands, I quietly sobbed. Roxanne was my best friend. Well, I was absolutely, privately, obsessed with her. I loved her more than I loved my own life. I was beginning to question my sanity. I was consumed with desperation.

I didn't want to hurt her. That was the last thing I could ever imagine myself doing. The words that came out of my mouth in her living room were not the words of her best friend. I had to admit that mostly, I was jealous. The other small percent was a tad bit of fear for her safety.

Luke was undeniably good-looking; I could not contest the fact. The way he looked into her eyes made me cringe, though I was more disturbed by the way she returned his gaze. Why did she never look at me like that? What was wrong with me?

I wiped my runny nose on my shirtsleeve. Using my palms, I brushed my tears away. When she hurt, I hurt. She needed time to calm down, then I would reconcile with her. When it came to her wants and needs, I was a pushover.

I tried the ignition and my truck rumbled to a soft purr. With my opposite shirtsleeve, I smeared the rest of my tears away. Glancing at my face in the visor's pull-down mirror, I could only laugh at how bad I looked. Turning my eyes back to the windshield, I was astonished to see Regan standing in front of my truck, staring at me.

She moved around to my window and tapped on it. Déjà vu struck me. Rolling down the window, I waited for her to speak.

"I told you it would make you upset. I know you better than you think." Her smirk conveyed *I-told-you-so*.

I couldn't disagree with her, as much as I wanted to. "You were right."

She was very smug. "Thank you! Finally someone acknowledges that I'm not always wrong."

I tried to suppress a smile. "I didn't say you were right all the time. You're still wrong nine times out of ten."

Regan reached through the window and touched my face with her cool hands. Placing my hand over her hand, I closed my eyes. Letting the moment linger only temporarily, I grabbed her hand and gently pushed it back through the window. "Not here..." I reminded her.

"Do you want me to come over?" she casually asked.

I hesitated. My conscience was beginning to kick in. Guilt was not something I handled very easily. "I don't know..."

She leaned into the window. I could feel her breath. "Oh, come on, Tyler. Don't you want some company?"

It was true. I did want some company. But Regan's definition of *company* differed from my own. I could be eased with senseless television or video games, but Regan had a different idea of how to make me happy. And she was so good at it.

"Okay," I agreed hesitantly, "Hop in." Was I going to regret this later? Oh, yeah. I always did. Unfortunately, the disappointment I would have in myself never kept me away from her for very long.

Our relationship was complicated. She hated her sister and if I couldn't have Roxanne, I would take the person that most closely resembled her. I had to admit that every time I kissed Regan, I pretended I was kissing Roxanne. Did that make it right? By no means was it the moral thing to do. I was letting myself be conquered by my desire to be with Roxanne, but because she was unavailable, I took the next best thing, her sister. Sadly, a part of me really didn't care. As long as Roxanne never found out, I would be in the clear. I wasn't kidding myself though; I knew my secrets would be revealed at some point.

Although Regan hated her sister, I knew she wasn't interested in divulging our escapades to her. From the start, we agreed that this association was solely between her and me. No one else would be involved. Our goal wasn't to hurt anyone else. We just needed *company*.

I glanced at her from across the seat. Unsurprisingly, she was staring back at me. She remarked, "It's been too long."

"It should have been longer," I corrected. I was ashamed of myself. There was no point in denying the truth.

Changing the subject, she said, "So, you don't like Luke, do you?"

My teeth automatically clenched together at the name. "I don't want to talk about it."

Regan quickly recognized my retreat. She moved her body closer to mine and leaned her head against my shoulder. I silently inhaled a deep breath, taking in the sweet scent of her hair, finally feeling calm. Why couldn't things be this easy with Roxanne? Why didn't she want me? I shook my head, trying to forget her name for the time being. I questioned my feelings for Regan. I wondered if I could ever be more for her, not that she asked or anything. Regan was not my type; I knew that. In addition, a relationship with Regan would tear my relationship with Roxanne into a million microscopic pieces. I couldn't have that.

For now, I would have to be satisfied with Roxanne's substitute. I wrapped my arm around Regan's body and held her tightly.

10

REGAN

I thrived on the fact that if he wasn't with her, he was with me. My sister *did* have to share everything she had. Oh, if she only knew.

Despite my own need to be cared about, I also considered that when Roxanne found out—and I was sure she eventually would—it would make my life worth living. I wouldn't tell her now, of course not. There was no reason to break her now. Someday I would need to bring this up. I would wait for the opportunity. The funny thing was that she would have nothing to argue about. Tyler had asked her out more times than I could count and she had continuously rejected him. Tyler needed to move on. Even though she wouldn't admit it, I knew Roxanne was secretly in love with him. She would never tell me that out loud, but I knew.

Sure, I liked Tyler. He was hot and very affectionate. Not dating material for me, though. He was too...nice. This was strictly revenge. Plus, he was such a good kisser.

Eventually, Tyler was going to get a girlfriend and Roxanne was going to have to get over it. He was a perfectly good boyfriend candidate. I longed for the day he would get married. I could only dream about her reaction!

Until then, I counted on continuing our little secret. It was fun, thrilling, really. Roxanne had no idea what she was missing.

I waited patiently on his bed while Tyler showered in his connected bathroom. He had only finished up working at the horse farm to check on Roxanne. The smell didn't bother him but I insisted. I wasn't going to complain; he always smelled like heaven when he got out of the shower. It made spending time together that much easier.

Lying back and stretching out my legs, I recalled how this relationship came to be. I remembered we were about sixteen. Tyler was always at our house, since as far back as I could remember. One day in the fall, after he had gotten his driver's license, he surprised Roxanne with a dozen roses and drove her somewhere to ask her if she would be his girlfriend. Tyler was convinced this time she would come to her senses and say yes. When he told me this initially, I laughed to myself. I wanted to tell him to stop lying to himself, that she was never going to change. But instead, I let the event unfold because I was shallow. I wasn't afraid to admit it.

As he dropped her back off at the house, I was lingering on the steps leading up to our front door talking to Stacy on the phone. Roxanne silently walked past me, not acknowledging my presence, which was typical. After a minute of distracting gossip, I looked back at our driveway and noticed Tyler had not left. His truck wasn't even running. I stood to get a better look in his direction. Tyler's face was planted on the steering wheel, clearly upset. I told Stacy I would call her back. Hanging up the phone, I slowly walked toward his truck. Opening his passenger door, I climbed into the cab.

Tyler did not move. I was worried he had suffocated himself and thought what a shame that would be if it were true. My sister was not worth dying for. I obnoxiously poked his arm. "What are you so upset about?"

Barely turning his head, he grumbled, "Where have you been for the last thirteen years?"

"I've been right here, watching your pitiful attempts to gain access into my sister's bolted heart. I'm telling you, she's a lesbian." I wasn't quite convinced this was true. She really didn't have any girl friends.

He laughed once out loud. "You know that's not true. You're just jealous that your sister is getting more attention from a guy than you are." His comment definitely stung.

I thought about my response momentarily. Cocking my head to the side, I tried to stare compassionately at him. "Maybe you're right. Maybe I'm just jealous that you're giving *her* all the attention."

Tyler caught the emphasis I was conveying. He wrinkled his forehead, trying to understand. "Wait, you're really upset that *I'm* giving *your sister* attention? As in... not you?"

I shrugged my shoulders. "Well, yeah. You've been after her since we were kids and have you ever looked twice at me?" My eyes floated to a point on the dashboard in front of me.

His mouth opened slightly, without speaking. Tyler's eyes were wide as he restated my accusation, "You're seriously jealous that I'm in love with your sister and not you?" There was an accent of pleasant surprise in his voice.

I tried to explain myself. "I mean, we're twins. What does she have that I don't?" I intentionally pouted my bottom lip, waiting for him to take the bait.

"Besides the fact that you two are completely 2000% different from each other—more different than two people from opposite sides of the world—you want to know what you don't have to offer?" He was definitely curious.

"Yes, what can't I offer you?" I asked.

"Regan, I don't know. You're not my type. We're just not alike," he proclaimed.

I moved closer to him and brought my face toward his. "Tyler, she doesn't want you. Why can't you even consider a girl that could be so much more than Roxanne can? You don't know what you're missing. She won't even give you the time of day..."

He finished my sentence, "...and you will?" Tyler raised his eyebrows disbelievingly.

I smiled. "I could at least be more than a friend."

Quickly, he responded, "Regan, I didn't even realize we *were* friends. And now you want to be more?"

Laughing, I flirtatiously pushed his shoulder. I said, "Of course we're friends, silly. You can't come to my house every day for the past thirteen years and not expect us to be *at the very least* friends."

He shook his head slightly. "Alright..."

"Close your eyes," I commanded him.

He angrily pulled his body away from me. "Why?"

"Please, just trust me."

"Why should I trust you?"

"Because my DNA matches my sister's."

"So what?"

"Just do it, please." I asked very nicely this time.

"Whatever." He obediently lowered his eyelids and sat patiently, hands in his lap.

Glancing out the windshield at my house, I made sure no one was peeking through the dining room windows. No one knew Tyler was still here, except me.

I shifted my weight to turn my body more directly toward his. He sighed. Gently, I placed my hands on each side of his face. His cheeks were warm. "Regan..." he warned.

I pulled his face into mine, locking our lips together. Tyler struggled at first, trying to push me away, but quickly gave in to the moment. He was enjoying this far more than I expected. After a minute of kissing, we both pulled away simultaneously. His face was blank. I wasn't quite sure what he was thinking.

He muttered, "What was that for?"

I smiled. "For being you. You are such a sweet guy. I don't know why you waste your time on my sister. She doesn't deserve you."

"I will wait for Roxanne until the end of time if I have to," Tyler declared.

"Well," I replied, "In the meantime, I'll be here." I turned to get out of the truck.

Grabbing my shoulder, Tyler said, "Wait..." He pulled me back toward him and kissed me.

Pulling away, his face was bright red. He bashfully admitted, "Sorry, I had to remember how it felt."

Grinning, I opened the door and jumped down. Before closing the door, I reminded him, "I'll be here." I heard his engine start and the truck back up as I skipped into the house. That was too easy.

Upon entering the foyer, Roxanne rose from the couch and met me with a look of fury. "Was that Tyler that just left?"

"Yup," I responded.

"What were you doing out there?"

"Oh, just telling him that you weren't worth all his trouble." I spoke the truth, just not the whole truth.

"Whatever," she grumbled, stalking upstairs to her bedroom.

I laughed to myself as I watched her disappear into her room. If she only knew...

My daydreaming ended when I heard the sound of water quit. I slid off the bed and stood quietly next to the bathroom door. I knocked twice.

"Can I come in before you put on your clothes?" I playfully asked.

"Quit it. I'll be out soon," Tyler called back.

"I think we need to move our relationship to the next level," I said, trying the doorknob. I knew it was locked, but I tried just in case.

Tyler lightly pounded his fist once on the door. "I'm going to move our relationship down a level if you don't go sit down."

I obeyed and went back to sit down on the bed. I wondered how long it would take before I got him to consent to more than kissing.

After a few minutes, Tyler opened the bathroom door. He had put on fresh jeans and a t-shirt for the occasion. As he came closer to me, I could smell the scent of his soap coming off his skin. "Mmmm," I hummed.

He smiled for the first time tonight. I was glad. Patting the spot on the bed next to me, I returned his smile.

"I don't think so," he quickly said, "let's go to the basement."

My smile faded. Even though he had a very nice, finished basement, I didn't want to go. "It's too cold down there."

"That won't be a problem," he muttered, almost to himself.

"Why can't we stay up here?" I asked, already knowing the answer.

"You already tempt me enough as is. And I'm not willing to give you something I can't get back," he said sternly.

"Are you saying that I'm irresistible?" I batted my eyelashes.

"More like impossible. Come on," Tyler grabbed my hand and pulled me out of his room and down the stairs to the basement.

He was ultimately right; being cold was not a problem for me with him so close.

11

TYLER

I lay on my side, elbow propped with my hand holding my head up, watching her sleep.

My favorite time to be with Regan was when she was the quietest. Sometimes it was very hard to be around her. She was the opposite of everything I wanted. I asked myself every day why I was using her. I didn't feel quite as bad because it was a reciprocal bargain. At least I hoped it was reciprocal.

I gazed at the light piercing through my blinds, streaking my bedroom walls. It was dawn and the sun was slowly rising. I longed for the simplicity of childhood—when all that mattered was who would be able to play that day and what there was for lunch. I was only eighteen, but I felt like I had lived much longer. I experienced the death of a man that played the role of my second father, as well as being blessed, and at the same time hurt, by the complications of love. There are people that don't believe teenagers are capable of real love. That was completely and utterly untrue. I knew what love was like...it blinded you and kept you coming back for more. I have been *changed* by love. Though, it hadn't been a completely positive experience for me.

Closing my eyes, I remembered a time when Regan, Roxanne, and I would play in their backyard while our parents gathered in the house. We would play house and of course, I was the father. Roxanne and Regan took turns being the mother. I never got to make any of the decisions though, because I was outnumbered. I would stay the night during the weekends or Roxanne would stay over at my house. As we got older and "more developed," our parents stopped that ritual. I laughed quietly at this memory, peeking at the girl who lay silently next to me. Even though our hormones raged and sometimes it was almost irresistible, I was still a virgin. I wasn't sure if Regan was or not. Although she seemed sure of herself, I believed it was all an act. There was only one person I was waiting for, and I vowed to wait for her for as long as it would take, marriage or not.

Spending time with Regan, at night especially, made things very hard for me. There was a very large part of my brain that was controlled by hormones. I had to make sure I had my head on straight or I would really regret this. We never used my bed for anything but for sleep, like now. After spending time together last night, we turned on a movie and Regan fell asleep on the couch downstairs. I picked her up and let her sleep in my bed. I slept in the living room. I couldn't attach myself to her any further.

I was addicted, but I knew this had to stop. We couldn't continue this in college and now was the perfect time to end this sick relationship. I didn't even really like her. In fact, she annoyed me more than anything. The only thing that kept me going was her physical likeness to her sister. I wondered if Roxanne would really kiss me the same. Or better? Would she touch me the same way? I opened my eyes to stare at the goosebumps on my arms that appeared every time I thought about her. I felt angry with myself. When Roxanne found out how desperate I was, she would never want me. She was much better than I was. I didn't deserve her.

Slowly getting off the bed, I closed the door to my bedroom and trudged into the kitchen to make breakfast. My parents were asleep. They didn't know Regan was here. In fact, they never knew when she was here. And they never would find out about us because I decided that this was the last time Regan was coming over.

Fixing a bowl of cereal, I sat down at the dining room table and stared blankly at the wall. Even after showering this morning, I felt disgusting. Although we never had sex, I had seen more of Regan's body than I had ever seen of Roxanne's, even after all these years of friendship. I began feeling sick to my stomach. Pushing my bowl away, I heard a creak come from a door down the hallway. Turning my head, I saw Regan stumble sleepily toward me. I looked down at the table in front of me. I didn't want to look at her.

"What are you doing up so early?" she asked, placing her hand on my shoulder.

I removed it quickly. "I should ask you the same question." My voice was noticeably flat.

She didn't recognize my lack of emotion. Sitting down in the chair next to me, she said, "Come back to bed."

"No, I'm taking you home. You shouldn't be here," I quickly whispered.

"Why?" Regan asked, perplexed.

"You should never have come over. This was a bad idea, the whole thing. Please, go grab your stuff and I'll drive you home." I covered my face with my hands. I felt ashamed.

I heard her stand and walk toward my room. A few seconds later, she came back with her purse and shoes. I grabbed my uneaten cereal and set it in the sink.

We silently walked out to my truck. I unlocked the doors and hopped in. Turning toward the passenger's side, I noticed Regan standing outside of the door. Mechanically rolling down the passenger window, I called, "What are you doing?"

"Nothing," she mumbled, opening the door and climbing in.

She was beginning to irritate me. "What's your problem?" I tried to ask nicely.

"I don't understand *your* problem," she replied.

I started the engine and buckled myself in. Wanting to get her home as soon as possible, I backed out of the driveway and headed north. "I can't do this anymore." The shame was obvious in my tone.

"Okay...but why so suddenly?" she casually asked. I could tell she was trying not to sound disappointed.

"Regan, it's not you. It's me," I froze, realizing how shallow I sounded. "No, really, I just can't bring myself to do this anymore. You're great...at making me feel good. But you're not my girlfriend and never will be. I shouldn't use you and you shouldn't use me. It's just wrong. We're better than this. We don't need to do this to make each other feel needed." I waited for her to disagree.

She nodded slowly. "Yeah, I guess you're right."

Surprise crept across my face but I instantly tried to hide it. "Thank you," I replied.

"I'm better than this," she repeated, the corner of her mouth curling up.

I slightly smiled. "Yes."

"So," she started, a smile breaking across her face, "I'm great at making you feel good?" It always had to be about her. I sighed.

"Yes, now please drop it. And also, you can't tell Roxanne about this," I reminded her of our previous agreement.

She shook her head, still grinning. "Oh, I won't. Not now, at least."

I nodded. That was all I could realistically hope for. "I'll take that."

When I arrived in her neighborhood, I pulled my truck along the curb close-to, but out-of-sight-of, her house. The engine continued to run.

Regan turned to me. "Are you sure?" she asked.

I tried not to think about my answer for too long. "Yes, I'm sure." I tried to sound convincing.

"Alright. Your loss," she shrugged. Regan opened the door and moved to jump out. Quickly turning back around, she paused, and then leaned toward me, placing her lips softly on mine. I tried so hard to push her away, but my body wouldn't move. After a minute, she broke away, smiling. "I'll always be here."

Shaking my head slightly, I replied, "I'll remember that."

She leapt out of the truck, slamming the door behind her. As I watched her walk down the street and turn into her driveway, I inhaled deeply. I felt like a three hundred pound weight had been lifted off of my shoulders. I could be myself again.

Turning off the engine, I closed my eyes and leaned my head back against the headrest. I felt like I hadn't made a smart decision in a long time. I could start over now.

I longed for Roxanne. I grabbed my keys out of the ignition and slid out of my truck. I walked briskly down the street, following the same path that I watched Regan take. Cautiously, I strolled up their driveway, but instead of heading toward the front door, I walked around the side of the house. The strong wooden ivy trellis that lined the side of the house was the perfect ladder. I carefully climbed up the fence and heaved myself onto the sloping roof. Three windows down, I gently pulled the screen off the sill and tugged the window open. I climbed onto the large sill, pulling back flowing curtains as I stepped into her room. The goosebumps covered the skin of my arms again. I stared down at Roxanne sleeping peacefully. Quietly taking off my shoes, I crawled onto her bed, lying on top of her comforter. I placed my arm around her body and closed my eyes. Her hair smelled like fresh flowers beneath my nose. It only took minutes to fall asleep. Now, I would only dream of her.

12

LUKE

Time was wasting.

The countdown had started. I needed to move quickly. The problem was that I had no idea how much time was left.

Would I ever get to tell Roxanne who I really was? Why I was here? Why she would be my obsession for the next so many months?

Part of her was not afraid of me. That's what I wanted, wasn't it? For her to trust me. But I knew the closer we grew together, the harder it would be for us to part.

Right now my only objective was to find out more about Roxanne and her life. I had to know her very well. That was the only way I would be successful.

I would have to deal with Tyler and Regan as necessary. They could *not* get in my way.

In the meantime, I needed to find a canine.

13

ROXANNE

I woke up early to find Tyler cradling me.

I had to admit I wasn't completely surprised to find him in my room. After a fight, it never took long to rekindle our friendship. I always feared he would break his neck climbing the side of my house, though. If my dad were alive, he would have killed Tyler for performing such a dangerous act. And more than that, the trellis could have broken.

Without waking Tyler, I grabbed my running attire and headed to my attached bathroom. After flipping my hair into a ponytail, I grabbed my running shoes and my portable music. I closed the door quietly behind me and crept down the stairs. Everyone else was asleep; it was still early for my household. In the kitchen, I strapped on my shoes and then locked up the house. It was a beautiful day outside, but that was no surprise. I could feel the humidity touching the air and was glad I was running early. Today would be a speed workout; I only had one month before soccer practice would start and was in no shape for two-a-day workout sessions.

I drove to the St. Francis trail, praying silently that I would have no unwanted visitors today.

When I returned home, I was dripping in sweat from a combination of the run and the weather. I could hardly move my lower body, so I walked slowly. As I opened the front door, I could hear banter in the kitchen, the intertwined voices of Tyler and my mom. My mother loved Tyler like he was her own son, or son-in-law. I rolled my eyes at the thought. The smell of delicious food entered my nostrils. Stepping slowly into the kitchen, I was greeted with smiles.

"Look who dropped by," my mother beamed.

I pretended I didn't know any better. Smiling, I said, "Mom, Tyler stops by all the time. In fact, if he didn't stop by, I would be worried for his health."

Mom was cooking her famous french toast and cheesy eggs. "Oh, honey, you're just being silly." Tyler was sitting at the dining room table, his gentle eyes staring at me.

"How was your run?" he asked, noticing my awkward stiffness.

I exhaled loudly. "I'm not sure I'll be able to get out of bed tomorrow."

"How far did you go?" Tyler questioned. "20 miles? 30?"

I shook my head, cackling. "Um, I ran about four miles," I replied.

Tyler raised his eyebrows. "That's all? You're slacking....And you really shouldn't complain; it's a sign of weakness, you know."

I quickly rebuked, "Maybe you should try running with me sometime and then we'll see who's complaining. I would like to see your butt run four miles as fast as I do." I crossed my arms in front of my chest, sticking my tongue out at him.

A sneer crossed his face, "Someone's modest."

"You're one to talk. You always took all your school awards and rubbed them in our faces!" I joked.

Returning the gesture, he gawked, "You really need to stop the high-pitched whining. It's not very becoming."

"Children, now, now," Mom jumped in. "Oh, honey, I forgot to tell you. You got something from the university. I think it has to do with your housing."

I raced over to the counter where the mail lay. Although I wasn't excited about class, I was looking forward to dorm life. Picking up the envelope with an alligator emblem in the upper left corner, I ripped the flap open.

Scanning the letter quickly, I laughed, "Listen to this, they have the soccer team staying in a dorm called 'Excellence.' How cheesy."

Mom and Tyler joined in the laughter. I couldn't wait to hear the names of the other dorms. Tyler spoke seriously, "*Excellence* is a bit much for a mediocre soccer team, isn't it?"

I punched his arm hard, smirking. "Very funny."

"Do you know where you're staying, Tyler?" my mother asked, flipping french toast onto two plates.

Without hesitation, I ripped open my sister's letter from the university. We held no secrets in this house. "If you think *Excellence* is funny, you're going to die when you hear where Regan's living."

Ignoring my comment, Tyler faced my mother, "Respect."

I turned my head and stared at him, "I don't have to respect my sister. You of all people should know that."

"No," he continued, "I'm staying in Respect. One of the dorms."

Holding my stomach tightly, I laughed so much I was crying. "That's hilarious!"

"They were really creative with the names, weren't they?" Mom remarked politely.

Tyler came to stand next to my mother, grabbing a full plate of food. "This looks wonderful," he told her. Facing me, he questioned dully, "So, where's Regan staying?"

I was glad someone finally cared to hear. "She's staying in *Responsibility*! Now *that* is funny."

"Wow, that one takes the cake," Tyler replied.

Mom scolded me, "Roxanne, you shouldn't open your sister's mail."

I shrugged. "Oh well, too late." Facing Tyler, I asked, "So how far is Respect from Excellence?"

"Not too far. I think we'll share a dining hall." His voice still sounded flat.

"Oh, good." I smiled. I knew I would only be able to take being locked up in a dorm full of college girls for so long. Having Tyler close was very refreshing. Even if he were across campus, I would walk the distance to get away from the inevitable drama.

I grabbed a granola bar from the cabinet above the counter.

Tyler commented on my food, "Do you always eat healthy?" He pointed to his heaping plate of delicious, fattening food.

"Tyler," I started, "You have known me for a very long time. Why would you ask a question you already know the answer to?"

He shrugged slightly, a smile breaking through his lips. "Because I just don't get it. Besides, the real question is *why* do you always eat so healthy? Fat and carbohydrates are good for you, you know."

"I eat healthy—listen carefully now, so you don't miss it— because being healthy is good for you. And I do eat fat and carbs. I thought you were smart?" I smiled.

"That's all you're going to eat?" he grimaced, pointing at the empty wrapper on the table as I finished my last bite.

"No, I plan on ordering a big pepperoni pizza right after this," I sarcastically remarked.

Tyler's voice heightened, "That's actually a great idea. I'll split it with you."

"So what are you kids doing today?" Mom asked us, sitting down at the table with a plate of food in her hands.

Tyler responded, "I've got to work today. Dad needs help with mowing and I told Mr. Stockfield I would go back down today and help him with the horses."

I pouted slightly. I was hoping we could spend some time together and smooth things completely out. I supposed that would have to wait.

"I guess I'll take Lucy to the dog park," I answered.

At the sound of her name, Lucy, my black German Shepherd, came trotting into the room. I got up and grabbed a treat from her treat bowl in the pantry. "Sit," I commanded. As she quickly obeyed, I gave her the treat and sat back down. "Go lay down." I watched her as she laid down on her soft doggy bed in the living room. She was extremely obedient.

"I wish I could get Max to do that," Tyler said.

Laughing, I said, "I'm not so sure it's the dog, rather than the owner."

After shoveling food down, Tyler left to go to work. As the front door clicked shut, I realized Mom was staring at me. "What?" I asked.

"Why don't you and Tyler get together?" she softly asked.

I sighed. "Mom, I told you. In fact, I've told you many times. We're just friends." I couldn't count the number of similar conversations we'd had in the past.

"He's in love with you," she stated, matter-of-factly.

"That may be true, but I just can't be in a relationship right now."

"Right now or ever?" she questioned.

"I'll decide when *ever* comes." I wanted desperately to drop the subject.

"He's a good kid," Mom said, "and he comes from a good family."

I was starting to get frustrated. "His family will always be my second family, no matter what."

She glanced away. "I know, I know."

Standing, she took the empty plates and rinsed them off for the dishwasher. She worked quietly until she announced, "You know, his parents are very fond of you."

"Mom!" I stood and walked over to her. "Enough, okay?"

"Okay, okay... as long as you know what you're doing."

Sternly, I replied, "I do." I wished she would understand. If there was anyone who could relate to my feelings, it should be my mother. She understood loss. In four years, my mother had not dated or considered it at all. We were in the same boat there.

Deciding to stay in my sweaty clothes, I called, "Lucy! Let's go to the park!"

Lucy was fast to come at the sound of *park*. "Bye, Mom," I said, walking toward the front door. I pulled Lucy's leash and collar off the hook by the door and tugged it over her head.

"Bye, honey," I heard my mom call back from the kitchen.

Loading Lucy into the passenger seat, I shut the door and climbed in behind the wheel. The park was only a few miles away, for which I was glad. Lucy licked my sweat-covered arm almost the entire ride there. "Gross," I told her. She didn't seem to mind.

Arriving in the little parking lot, I noticed only a few other cars. My attention was held by one car in particular, a red Mustang. Although I was happy with my Xterra, I had always wanted a Mustang. Tyler would definitely approve of the American-made brand. He was not a fan of my Nissan and its foreign features.

I locked my car and we walked toward the fenced-in dog park. The park was in an L-shape, sitting up against a lake. Lucy loved to swim. The park was scattered with trees and benches, providing shade and rest to the dog owners.

Approaching the entry gate, I recognized a Husky running in the distance. I found that I could usually only remember the names of the dogs, rather than the owners. Once inside the fence, I unclipped Lucy's leash and set her free. She ran toward the Husky and its owner. I walked at a snail's pace, my muscles still tight from the morning run.

I socialized with the different dog owners as Lucy and I traveled around the park. The lake that bordered the dog park sat still, inviting curious canines in. Hopefully, Lucy would be so preoccupied with everything that she wouldn't take a second glance at the water. I knew it was an impossible plea.

As Lucy and the other dogs ran around chasing each other, I parked myself at a bench beneath some trees to shelter myself from the hot sun. When a minute of peace passed, I was startled by a small rat terrier and it's constant, annoying bark scratching at my eardrums. I shook my head at the little dog, searching around the surrounding area for the owner.

"Where's your owner?" I asked the dog.

He continued to bark back at me.

A male voice called from a distance, "Hey, sorry about that!"

My eyes glanced up at the owner, walking briskly toward me. Immediately, my heart stopped.

Approaching me, Luke remarked, "Devilish little thing, isn't he?" His bright smile was unwavering.

"Like owner, like dog," I commented, standing and walking away from him and his poor, stupid dog.

"Ouch, that one hurt." Luke replied, sprinting to catch up with me. The piercing bark followed behind us.

"Where did you get the dog?" I turned and asked him. It was obvious the dog didn't belong to him.

Shooting me a troubled look, Luke said, "My house."

"Or, someone's yard?" I corrected, continuing to walk at a quick pace.

"Are you suggesting that I *stole* this dog?" Luke asked, a flash of shock crossing his face.

Without looking at him, I answered, "Yes, I am."

"Well," he started, "If I did steal the dog, would you like me better?"

My eyes glared at him. "No. Not at all."

"Oh, good," Luke sighed loudly. "I have a streak going and I don't want to mess that up."

I rolled my eyes. "Of course, you would think that."

"Why don't you give me a chance?"

I realized Luke was not walking next to me anymore, his voice a bit distant. Slowing, I barely turned my head to look back over my shoulder. He wasn't standing behind me. He was nowhere in my periphery.

"What are you looking for?" Luke's voice was now in my opposite ear.

I swiveled on my feet to glare at him. "How did you do that?"

"Do what? Look ridiculously good-looking? Well, my mother says I get it from her side of the family..." Luke rambled on.

Folding my arms in front my chest, I let my head fall toward the ground and closed my eyes in annoyance. After inhaling deeply, I opened them. Again, as if by magic, Luke was gone.

Spinning around, I found him, looking unusually smug. "What's with the disappearing trick?"

"Are you amused?" he asked, baring his white teeth at me.

I shook my head. "Nope."

"So, are you going to answer my question?" Luke asked, returning to my side. I continued to walk toward a group of dog owners congregating.

"Nope."

"Do you even remember the question?"

"Nope."

He chuckled. "Now, that's not fair."

I glowered at him. "Hasn't anyone ever told you that life is not fair?"

Luke's dog started barking furiously at an older couple. "Fido!" he called after the dog. The dog's barking did not falter. I didn't blame the poor dog; I wouldn't answer to a fake name either.

"Fido?" I laughed. "Real original."

Shrugging lightly, Luke grinned. "I save my creativity for ways to annoy you."

I wrinkled my face. "Why, thank you."

"You're welcome," Luke offered.

Fido began running in circles around the innocent couple, his loud screeching clearly uninvited.

"Fido!" Luke called out again, jogging toward the dog in his flip-flops. The dog was not about to be controlled though, as he was definitely quicker than Luke. Luke had no chance of catching this little dog, especially when wearing flimsy rubber, but the chase was very entertaining. The dog swerved in and out of other dogs and owners, making everyone laugh at Luke's expense. Suddenly, Luke stopped, seeming exhausted. He leaned against his knees, wiping his brows with his forearm. I could only smile in response. Finally, someone else annoying *him*.

Lucy nudged her nose against my dangling hand beside me. Kneeling down beside her, I scratched the backs of her ears. Her licking kisses in my hand were sloppy and wet.

"Life *is* fair, actually," his sweet voice announced his returned presence.

I looked at Lucy and shook my head, thinking: *don't ever waste your time on boys*. If only she could read my thoughts.

Standing, I stared at him curiously. "Life was not meant to be fair."

"Well," Luke chortled, "it certainly is."

"How so?" I gawked at him.

"We are given what we deserve," he proclaimed.

I couldn't believe my ears. *So*, I thought, *I deserve to suffer unimaginable pain through the loss of my father*. If his theory was true, what was the point in living?

He explained further, "We have done nothing to deserve anything. We don't make our own destiny."

I frowned. "I don't need you to preach to me."

"Then what do you need?" Luke responded. His eyes were slicing right through me. He was trying hard to read me. If he only knew that my soul was bound up tight, he would realize that his effort wasn't worth it.

I touched my chin in exaggerated thought. After a minute, I looked him square in the eyes. "A new identity."

A momentary silence elapsed, Luke standing statue-like. His eyes were in a trance, unblinking. I couldn't detect a breath; I was a little concerned.

Abruptly, the edges of Luke's mouth curled into a smile. "You're funny, Roxanne."

I enjoyed the sound of my name on his lips. "I'm glad you think so," I calmly commented.

Without further words, Luke began walking forward again. The little dog he brought was now trotting around the length of the dog park aimlessly. At first, it seemed that Luke was going to retrieve the troublemaker. It soon became obvious that he was headed in no particular direction. I watched his movement from afar, trying to analyze his next step. He was unusually unpredictable.

Eventually, the dog wandered back to Luke, as if summoned mentally. Luke bent down to grab Fido's collar and attached the leash.

"C'mon Fido, let's go home," Luke muttered within earshot of me.

Anxiety came over me and I couldn't help but protest. "Wait!" I called, jogging after him. The whole way I was kicking myself for my curiosity.

A satisfied look crossed his face and I was instantly disappointed in myself for my momentarily lapse in judgment. When I had caught up to him and Fido, I wasn't quite sure what my plan was.

"I'm sorry," Luke began, "but I can't give you a new identity. But, I can help you improve your current one."

"Before you tell me how to do that, I have some questions for you. The only thing I know about you is your name. And I'm not even sure it's your *real* name. I have no idea where you're from or how you know me. I want to know why you keep showing up at the same places that I'm at."

Surprisingly, Luke admitted, "You're right."

I raised my eyebrows. "About which part?"

"My real name is Lucio Castelli," he affirmed.

That answer was not what I was expecting. "But you go by Luke?"

He carefully shook his head. "Not really."

"Then why would you lie to me?" I felt hurt, sort of. His presence was finally starting to grow on me, as was his trust.

For once, it appeared Luke didn't have a good answer. He shrugged his shoulders, refusing to look into my eyes. "I don't know. But I kind of like the sound of it."

My eyebrows pinched together. "Okay..."

"Want to know something else?" He offered, lifting his eyes to meet mine.

Bewildered, I shrugged. "Sure, why not?"

"I'm Italian, as if that weren't obvious... from Venice. And I'm eighteen. I'm attending the University in Gainesville this fall, major undecided. I'm staying with some friends of the family in the city." His answers flowed off his tongue so naturally that I almost wondered to myself if I had asked him any questions.

All I could manage was, "Wow." My response was less than enthusiastic, although all the new information was intriguing. It seemed I wouldn't be escaping my stranger very quickly after all, seeing that he was going to Gainesville in the fall.

Luke's eyes dropped, frowning. "You don't care, do you?"

I sighed heavily. "It's not that. I just don't understand why you're telling me all this."

"Well, you told me you didn't know anything about me. And to top it off, I'm a harmless guy. Do you feel better now, knowing more about me?"

I hesitated before I answered. "Better," I told him, surprised at the truth. I did feel better. But there were still so many unanswered questions.

"You forgot to answer one question," I reminded him.

He glanced at me suspiciously. "Did I?"

"How do you know me?" I asked him. This was the foremost important question, above all others. My thoughts drifted back to our initial meeting on the trail. He spoke my name like he knew me.

"I don't know. Lucky guess?" he offered.

I blinked, irritated. Quickly, I tried to dissolve my impatience, remembering my other dire question to be asked.

"Now, tell me, Luke. Can I call you Luke? If you don't know me, then how is it coincidence that two people run into each other so often?"

"Maybe we just have more in common than you would like to admit," Luke stated, matter-of-factly.

I realized I wasn't going to get an honest answer from him. "Maybe."

After freeing Fido from his leash again, Luke and I walked quietly around the dog park, not really looking at each other but always aware of the other person's presence. It was borderline awkward. I welcomed the silence, though.

After awhile, I felt Luke's eyes on me. I turned to look at him and met his beautiful brown eyes with wonder. I couldn't help but linger on why this guy was here at the dog park with me. My perplexity was certainly showing on my face.

"So," Luke broke the silence, "tell me about yourself."

Although I wasn't really interested in telling my entire life story, I couldn't resist the attention. The only other boy who was ever interested in me happened to be my best friend. Tyler could probably talk about my life in far more detail than I could.

"What would you like to know?" I asked him, hoping he would initiate the questions.

Luke cleared his throat in preparation. "Alright, question number one: why don't you get along with your sister?"

The question threw me off guard. I was taken aback at how little time it took for Luke to conjure up such a personal question. My sister must have given him a hint about at how close we were, or the lack of closeness, I should say.

"Luke," I hesitated.

"Roxanne, don't be afraid of the truth," he encouraged.

I shook my head. "You don't understand. It's a long story."

"I have approximately 70 or so years before I kick the bucket. I believe I have the time." Luke seemed genuinely interested in me. My former impressions of him were beginning to fade. Although I was beginning to trust him, I tried not to let my guard down quite so fast.

I shook my head again. "Not now, okay? It's such a nice day and I really don't want to dampen it."

"Oh, don't worry, the air is damp enough as is. But I empathize with you. I will wait for the *long* story until you decide to share it with me." His eyes twinkled with each word.

The sun was at its highest point overhead, the heat blazing down on us and everyone else outside. I didn't realize it before, but the humidity was becoming almost unbearable. The sweat under my arms was accumulating, firstly from my early morning run and now from the increasing heat. Suddenly, I was feeling self-conscious. The feeling was relatively new to me. Attending an all-girls Catholic high school had provided the perfect excuse not to wear make-up or dress up to impress dumb, immature boys who probably wouldn't pay attention to any of it anyway.

So now, in the middle of the summer before I get shipped off to college, I meet this guy, who seems very different from all the others. I knew it was all too good to be true and soon enough, I'd be proven right. It was only a matter of time.

Wiping my mouth with the rim of my t-shirt, I let out a deep breath. The thick air was definitely taking its toll on my lungs.

"You okay?" Luke asked, concerned.

I nodded. "Yeah, I think it's time Lucy and I leave. *I'm* not the one with layers of fur on out here."

He chuckled then began looking around the dog park for Fido. It seemed that the dog was nowhere to be found. I also joined in the search, scanning the various spots of the park he could be lounging. Neither of us could spot him.

In the near distance, I heard a squeaky bark and instantly recognized it. Luke and I both turned our heads toward the sound. We couldn't help but laugh at the sight of Fido swimming in the murky lake that surrounded the park. I knew that the lake was rather disgusting, having been the swimming hole for all types of dogs for years. I grimaced at the thought of pulling him out if Fido didn't cooperate.

With Lucy following behind obediently, Luke and I made our way down to the lake's edge. Fido was approximately twenty feet out, looking like he was having the time of his life.

"Fido!" Luke yelled.

"His name isn't Fido, Luke," I declared. The dog swimming leisurely in the lake didn't acknowledge Luke's call at all.

"I," Luke paused, struggling to find the right words, "know."

"A-ha! I knew it. You stole this dog, didn't you?" As I turned my eyes from the dog to Luke, a wave of water flew at me. The temperature of the sun didn't change how cold the water felt. Suddenly, my face and the front of my shirt were drenched with lake water. The smell was unavoidable.

"Ah!" I screamed, grabbing two palms full of water and throwing it back at him.

Laughter and water filled the air between us. I couldn't believe what was happening, but I was all about revenge. By the end of the water fight, we were both drenched from head to toe, smiles plastered on our faces. Luckily, the dog decided to come back to shore and sat right next to Luke. I was beginning to get suspicious—the dog was a little too odd for me.

The sound of happiness quickly died. Luke scooped up his dog and tethered him to a leash. Setting him back down, Luke grinned at me.

"I believe it's time that I get this dog back to its owner," he proposed, nonchalantly. Luke began walking toward the park entrance.

Frozen still, my mouth gapped and my eyes widened in disbelief. "I knew it!"

"So why do you look so surprised?" Luke asked, proceeding forward.

Racing after him, I shouted, "I can't believe you really stole that poor dog!" Some heads of bystanders turned toward us, shock drawn across their faces. Smiling with embarrassment, I tried to cover up the situation.

Whispering, I continued, "How could you?"

Luke, mimicking my actions, whispered in return, "I thought you knew."

Rashly, I crossed my arms in front of my chest and glared at him.

As we both approached the entrance gate, he touched my shoulder lightly. His touch felt strangely different from Tyler's. It was much softer, gentler. Desperately trying to hold my stern face, I concentrated on his eyes. To my dismay, his gaze only put me at ease.

"Roxanne, sometimes courage isn't enough," Luke professed.

"I don't understand."

We both ambled into the desolate parking lot, only a few cars remaining. I again admired that red Mustang as it sat handsomely across the lot from my Xterra.

"You like?" Luke pointed toward it and grinned. Disbelief was clear across my face.

Unaffected by my obvious surprise, Luke continued to stare at me. Picking up little Fido in his arms, he moved closer to the new, shiny car. Desperately musing over a variety of simultaneous feelings, I knew I didn't want to wait for his answer any longer. I eagerly wanted to understand what he originally meant before I got distracted by his change in choice of transportation.

Arriving beside him at his car, Luke placed the dog in the passenger seat. After shutting the door, he came to stand within inches from me. Leaning in towards my face, Luke tranquilly disclosed, "Sometimes one has to go to great lengths to get what one wants."

14

REGAN

Ah, the smell of coffee was intoxicating.

As I sat at my booth in a local coffee shop, I stared around at the different people enjoying their choice of beverage and pastry. The variety of smells—espresso, mocha, and caramel—wafted toward my nose, deepening my sense of relaxation. Although the combination of conversation and the bustle of workers provided a lot of background noise, it was well received. I always enjoyed being around a crowd, never totally alone.

Laptop on the table, I perused countless online stores searching for a particular style of music. Leah was planning on meeting me here soon, so that we could catch up on the latest gossip. It would only be a matter of weeks before she would be heading off to South Carolina to study fashion. If everything worked out as planned, in ten years, Leah would be sporting a chic clothing line, I would be reporting the latest news on CNN, and our friend Stacy would be curing childhood cancer. We had already decided that no matter what, we would remain friends.

"Here you are, miss," the barista sat my caramel macchiato next to my computer.

"Thanks," I told her, as she headed back around the counter.

Searching through the different categories, I spotted the specific band I was looking for. Grabbing my purse, I struggled to find my credit card. *Where did I put that darn thing?*

"Aha," I said aloud, brandishing the card in my fist.

"Hey, Regan," spoke a familiar voice from across the booth.

"Ah!" I blurted, overtaken by surprise at the sight of Luke.

A smile struck his gorgeous European face.

"Luke, you scared me!" I confessed, feeling my heart rate begin to slow.

His expression didn't falter. Luke always seemed to be unnaturally calm. "I'm sorry. Are you sitting with anyone?"

Before I could answer, the same barista came back to our table and placed a drink in front of Luke. He winked at me.

"Caramel macchiato for you, sir," she said happily, smiling from ear to ear.

"Thank you very much."

Once the barista left, I stared crookedly at him. I watched him take a sip from the paper cup, not grimacing once from the drink's hot temperature.

Licking his lips, he commented, "This is delicious. What are you drinking?"

Cautiously, I asserted, "Same."

"You have good taste."

"Thanks... what are you doing here?" I asked, hoping not to offend him by the blunt question.

His eyes went flat. "I can leave, if you'd like."

Quickly, I replied, "No, no. I was just curious."

He shrugged. "I heard this place was good, so I wanted to try it." He took another sip.

"Isn't that hot?" I asked, extremely curious. It always took me a few minutes before I could venture to drink any hot coffee.

Downing a large gulp, he grinned, leftover liquid lining his top lip like a mustache. "Nope."

"That's odd," I said, eyeing my own cup, "Because mine is still scorching."

He gazed at me carefully. "I must not be as sensitive." Snatching a napkin off the table, he dabbed his mouth.

"Okay..." I slowly mumbled.

Pointing at my laptop, Luke asked, "What are you shopping for?"

"How did you know I was going to buy something?" I wondered, suspiciously.

Luke nodded his head toward my hand. Although my credit card was still clenched beneath my fingers, I had completely forgotten about it when I saw him. He always took the breath right out of me. Luke was definitely attractive, but I prided myself in having self-control regarding the male population. The boys need the girls, not the other way around.

"Oh, right," I put my card down on the table. "I'm buying music. I've had a hard time finding it in stores here."

"So, what *do* American college girls listen to?" He eyed me curiously, but I knew what kind of information he was looking for.

Cocking my head to the side, I probed, "You mean, what does *Roxanne* like to listen to?"

"Well, since you brought her up..."

"I'm the wrong person to be asking. I told you we don't really *hang out* or anything." I took a swig of my drink to distract away from the start of an awkward conversation. The liquid was still hot, but manageable.

Luke looked down at the coffee cup in his hands. He seemed to be considering something.

"I have a question for you," he stated after a brief period of silence.

"Shoot," I said. I was desperately hoping it wouldn't have anything to do with Roxanne.

Meeting my gaze with soft eyes, he asked, "What's up with Roxanne and Tyler?"

Strangely, my pulse began to race at the sound of Tyler's name. Was it that I really had feelings for him? Or did I just feel enthralled with betraying my sister? I couldn't decide which; maybe it was a mixture of both.

"Tyler?" I mumbled in a haze.

Luke nodded suspiciously. "Yes, Tyler and Roxanne."

I took a deep silent breath and cleared my throat. "You have nothing to worry about."

Shaking his head, Luke reminded me, "That's not what I asked."

After momentarily closing my eyes and wagging my head, I opened them to refocus on Luke's face. "Can you repeat the question?"

"Alright," Luke began slowly, "Is there anything romantically happening between Roxanne and Tyler?"

I gulped. *What was wrong with me?* I anxiously thought. To buy some time, I took another drink from my cup. Another deep breath and I would be okay.

"No and yes," I finally answered.

Luke's eyebrows furrowed together in confusion. "What do you mean?"

"Yes for Tyler, no for Roxanne. At least that's the way it seems." Everything I said was true to the best of my knowledge. I knew Tyler was madly in love with my sister. I also knew that in public, Roxanne clearly refused to date Tyler. The mystery was how she actually felt about him.

"So, Tyler's going to be difficult," Luke said, more to himself than to me.

"You don't have to worry about Tyler," I affirmed.

Returning to the present, Luke muttered, "Why not?"

I slightly shrugged my shoulders. "Because it's Tyler."

"What's that supposed to mean?"

"Oh, I don't know. Tyler is...all bark and no bite."

"I don't understand..."

I rolled my eyes. "It's a metaphor, foreigner. It means, he may seem tough, but inside he's as gentle as a lamb." My voice was noticeably softer toward the end of my sentence. I hoped Luke wasn't paying close attention.

"Tyler seems far from soft. How would you know, anyway?"

There was the question I was desperately praying to avoid. He's right; how *would* I know if Tyler was soft at heart if I hadn't clearly spent time with him? He was my sister's best friend. Since Roxanne and I were far from close, there was no good explanation for hanging out with Tyler. He should technically be the enemy. In my world, Tyler was more like a traitor to the other side. Although Tyler had severed our secret relationship, he had worked for *my* side, an obvious faux pas.

I quickly made up a reasonably true story. "I've been around Tyler long enough to know. Although it's hard to believe, Tyler, Roxanne, and I used to be like the Three Musketeers."

"Who're they?" Luke asked, ignorantly.

"The Three Amigos?" I rephrased.

He was unmistakably bewildered. "I have no idea what you're talking about," Luke confessed.

"Never mind," I waved him off. "Anyway, the three of us used to be the best of friends. We were always together, no matter what. We always had so much fun."

Setting his chin into the palm of his hand, Luke grinned. "You're smiling."

I straightened up at his comment, distinctly frowning in the process. "I am not."

His smile met his brown eyes. "Oh yes, you were."

"Why would I be smiling?" I grumbled.

Leaning forward, Luke's stare burned into my eyes. "Because you know as well as I do that you and your sister shared a fun childhood. I can tell by the look on your face. I bet you two were inseparable. When did that all change?"

I was hoping that today would be relaxing. Luke and I had been sitting there for less than ten minutes, and I was already beginning to stress out. Talking about my family, particularly my inept twin sister, was not a calming subject. Discussing the past was usually evaded in our household, one thing we both agreed on. Our mother was the only true stronghold of our threesome. Without her, there was no hope for tying loose ends or keeping from burning old bridges.

Sighing heavily, I rolled my eyes. "I really don't want to talk about it."

Quickly, Luke responded, "Why not?"

"It's all irrelevant."

"You're just like Roxanne," he mumbled.

"What!" I exclaimed, appalled. Comparing me to my sister was the biggest insult.

Before he could answer, I continued, "I am *not* like my sister."

He responded quietly, "I'm sorry, I didn't mean to offend you. It's just that you both hate talking about the past. What in the world happened?"

I decided there was no point in escaping the truth any longer. Luke would get the information out of me sooner or later.

"Our dad died when we were in eighth grade. Of course, it was hard on all of us. Roxanne and I were both close to our father, but more so Roxanne. I got along better with our mom since we're more alike. Roxanne and dad were always playing sports and watching football on TV. His death was a lot harder on her."

"I'm so sorry to hear this news." After sitting silently for a minute, Luke continued, "So, his death drove your relationship apart?"

I nodded. "We all mourned, but it seemed like her mourning period never really ended. She never really accepted it. After his death, she really wasn't the same person. I'm surprised Tyler stuck around. She really was awful to everyone for a long time. She still hates me, but at least she acknowledges other people."

"Why does she still hate you?" Luke asked.

"Actually, I have no idea. I guess because his death didn't affect me like it affected her. She probably resents the fact that I was able to move on when she couldn't even think about the next hour of her life. I was able to go back to school shortly after his funeral, but she wasn't mentally functioning until a couple weeks later."

Luke considered the information and then asked, "What about her friends? Did she still hang out with them?"

"She was pretty rude to everyone. Roxanne spent the second half of our eighth-grade year locked up in her room. The only time she got out was for soccer. It was probably the only thing that kept her from going crazy. As a matter of fact, it was the only thing that kept the rest of us from going crazy. Tyler spent a lot of time at the house then. He also had a big part in keeping her sane."

"Tyler," Luke repeated, staring down at the table.

"Yep, Tyler," I also reiterated.

"He's been a good friend," he stated, matter-of-factly.

"I guess so," I dully agreed.

"So, where does that lead us?"

I cocked my head at the question. "Is that a rhetorical question?"

He shook his head, "Nope."

"Well, then, I don't know."

"That leads us back to Tyler and Roxanne."

I sighed. "Okay..."

"So, to recap, you three used to be close, but then your father died, and now you're not. Did I miss anything?" His eyebrows arched as he rattled off the summary of our conversation.

I looked upward as if in thought. Returning to meet his gaze, I said, "That pretty much sums it up. Without all the heartache and tears, of course."

He confirmed, "Right. Now continue on about Tyler."

"Alright. Well, after dad died, Roxanne all-of-a-sudden couldn't date anyone. Technically, she wasn't allowed to date until she was sixteen, but our parents loved Tyler. He's one of those boys you could definitely bring home to mom." I noticed Luke's lips tighten as I spoke highly of Tyler. *He must really be jealous*, I thought.

I continued, "I don't really understand any of it. Let's just say, Roxanne doesn't really fill me in on her personal life. Tyler is perfect for her. Well, I say that mainly because he's the only guy I know that can put up with her for long periods of time."

Luke's face was stern.

"Well, except for you," I corrected.

His head wagged back and forth. "I haven't spent long periods of time with her."

"Let me rephrase," I began, "You two are the only guys that can put up with her, period."

Thankfully, Luke smiled. The weak happiness vanished quickly, though.

"Keep going," urged Luke.

"So, although Roxanne considered herself off-limits, Tyler didn't quit. He was, and still is, determined to make her his girlfriend. He doesn't seem to bother her with the subject very often, but he must try, like...at least once a month."

Luke cleared his throat. "If Roxanne doesn't tell you anything, how do you know all this?"

There was that awful question again. *Why do I keep digging myself in deeper?* I thought to myself. I would not tell Luke about my forbidden relationship with Tyler. Luke was not on *my* side. He was clearly for the enemy.

"Tyler's pretty public about his feelings," I said. I wasn't lying, I just wasn't telling the whole truth.

Luke seemed to accept the statement without further question. "Okay," he replied.

He brought his drink to his lips and gulped down the rest of the coffee. After licking his lips, he asked, "So, Tyler won't be a problem?"

"I don't think so," I offered. Compared to Luke, Tyler looked like a boy.

Unexpectedly, Luke leaned forward and clasped his hands together tightly in front of his face. His eyes pierced right through me. He then asked, "What do you see in me?"

Taken aback, I stuttered, "E-excuse me?"

"Obviously, you think I have a chance with Roxanne, while Tyler does not. Now, why would a stranger like myself be a better candidate than a friend she's known for years?"

Rapidly, I randomly asked in return, "How do you have such good English?"

Although surprised, Luke wasn't giving up. "Practice. Now please answer the question."

I stupidly spoke the first thought that came to mind, "Fresh meat."

Luke chuckled loudly. Sighing in relief, I tried to smile back in chagrin. He continued to laugh while I sat awkwardly quiet.

"You're so funny," Luke started, "I really like that about you. You're honest."

"Well, you know, I try," I playfully laughed, still uncomfortable.

Through a laugh, he said, "I'm sure you do."

Taking a sip of my own drink, I conjured up another question to ask. "So, what about you?"

He looked confused. "What about me?"

I clarified, "What's the next step for you?"

The corners of his mouth slowly formed a grin. "Sweep her off her feet, of course."

15

REGAN

"Hello?"

"Hey, Tyler," I responded lightly.

His voice falling to a whisper, Tyler said, "Regan, why are you calling me?"

"Why so mean?" I asked.

"You don't call me unless..." he paused, then continued, "you need something."

"That's true, but not this time."

"Alright, so, what's up?" he lightened his tone a bit, obviously relieved.

"I just thought I would warn you," I told him, an edge in my voice.

He laughed. "Warn me about what?"

"You have some competition."

"Competition for what?" he asked, more cautiously.

After a momentary pause, I answered, "For Roxanne."

"What do you mean?" Tyler slowly mumbled, confused.

I informed him, "Luke likes Roxanne."

"So what?"

"You don't care?"

"There's no way she likes him," Tyler asserted.

"They're going on a date," I lied.

Silence filled the space between us. I could almost hear him breathing on the other end of the line.

Suddenly, Tyler said, "I don't believe you."

"Fine. Don't believe me. You'll see. She likes him, you know."

"How would you know? You never speak to Roxanne."

"But I talk to Luke."

"Luke means nothing to me."

"He will when you lose Roxanne to him."

"I will not!" he yelled.

"You know that she'll fall for him. I can tell in your voice."

"Stop, Regan."

"Stop what?"

"Bothering me with your stupid lies."

"You can ask Roxanne for yourself if you don't believe me."

"There's no reason to ask her. She tells me everything."

"Just like you tell her everything?"

"Regan..." His voice was stiffening as his irritation with me rose. I smiled to myself.

"Tyler."

"Unlike myself, Roxanne doesn't need to hide secrets."

"And she doesn't deserve you," I boldly pointed out.

Speaking rigidly through his teeth, Tyler forced out, "Yes. You're right. But no one is good enough for her."

"Whatever you say," I coyly added.

"Exactly. Whatever *I* say. Is this all you called to bother me with?" He was angry.

"Yup," I replied. "I just thought you would like to know. I'm doing you a favor."

"No," he said, "You're not. You're being a royal pain."

"Fine, next time I won't warn you," I cautioned.

"I'm a big boy, I don't need a babysitter."

"Okay, well, I'll make sure to tell you *I told you so* at the appropriate time."

"Whatever."

Click.

I gave my phone a smug look. Guilt was not a part of my vocabulary.

16

LUKE

I needed to leave for a while.

Roxanne was skeptical about the cars, the dog, and me. I was concerned my plan wasn't going to come together as planned. The balance between mysterious and trustworthy was harder to accomplish than I imagined.

I knew it seemed childish, but leaving was the only way I could justify my actions. I would return soon enough.

There was something about Roxanne.

I was disappointed and frustrated with myself, all at the same time. How foolish I was! I was put here to accomplish one task and one task only. It was clear: I was not to be distracted. How could I let this happen?

She wouldn't even know I was gone. Though, I secretly hoped she would.

When I took this job, I knew there would be struggles and grief, but I was so ignorant. Thoughtlessly, I took the task on with pride. Of course I was scared, but this was so much worse. It was overtly important to remember that she was not the only one I needed to impress.

How was it even possible for me to feel this way? I was so good at acting, but I couldn't deny that I had some feelings for her. It had been so long since I had such thoughts for a girl. Why *her*? Why *now*? If only...

I knew I couldn't live in an *if only* world, so I shouldn't kid myself.

But she was so pretty and troubled all the same! It made for such a good project.

What was I saying? A girl shouldn't be a project. She did need work, though.

I just needed to help her, that's all. More than need, I *wanted* to help her.

I was starting to care for her.

Was that so wrong?

Stage Three

BARGAINING

17

ROXANNE

It had been one month since I had seen Luke.

I laid across my bed, staring at the ceiling in intense thought.

Part of me wanted to be relieved. Another part of me wanted to be disappointed. I was torn. How unfair that a guy I hardly knew could have such an impact on me.

It shouldn't surprise me that a guy was the source of my unrest. The male population in general couldn't be trusted to follow through. I needed to give Tyler credit, though. He had never let me down. My father couldn't even help me. Even being upset, I knew I shouldn't blame him. No one lived forever.

In reality, I shouldn't hold Luke accountable. He never promised me anything. I didn't have his phone number and he didn't have mine. How would I contact him, even if I wanted to? Thinking about it all was absolutely useless, but it still consumed my thoughts.

His safety barely crossed my mind. Maybe I should be more concerned. What if something *had* happened to him? Would I ever see him again?

I knew I couldn't live hypothetically, but it was difficult to escape the *what-ifs*.

He knew where I lived. He could have stopped by. What if he didn't remember how to get here?

The list could go on.

In the past, I would get annoyed when girls at school would worry over guys and what they thought. They would analyze every conversation, every single gesture. Sadly, I could now say I understood. The obsession wasn't quite as involved, but at least I could sympathize.

It all didn't really matter. I knew it shouldn't matter if I ever saw him again. But I couldn't deny that I cared if I never again coincidentally ran into him.

I knew little about Luke. He was from Italy. What else did I know? He stole cars? He stole dogs? He sounded like a real winner in any mother's eyes. The little I did know about him could be completely false. Although this was a possibility, I didn't want to admit that he might be a good actor. Even worse, he might be a good criminal. But not once had he tried to hurt me or even mention anything of the sort.

My mind raced through the mixture of feelings, good and bad. Whoever said being a girl was easy was obviously not a girl. I needed to distract myself.

Searching my room, I picked up the folder marked "College" across the top. Opening it, I pulled out the first two pages lying inside. The map of campus and my schedule of courses needed attending to. With only a week before heading to campus to start training for soccer, I still wasn't quite sure where the necessary facilities were located. Namely, I needed to find my dorm, the dining hall, and the athlete's recreation complex on the map. I knew this wouldn't take long, but I needed to pull my mind away from Luke and place it on the future.

After spending only a few minutes with the map, I was bored. I could look up my class schedule before school started in August, which was a little over a month away.

My thoughts moved to what I imagined soccer practice and dorm life would be like. The only thing I really knew was that we would be practicing twice a day and it would be hell. In the weeks leading up to the start of practice, I had increased my daily running mileage in hopes that my transition to Division One sports would be less daunting. Thankfully, I had sustained no more injuries on the trail.

My roommate's name was Allison and she was a freshman on the team as well. I had phoned her a few days ago to make the necessary arrangements for furniture and to get to know her a little better. The first thing I learned was that she was from southern Florida. She was going to study nutrition and fitness, so I knew instantly we would get along. Her field position was defense, while I was offense. She also informed me that she was a bit of a cleaner and would probably spend most of her time off the field in the library because she enjoyed studying. I could handle clean and I could handle the room to myself. I believed that this new relationship would work out perfectly.

Tossing the "College" folder back onto my desk, I sighed. As much as I didn't want to admit it, I was actually beginning to get excited about school. Well, I used the term lightly. For me, school encompassed many different things. I knew soccer would only be part of my new life in Gainesville. Unfortunately, I couldn't forever hide behind sports, like I did while in high school. Starting college meant starting a whole new me. That was a person I was looking forward to getting to know.

I plopped myself back on my bed. The freedom I would encounter at school was one of the main excitements. No more sister rummaging through my things, no more annoying voices in the hall outside my bedroom door, no more stupid phone conversations about purses and lip gloss to listen to. As I thought of a number of other things my sister did to irritate me, I realized something. What if my own roommate did these very things? I didn't really know Allison and she couldn't be completely trusted from the start. My mind began racing with all the horrible possibilities that faced our new relationship.

Inhaling deeply, I let out a large breath of air. My worrying needed to stop. The anxiety of dorm life would have to wait. There was no reason to start freaking out right now.

I turned my head sideways to stare at my mirror. A photo, stuck into the rim, caught my eye. The picture was a still-shot out of one of my favorite movies, *Gone With The Wind*. A handsome Rhett and a beautiful Scarlett, embracing each other, stared back at me. My head shifted to the clock above the mirror; it read eleven o'clock. My thoughts had carried me so far from reality that I didn't realize how late in the morning it was.

Turning my attention back to the black and white photo, I sighed. *How fitting*, I mused. I felt that Luke had just gone with the wind. Smacking my forehead, I tried to erase the mental image I had of him. Escaping his natural, Italian lure was not an easy task to accomplish.

My memories of him were simple pictures, even videos in my head. I couldn't depend on these images; the false sense of hope they provided.

Unlike the less-than-tangible pictures in my mind, Luke was *definitely* real. And I was *definitely* struck by his absence.

Suddenly, a vision of us on the trail popped into my mind. Maybe, just maybe, I would find him there with an early morning run.

If I didn't see him running, I would have to wait until classes started in August. The university was so large, I doubted I would ever bump into him. There had to be a way...

I would find a way.

18

TYLER

"Aren't you excited?" I asked her, reaching over next to me and patting her on the knee.

"Yeah, I guess," Roxanne answered timidly.

"What's wrong?" I responded. She had been acting strange for the past week, but had never confessed the problem.

"Nothing," she glanced at me with soft eyes and continued, "I guess I'm just nervous."

I cackled. "Nervous? Roxanne Olivia Clarke is never nervous."

"Tyler, I'm serious. What if my roommate is a real psycho?" Her eyes were filled with worry.

"Well, then, you two will get along perfectly! You couldn't ask for a better match!" I caught a glare from her. It was obvious she didn't enjoy my sarcasm.

Checking my rearview mirror, I saw her mom wave from the car behind us. We were on Interstate 75, headed north to Gainesville. Although the official move-in date for the general student body wasn't until the end of August, the soccer team was starting practice and therefore needed to move in sooner. Her mom was driving Roxanne's SUV, with blankets, pillows, and clothing filling every available space. The back of my truck was loaded with furniture and, well, who-knew-what else.

Roxanne turned suddenly when a clicking noise sounded beneath the cab.

"What is that?" she asked, obviously concerned.

Shrugging, I said, "Oh, probably nothing. It does that now."

"You need to get a new truck. This one's, like, twenty years old."

"It is not!" I exclaimed. "It's only ten years old."

Roxanne folded her arms across her chest, an odd look on her face. "Tyler, I think it's time to trade in Ol' Red."

"Ol' Red is just fine. Plus, not all of us can afford new cars like your family. This truck has to last me until I graduate." My family's economic status was well below that of Roxanne's. Her dad had been the CEO of a big-time financial company, while my dad owned a lawn-mowing service. Her mom was a real-estate agent for pricey homes, while my mom managed the bakery department at the local grocer.

"Until you graduate college?" She was shocked.

"No, until I graduate obedience school. Of course, college!" Sometimes she disappointingly reminded me of her sister, but I wasn't going to mention that to her.

"Well, you better treat Ol' Red well then," Roxanne suggested.

Chuckling, I said, "You don't even know how to check your oil or change a tire."

"That's why I have you," she stated, smiling.

We drove down the highway without any further conversation. The silence in the air was ironically deafening. Peering at Roxanne, I noticed her attention was out of the passenger window. I noticed a black Dodge Charger race by, passing in front of me.

"What'r'ya thinking about?" I asked, hoping to get an informative response.

After a moment, she seemed to relax. She let out a long sigh, "Nothing, really."

I had to lighten the mood. "Just think," I started, "When the coaches and all the players see how good you are tomorrow, they're not going to know what to do with themselves."

She laughed out of mockery. "That's funny."

"C'mon, you're probably the only one that can run like, a million miles." I didn't have to get technical for her to get my point.

A smile slightly emerged across her mouth.

"There's the smile I have come to so greatly admire and adore." I placed my arm around her and pulled her toward me.

It would do no good to admit that I was going to miss her for the next three weeks. I would compare it to torture. Being apart from her was like temporarily losing a piece of myself. While she was away, I knew I would have little contact with her. Although the distance wasn't far, it would feel like we were worlds apart.

Maybe the limited contact would be to my benefit. I wondered if missing me would make her see me differently. If I purposefully didn't try to keep in touch, would she notice? Would the absence make her heart grow fonder?

She laid her head back on my shoulder. Turning to face me, she asked the question I was about to ask myself, "So, what are you going to do with yourself for the next few weeks?"

Jokingly, I said, "You know, sulk around...wallow in self-pity...the usual." There was a hint of truth in my statement.

"You'll be fine," she commented, returning her eyes to the ceiling of my truck. Roxanne knew I wasn't happy about the separation.

I nodded, "I know."

After the forty-five minute drive, we arrived at the University of Florida campus. A brick wall etched with the name of the school welcomed us. Even though I wasn't moving in, a chill of excitement went through my spine. Following the map sent in the mail, Roxanne and I found the right way to her dorm, with her mom in tow.

Pulling up to the curb outside of her residence hall, Roxanne seemed to recognize the others who were unloading and hauling belongings. She perked up, rolling down her window and hollering out, "Hey!"

I could only smile. I wanted her to be happy, even if it meant being apart for a while. This was her chance to start anew and I wasn't going to jeopardize that. Selflessness was so incredibly hard sometimes.

We parked and jumped out of the truck to begin the move-in process. As I scanned my surroundings, I was astonished to see so many big guys around. When I looked a bit closer, I could read their t-shirts: Gator Football. *Great*, I thought. I guessed that these brawny guys were helping move in the soccer girls. I looked like a twig in comparison.

The twinkle in Roxanne's eyes at the sight of the football team could only mean bad news. I doubted that this would be the last time she would be around them. Holding my tongue, I tried to keep my jealousy invisible.

"Let's go check out your room," I suggested, grabbing Roxanne's hand and pulling her toward her dorm's entrance. It was all I could muster to distract her from what was happening.

After registering with the move-in staff at Excellence Hall, Roxanne led the way to the fourth floor, room 423. Once I realized that there was no elevator, I was quickly relieved that the football team was there to assist.

"Tyler," Roxanne began as she arrived at her door ahead of me, "Allison's here."

As I stepped into her room, it was clear that her roommate was definitely here already. In fact, it appeared that Allison was completely moved in, every single thing in its exact place. The sight was eerie.

"She told me she was clean, but goodness," Roxanne said, walking around the tiny room.

"Clean...is an understatement," I remarked.

We were virtually undisturbed by her roommate's presence as the three of us moved all of Roxanne's stuff into the room.

"I wonder where she is," I wondered out loud.

"Who? Allison?" Roxanne asked, shoving clothes into her closet in no particular order.

"Who else? We haven't seen her at all."

"Well, I'm sure she's around here," Roxanne ventured to guess.

Putting everything away was the tedious part. Roxanne was shouting out orders to her mother and I about where to put things. As her mom threw me her comforter from across the room, we could hear talking and footsteps getting closer.

A short girl with fiery red hair and medium build walked into the room, a smile plastered to her face. "Hey, I'm Allison."

"Hey, I'm Roxanne," Roxanne greeted her, shaking the girl's hand. "And this is-"

Allison interrupted, "Is this your boyfriend?"

Roxanne and I laughed nervously together.

"No," we both said simultaneously.

"Brother?" she guessed again.

Roxanne shook her head. "No, this is my friend Tyler."

I held out my hand to shake.

"Hang on," Allison said.

I watched as she moved carefully over to her desk, where a bottle of hand sanitizer stood. She squirted it into her hands and rubbed them together.

Crossing the room back to where I stood, she accepted my handshake. "Nice to meet you, Tyler."

She repeated the same sterile routine once our handgrip loosened.

I exchanged a look with Roxanne while Allison wasn't looking.

When she turned back around, Allison stated, "And this must be your older sister?" A cheesy grin spread from each corner of her mouth.

Roxanne's mother blushed and made a slight wave in Allison's direction. "You're so sweet. I'm Rebecca. Are your parents around?"

Allison shook her head. "Nope, they left awhile ago. Headed back to Miami."

"Miami? I hear it's nice down there," Rebecca commented.

Without meeting her eyes, Allison agreed, "Oh yes, I love it there. But I'm sure Gainesville will be great." She deliberately poured a cup of paperclips out onto her desk. The three of us watched her carefully, wondering what she was doing. Picking up each paperclip, she muttered something under her breath and placed it back into the cup.

"Are you counting paperclips?" I blurted out.

Roxanne nudged me, glaring.

Allison smiled at us. "Sure am."

"Okay," I quickly stated. Sure, of course it was normal to count paperclips.

Gesturing toward Allison's side of the room, Roxanne stated, "Looks like you're all moved in." I hoped her attempt to change the gauche subject would work. Drawing awkward attention to her new roommate was not something Roxanne would appreciate.

Allison laughed and sat down at her desk. "Yeah, I can't stand for my things to be out of place. It's kind of an obsessive-compulsive thing."

Maybe Allison is crazy after all, I thought to myself.

After Roxanne settled in, her mom and I regretfully left to head back to Ocala. Rebecca and I had completely different reasons for our departing sadness, but we shared a commonality. Neither of us wanted to leave Roxanne. For me, I could barely stand to be separated from her. For her mom, it was the beginning of a life without dependent children. The twins were her responsibility, her company, and, essentially, her life. Now she would return to a home reeking with emptiness. Although I was pretty torn up about leaving Roxanne, at least I would get to see her soon. With Roxanne's soccer schedule, the likeliness of returning home often was slim to none. I couldn't resist feeling sorry for Rebecca.

With anyone else, the forty-five minute drive home would have been slightly awkward. Thankfully, Rebecca was like a second mother to me. Our conversations were similar to the ones I had with my own mom.

"So, Tyler, when are you and Roxanne getting together?" This was not the first time she had brought up this issue.

I chuckled at her question. Accelerating onto the highway, I turned over my left shoulder to check for traffic. "Why are you asking *me*?"

"You're such a handsome boy. I don't understand." I noticed a concerned look come over her expression.

In a joking voice, I said, "Are you saying that the only thing I have going for me are my looks? I mean, I'm flattered at the compliment, but a bit disappointed at the same time." I flashed a grin full of teeth her way.

She smacked me lightly on the shoulder, in the same way Roxanne did. "You know that's not what I meant. I'm just concerned for her."

"Why?"

"I'm not sure that she's ever going to get married."

"Rebecca, she's only eighteen. Give her a break."

"Tyler, you know as well as I do that her age isn't the problem."

I nodded in agreement. "I know."

"You're the best one for her, I just know it."

"We'll see."

"Just know that I'm rooting for you."

"Thank you. I'm glad I have your blessing."

"You've had my blessing since kindergarten." I loved her warm, motherly smile.

"I *was* a pretty cute kindergartener."

We drove along for a while in silence, listening to old country songs over the radio. I was more into rock music myself, but I knew Rebecca's taste. I could tell she appreciated the thought.

"So," she began, "How're your parents?"

I shrugged, wanting to reveal little on the subject. "Fine."

"Oh. That's good..." She was staring at me, fishing for more information. "I haven't heard from your mom lately; is everything okay?"

"She's fine."

"Tyler..." Her voice was serious.

"Rebecca..." I mimicked her.

"Does Roxanne know?"

"Know what?"

"Know what's going on?"

"With what?"

"With your parents."

Suddenly, I realized she was trying to get me to confess something. "I don't know what you're talking about."

She turned her whole body to face me, her face stern. "Tyler Christopher Hansen, tell me why your parents have avoided my family for the past few months."

I sighed, rather loudly. "No."

"Excuse me?" She was offended.

"Sorry... it's just, not something I want to talk about."

"Honey, it's alright. I care about your family."

"I know..."

"Please?"

"It's nothing really," I said, trying to sound nonchalant. Rebecca would see right through my act, but I had to try.

"Tyler," she warned me.

I gave up. "Mom and dad have been fighting a lot lately."

The cab of my truck got awfully quiet. I guessed she was taking the new information in and considering what to say.

"I'm sure it's nothing," she asserted, more to herself than to me.

"It's not nothing. They've mentioned the *D* word....," I said, solemnly.

Her eyes widened, struck by the seriousness of the situation. "Do you know why?"

"I try not to listen. I don't want any part of it."

She looked down. "I can understand that."

"It's hard... you know... seeing them so angry with each other. If I could just say or do something to change their minds. I would give anything to keep them together. Did you and Dan ever fight?" I wasn't sure if the question was too personal, but I decided to ask it anyway.

Casually, as if Dan was at home waiting for her to arrive, Rebecca spoke, "Oh, every now and then. It was always hard when he left for business, but we made it through."

I sat silently in thought, staring at the cars along the highway.

Rebecca placed her hand on my shoulder. "Tyler, it'll be okay. I'll invite Marie over for lunch and maybe she'll open up. Maybe I can convince her to reconsider. I wish she would have said something to me..."

"Don't take it personally, my mom would never want to seem dysfunctional. You know that."

"Of course she wouldn't. I completely understand."

Then, there was another pause of silence.

"Talk to her for me, will you? I'm worried."

Rebecca gave me another comforting smile and said, "Of course I will."

19

REGAN

"Kappa Alpha Kappa!" I yelled harmoniously at the top of my lungs.

I was standing alongside a group of girls, all of us learning to sing the sorority chants.

After moving into the dorms a week early at the University of Florida to participate in the sorority rush, I was chosen to become a Kappa, along with twenty-nine other girls. I would now consider these girls my Kappa sisters. My christening into the fall pledge class happened on my birthday. I couldn't have asked for a better gift.

Since high school, I knew I wanted to be in a sorority. What was better than having one hundred close girl friends? I couldn't think of anything that could even compare. We would go shopping together, talk about boys, go shopping again, dress up, and go out. What a great thing this sorority would be for me.

Since Roxanne moved away a few weeks ago, I hadn't spoken to her. Oh, the freedom! The feeling of not having to see her every single day was a relief in itself. It was an added bonus that I didn't have to talk to her at all.

Joining the sorority meant that I would be able to live in the house, instead of the dorm. I would get to be around my new friends, or sisters, all the time! It was going to be fabulous!

A sudden flash of old birthday party memories from childhood came to mind. Although I was glad I didn't have to be around

Roxanne, it was impossible to forget her birthday. Unfortunately, being a twin meant never being completely independent. There would always be something to remind you of her, like your birthday. Yet another thing we had to share.

"Kappa, kappa! Alpha, alpha! Kappa, kappa!" We shouted, in sync with our clapping hands.

I had thought of Luke's disappearing act a couple of times. I bet that he was sick of Roxanne. Who wouldn't be?

It did disappoint me, though. I enjoyed his company. He was always so sweet.

Too bad my sister had to scare him off.

At the thought of Luke, I couldn't help but think about the numerous males on this campus. *The world is my oyster*, I thought, grinning.

"Sing louder!" the pledge class teacher criticized. I liked to call her *Nazi* in my head.

"KAP-PA, AL-PHA, KAP-PA!" We sang, straining our voices.

Although I couldn't deny that having a boyfriend would be nice, I didn't really want one. I wanted to have fun and I knew the tragedies that came with a relationship. I would rather just kiss and tell. That was more fun, anyway.

"Now add the dancing!" the pledge class teacher commanded.

Unfortunately, school would be starting in a matter of days. I was excited about college, but not about class. I knew I needed to get decent grades or my mother wouldn't be as giving with her money. At least none of my classes required me to be up before noon.

"Now clap your hands!" We heard her scream in our ears as she walked behind each of us, critiquing our postures and our clothing.

Tonight was the Kappa Date Dash. The event consisted of the pledge class randomly asking guys to go on a group date. The catch was that we were timed, allowing only ten minutes to persuade a stranger to come with us to a designated location. If anyone failed to complete the task, the girl would be forced to sleep outside in the middle of the house yard in a bikini. Although I looked great in a bathing suit, I was not going to be subjected to the embarrassment of not finding a date.

"Don't forget your smile!" She yelled.

At this point, I was about all smiled out. I nervously glanced to both my left and right to estimate how my neighboring sisters were holding out. Surprisingly, they were fine. I wiped the sweat off my forehead and straightened up.

"Alright, that's enough. Good job," the pledge class teacher commended us.

I sighed quietly in relief. I didn't think I would be able to speak tonight for the dash. It wouldn't stop me from getting a date, though. I would do whatever it took.

She continued, "Okay, girls, don't forget to be at the house tonight at six o'clock sharp. Shortly after, we will begin the biannual Kappa Date Dash. Be sure to wear the appropriate attire. Do not do the Kappa name an injustice. Have a positive attitude, and you will succeed! You're dismissed."

The pledge class broke apart, tiredly heading into the house. I followed a few other girls up the stairs to my room. I shared a large room with five others. It was a hard adjustment from my single room at home. Unregretful, I had to smile at the future of fun that lay ahead of me.

Peering at the clock on the wall, I gasped. We only had two hours to get ready for the dash. I would have to hurry!

At two minutes to six, I was lined up next to my pledge sisters outside our house. I tried not to laugh at the scene. Bystanders passing by had stopped to stare. We all looked ridiculous.

Each member of my class was given a slip of paper earlier in the evening. Each slip was unique. Until instructed to do so, we were not allowed to look at the paper. I knew each one of us was nervous at the destiny that awaited, written beneath a simple fold.

Before we began singing Kappa chants, I could remember when we were given the cue.

"On my call, you can look at your paper. Ready? Go!" shouted the pledge class teacher.

Hurriedly, we all unfolded our papers. Dumbfounded looks followed.

My slip read: Farmer.

The girl next to me held a slip that read: Hunter.

We all swapped confused glances.

"Teacher, am I supposed to find a firefighter for the dash?" a fellow pledge asked, bravely.

"Ha! You're so simple-minded. No, girls. You do not have to find a firefighter, or librarian, or mechanic for the dash. *You* are to dress as the occupation listed on your slips." The smug look on the teacher's face was indescribable.

I remember the quiet shrieks that filled the air. Abrupt *hushes* followed. We didn't want to seem too ungrateful.

So, as designated, I was dressed as a farmer. In a desperate attempt to look cute, I put my hair in pigtails and painted small brown freckles on my cheeks. Luckily, I happened to own a pink cowboy hat, which I donned for the occasion. I bought denim overalls, manually cut into short shorts. One of my roommates owned a pair of brown cowboy boots, which I was able to borrow. Overall, I thought I looked the part, adding my personal touch to enhance the effect.

Many of my fellow pledges had also altered their original occupational attire. Each girl transformed her assignment into a challenge and was able to conquer it. Although we were all supposed to look like men, I thought we looked fabulous. Who wouldn't date us?

"Three...two...one...Go!" sang out the pledge class teacher. The time to dash had come.

As she walked backward into the house, I could hear her voice again, barely audible with the new commotion, "You have ten minutes."

Panicking, all the girls in my pledge class scrambled from the front yard of our sorority house. It was a hectic scene. It reminded me of standing outside a department store in the early hours of Black Friday in November, waiting for the store to open. Once the clock rang out, everyone spilled into the store in a rush, trampling those less worthy and heading for the best sales. Yes, we were each headed for the best deal on campus.

Time was against me. I could hear the seconds count down with each heartbeat. Sweat broke out across my forehead. I scanned my surroundings, moving with precision through the streets of Greek Town, where all the fraternity and sorority houses sat. I watched girls flee in all different directions. Trying to keep my cool, I picked up a slight jog. Out of the corner of my eye, I spotted a guy at a close street intersection. He appeared handsome and alone.

As I began to dart across the street, I heard my name being called from a distance. I looked around, finding no one to my dismay.

"Regan!" he called again.

I flung my head around, to find the best-looking guy on campus jogging toward me.

"Luke!" I exclaimed, a mixture of confusion and surprise rolled into one.

He approached, not winded at all. Atop his head was the same old hat he wore every time I saw him.

"What are you—?" I started.

"What are you—?" he asked, gesturing toward my outfit.

I posed, girlishly.

I realized I was still on a mission; I didn't have much time. "Luke, I don't have time to talk. I have to—" I lost my words again, looking back to see if my target had fled. To my disappointment, he was gone. There wasn't another male in sight. What was I going to do? *But then again...*

Peering at Luke, I considered the idea. He was definitely good looking. The other girls would die just to be seen with him. I would be envied, and I liked the thought. Plus, if Roxanne ever found out, she would flip. It would be perfect.

"Come with me!" I grabbed his big, muscular hand and dragged him back toward the mansion I called home.

"Where are we going?" he asked through a laugh, intrigued by my actions.

"I'll explain later. Now, we have to hurry!" I gave him another yank to reinforce my words.

Suddenly, I felt his hand slip out of mine. He was now running alongside me. Luke led the way straight back to the house. *How did he know where I lived?* I briefly wondered. The thought dissipated once we reached our destination.

I tried to catch my breath as we stepped through the large double doors. Again, Luke was perfectly fine, probably without even an increase in pulse. I took my eyes off his gorgeous face and recognized quite a number of the girls in my pledge class with dates, random guys who looked awfully confused. Grinning, I winked at one of my roommates, who was motioning slightly toward Luke and mouthing, "Hot!"

I nodded and watched as more girls waltzed through the door with their dumbstruck dates. Eventually we were ushered to the basement, where a three-course catered meal awaited us. Explaining to Luke the theme and the reason for the chaos, I tried to keep from blushing. After a stream of compliments from him, butterflies filled my stomach.

"Let's sit," he suggested, pulling out a chair for me to sit in.

"Thank you," I said, biting my lip.

He sat in the chair adjacent to mine, dragging it closer to me. I tried not to stare too often at him, so he wouldn't think I was weird. This was difficult because every time I looked into his eyes, he was staring at me. Not a normal stare, but a *gaze*. I would have guessed he was trying to solve a puzzle.

"You know... you look just like your sister tonight," he remarked.

My mouth dropped slightly. "W-what?" I mumbled, horrified.

"You are beautiful. You really don't have to wear this," he pointed at my outfit, in particular my hand-cut shorts. I thought I had done a good job.

Baffled by the half-compliment, half-insult, I shrugged. "I thought guys liked a little leg."

His hand touched my knee, his eyes piercing into me. Luke was holding onto the back of my chair. I had no way to escape, even if I wanted to.

Slowly, he slid his smooth hand up from my knee to my bare thigh. Goosebumps prickled my arms, and he could surely feel them on my leg. His locked gaze didn't falter; it made me afraid. I felt his fingers cradle the muscles on the top of my leg as he approached the denim. A chill ran down my spine.

Once his fingertips reached my shorts, he peeled his hand away easily. Using the same hand, he cupped his chin and rested his elbow on the table.

With a stern affect, Luke commented, "It's hard for males to resist when you wear revealing clothing."

"Isn't that the point?" I chuckled, unsure if I was supposed to laugh.

"No."

I kept silent, bringing my eyes down to my hands fidgeting in my lap.

His hand touched my chin, lifting my head so our eyes would meet. "Regan..."

"Luke...," I muttered, feeling a bit embarrassed.

"Don't feel bad. I'm trying to let you know that sometimes, being sexy is inappropriate."

"Oh, 'kay." I wanted to pull my face away from his touch, but couldn't seem to muster up enough force to do so.

"I'm serious," Luke retorted.

I nodded, feeling his grip loosen.

He let go of my chin, resting back in his chair.

I let out a sigh of relief. I *wanted* to be sexy. Why was that so wrong?

For once, I wanted the attention off me. "Why do you always wear that stupid hat?" I poked his head.

Luke made a funny face and put his hand on top of his head. "What? This?"

I nodded, "Yes, you always wear that old thing."

"I like it..." he said, trailing off. He sounded discomfited.

"It's old. You need a new hat," I ordered.

Paternally, Luke said, "Now, Regan, how would you like it if I told you that you needed to discard your favorite *Coach* purse that you always wear?"

Folding my arms across my chest, I grunted. "Not the same."

He raises one eyebrow disbelieving, "And why not?"

"Because my purse doesn't smell."

After eating a delicious meal and chatting with those sitting near-by, everyone headed to a different area of the basement to play drinking games. Luke declined the alcohol, but played regardless. He looked like he was having fun. I hoped so. Since I only had to make it up two flights of stairs, I didn't hold back on the beverages.

As the night lingered on, I mingled with the different girls in my pledge class while Luke did his own mingling. Every time I saw him, he was conversing with a different girl. I knew that the girls couldn't help but be drawn to him. At least I could rest on the fact that he was *my* date tonight.

When I was less capable of watching Luke from afar, I started moving in his direction. On the way, I felt an arm swing around my waist. As I turned to determine the culprit, I recognized him as the random date of one of my roommates.

"Hey, baby," he said.

"Hey." I laughed nervously.

He held me close to his body. "What's your name?"

"Regan," I answered, trying to gently squirm out of his hold.

"Well, Regan," he grinned, "I'm Todd." Pulling me even closer, his hand dropped from my lower back down to my butt.

"Whoa, buddy! That's enough," I shoved away from him, struggling to put distance between us.

"Oh, come on. You must be needing something...."

His suggestive nature made me cringe. I shoved again. "Get off!"

Todd only gripped me closer. I was considering decking him in the face.

"She's going to hit you if you don't stop," Luke offered to Todd, appearing next to me.

Todd's face scrunched together in anger. "Get your own."

"I'm sorry, but you have mine," Luke corrected, grinning at me.

"Yeah, whatever," Todd remarked, hesitating to make any further movement.

Luke unwrapped Todd's hands and put his own arm around me. I folded into him, letting him wrap me up. It felt comforting after what had just happened.

"Let's go outside," he whispered into my ear, leading me to the front doors.

I nodded, letting him support much of my weight. The alcohol was definitely starting to affect my sense of awareness.

Once outside, the night air felt refreshing. I could hear the cacophony of sounds around us, but I felt far away at the same time.

"Hey," Luke began, turning me around to face him, "Are you okay?"

I was quiet for a brief period, then answered, "Yeah, I'm okay."

"I have to tell you something," he said.

My heart leapt. "Yes?"

He leaned forward, eyes secured into mine. With a soft voice, he said, "I told you so."

I jokingly pushed him away. "Thanks," I sarcastically stated.

"Well, I *did* tell you so."

Nodding, I leaned back into his chest. "Thank you."

"For what?" Although all other noise seemed distant, I could tell his lips were right next to my ear.

I turned my neck to gaze up at him. "Protecting me."

"Of course," he firmly said. "Promise me something?"

"Anything," I offered, my voice increasing an octave.

"Please, please, don't look that sexy in public again."

A smile broke across my mouth, "Sure."

"Thank you."

"Promise me something?" I asked.

"Sure."

I gulped. The butterflies fluttered. "Promise not to leave again."

I didn't want to see the expression on his face but I had to look. His eyebrows were turned down, his mouth in a frown.

Silence filled the awkward space between us. He thought for a few minutes on what I had said.

Then, he asked, "Why do you say that?"

I didn't have a good answer. He should know I was thinking the same thing inside my head.

"I don't know," was all I could come up with.

A pause of silence, filled with only the sound of his breathing. "Okay. It's a deal."

Someone brushed up against my arm. I recognized the long brownish-blonde hair.

Sluggishly, I called out, "Alexi! Where are you going?"

She waved at me, and winked, as she kept walking away from the house.

Luke's warmth was burning into me now. It invited me in. The next set of events happened in a blur.

Without really realizing my actions, my hand reached behind his head and pulled him closer. I gently forced my lips onto his and we kissed, experiencing a moment I could only visualize in a dream. It was indescribable. The seconds that we were interlocked seemed to last forever in a good way, but I couldn't be sure how long it actually occurred. All I knew was that he wasn't pulling away. Or maybe I wasn't letting him pull away.

The only thing that broke my fantasy experience was a loud yell from across the yard.

"Luke!" Roxanne yelled, clearly furious.

A smile spread across my lips as Luke pulled away.

20

ROXANNE

H appy Birthday to me, Happy Birthday to me, Happy Birthday to Roxanne, Happy Birthday to me.

Every year on this day, I'm reminded that I have to share my world with my sister. But I wouldn't let this fact destroy my first birthday of independence.

The only thing that made this particular birthday disappointing was the fact that I wasn't able to play in the first soccer game of the year against Ohio. My coach dismissed the freshmen from traveling. I had hoped that she would change her mind about that rule, at least for my sake. I had something to prove on the field and I had been waiting for that moment for a long time. I guessed my chance to shine would have to wait.

On the other hand, I didn't have to spend my birthday on a large charter bus with thirty grouchy, sleepy girls. Plus, school would be starting on Monday and I was looking forward to a relaxing weekend with my new friends before my stress would start to pick up. I had made a lot of friends on the team—especially the freshmen—and they were looking forward to celebrating my birthday with me. Unfortunately, this meant that celebrating with Tyler would have to wait. I felt like I had to put him on hold for the last month, due to long and tiring soccer practices and team get-togethers. Hopefully, all that would change once school started up and my schedule evened out. I had hope, but I didn't know if it was realistic.

Tyler was not the only boy I hadn't seen in a while. Luke had disappeared now for quite a few weeks. I missed them both, in different ways. Tyler had always been my safe haven and comfort; Luke was still a mystery to me. I understood Tyler; I didn't understand Luke at all. I liked them both for these polar-opposite reasons. I couldn't explain it. I knew it didn't make sense.

In between soccer practice and hanging out with my new friends, I had contemplated many times how I would get to see Luke again. Maybe the ordeal with Tyler pushed him away. Tyler could seem very intimidating when he was protective. If Tyler weren't my friend, I wondered if Luke wouldn't have disappeared. The thought made me sad.

Thankfully, dorm life with my fellow teammates was better than I expected. With a count of only a few dramatic events a week, our friendships were holding strong. We were all going through the same hell—two-a-day practices—and consequently understood each other. Most of the girls that lived on the soccer floor were freshmen, but there were a scattered bunch of sophomores. I wondered if they thought we were bothersome because of how we acted. This was our first time away from home and boy, did we embrace it! I'm sure we were obnoxious and sometimes downright annoying, but hey, we were having fun.

Adjusting to all-you-can-eat buffet-style dorm food was definitely difficult. I wasn't used to the small selection of healthy options. Eventually, salad and fruit would get old. I had to hold strong for as long as I could. With the increase in energy expenditure, I was constantly looking to fulfill my carbohydrate appetite but my only options were pizza and hamburgers. That just wouldn't do. There had to be another way. Because I wasn't able to eat as much as I needed, I had already lost five pounds. At least I could look forward to a good meal one day a week: Pasta Fridays at the dining hall were my absolute favorite. I had also decided to make a diet exception for my birthday. Oh, that cake was going to taste so good!

My birthday plans were a surprise, planned by the girls in my hall. I loved surprises; I was so excited! The only thing I had to do was be dressed by five o'clock and the rest would fall into place. Looking at my watch, I decided it was a good time to start preparing. Due to the occasion, I permitted myself to wear make-up and fix my hair. Although I knew how to accomplish the task, getting fancy was a rarity. In fact, I had to burrow clothing for the occasion. I would much rather wear a t-shirt, shorts, and flip-flops and pull my hair into a hair tie behind my head.

My roommate was out running errands, so I had the room to myself. Flipping on the radio, I grabbed a nice pair of dark jeans I had rarely worn, a real bra that was all but new, and a sleeveless dressy shirt that Allison lent me. As I began to change, my cell phone rang.

I smiled; it was Tyler. "Hey!" I answered.

"Roxy! Happy Birthday! Do you feel old?" Tyler joked. The enthusiasm in his voice was unmistakable. He enjoyed birthdays just as much as I did.

"Oh yeah," I laughed, "Real old. But you should be the one to talk. Don't forget you're older than me."

"The older, the wiser, they say. What are you doing?"

"I'm getting ready," I said.

His tone changed. "Getting ready for what?"

"My friends from the team are taking me out, I guess," I truthfully told him.

"You guess?" Tyler asked, curious.

"It's all a surprise. I have no idea what's going on."

As if in relief, Tyler's voice lightened. "Oh, I see. Well, I have your gift. Can I come over?"

I looked at the clock. I had an hour before I was getting picked up. Surely that was enough time. "Sure, but I'm leaving in an hour."

"That's plenty of time. See you soon." *Click.*

Staring at the phone, I shook my head. That was awfully strange. Shrugging, I threw my phone on my bed and got back to work.

A knock at the door came only ten minutes later. Luckily, I was already finished getting dressed. When I opened it, I found Tyler out of breath. "What's wrong?" I asked, slightly worried.

"I. Ran. Up. The. Stairs," he panted, inhaling in between words. He stepped past me into the room.

Shutting the door behind him, I laughed. "Why'd you do that?"

He shot me a glare. My smiling immediately ceased.

He explained, "I didn't want to make you late. *You're* the one that has plans."

"Okay, okay, fair enough."

Once taking a better look at Tyler's face, I realized something was drastically different. "You have fuzz!" I grabbed his chin and scratched his skin lightly.

He chuckled, still with labored breathing. "You like?"

"I'm not sure...I have never seen you with facial hair before." In the many years I had known Tyler since puberty, he had always worn the clean-cut look. Looking at him now with a half-goatee-half-dusty beard, I wasn't sure what to think. It didn't look like Tyler.

Tyler brushed his hand over his cheek. "I kinda like it."

"What made you decide to grow it out?"

"Lack of parental supervision. My mother would never have let me do this."

"So," I began, "you don't really want a beard...you're just adjusting to your new-found freedom."

He smirked. "Something like that, I guess. You don't like it, do you?"

I sighed. "Tyler, you could probably look good with pink hair. I'm sure it'll grow on me. No beard though, okay?"

"I promise, no beard. Just a little five o'clock shadow, that's all."

"I think I can live with that."

Now that my attention to his facial hair had ceased, he thoroughly took in the situation. Cocking his head to the side, Tyler looked me over appreciatively, giving me a gentle smile. "By the way, you look absolutely beautiful."

"Tyler," I started, feeling my cheeks blush pink.

"Now, how does a guy like *me* even stand a chance when a girl like you, dressed like *that*, goes out in public?" He winked at me.

"No matter what I wear or where I go, you don't have a chance," I said sarcastically, adding a cackle at the end.

"Ha, ha. Very funny."

"So, where's my gift?" I held out both my hands in a receiving manner.

His eyes softened. A meek smile crossed his mouth. "Close your eyes," Tyler demanded.

I closed my eyes and listened. Suddenly, I felt a cold metal touch my neck. It tugged at my skin as Tyler clasped it in the back. He lifted my hair out from under its grasp.

I could feel Tyler's breath close to my ear. "Okay, open your eyes," he whispered.

After I opened my eyes, I touched the necklace on my neck. Although I couldn't tell what it was, I was thrilled. I raced to the little mirror on the wall.

The silver necklace was the outline of a soccer ball with the number 16 in the middle – my jersey number. It was wonderful.

After a minute of silence, Tyler spoke, "Do you like it?"

"Tyler, I love it!" I exclaimed, throwing my arms around his neck.

He chuckled. "Good, I was getting worried when you hadn't said anything."

"It's the best present ever," I proclaimed, pulling away from his arms.

"I'm glad. Happy Birthday." His glistening smile was contagious.

I paused again to stare in the mirror. I was so happy.

Feeling Tyler standing right next to me, I turned to look at him. His face had changed.

"I'm still mad at you, you know," he asserted.

"For what?" I asked.

He was quiet for a minute. Then suddenly, he spoke, "For spending your birthday with your dumb friends instead of me."

I grabbed his shoulders and gently shook him. "For one, my friends aren't dumb. You haven't even gotten the chance to meet them. Secondly, I promise we will celebrate this weekend."

He squinted his eyes. "Promise?"

"I promise," I pledged.

His smile eased my angst.

"So," Tyler began again, sitting down at my desk, "Why don't you ever look like this?"

My eyebrows scrunched together. "What do you mean?"

"Don't get me wrong, you're pretty no matter what. I just don't know why you don't wear make-up and dress up more often."

I put my hands on my hips and glared at him. "Tyler, you know why."

He shrugged. "Okay, I know you think it's stupid to try and impress people. But you look so good."

"My friends will like me for who I am, not what I wear or what my face looks like," I announced.

"I get it, I get it." Tyler almost always agreed with me to get out of an argument.

I took a seat on my bed. Staring outside at the fading daylight, my birthday anticipation for the night was building. I needed to distract myself.

"So, did you get all moved in?" I asked, not really interested.

He nodded. "Sure did."

"How's your roommate?"

"Boring. Lazy. He's currently sitting in our room drunk." Tyler's expression was unenthusiastic as he spoke.

"He is? Isn't it a little soon to be getting plastered already?"

"Guess not," Tyler said.

"You're not going to be influenced by him, are you?" A slight look of worry creased my face.

Laughing, Tyler answered, "No way. Maybe he'll change when school starts. It doesn't look promising though."

After a small pause, I continued to question him, "What are you going to do if he brings in a bunch of drunk, naked girls every night?"

Grinning, he said, "Thank him."

Folding my arms in front of my chest, I gawked at him. "You wish."

"You're right," he said. I wasn't quite sure how serious he was.

I had a bright idea to change the subject. "You know what? I should set you up with one of the girls on my team." I had to admit to myself that I didn't really think the idea was foolproof. The thought of Tyler dating someone, especially someone I knew, would put me beside myself.

Trying to conceal concern, Tyler stared at me. "Really?" He was disbelieving, of course.

"Sure, why not? They're all really great."

"I don't think so."

"Why not?" The idea only seemed amusing because I knew Tyler wouldn't go for it. Part of me wanted him to be happy with another girl, but another part of me wanted him single, forever. But I couldn't let him know I felt that way.

"I don't want to date anyone right now." His eyes were almost pleading. Tyler could declare his abstinence from dating as much as he wanted, but I knew the truth. He wasn't interested in dating anyone *except for me*. It was obvious he wouldn't be saying this out loud.

I recommenced my ignorance, "Alright, well, let me know when you're ready."

Tyler averted his gaze away from me. "Sure," he mumbled meekly.

After a moment of awkward silence, he asked in a lighter tone, "So, what's on the agenda for the birthday girl tonight?"

I shrugged. "I have no idea. It's supposed to be a surprise."

"Right," Tyler pronounced slowly and warily.

Glaring at him, I rebutted, "I promise!"

With a slight grin crossing his lips, he shook his head. "I bet you'll start at the male strip club, followed by the bar where you'll display your own dancing abilities atop a table, and you'll end the night in a hotel making out with your roommate and running nude across the campus."

I put on the best smug look I could muster. "You got me! How'd you know?"

He laughed. "Well, you know, I have a good sense of the girls in town."

"Right," I mocked him.

Startling me, my phone rang from across the room. I hurriedly grabbed it and flipped it open.

"Hey!" I exclaimed into the receiver.

"Hey birthday girl," my friend Meghan answered.

I stared at Tyler as he made funny faces at me. "What's the plan?"

"I'm headed over, is that okay?"

Covering up the speaker, I leaned closer and whispered to Tyler, "Meghan's coming to get me, is that okay?"

His face flat, Tyler responded, "She's your friend."

I rolled my eyes. "I feel bad that she's coming early. Sorry we can't spend more time together."

"It's alright. You owe me a date, though." By date, I knew he meant a *friendship* date. It was the least I could agree to, seeing how I hadn't spent a lot of time with him since I moved to Gainesville three weeks ago.

"Sure, sure," I agreed, smiling at him.

Removing my hand from the speaker, I continued, "That sounds great. You'll get to meet my friend Tyler."

"Is he hot?"

"Oh, yeah," I laughed, winking at Tyler.

"What?" he mouthed, a look of curiosity flooding his face.

I shook my head.

"Well, then, of course I would like to meet him." I could sense the smile in her voice. An internal laugh escaped. As much as I liked Meghan, she wasn't good enough for Tyler.

"See you soon," I said.

"See ya!" Meghan squeaked.

A knock at the door erupted only a few minutes later. As soon as the door was open, Meghan flew in to give me a hug and quickly greet Tyler.

"Hey, I'm Meghan," she bashfully waved. As much as she was trying to appear shy, she wasn't convincing enough.

"Hey. Tyler," he nodded casually. I watched Tyler scan her over. It was a little weird to watch the scene. Meghan looked somewhat clueless, but that could have been a part of the act.

Throwing her designer purse down on my bed, Meghan gushed, "Roxanne's told us so much about you!"

He flashed me a grin. "Oh, really? Like what?"

"Don't hurt his feelings, Meghan," I joked.

She bit her bottom lip and giddily said, "It's all good things, I promise."

"Well, in that case," Tyler turned to look at me, "I'm disappointed in you."

I gave him a haughty stare.

"Well, are you ready?" Meghan asked. "You look fabulous."

"Yes, just fabulous," Tyler teased. Meghan was giggling like a small child.

"Yep," I grabbed my key and threw it into the clutch I burrowed from my roommate.

As the three of us walked out of the room, I turned to Tyler. "I'll call you soon, okay? I'll be here all weekend so we should hang out."

He pushed his finger onto the tip my nose. "You be good."

I nodded, smiling. "I will."

"Nice to meet you, Meghan," Tyler held out his hand.

"Same here," she shook it gently.

According to Meghan, the first stop on our list was at our friend Laura's house. Thankfully, Laura lived close to campus, right on the other side of the Greek Town. I wasn't sure how long I would be able to walk in my heels. There was a good chance I would be parading around without shoes most of the night.

Although it was early in the evening, the members of the Greek community were already starting their weekend. Being the weekend before the start of classes, there was reason enough to celebrate. The smell of barbeque wafted toward my nose, making me realize how hungry I was. Fraternity brothers crowded their house yards, throwing footballs back and forth. Sorority girls pranced from house to house in higher heels than my own, wearing short skirts and sparkling tops. I thought, *there's no way my legs would look good in that*. My jealousy didn't last long though, with the realization that many pairs of male eyes were staring at Meghan and I.

We tried to smile casually and continued to walk forward. I wondered if it were obvious we didn't fit in with that crowd. From what I gathered from the upper classmen on the soccer team, the collegiate athletes generally didn't fraternize with the other social

147

groups on campus. I guessed we led completely different lives. As one girl put it, "While we're working our butts off to do well on the field as well as in the classroom everyday, they're going to school for the weekends." I knew she was being overly judgmental. I also knew that my sister was now a sorority girl and I couldn't deny her priorities. But there were probably a lot of smart people in the Greek community.

We arrived at Laura's house quickly. She lived with four other girls from the soccer team in a nicely sized five-bedroom house. The décor and furniture yelled *cheap*, understandably. Even with the less elegant look, the house still felt fairly cozy.

"Where is everyone?" I asked, scanning the desolate house.

"They're all at the game," Laura replied. The roommates were all upper classmen, including her older sister. Shannon was the only reason Laura was able to live in the house. Without her sister's approval, Laura would have been stuck down the hall from Allison and me. I silently wished my relationship with my sister were filled with love and kindness. On a more considered second thought, I was fine living without her. She would have only annoyed me.

Soon after our arrival to the house, ten other freshman girls showed up. Together, we went out to dinner and ate delicious birthday cake. Even though I normally wouldn't eat that much sugar, I let myself go. It was my birthday, after all. After the indulgent activities, Laura led our caravan back to her house. I was surprised; I didn't expect to head back to the house so soon.

"What's going on?" I asked Laura as we walked back up her steps.

"Just wait, you'll see," Meghan responded.

As we stepped inside the dark foyer, a small overhead light flashed on. Suddenly, music blared over a loud speaker, surrounding us with dance beats. I looked around, noticing a smile on everyone's faces. It was obvious that this was a part of the surprise.

"What—?" I started to ask, unable to finish in my bewilderment.

"You don't need to ask what, but when?" From the back, my friend Kristen placed her hands on my shoulders.

"When?" I rephrased, still confused. It was more of a question about the question.

"Exactly. Now!" she yelled.

A bright flow of brilliant lights flooded the living room. There stood another handful of girls from the team, sporting bright smiles. "Surprise!"

The living room had been transformed from a dining area to a bar. On one side of the room held a long table, covered with bottles of liquor and an assortment of other drinks, as well as cups and shot glasses.

"Oh my goodness!" I squealed, unsure of really how to respond. I wasn't really a drinker in high school, except for the occasional homemade margarita from my mother.

"It only gets better," called out Allison next to me.

At the command of a control, the television screen flashed on. A luminous blue background appeared, with black words scrolling across.

"What's this about?" I asked, turning to look at my friends.

"What else but karaoke?" Laura said, knowingly.

"Oh, no... I can't sing!" I exclaimed. No one would want to hear me sing.

"Well, seeing how this is our only glimpse of freedom for the next...who knows when...we figured we would get a little...crazy!" Meghan responded, unscrewing the caps to the bottles and pouring some in each of the cups. She continued, handing me a shot glass of clear liquid, "Don't worry. After a few of these, no one will care what your voice sounds like!"

"Good thing there are no boys," I laughed, staring uncertainly into the small glass in my hand.

"You should invite Tyler," Meghan suggested, winking at me.

"Oohh, Tyler," a few girls commented.

I felt the blood rushing to my cheeks. "He's just a friend."

"A *special friend*, I'm sure," Laura added.

I shook my head lightly. "It's not like that."

"Then can I have dibs?" Meghan asked, as she downed a shot of her own clear liquid.

"Yeah, what about me?" another asked.

"And how about me?" someone else questioned.

I could tell everyone was joking, but it made me a bit jealous. Tyler's dating status shouldn't be any of my business. I should let him be free while he had the chance to meet new people easily. *Let it go*, I forced myself to think.

"Yeah, yeah. How am I supposed to drink this?" I asked, hoping to turn the subject away from Tyler. Looking guardedly into my cup of clear liquid, I wondered how crazy the night was going to get.

"Just put it to your mouth and drink!" Meghan cried out.

"Here," Allison gingerly handed me a can of soda. I almost sneered at the sight of the sugar and carbonation.

Noticing my distaste, Allison added, "Don't worry, it's diet."

I weakly smiled as everyone chanted for me to drink. As I threw the liquid down my throat, the burning immediately took hold. As quickly as possible, I drank the diet soda to neutralize the awful taste.

"Here's your microphone," Laura added, forcing it into my free hand.

"C'mon, birthday girl first!" cried Kristen, nodding at the microphone.

That was the first sign of a long night ahead of me.

Stumbling out of the house, I yelled an obnoxious goodnight to Laura and clumsily began walking back to my dorm. With a sober Allison in tow, I tried to focus on where I was roaming in the darkness. I could make out the skewed outlines of the Greek mansions, so I knew I was headed in the right direction. I carried my heels in my hand. Less aware of my surroundings, I stubbed my toe once or twice on the sidewalk or curb. The feeling of carelessness was well accepted. I was typically a cautious and organized person. Tonight, all my less important inhibitions were gone.

"C'mon, Allison!" I called behind me.

"Even when you're drunk, you're fast!" I heard her say, although it seemed she was further away than I thought.

My senses were still intact enough to know that the Greek parties were still in full swing. I guessed my tolerance for alcohol was probably less than most, consequently ending my night early. The blurry sight of the various people made me feel dizzy.

As we passed what looked to be a sorority house, I heard a familiar shrill voice.

"Alexi! Where are you going?" My hearing instantly picked up on the annoying tone.

Regan, I thought. *What a coincidence.*

Concentrating on focusing my eyes on her figure, I couldn't decide how far away she was. Without much thought, I moved in the direction of her voice. I wasn't sure what I was going to say to her, but I knew there had to be something mustering up inside me.

As the distance closed between us, my eyes were able to better adjust. When I could finally see clearly, I instantly wished I was blind. My mouth dropped.

"Rox, where are you going?" I heard Allison call out to me.

I blinked twice to make sure I wasn't hallucinating.

No, what I was seeing must really have been happening.

There he was, kissing my sister.

Luke.

21

ROXANNE

I had no idea what to do or say.

All I could do was drunkenly stare at Luke and Regan. My cheeks were red with fury, my throat shut from the bubble that had emerged there. I wanted to cry, whether from sadness or anger I couldn't decide. How could Luke do this to me?

I was torn about what to do next. Should I start yelling and screaming? Should I run away? Should I pinch myself to make sure I was conscious?

Was Luke really worth this pain? Maybe all I was to him was a gateway to my sister. I expected this kind of behavior from her, but I trusted Luke. Well, I had just started trusting him before he left. *He left me*, I reminded myself. *He left me.*

I turned around, a frown sewn on my lips, and stormed off toward Allison. She had the most confused look on her face, which was understandable. I would have to explain later. In the background, I heard my sister scream in our direction, "Luke! You can't leave me! You'll regret this!"

"I want to go home," I choked out.

"What's going on?" she asked, jogging after me.

"I-I..." I started, but couldn't find the right words.

"Roxanne, slow down!" Allison cried after me. I didn't realize I was walking so fast. All I knew was that I wanted to get away.

"Roxanne!" I heard a different voice call.

I don't want to talk to you, I thought. I wished I had the words to speak my thoughts.

When Luke finally caught up to Allison and me, he grabbed me by the shoulders and spun me around to look at him. He was ignoring Regan.

Diverting my eyes away from his, I could feel the tears budding up. *You cannot cry*, I reminded myself.

"Look at me," Luke commanded, holding my jaw straightforward.

"No!" I mumbled, pulling away from his grip.

"Yes."

I couldn't resist his strength, so I was forced to look at him. How could those wonderful brown eyes deceive me?

Using both my hands to pry his away from my face, I firmly said, "Leave me alone." His hand gave way immediately.

"Roxanne," he whispered, barely audible.

"What do you want?" I asked harshly.

"Can we please talk?" Although I didn't want to admit it, Luke's face was sincere.

I looked at Allison, who was still baffled by the situation. She was trying to decipher my expression, whether she should leave me in the hands of this stranger.

I nodded my head in agreement. *You're crazy*, I thought about myself.

"I'll meet you back at the dorm," I informed her, a little unsure of my own decision.

"Thank you," Luke stated, grabbing my hand.

Allison's face scrunched together anxiously. "Are you sure?" she mouthed.

"Yeah," I muttered, biting my lip.

I watched Allison walk solemnly toward our dorm. She turned once to look back in our direction, and I nodded confidently to her.

Luke brought my attention back to him, "Can we walk?"

I nodded, slipping my hand out of his. I was definitely still mad at him.

We walked wordlessly through Greek Town and then back onto campus. There was no particular course to our path, so we wandered aimlessly.

"Can I tell you something?" he finally asked.

"Please do," I encouraged. He had a lot of explaining to do.

"I know what that looked like back there…"

I couldn't withstand not voicing my opinions, so the words just spilled out. "Yeah, I know what it looked like. It looked an awful lot like you kissing my sister. It looked like you were hanging out like you two were old friends, when I haven't seen you in more than a month. It looked like a lot of things back there."

"Even though you won't believe a word I say, and that's completely justified, I would like to tell you the truth."

I interjected, "The truth would be good."

He nodded. "So, here it is. Regan kissed *me*."

I cackled loudly. "*Right*."

"I told you, it's the truth."

"Why should I believe you?" This was not the first time Luke would have lied to me.

He gazed into my eyes with pure innocence. "Because I'm asking you to."

I folded my arms across my chest stubbornly.

Luke added, "What can I do to make you understand?"

"Answer me this: what would my sister say if I asked her what happened?" My face was smug.

"She would most likely lie. Why would you ask her anyway? You trust me more than you trust her."

I considered this for a moment. Luke was 100% right. My sister *would* lie to me, no matter what I wanted from her. I speculated on the fact that he seemed to know my family so well, even though he barely knew us. Were we that dysfunctional and transparent?

I grudgingly admitted, "Okay, so she kissed you. What were you doing with her in the first place?"

"Again, believe me if you will. Earlier this evening, I was actually trying to find your sister so that she could tell me where you were. I didn't have your phone number and I didn't know which dorm you were in. I knew where to find her because she told me she wanted to be a Kappa this summer. Good guess."

"Okay, continue," I urged him, still wary.

"When I ran into her, she needed to find a date for this thing... I still don't really understand it...anyway, so, I was actually doing her a favor. When you saw us, she was more than inebriated. I promise I didn't initiate it."

Suddenly, as if turned on by a switch, the briskness of the cold air made me shiver. I guessed in all my frustration, in addition to my decreased inhibitions, I didn't realize how chilly it was outside.

Luke immediately picked up on my discomfort. "Here," he stripped off his lightweight cotton jacket and draped it around my shoulders.

"Thanks," I offered, unsmiling.

Although I wasn't quite ready for the answer to my next question, I knew I needed to ask it. I really didn't want to seem desperate. I didn't want him to know I cared. I wanted to pretend I was more independent than I actually was. In a rush of words, I asked, "Where have you been for the last month?"

Surprisingly, he laughed.

That irritated me. "What?"

He eyed me, a grin plastered across his face. "Was that hard for you to ask?"

How did he know? How did he always know?

He didn't allow me to answer. "Roxanne, I've thought a lot about you since we last met."

I didn't want to tell him that I felt the same way. I forced myself to bob my head up and down in agreement.

"*A lot,*" he emphasized.

I was fully aware that he didn't answer my question. So, I decided to ask a slightly different one, hoping for an adequate response. "Why did you leave?"

Luke paused before he finally answered, "I, uh, had to."

"I don't believe you."

He grunted. "I'd give my left hand for you to believe me right now."

I tried not to get caught up in his bargains. "Where did you go?"

"Home." His answer came out so quickly it appeared that he knew the question before I asked it.

"Home?" I asked. Suddenly, I was feeling a little sick to my stomach.

"Home...to Italy. I wanted to see my family before I started school."

"Alright," I dully said, placing a hold on any further questioning. I knew that his answer was a legitimate excuse to be absent from my life for over a month. Even though this was true, he still didn't tell me he was leaving. I continued to be suspicious; I had to be.

"Are you okay?" Luke asked, noticing my discomfort.

Silently, I nodded my head. I didn't want to speak, concerned I might feel worse.

His eyes smiled at me. The corners of his mouth peaked, ready to flash a brilliant smile but waiting for something. "Forgive me?"

Of course he would ask me to forgive him. What was I going to say? *No?*

I nodded a little bit. "Sure."

"Sure?" He was displeased.

"I mean, yes. I forgive you." I wondered if I actually believed that myself.

"Thank you. That means a lot to me." His smile wasn't shying away anymore.

His attitude was so light and carefree. Luke was the exact opposite of me in that respect. I realized I didn't want to upset him, no matter what. I figured out that when he was happy, I was satisfied. Would his relaxed nature eventually annoy me? I hoped not.

After a few more minutes of nice, quiet walking, Luke tried to make easy conversation. I wished I didn't have to answer any questions, but rather just listen to him ramble on. He didn't seem to pick up on my angst.

"So, what have you been up to for the last month?" he asked. I almost gawked, but caught myself before the embarrassment was inevitable. Did he know how much this question stung? It was as if his leaving really wasn't a big deal. Well, I knew it shouldn't have been, but of course it was.

As I thought about the last five weeks, I realized that not a lot had happened while he was away, except for moving to school and starting practice. Well, maybe that *was* a lot to undertake. It wasn't the easiest transition.

I finally answered, a little meekly, "Nothing too exciting. Just starting soccer, I guess."

"Soccer?" he asked, confused.

I stared at him before answering, calculating his question. Did he really not know that I was on the soccer team? Surely I had told him that.

"Yeah...didn't I tell you I was playing soccer?"

Luke was still baffled. "Soccer?" he repeated.

I smiled at his ignorance. "Yeah..."

His facial expression cleared, but a hint of perplexity was still apparent. "Oh, you mean, *fútball*...how's that going for you?"

"Right, football...it's alright. We've been practicing twice a day for a while now. It's sort of exhausting, actually." I sighed loudly just thinking about the previous week and how drained I was. I wondered how much school and soccer would clash. Would I be able to make it?

Luke picked up on the slight worry that showed on my face. "You'll be fine." He was so good at reading me.

I rolled my eyes in response. "We'll see."

He shook his head, a smile on his lips. "No, I promise. You'll be fine."

"Whatever you say, Luke."

He bit his lip and looked at the ground, an obvious grin yearning to explode across his mouth.

"What?" I asked. I really wished I could read him the same way he read me.

"I love it when you say my name."

My eyebrows furrowed together, "You mean, your *other* name?"

"I really like Luke. Let's keep it." His cheeks were pink. I couldn't tell if he was blushing or if I just never noticed their color before.

"I don't know about Italy, but in America, you can be called whatever you want."

He laughed. "Well, thank God for America." Then he winked. My heart almost stopped. Why was I such a girl?

Jokingly, I gently pushed his head away. Motioning to his hat, I asked, "Do all Italians like the Los Angeles Angels?"

Sarcastically, he said, "Oh yeah, we're all *big* baseball fans. Didn't you know the Italians came up with the game?"

"You're such a liar!" I exclaimed, followed by a laugh. "It's definitely the American pastime."

He nodded, chuckling. "No, we're definitely more into fútball...I mean, *soccer*."

I laughed at his ignorance.

"I'm sorry," he apologized, "I don't mean to seem stupid."

I sighed. "Luke, don't ever feel stupid around me. Got that?"

He saluted me like a soldier. "Yes, ma'am."

"And never call me ma'am."

"Yes, sir." He grinned.

I puckered my lips together and squinted my eyes. "Have I told you how funny you are?"

"No, please tell me again." His white teeth were glowing and it was hard to look away. I could stare at him all night long.

Another round of silence filled the air as we moseyed down the paths that students took to class during the week. Campus was beautiful, especially at night. The cool breeze was refreshing, though it was still pretty warm in August. I made a mental note of all the small things I enjoyed—the miniature trees that lined the middle of the path, the scattered patches of red and white lilies, the way the brick path felt against my bare feet. I inhaled the air. It was so refreshing.

As we rounded the corner of one of the buildings, Luke suddenly spoke, "May I promise you something?"

I shrugged. "Sure, anything." As soon as the words escaped my mouth, a combination of my inhibited balance and pure clumsiness made me stumble.

Grabbing me before I could hit the ground, Luke cried out, "Whoa! Are you alright?"

"Too much to drink...bad idea..." I mumbled, steadying myself against him. Bending down, I rubbed my feet, brushing off the acquired dirt.

Luke quickly commented, "So, that's the smell."

"My feet don't smell!" I punched him lightly in the arm.

"No, not your feet. Your breath; I can smell the alcohol. What is with you sisters? How much did you drink?"

I scowled as we started walking again. The cold brick sent a chilled sensation through my feet.

"I don't know. Too much?" I was hoping that I wasn't too obviously drunk. I was actually starting to feel a better grasp on my surroundings. I had been hoping all along that Luke wouldn't be able to notice my diminished perception.

"I would say too much, if my opinion counts."

I pouted.

"I promise I won't leave you again. Without telling you, I mean."

I was shocked, not expecting him to promise me *that*.

I pretended like it didn't matter, using my hands for emphasis, "What? Oh, no! It wasn't a big deal. I mean, we hardly know each other."

"But you must promise me something," Luke advised.

I gulped. "What would that be?"

He narrowed his eyes to me. "Promise me you'll always trust me. No matter what."

Biting my bottom lip, I contemplated this negotiation. It seemed like a harmless enough request.

"Okay," I nodded.

Grabbing my hands in his, he smiled. "I want to get to know you better. It's clear there's so much more to learn."

I didn't believe that there was much more to learn about me. My life wasn't that interesting. I could sum up my life in a few phrases: My dad died, I had one best friend, I hated my twin sister, and I played soccer. Wow, what a real-life fairy tale. *Not*. Actually, my life seemed pretty dysfunctional. I wouldn't know what to do with a life devoid of some kind of drama.

"Why do you want to learn more about me?"

"Because you're interesting."

Of course I am, I laughed to myself. I shook my head. "Not really."

"Well, I don't know who told you that but I think you are."

"And you're the only one that matters, right?"

Luke smiled. "Why, thank you, how sweet of you to say that."

I had to laugh. "Have I told you that you speak great English?"

Immediately, he responded, "Have I told you how beautiful you are?"

That caught me off guard. I was unable to speak.

Without waiting for my answer, which may have taken hours, he continued, "Well, you are, especially tonight. I mean, don't get me wrong, you are definitely hot when you're dripping sweat and have gravel dust on your calves, but look at you!"

I watched him look me up and then down. He was pointing at my outfit. I had to admit I thought I looked nice. Maybe not *hot*, but nice for sure.

"Thank you?" I said, not quite sure what to say.

Laughing, he pulled me closer for a brief moment, "No, seriously, you look stunning tonight, Roxanne."

Bashfully, I stared at the ground. "Thank you, Luke."

After letting go of my body, he brought his hand to my chin to lift my eyes back to his. We kept walking.

"And by the way, English is easy!" he exclaimed, answering my previous question.

I smiled at his change of subject. Maybe he could tell I was a bit uncomfortable. I was hoping that would change eventually. "Really? I've heard otherwise. Maybe Italians are smarter than the average human."

"Well, duh," he said sarcastically, ending with a chuckle. Then he added, "So, why *are* you all dressed up?"

I couldn't resist laughing. "It's my birthday!"

Luke stopped mid-step, his mouth gaping open. "It is?"

Happily, I nodded my head. "Yeah!"

Luke's eyes lit up. "Oh, wow! How great. Well, Happy Birthday!"

"Thanks," I said, still laughing. I found it funny that we had been walking for quite a while and he had no idea. Conversations with Luke were somewhat odd—the questions and answers appeared to have no sequence. I liked the unconventional way our friendship worked. I was convinced that I probably would never fully get to know him, even if we spent a lot of time together. There was a certain enigma about him. I couldn't decide if I liked that characteristic about him or not.

"If I would have known..." Luke trailed off, looking dumbly around.

Perplexed, I stared at him. I followed his movement as he weaved around the walkway, his shadow absent in the lamp light from above, and watched him bend down and pick something up from the ground. Turning back toward me, I gazed into his caring eyes. He held out his hand to me, palm up. A beautiful red lily lay across his hand, offering me its color and brilliance. I took it slowly from his hand, closed my eyes and smelled it. That particular one had the most breathtaking scent. It was almost overwhelming.

"It's...amazing," I said, beaming at him.

He shrugged, holding back a smile. "Sorry, it's all I have to offer you."

Shaking my head, I said, "It's more than enough."

The only flowers I had ever received from a boy were from Tyler, and those didn't count. Flowers were to Tyler like presents to Santa Clause. The art of his giving was second nature. Although I appreciated each and every rose he gave me, the surprise of the gift wore off after the first ten bouquets. After knowing him for fifteen years, I couldn't even count the number of dozens of flowers I had received. But this one, simple lily was different. There was more to it then what I could even comprehend.

The flower in front of my face, I peeked at Luke through the petals. He glimpsed down at the watch on his wrist. His facial expression concerned me.

"Do you need to go?" I asked, a hint of attitude in my tone. There was a chance I would be angry if he left me now, after our reunion, his homecoming.

He contemplated his response without looking at me, checking his watch again. As if weighing two options in his mind, he moved his head side to side. I just stared, waiting for an answer.

"Let me walk you back to your dorm," he finally suggested, moving in the direction toward my dorm.

"Why?" I called after him, trying to catch up in my bare feet. The bits of rock along the path slightly stung my calloused skin.

"Church in the morning," Luke answered, matter-of-factly.

Baffled, I said, "Oh, okay."

Raising one eyebrow, he asked, "Want to come?"

"I don't know..."

"Why not? There's always the late service."

"How late is 'late'?"

"Eleven o'clock. And I promise no one will ask you to pray or speak in tongues or sing in front of anyone."

"Sounds harmless enough. Although, I was hoping to try my hand at the whole speaking-in-tongues thing." I half-smiled, hoping he recognized my sarcasm.

"It's fun," Luke offered.

I chuckled, hoping he wasn't serious. Picturing the scene was difficult, but I couldn't hold anything past Luke. He was different.

"Isn't it bad to come to church with a hangover?"

He shrugged, grinning. "Well, you can take that up with the Lord."

"Oh, *okay*," I joked.

"He's the only one, other than myself, that will know. Just don't puke. That might give you away."

"No puking, check."

"And shower."

"Shower, check."

"And don't look too nice."

"Why?"

"So that the other guys don't notice you."

I blushed, a smile on my lips, looking at the ground in modesty. Luke certainly had a way with words. "I'll try not to."

"Please don't," he pleaded.

22

LUKE

I sensed her footsteps behind me.

Opening my eyes, I barely turned my head to acknowledge her. She stared at me, confusion across her face.

"I didn't expect you to show, especially this early," I bluntly said.

Without smiling, she shrugged her shoulders. "I'm here, aren't I?"

I nodded to her attire, "And dressed appropriately."

"Where is everyone?" Roxanne was referring to the empty sanctuary that surrounded us.

My eyebrows furrowed. "What do you mean?"

She sat timidly beside me on the wooden pew, though I was kneeling on the ground. Her voice dropped to a whisper. "Luke, we're alone."

I immediately looked upward, a slight grin emerging on my lips. "Not exactly."

Roxanne rolled her eyes. Oh, those beautiful eyes. Blinking, I tried to snap out of my admiring haze. I wasn't here to silently gawk over her, as I normally did. I was here to rid myself of my selfish thoughts and wishes. Suddenly, I regretted inviting her. Her presence would cancel my pure motives. How could I not think of her with her right next to me?

"Funny," she responded.

No, I tried to convince myself, everything would be fine. I would be able to concentrate. She *would not* distract me.

When I didn't answer any of her comments, she probed, "So, what are you doing?"

I kept my annoyance beneath my skin, holding my breath to prevent a sigh from escaping. I had no reason to be irritated, except I did.

Calmly, I replied, "Roxanne, just close your eyes and relax. It's too early for service."

Now she was curious. "Then why are we here?"

I took a deep breath. "Because this is the best time to come." Maybe the questions would end there.

Silence. I closed my eyes.

When I was satisfied with my time, I opened my eyes to find her staring strangely at me, her arms crossed. I couldn't help but quietly laugh.

Patting the empty space of floor adjacent to me, I said, "Come."

With a bit of apprehension, Roxanne followed my order.

She nodded expectantly, waiting for more direction. It was clear she wasn't experienced at praying.

I leaned close to her. "Close your eyes. Let the moment take you."

She smirked, obviously not intrigued.

"Hey, you came down here of your own free will."

She didn't argue, though I thought she might. I watched her eyes close, a vulnerability surfacing over her face.

I waited for her. It took longer than I imagined.

Finally, I saw sun through the stained glass window, reflecting off the blue in her eyes. And finally, she looked peaceful.

"Can I ask?"

"Ask what?" she wondered.

"What you were praying for? About?"

Her eyes diverted toward the floor. "Isn't it true that if I tell you, it won't come true?"

I grinned. "I believe that's only true for wishes."

"Wishes, prayers, same thing, right?"

Eyeing her, I said, "Not quite."

"Well, okay... I prayed for..."

I waited patiently.

"My dad's approval."

I was strong. I knew I was. So, why did Roxanne make me feel so weak? If I didn't get so involved with her, my task wouldn't be so difficult. In order to do my job, I had to keep my head on straight.

My break helped me regain my senses. Leaving again was not an option. I would not be granted another chance. I could not be a letdown.

I had never felt so at ease with anyone before. Did I never have feelings for a girl back in Italy? Of course I did. But she's different. So very different.

Did my assignment interfere with the feelings I had for Roxanne? I couldn't decide. I knew I couldn't let Roxanne know about this. I had to stay strong.

I had a purpose to accomplish. If it were not Roxanne, would I care so much? I couldn't be so sure. She made my objective more real, more important. I wanted to do this for her more than anything.

23

TYLER

The annoying sound of my alarm clock reminded me that it was the first day of classes.

I sluggishly climbed out of my too-small twin bed and dressed in the dark. My roommate was not up yet. Grabbing my toothbrush and paste, I headed down the hall to the community bathrooms. When I opened the door, trying not to look at the urinals, I crossed the cold tile floor to a sink. I stared at myself in the mirror while brushing my teeth—I still looked asleep. I couldn't believe college had already begun. It felt like I had just graduated from high school yesterday. I heard the door to the bathroom open and I nodded at the guy that walked in. He also looked as if he were sleepwalking.

Capping my toothpaste, I swung the door open and stepped into the empty hallway. My room was three doors down. Trying to be as quiet as possible, I opened the door. My roommate was sprawled over his bed, feet hanging off the edge. Like mine, his bed didn't accommodate his height. A snore erupted from his mouth, startling me. Had he snored like that all night? Maybe I was a heavy sleeper. I could see how that characteristic would help tremendously with dorm life.

I slipped on my tennis shoes and pulled my backpack over my shoulder. Searching my small wooden desk for my class schedule and campus map, I spotted them and shoved them into my pocket. Locking the door behind me, I took a deep breath. Hopefully this experience wouldn't be completely overwhelming. Freshman Week was great— meeting new people, taking advantage of free campus activities, and becoming acquainted with the enormous campus. The only bad memory that stuck in my head was not seeing Roxanne's face everyday. Every time I talked to her, she was either busy practicing with her soccer team or doing "team-building" activities. It had to lighten up soon, right? Maybe this was a good time to make some guy friends. And maybe if she noticed I was spending more time with guys than with her, she'd realize what she was missing. So far, the guys I met played video games, the guitar, watched obnoxious television, and played more video games. I think I could get the hang of the whole video game thing. Roxanne hated video games.

Walking out into the fresh Florida sunshine, I realized that although I was the only one in my hallway awake, this was not the case with the rest of campus. People buzzed on every corner. Smiling to myself, I decided to join in. My first class was physics— *what a great way to wake up the brain*, I sarcastically thought. Pulling out my schedule, I glanced at the building name and then at the map. My physics class was held in the New Physics Building. I couldn't help but laugh at the lack of creativity.

Once I arrived at the building, I thanked myself for leaving early. The building was practically on the opposite side of campus as my dorm. Checking my schedule again, I etched the room number 325 into my brain. The less I looked like a lost freshman, the better. The distinction between the underclassmen and the upperclassmen seemed obvious. Hopefully my height would work to my advantage.

Climbing the three flights of stairs to my class and becoming almost completely winded, I decided that after my classes ended, I would go to the gym. I was forced to pay for it regardless of whether I ever stepped a foot in there or not. Luckily, room 325 was the first room I came to. I checked my watch— ten minutes until class started. Looking through the small vertical window in the door, I noticed a few heads scattered throughout the medium-sized classroom. I walked inside, relieved I wouldn't be the nerd that was always the first one to class. I mean, it was only the first day, right?

I made sure to sit in the front. This was the only way I could pay attention. Even though I was undoubtedly the only one seated within the first few rows, I tried not to care. After all, college was not about impressing others, it was about doing well academically. No, I had it all wrong, college was *completely* about impressing others, whether I wanted it to be or not. I shook my head; peer pressure was already consuming me and no one was even within ten feet!

As the ten minutes dwindled, people trickled in one after the other. To my relief, I wasn't the only one sitting in the front row. It seemed like this would be a full class and inevitably, the front row would have to be filled. Everyone seemed to know each other. Was I the only freshman?

The professor arrived at exactly the start of class. He was a short man, with bottlenose glasses. His gray hair and mustache were streaked with strands of white. His eyes were too big for his head. When he spoke, his voice didn't match his appearance. The only two words I could use to describe his speech were funny and fast.

"Good morning. I hope everyone printed off the syllabus from the course website," he started, quickly. "My name is Robert Bird and my office hours are..."

My attention shifted when a guy entered the classroom and noisily sat down in the only open seat, which was next to me. The teacher stared at him, clearly bothered, but kept talking without interruption. When the guy noticed I was looking at him, he whispered, "Hey." I slightly smiled and nodded my head. Turning my head back to the professor, I realized he was flying through the syllabus, mumbling through less important parts such as disability services and especially exaggerating academic integrity (which I learned meant no cheating). Before I could even flip to the right page, he had finished.

"Alright, I'm sure you will all be pleased to know that we're starting full force today. Ha, ha...force..." he chuckled to himself, staring at the class for a similar response. "Get it? Force...physics...Anyway, as you can see on the first page of the syllabus, you have homework due on Wednesday."

The rest of the class was a blur. The professor spoke so fast I could hardly read my notes. I didn't have legible handwriting to begin with, and now, it appeared to be just plain scribbles. I prayed I would find a study group that would help me decipher the formulas and the laws. When the professor finished five minutes late, the entire class erupted into talk. I stood to put my things back into my backpack.

A hand shot in front of my face. "Hey," the familiar voice spoke again. I tried to smile as I looked into the face of the less punctual guy next to me. He continued, "Colten McCoy...call me Colt."

The guy named Colt stood at about the same height as me. It was obvious that he worked out. Maybe I would look like that after a couple months in the gym. I could only hope. He reminded me of my high school's football quarterback, but older. I guessed that he was probably the most popular kid and hung out with all the jocks. I doubted he was a nerd like me. He wore a bag around his left shoulder that hung on his right side. He definitely didn't portray a geek by his attire, as he was equipped with aviator sunglasses hanging from his shirt neckline.

I returned the handshake. "Tyler Hansen." I was at a loss for what else to say.

He spoke quickly, delaying any awkward moments. "So, do you get this stuff?" Colt gestured to the chalkboard where the professor had sloppily scribbled letters and numbers and a lot of unreadable symbols.

"Well, it's only the first day...but I took college-level calculus in high school, so I guess it won't be too bad." I watched as students for the next class began filling the room. Grabbing my backpack, I started walking toward the door. Colt followed.

"Wow, are you only a freshman?" he asked, surprised.

"Yeah, almost a sophomore by credits," I replied.

"I'm impressed. This is supposed to be an upper-level class." Colt led the way out of the building and onto a busy pathway filled with students heading in all directions. I smiled at the scene; I felt grown-up. The sun was warm on my back and the humidity was rising. I hadn't looked at my schedule to see where my next class was. I wasn't in any hurry to go anywhere specific; I remembered I had a break between my first and second class of the day.

"So, what are you majoring in?" I asked him, following closely beside him. I was making sure to dodge other students when necessary.

"Aerospace engineering," Colt responded, smiling modestly.

"Really?" I was shocked. "That's...wow, that's cool." I couldn't imagine how smart you would have to be to graduate with that degree. Surely physics would be easy for him.

He suddenly laughed. "Nah, man. I'm just kidding. I don't even know how to spell aerospace. I'm biology. My advisor thought it would help my chances of getting into medical school if I had a class like this under my belt."

Too quickly, I replied, "Aerospace: a-e-r-o-s-p-a-c-e."

Colt shook his head, his eyebrows furrowing together. Did I say something wrong? Apprehensively, he asked, "What's your major?"

"Mechanical engineering." I watched as his face relaxed.

"Figures," he said, smugly.

"What do you mean?" I was confused.

"You're smart, that's all. I should have known from the fact that you're taking physics with calculus as a freshman. Freshmen are supposed to party and get in trouble. You know, you're free now...from parents and responsibility." It sounded like this was a rule and I was the only person breaking it. Again with the peer pressure!

When I didn't respond, Colt continued, "Look, you seem like a cool guy. I'll help you settle into college life if you help me in physics."

I shook my head, "No cheating, right? You heard what the guy said about *academic integrity*." I laughed a little too loudly, trying to show that I was joking. I was only half-joking.

His face was serious. "No, nothing like that. I might just need some tutoring. I have to apply to med school next spring and I need to keep my 4.0."

Chuckling, I said, "You won't need me to keep your 4.0, but I'll take you up on the settling into college part."

"Alright, but I'm telling you, I will need help."

"Why do you say that?" I couldn't believe this guy was asking *me* for help when he clearly could be *my* tutor.

"Let's see... I'm also taking Biochemistry, Cell Biology, Organic Chemistry 2, Human Physiology, and Medical Ethics." His voice was cool. He didn't sound worried at all about his monstrous schedule.

My jaw dropped slightly. "Are you kidding me? You're taking all those classes?"

Colt's mouth moved into a half-smile. "Yeah, no big deal. But like I said, I might need some help."

I had to ask, "How are you going to have time for anything but school?"

He shrugged and nonchalantly replied, "I work hard during the week and play even harder during the weekend. You can imagine the stress relief I need by Friday."

"Well, yeah. I would imagine. What branch of medicine?" I pulled out my schedule, scanning the printed words for information about my next class.

Stopping, Colt put his hand on my shoulder. He seemed so much older; so much wiser. He was my role model. "Do you need help finding your next class?"

"Um," I mumbled, finding my map in my pocket and searching it, "I'm heading to Tebow Hall."

Grabbing my schedule out of my hands, Colt checked it over. "General Chemistry, eh? That's a piece of cake. The lab can be fun, if you like that kind of stuff. English Composition is a breeze, too. Watch out for plagiarism, though. Oh, and General Psychology is pretty interesting. Don't get depressed when you find out that you have all the symptoms of schizophrenia, psychosis, and bipolar disorder. It's all in your head. Literally." Laughing at his own wit, he handed me back the schedule. "Here, I'll point you in the right direction."

I was glad for this new friendship I had gained. Meeting new people wasn't so scary, after all. Colt seemed like the kind of guy I wanted to be. Smart and focused, but also laidback and carefree. Could those four characteristics possibly coexist together? I hoped so.

As we leisurely walked, I stared around at the buildings. We passed the student recreation center, for which I was appreciative. After being seen standing next to Colt, it was clear I needed to shape up. Quicker than I expected, we arrived at Tebow Hall, where my chemistry class was held. Most of the other classroom buildings looked relatively new, except for this one. In front, the flowers and bushes were dying, the color fading even in late summer. The stone walls were washed out. The facade of the building mirrored my feelings toward the subject of chemistry: unpleasant and crummy.

"Here we are, good ol' Tebow Hall," Colt pointed to the entrance.

"Thanks. I'll see you around?" I asked him.

"Yeah, sure. Wednesday morning, bright and early. Don't forget that homework." He smiled, stepping backward.

"Thanks," I repeated, waving my hand at him. Heading into the building, I was glad my class was on the first floor. I easily found the room, but it was much larger than my first class. This was an auditorium. It was empty, of course, because I was fifteen minutes early. The weather was still tolerable, so I decided to sit outside and soak in my new surroundings.

Parking myself on a bench, I pulled out my cell phone. Flipping it open, I was disappointed to find no voicemails, not even a missed call, and no text messages from Roxanne. I missed her, terribly. I wanted to call her, but I didn't want to bother her. She was busy adjusting to her new life. As I moved to flip it closed, my phone dinged.

1 NEW MESSAGE. What a coincidence. I pressed ACCEPT and found it was from the very person I was hoping for.

I SEE YOU, CAN YOU SEE ME?

I frantically searched the immediate vicinity for her. I quickly text messaged back: ARE YOU HIDING?

Within five seconds, another ding.

NOPE.

Exhaling, I searched again. There was no one that resembled her at all.

Ding. YOU'RE NOT LOOKING HARD ENOUGH.

This time I stood up, turning to look behind the bench. There she was, as beautiful as ever. Her long brown hair was pulled into a tight braid that hung down over her shoulder. She was wearing a t-shirt and sweatpants, which wasn't very different from her usual attire. But something was missing. Appraising her neck, I instantly noticed she wasn't wearing the necklace I had given her only a few days ago.

"Hey," I smiled, trying to push the necklace from my mind. I wanted to avoid an argument since I hadn't seen her in a while.

She returned my smile. "Hey." Moving around the bench, she sat and patted the seat next to her. The gesture reminded me of a time early this summer at the lake. I hoped the conversation would be different.

I sat next to her and looked at my feet. We hadn't talked since her birthday even though she promised we would hang out. There was a certain awkwardness between us now; I didn't think that was possible.

"How's your first day been?" Roxanne asked.

"Pretty good, and you?" I asked her in return.

"It's great! I love the large classes. They don't expect you to answer questions...there's no pressure..." She looked genuinely happy.

"Really?" I asked her. "The whole class thing is kind of stressing me out."

"Why? It's awesome, but very inconvenient." She was never the most ideal student.

"Roxy, I know it may not seem worth your time, but you have to be a student to play soccer here," I grinned, playfully mocking her.

She sighed, too loudly to be serious. "I guess..."

"Going back to the stress thing, I just feel the eyes of everyone on me. I don't know. It's hard to explain, I guess."

Her hand reached up to embrace my arm. In slow strokes, she comforted me. It felt like time slowed down during those few seconds of her touch. My stomach churned. All I wanted to do was hold her in my arms.

To divert my yearning thoughts, I changed the subject. "How was your birthday weekend?" I asked, pretending to sound interested.

She let out a grunt, pulling her hand away. "It would have been better if the freshman could have gone to the game on Friday night. It's not fair." I distinctly remember having a very long conversation last week with Roxanne about missing the first game of the season on the coach's orders. It wasn't really a true conversation; I mostly listened. I tried to be sympathetic but it was hard. All this soccer talk was beginning to really irritate me. I never imagined it would be worse in college than it was in high school. It was only slightly bothersome then. Now I wanted to scream.

Flatly, I replied, "Yeah, that does suck."

She looked at my squarely. "I'm sorry I keep bringing it up. I need to shut up about it." Roxanne was more perceptive than I gave her credit for and for this, I was thankful.

I shrugged. "Not a big deal. But you had a good birthday?" I knew how important birthdays were to Roxanne.

She looked down at her hands in her lap. A smile emerged onto her lips. "Yeah, it was good."

"What's up with that look on your face?" I asked, very curious.

She shook her head, still averting her eyes. "I had a good time."

"What'd you do? Watch Titanic and drink Cosmopolitans?"

"No, of course not. We played strip poker and drank Tequila."

My eyes grew wide. "W-what?"

Roxanne broke out into laughter. "You're gullible, you know. Could you see *me* playing poker? And strip poker, at that."

A mental image flooded my mind. I could feel my cheeks flush. I would never admit to Roxanne how many times I pictured her privately in my mind. After all, I was only a man. What did she expect?

"Right, poker," I muttered, silently praying she wasn't being too observant.

After momentary silence, Roxanne said, "We hung out at Laura's house and sang karaoke, in case you were wondering."

I cleared my throat. "Sounds fun," I said awkwardly. Checking my watch, I realized class was starting within minutes. "I better go. My next class is about to start. When am I going to get to see you?" I wanted to bring up her broken promise but didn't have the time to argue.

Placing her hand on top of mine, she smiled weakly. "Soon, soon. I know we have hardly seen each other since I started practice. I'm sorry for that...I miss you, Tyler."

I stared into her radiant green eyes. "You know I miss you."

Standing, she threw her bag over her shoulder. "I'll call you later, okay?"

I nodded, also standing. "Sure. Have a good rest of the day."

"You, too. See ya!" And she walked away, without another glance. I felt like she was walking out of my life forever. What was wrong with me? I was obviously too dependent on her. That had to stop. I needed some male friends, badly; meeting Colt was a good start.

My voice cracked before my brain could process what I was doing. "Roxanne!" I called after her.

She turned back around, a beautiful smile resting on her lips. Her head cocked in puzzlement.

I looked around to make sure no one was within earshot. "I miss you," I mumbled to her. Did she even hear me?

Roxanne walked back toward me, carrying a soft expression on her face. Without saying anything, she brought her arms around my waist and rested her head against my chest. Reflexively, I cradled her, her body warmth immediately penetrating my skin. I wanted to stay in this position forever.

Her head still against my chest, she whispered, "I miss you."

Eventually, without my consent, Roxanne pulled away and cupped my face in her hands. "Don't worry. Soon, soon," she reiterated. She turned around and started back off in the opposite direction.

Slowly making my way back into the eerie building, I found the room quickly and took a seat close to the front. There were probably five hundred seats in this auditorium. I wasn't sure if this would be a good or bad thing. Maybe Roxanne was right. At least the professor couldn't call on you for an answer. Did they even do that in college? I was recognizing that I was very naïve about this whole college experience.

As with my first class, I watched the other students take their seats and soon the professor joined us. Even as the professor began with the same introduction as my physics professor, I couldn't pay attention to what he was saying. Roxanne's face was the only thing I could focus on.

24

ROXANNE

The ground beneath my feet had never felt so unfamiliar.

The morning air through my lungs was immensely refreshing. It was the dawn of a beautiful, cloudless day in September. The campus was barely waking. Although I didn't mind the large number of students that attended Gainesville, the morning was always my favorite time of day, the desolate campus feeling more like home.

The stillness in the air was comforting. As I passed the outdoor track in the middle of campus, I could hear the shouts of the campus military group. Their voices were the only noises piercing the silence that surrounded me. I realized I wasn't the only one exercising so early in the day. I assumed that being a part of their military group was similar to being on the soccer team, being forced to mindlessly exercise on command. Shaking my head, I tried to clear the useless thoughts from my head.

Making a complete circle around the outskirts of the campus, I decided my endurance wasn't quite challenged enough. Another lap around was on the agenda.

As I approached the outdoor track again, I heard no voices this time. It was a very distinct silence. *Where did they go?*

Suddenly, as if on cue, waves of people in uniform jogged past me on both sides. I felt solely enveloped in an army of foreign people. My head turned, staring at each new person that passed me. To my

179

dismay, their pace left me in the dust. I felt self-conscious, which was a rarity when I was exercising.

When I was sure that the mass of people had left me trailing, a few stragglers sprinted to catch up. Maybe I needed to join this group in the morning. They seemed to be in very good shape.

Another pair of footsteps echoed mine from behind. *Are there more?*

I kept my gaze straight ahead, trying not to rudely stare.

The figure met my running pace and stayed next to me. I turned to see who it was.

"Hey!" I called out to Luke, blissfully running beside me in a tighter white shirt and black running shorts.

"Good morning," he called back, smiling wide.

"What are you doing here?" I asked, returning the smile.

"Well, I'm not sure about you, but I'm running."

I pushed him gently, just enough to throw off his balance and slow his steps. "Funny."

"How long have you been running?"

"Oh, about an hour. You?"

"Just started. It's fate I found you out here." His smile reached his eyes.

I rolled my eyes. "I don't believe in fate."

He gawked, "Well, why not?"

I shrugged my shoulders slightly. "I just don't. We have complete control over our actions."

He crudely laughed. "You're such a silly girl."

A silly girl? I thought to myself, offended. That's what little boys said about the girls in their first grade class. I was *not* silly.

Luke corrected himself, "You're just mistaken. That's all."

"Prove me wrong."

"I'm not sure that's quite possible, but I'll give you an example, if you wish."

"Hit me."

"Why would I do that?" He stared at me, a curious expression across his face.

"Luke, it's just a term we say. Give me the example." He took things so literally at times.

"For example, us meeting."

"What do you mean?"

"Fate brought us together, don't you think?" Luke's voice was hopeful.

Sternly, I stated, "No, it was coincidence."

"I beg to differ."

"Why?"

"God brought us together, Roxanne. I was meant to be in your life."

I waited to speak. *I hate it when he says things like that*, I thought. He was entitled to his opinion, though.

"Alright..." I said, dumbly.

He laughed. "Don't worry about it. You'll see someday."

I barely smiled.

Then, he asked, "So, how was your night?"

"Well, let's see. I slept...so, it was good. And your night?"

"Unfortunately, I didn't sleep very well."

"Why not?"

"I couldn't stop thinking about you."

My heart skipped a beat. As his words hit my ears, my pace immediately slowed to a walk. I wasn't sure if I should stare at my feet or look to him for an explanation. When had our relationship moved past friendship? Had we even been *friends*, to speak of? It was all so movie-like, so fairy tale. It was very hard to believe his outlandishly blunt comments.

Finally, I spoke, when I realized he wasn't going to, "...really...?"

"Really." His response was firm, calculated.

"Why?" I was very curious now.

"I can't answer that because I don't know. You're all I think about, Roxanne. Isn't that strange?"

I thought it was strange that he was asking me if I thought it was strange. We were definitely on the same page about this new fondness. Nodding, I kept my eyes at the ground in front of me.

I started to worry about what he might ask me in return. Before I could begin to fret, Luke pursued the idea himself, "Do you ever think about me?"

Luke was so frank and honest, it was overwhelming. The people I encountered on a daily basis tended to mind themselves, making every effort to mask their true feelings hidden within. I did not frequently make my opinion obvious to those around me. I didn't ask for many opinions, either. I minded myself. I liked it that way. Luke was different.

A brief period of silence elapsed before I could find my voice. "Yes, I do."

"You do?" He sounded surprised and hopeful.

Inhaling a deep breath, I forced myself not to let my emotions take me away. "Yes."

As he reached his arm around my shoulder, I could feel my sweaty shirt stick annoyingly to my back. I tried to ignore the awful sensation and concentrate on the touch he was providing. He pulled me closer to him, in a child-like manner. The scent that radiated off of his body was like nothing I had smelled before. I flinched away, knowing that I smelled ten times worse than he. Luke didn't let me go.

We walked in unison for a while, following along the same path we had just ran. The various emotions coursing through my veins were tremendous. I felt awkward, being so physically close to him for so long. I was being faced with indecision. I honestly didn't know what to do. So, I stayed put.

Eventually, his arm fell back down to his side. "Let's run."

Fixing my slightly ruffled hair, I said, "What for?"

"Well, the sun's about up and you didn't get to finish your workout."

I shook my head, "It doesn't really matter."

"I believe it does matter to you."

How does he know me so well? I wondered. Did it really even matter at this point?

"Okay, where do you want to run?"

"Back to your dorm."

"Why my dorm?"

He grinned. "Can I see your room?"

I knew I wouldn't be able to tell him no easily, so I agreed. I was without good reason, anyway.

Leading the way, we jogged side-by-side back to my dorm. I wasn't used to having a running partner, but I had to admit it was nice. We briefly chatted about class and soccer along the way. I learned that he had a desire to become an interpreter for the government some day. He liked Florida a lot, but admitted he was homesick. He missed his large family back in Italy. He was staying in one of the older dorms on the far side of campus, where his roommate was frequently found lounging in their room.

Once inside my dorm, I led him to the stairwell. Eyeing him playfully, I asked, "I'll race you."

"What floor are you on again?"

As I opened my mouth to answer his question, I watched as he broke out into a sprint up the staircase. He didn't leave me much time to react. I briskly followed in his footsteps.

"Fourth!" I yelled.

Luke was waiting at the entrance to my hall. He seemed to be breathing normally.

"How...are you...not...out of breath?" I asked, sucking in as much available air as possible. I had never climbed stairs so fast for fun before.

He shrugged, which irritated me. Luke looked perfect, while I looked disheveled. *He must do this in his spare time.*

"Lead the way," he announced, holding open the door leading out of the stairwell.

A few steps before my dorm room, I heard Allison's voice. "Yes, mother. Yes, uhuh. Yes, of course..." I assumed she was on the phone.

The door opened before I could even reach for the handle. Allison, phone glued to ear, rushed out with her purse in hand. "Mothers," she mouthed to me while rolling her eyes. I noticed the glance that Allison flashed me after seeing Luke standing next to me. She stared at me, questions floating around in her eyes. She knew she would have to wait for the answers. She didn't know it, but she might have to wait a lifetime.

I pointed at Allison as she hurried down the hall. "That's my roommate, Allison. She's on the team with me."

Luke peered down at his watch. "I recognize her from your birthday night. Where is she headed so early?"

"She has an eight o'clock class."

"It's not even seven yet."

"Well, Allison's a bit anal-retentive about time. She always has to be early to everything."

"She sounds...interesting."

"I like her. She's a good friend."

He smiled. "Everyone needs at least one of those."

We stepped into the tiny space Allison and I shared, our room. "That's my bed," I pointed out.

Clearly distracted, Luke shifted to the opposite side of the room. "What's this?"

His hand was outstretched, ready to pick up Allison's bottle of hand sanitizer that she worshipped.

Quickly, I said, "Oh, make sure not to touch anything of Allison's."

Luke's hand retracted back to his body. "Why not?"

I hesitated for the right word. "She's a bit...crazy...when it comes to her things."

"I see. Alright then, no touching Allison's stuff."

"And to answer your question, that's hand sanitizer. She's freaked about germs."

His eyes widened. "How do you live with this girl?"

"She keeps life interesting, that's all." I couldn't have asked for a better roommate than Allison. She studied, she was clean, and she cared about my wellbeing.

"When in Rome, I guess," Luke said.

"Luke..." I shook my head at his choice of words.

"What?" He was puzzled.

"Oh, never mind..." I couldn't help but laugh at him.

I slipped my running shoes off and threw them in my makeshift closet. Wiping my forehead with the back of my hand, I realized how sweaty I was. I was absolutely gross. Being dirty didn't bother me when I was by myself or around other girls, but Luke made me feel more insecure than I was used to. I was embarrassed to realize I had looked similar to this on many occasions where Luke and I crossed paths. If I weren't so grungy every time he saw me, maybe he would show more consistent interest.

"I'm sorry I'm so disgusting right now," I re-wiped my forehead with the rim of my t-shirt. My face definitely needed to be washed.

Luke leaned his upper body against my computer desk. A grin broke out across his lips. "Don't apologize. You're kind of cute like that."

"You're so weird," I laughed.

"When in Rome," he repeated.

"Luke!"

A loud laugh erupted from his mouth. He knew how to jokingly frustrate me. "I know, I know...*I don't use the right American lingo.*"

I plopped myself on my bed, my back resting against the wall. "It's okay. If nothing else, it's a good laugh."

Following, Luke sat next to me. Our legs looked funny next to each other. His feet dangled off the bed further than mine did because of his height. We stared absently out the window at the beautiful sun rising. I wondered what he was thinking about, being with me here in my dorm room. I wondered if he was wondering what I was thinking.

"What are you thinking about?" he asked, to my surprise.

"I don't know...whatever you're thinking about."

He slightly chuckled. "I wish."

I pushed my shoulder into his. "What is it?"

Before I could analyze his moves, his hand was cupping my jaw. His face was so close to my face that I could hear him breathe. Our eyes were locked for an uncountable amount of time. I knew he wouldn't be able to hear any air escape. I was holding my breath.

As if time had slowed, he leaned in closer to my face than he already was. I closed my eyes. Should I lean forward? Should I touch his face? Should I hold my breath? I didn't know what I was supposed to do.

After what felt like fifteen minutes, I felt his nose touch mine. And that was it. He had stopped.

What's going on? Do I open my eyes now? I'm confused...

Slowly, he moved his hand and drew back. I didn't have to have vision to realize he wasn't centimeters from my lips anymore. I was more than slightly disappointed.

My eyes opened, unsure what to expect.

To my surprise, Luke was smiling, like he always did.

I wanted to speak, to ask questions, but I couldn't.

"Roxanne," he began.

I could only nod. *Breathe*, I coerced myself.

I watched his mouth as the words came out slowly. "Will you go on a date with me?"

25

LUKE

I thought I had a plan. But I didn't.

When Regan kissed me, I knew it was wrong. But was it so wrong that I wanted to keep kissing her? It honestly had nothing to do with who she was. She was my first kiss. In Italy, I was waiting for my wife, as silly as that sounded. But now, none of that mattered.

Even more so, touching Roxanne's face and being so close made it difficult to resist her. I liked Roxanne, which was obvious. I wanted to experience my first kiss with her, but that wasn't in my hands. The kiss just...happened. I recalled the anger in Regan's voice as I left her for Roxanne that night. I sensed she would never forgive me, but I paid no mind.

I knew in my heart that I shouldn't kiss Roxanne. I knew I shouldn't be so involved. Why was this so hard for me to understand? She was so easily falling into my hands. I guessed that was the whole point. I needed her to completely and utterly trust me. She needed to trust me with her life.

How long could this act possibly go on? As much as I wanted it to end, I wasn't prepared for what would be in the immediate future. I wasn't allowed to know any details, to my dismay. I would know when it was happening, that's all.

Well, for now, I had to keep up my end of the deal, which was to *do as the Romans do*.

26

TYLER

I waited to hear her voice on the other line.

"Hey, Tyler," Roxanne finally answered.

I thoroughly enjoyed listening to her speak. "Hey, what's up?" I asked her.

"Oh, not too much. What about you?"

"Same. What are doing tonight?" Surely she wasn't busy *every night* of the week.

There was a pause. "Uh," she started, without continuing.

"You're kidding me..." I sounded disappointed, less disappointed than I felt.

She sighed softly. "Tyler, I'm sorry."

"You don't have time for me anymore."

"No, Tyler, it's not like that."

"I wanted to cook you a home-made, store-bought pizza. I can count on my right hand the number of times I have seen you since school started. Since we were little, I have seen you every day. You don't know how it kills me not to see you..." I let more slip out than I normally allowed myself.

Another long pause filled the emotional space between us. Finally, "I'm sorry," she repeated.

"What are you even doing?" My voice was vengeful.

She spoke more quickly this time. "Oh, just hanging out."

"With who?"

"No one special."

"With who?" I asked again. She was definitely hiding something.

She sounded angry, "Why do you care?"

"Because I want to know who you're ditching me for."

Slowly, but with power, she said, "I'm hanging out with Luke."

"Luke? That guy from this summer?"

"Yes."

"You don't even know him."

"That's the point of hanging out."

Oh, no, the question was inevitable. "Is it a date?" Did I really want to know?

Another quick response, "No."

"Have you ever been on a date with him before?" I couldn't help but recall what Regan had said to me a few months back on the phone. I didn't want to believe her, but the doubt was there.

"No, of course not. Why did you ask that?"

"Oh, just something Regan had said to me..." I knew it was a bad idea to bring up Regan.

"What?!" she yelled.

"Calm down, it's nothing..."

"Nothing? What did she say?" Roxanne was fired up now.

"If you cancel your date, I can come over and talk about it with you." Maybe she would buy the ploy.

"I don't think so, and it's not a date!"

"*Riggghhttt...*" I prayed to God that it wasn't a date.

"What did Regan say?"

"She told me that you were dating Luke."

"When?"

"In July."

"What a big, fat, lair..." her voice trailed off.

"You know your sister," I reminded her.

"Wait, when did you see her?"

"She called me," I stated, nonchalantly. *Whoops.*

"Why does she have your number?" she asked, simultaneously confused and accusatory.

"Oh, I don't know. I guess for emergencies." I hoped that I sounded convincing.

"Okay..."

"So, you coming over?"

"Tyler, I'm going to hang up now."

"No, don't!"

"I promise we'll get together soon."

"You promise that, like, every time we talk. When are we *really* going to hang out?" I was beginning to think I wouldn't be seeing my best friend anytime soon.

"I'm a bad friend, aren't I?"

I nodded my head. "No, just too busy for your own good."

"I miss you, Tyler."

"Roxanne, words can't describe how much I miss your face. Call me soon, okay?"

"I promise." *Click.*

I desperately wished she would fulfill her promises.

27

REGAN

H aving a fake ID was amazing.

Dressed in my sexiest low-cut shirt and my most fitting low-rise jeans, I was headed out to the bars with some girls from my pledge class. It was my first bar experience. I was determined to have a good time, especially after a long week of tests.

"You look so hot," my friend gushed from the back seat. I had no idea why I was driving. I was already sure of the fact that I wasn't going to be coherent enough to drive home later.

I loved my new friends. They were just like me. We read a lot of *Glamour* magazine, exchanged clothing and shoes, borrowed music, and shared stories about the boys in our lives. I always had someone to talk to. It was a built-in family, similar to the relationships I had with Stacy and Leah in Ocala. Who could want anything more?

Once I parallel-parked my BMW a few blocks away from our destination, each of us checked our mirrors and made last-minute changes to our already perfect looks. Grabbing my silver clutch, I shut my door, following after the other girls to the bar. Tonight was going to be very exciting. I wondered if I would remember any of it.

The place was everything I imagined a bar to look like. People were everywhere, inside and outside, socializing the night away. More important, gorgeous men were not in short supply. Drinks were flowing from cups and bottles. Hips were swinging to the rhythm of the music.

My friends and I moved closer to the bar. As expected, random, cute guys bought our first drinks for us. Hopefully I wouldn't be spending any actual money tonight. The thought of having to pay for my own drinks made me irritated.

Out on the dance floor, all of the girls in my group started dancing with each other. I was hoping to attract a crowd of guys standing near the wall adjacent to the bar. Stealing a few glances, I tried to lure the unsuspecting boys with my eyes. I spent the majority of the time playfully grooving to the fast beats of the music coming from the speakers above us. We only had to dance solo for a small amount of time. Soon after we hit the dance floor, we all had our own dance partners. Another round of drinks followed.

I felt like every guy I saw was drop-dead stunning, but that might have been the alcohol. I'm not sure how often I gave my number out, but eventually, my friends had to step in and escort me away. Realistically, I couldn't keep up with that many boys!

I was leaning against the bar flirting with an older man when I saw him.

"Tyler!" I practically screamed, running up to him and throwing my arms around his neck.

"Whoa, hey, Regan," he said.

"Who's this?" his friend asked, eyeing me. Although my vision was a little blurry, I could still tell he was very handsome as well.

Tyler pointed to me. "This is Regan. Regan, this is Colt."

Colt raised his hand to me. His large, strong hand felt nice in mine.

He was grinning. "Nice to meet you, Regan. You look awfully familiar."

I giggled, although I didn't know why. Smiling back at him, I said, "Maybe I've seen you around."

Tyler turned to Colt and muttered, "This is Roxanne's twin sister."

Colt understood. "Oh! Okay, that makes sense now."

A look of disgust was plastered to my face. "I'm *so* sorry you had to meet *her*. She's not here with you, is she?" I didn't imagine Roxanne as much of a party girl.

Tyler answered, "No, don't worry." I let out a sigh of relief.

Colt replied, "I haven't met her, just seen pictures of her. I didn't realize she had a twin."

I pushed Tyler's chest gently. "You didn't tell him about me? Shame on you."

"Yes, shame on you," Colt agreed. He raised his eyebrows up and down. He had a funny look on his face.

"Let's get something to drink," Tyler suggested, moving forward through the crowd toward the bar. I recognized a slight roll of his eyes.

"Hey, you're not twenty-one. How'd you get in?" I couldn't imagine Tyler using a fake ID.

Colt spoke before Tyler could answer, "I know the guy that runs this place."

"Wow," I said, batting my eyelashes, "Must be nice."

Colt brought his arm around my shoulder. "You don't even know." He moved us forward, following Tyler. The scent of his cologne was intoxicating.

At the bar, Tyler ordered himself a beer. I pretended to be distracted when I saw Colt lean over and whisper to Tyler, "And she has a *twin*? Dude, you've got it made in the shade!"

I couldn't see Tyler's response, but I bet he agreed.

Colt offered me his hand to dance after he took a swig of Tyler's beer.

"I'm kind of thirsty," I admitted. I wasn't planning on buying my own.

"Let me get that for you," Colt proposed, winking at me.

After downing my umpteenth shot, Colt led me to the dance floor. He was a great dancer! It was extremely hard to focus on the music though, because the room was spinning with all the people and lights.

Every now and then, I peered at Tyler, standing at the bar. Although the scene was somewhat fuzzy, I could tell he was analyzing every move I was making. His face was stout. He was probably jealous of Colt. Who wouldn't be?

I danced with Colt for a few more songs before he said, "I've got to head to the little boy's room real quick."

"Okay," I said absentmindedly, absorbed by the thought of finding Tyler.

Once Colt was out of sight, I immediately searched the bar area to find him.

"Tyler!" I called, once I spotted him.

He nodded his head toward me as I approached. Placing my hand on his chest again, I gazed into his eyes. "Let's dance!"

Tyler shook his head.

I pouted my bottom lip. "Please?"

"No, thanks."

I ran my hand down the side of his body and circled around, accidentally grabbing what seemed to be his wallet. "Oh, come on."

Looking away, Tyler hesitated before removing my hand. When his eyes returned to mine, I couldn't read them. He was a mystery to me, which only heightened the chase.

I pulled on his hand, escorting him to the dance floor. He seemed to waver, but only for a moment. Soon he would be completely under my control.

My persistent tugging finally resulted in reaching the middle of the dance floor. I wrapped my arms around his neck and pressed my body against his. I tried to find his eyes but he was staring in another direction. There was no expression to his face. I couldn't detect any moving in his legs or hips. He was standing completely still.

"Tyler!" I shouted over the music.

He gazed blankly down at me. "I just can't."

Removing my arms, he gently pushed me backward, breaking the seal between our bodies. My mouth gapped wide open. I stood flabbergasted as I watched him make his way through the sea of people and out of sight. I was rejected!

Before I could even contemplate running after him, Colt found me and wanted to pick up where we left off. I *was not* going to let Tyler ruin my night of fun. It was his loss. Colt was probably a better dancer anyway.

I'm not sure how or when it happened, but eventually, I ended up dancing on top of the bar with three other Kappa girls. I was having the time of my life and yet an out-of-body experience at the same time.

After some dancing with the girl next to me, I felt warm hands on my arms from behind. A large fraternity guy had climbed onto the bar and felt the necessity of dancing with me. Embracing the opportunity, I willingly partook in a lighthearted exchange with the seemingly harmless guy.

To my dismay, the intoxicated man behind me was looking for something more than a dance partner. He teasingly grabbed me at first, but then his hands started to move in inappropriate ways. I wasn't sure if he was in control of his actions or if it was mainly the alcohol. I quickly realized that it didn't matter.

I tried to politely push him away, but my efforts were useless. He only gripped harder. As I pulled away from his grasp on my arm, I lost my footing and toppled off the bar.

My eyes must have been closed the whole time, because I didn't know how it was possible that I wasn't on the ground weeping in pain.

Slowly, I opened both eyelids, only to find Tyler's concerned face staring back at me. *Finally*, I thought anxiously, *he's showing some emotion!*

"Wow! Good catch!" I exclaimed, laughing.

Unbeknownst to me, Tyler had been standing fairly close to the bar, watching me. I wondered if he knew something might happen to me. I was surprised I hadn't noticed his presence, but my surrounding environment wasn't a concern to me while dancing atop the bar. My inhibitions were close to gone at that point.

I had to admit it felt nice being cradled in Tyler's arms. His cologne also smelled amazing. Suddenly, I had a longing to be embraced by Tyler more often. I couldn't describe the sensation, only that it resembled the feeling of caring. I wanted him to care about me.

"Are you okay?" Tyler asked, setting me onto my feet.

I nodded, not wanting to let go. On my feet, I felt unsteady, an excuse to cling even closer to him. Thankfully, he didn't move away, but instead supported me until I could catch my balance.

Without taking long to recover, I was ready to dominate the dance floor again. Grabbing both of his hands in mine, I waded backward through the crowd, stringing him along. "We're dancing!" I proclaimed, not giving Tyler the chance to decline.

Although there was clear hesitation in his eyes, Tyler didn't refuse. Tyler was pretty shy; I knew he had really wanted this all night but couldn't muster the courage.

At first, Tyler kept his distance. We were two completely separate entities, only dancing to the same music. It was disheartening, but it didn't bring me down. Within minutes, our bodies slowly began moving together synchronously. All of Tyler's reserve flowed out of the bar along with the people leaving. His hands traveled along my back, my own gripped around his shoulders. Our movement was so fluid; it felt like we had done this all night. There was an undeniable chemistry between us. It was coursing through our bodies.

I ran my fingers up his neck and then through his hair. His bright blue eyes were piercing as the overhead lights shown down. The proximity of our bodies let me rest my cheek against his. I rubbed my nose along his skin softly. Eventually, my mouth found his lips. Tyler didn't resist, like I expected him to. Surprisingly, it was a very natural reaction. He didn't even flinch.

All too soon, I heard Colt's voice close by, "Hey! I leave for two seconds and you two are making out. Not cool, Tyler, not cool."

We heard his complaint, but that didn't stop us.

Pulling away slowly, I inhaled a deep breath. "You're *such* a good kisser."

Tyler was kissing my neck, brushing away the hair from my shoulder. I giggled because it tickled.

He worked his way up my neck to my ear. Tyler whispered, "Come home with me."

"I thought you'd never ask," I said, smugly. My judgment was never very good, even sober.

Hand in hand, Tyler walked me to Colt. "We're going to get out of here."

Colt raised his eyebrows. "Are you sure, Tyler?"

Tyler and Colt exchanged a look I couldn't decipher.

"Alright...give me a ring later."

Tyler nodded and squeezed my hand. As we headed for the door, I waved goodbye to my friends, who looked confused. I gave them the thumbs up so they knew I was okay in Tyler's hands.

My car was the only available ride, since Tyler rode with Colt. He gladly took the keys from me, since he hadn't had as much to drink. After a safe ride and parking my car in the parking garage, we joyfully got out and practically skipped to his dorm. I silently questioned how sober he really was. I wasn't used to the loose and free Tyler.

With our fingers interlocked, we jogged up to the door and rushed inside. A few people lounging on the main floor gave us goofy looks. The stair climb to the second floor was thankfully quick, not requiring that I remove my heels.

As we arrived at his room, Tyler already had his key in hand. Peering cautiously into his dark room, he flipped on the light and allowed me in.

"My roommate's gone," he declared, tossing his keys onto his desk.

Jumping up onto what I assumed to be Tyler's bed, I kicked off my heels and watched them fall to the floor. "Aw, the more the merrier," I joked in response.

Tyler let out a slight laugh and faced the door as he removed his own shoes.

I lay back on the bed, sinking into the thin mattress. Closing my eyes, I took a deep breath.

When I opened my eyes, it was morning.

28

TYLER

When I had agreed to go to the bar with Colt, I had never imagined returning home with Regan.

What was I thinking? I wasn't, that was clear.

I tried to resist the temptation of her lips, her body, her everything. I just wasn't strong enough. The entire night I was in a constant struggle about what to do. Watching her reckless actions, I felt an innate urge to protect her. Although Roxanne would never admit it, she would expect me to keep her sister safe if I could help it.

I considered leaving, about a million times. I considered kissing her, about a billion times. I was only slowly gaining a tolerance for beer. Hiding the effects of the alcohol was the easy part. On any other day, I might have been able to say *no* more than once. Last night was a completely different story.

Although not an excuse for my actions, I missed Roxanne so much my stomach ached. I might compare it to drug withdrawal, if I had ever experienced it. The thought of not being close to her made me sick.

When my withdrawal symptoms from Roxanne were mixed with beer as well as her exact look-a-like, I knew I would be doomed for a bad situation. Though, I was not prepared to see Regan in those exact conditions.

Colt was a great friend. At the same time, he was definitely a male. I had filled him in on my liking for Roxanne, but not nearly in as much depth as I experienced. He had no idea of the history between

Regan and I, and how I had cut myself off from exploiting her. Or so I had thought.

The way she looked, the way she moved, the way her gloss shined off her lips, the way she needed protection...it was all a recipe for disaster in my world. I couldn't overcome the devil's pleas on my shoulder. If only the angel had been a bit louder.

As we drove back to my dorm, she couldn't keep her hands off me. She would have broken through handcuffs if I had entrapped her wrists. Roxanne was *not* off my mind, but I found it very hard to concentrate. My conscience thoughts were flying back and forth in my mind. I turned the music up loud so we wouldn't have to talk. Talking would have only made the situation worse.

My adrenaline subsequently increased once we left the car. Although Regan's hair was dyed blonde, her resemblance to Roxanne was unmistakable. When I looked into her eyes, all I saw was my best friend and ultimately, the love of my life.

When I wasn't thinking about force vectors and chemical compounds, my mind always wandered to her. I was in a constant mode of emotion. I had to admit to my desperation. All I wanted was to be loved. Was that so wrong? I had never had a girlfriend. Yes, maybe I could have had one if I had tried a bit harder. Roxanne was the only girl I wanted. There was a chance— probably a good chance— that Roxanne would never consent to being with me. Was I ready to accept that? Not by a long shot. Would I have to deal with the repercussions until the time of her final decision? Well, the answer should be yes, but I savagely decided to take a lesser route.

Opening my dorm room door, I checked for my roommate's presence. Regretfully, he wasn't around. I'm not sure that would have skewed Regan's plans, though. When I realized that I was proceeding to the next step, I silently inhaled and held my breath for a few seconds. Slight anxiety was taking over— flight or fight response, maybe. In this case, flight was not an option.

I tried not to say anything as I heard her gleefully take over my bed. I asked myself over and over again: *What was I doing?*

I pictured evasive tactics in my head, unsuspicious ways to avoid the forthcoming events. Rubbing my forehead, I slipped off my shoes, delaying the inevitable as long as possible. Silently praying, I begged for a way out of the terrible mistake I'd made in bringing a drunk Regan to my room. I would do anything to avert the crisis that lay before me.

Inhaling again, I let out a deep breath to help relax the pained look on my face. Then, I turned around to meet my unwelcome destiny.

And there she was. Regan was sound asleep sprawled across my bed.

Falling quietly to my knees, I thanked God for a miracle. I held my head in my hands and tried to breath evenly. Raising my head up, I gazed at Regan for a couple minutes, making sure that she was truly asleep. My initial impression was right; she was definitely out for the night.

I thought about sleeping in my roommate's bed, but I couldn't force myself to do it. He was certainly not the cleanest guy in the hall. Grabbing a stray pillow off my bed, being mindful not to make very much noise, I settled onto the floor for the remainder of the evening. Curled into the fetal position, my mind raced with thoughts about the whole night, about going to the bar, about seeing Regan, watching her dance with other guys, about staying close to her just in case something were to happen. The image of kissing and dancing with Regan stuck in my head like a bad dream. I couldn't distract my mind away from her face. Why did I invite her back here? What was I expecting? It was a wonder that she fell asleep and I didn't have to deal with the consequences of my actions.

Eventually, my racing thoughts cooled down and the images became hazy.

I opened my eyes, staring blankly at the wall where the sun shown through my small dorm window. Only after the second knock on the door did I realize that the first knock had woken me up. Rubbing my sore back, I got up from the floor and trudged to the door.

Barely awake, I pulled the door open. My eyes widened at the sight of my visitor.

"Roxanne," I barely uttered. She was drenched in sweat, obviously making a stop on one of her morning runs.

"Tyler!" she squealed, pushing the door open to give me a hug.

Before the door could open any more than the width of my body, I hurriedly stepped out of the room and shut the door quietly behind me.

"Why can't I come in?" she asked, confused at my secretive attitude.

I had to think quickly. "Oh... it's just that my roommate likes to sleep naked. It's not a pretty sight, as you can imagine." I added a muffled laugh at the end so that she would believe me.

Lying to Roxanne was not my first choice of actions, but there was no way I could let her see her sister in my bed. It was so hard to look into her eyes.

She looked so beautiful, even in her running attire. "Oh, that's gross!"

I nodded in agreement, "I know, I know."

Roxanne cocked her head to the side. "Tyler, why are you so dressed up?"

I looked down and realized I was still in the same clothes from last night. "I guess I just came home and fell asleep last night."

Leaning toward me, she sniffed my shirt collar. Roxanne curiously asked, "Tyler, you smell like beer. What did you do?"

I shrugged. "Just hung out with Colt, that's all."

"Hung out where? I know guys don't usually dress up for each other." She had a knowing look on her face.

"We went out, that's all." I didn't want to say any more than that, but I knew that wouldn't be enough to satisfy her curiosity.

"Went out?" she asked. Of course, she would wonder.

"You know...*out*..."

"Like, to a bar?"

I slowly nodded. Would she think of me differently now that she knows I do those kinds of things? Roxanne and I never experimented with alcohol in high school. It wasn't something we were into. Would it matter to her if that changed?

"Oh," she replied. Against my expectations, she continued, "I need to meet this Colt guy. You keep talking about him."

Her response surprised me. "What?" I asked hollowly.

"I need to meet Colt. You two seem to be close."

I was still shaken by her unconcern, but I wasn't willing to discuss my new drinking habits. It was time to focus on Colt.

I smiled to myself, thinking of how often Colt reminded me that he hadn't met Roxanne yet. "Yeah, he feels the same way about you."

She grinned. "No blind dates, though, okay?"

I shook my head, reminding myself that she was just joking. For an instant, I recalled last night when Colt and Regan were dancing. I bet he would date both of them, maybe even at the same time. I guessed most guys had a thing for cute twins. Colt had no idea how different this pair of twins was. I doubted he would want to be involved, like I was. Then again...

"No worries," I finally answered, realizing I had forgotten to answer her. "So what brings you here so early? You probably have like, another twenty miles to run or something, right?" I slightly grinned. It was way too early in the morning for being conniving. As much as I loved her company, and how surprised I was at her appearance, her timing was ironically bad.

"That's on tomorrow morning's agenda. I'm just running fifteen today."

Leaning against the doorframe, I tried to smile, but knew it probably looked fake. I was praying that this visit was merely a nice gesture and short in nature. Although I had no idea of what time it was, I knew from experience that Regan was not a particularly light sleeper and could be woken easily.

"So, really, what's up?" I pushed.

She shrugged. "Just haven't seen you in forever." Shifting her weight between her feet, Roxanne seemed antsy. I could sense there was a very specific reason for her visit this morning.

I glared at her. "Roxanne, I, unlike you, enjoy my sleep and you know that. Please, tell me what's on your mind."

As she averted her eyes for a moment, I suddenly became nervous. Why was she being so quiet? What was she afraid to tell me? A million different ideas ran through my idea, namely about the girl sleeping in my bed. Had one of her friends seen me last night? Had she figured it out?

Looking at her feet, Roxanne tapped her toe against the floor. "I need a girl friend."

Puzzled, I cleared my throat and said, "I, uh, can't help you there."

She shook her head. "No, you don't understand. I need my best friend."

"I'm right here." I was clueless.

"I need you to be more like a girl."

"*Excuse me?*"

She let out a sound of frustration. "I need to talk about girl things!"

Now I was definitely not interested. "Talk to Allison, she's a girl."

"I can't; it's not the same." In that instant, her eyes pierced right through my soul. There was clear distress in her expression.

I noticed she began fidgeting again. I rubbed my head. "This can't wait until I'm fully awake?"

As soon as I spoke, I knew I had said the wrong thing. Roxanne folded her arms across her chest and glowered at me. Without giving me a chance to repent, she spun around and headed quickly down the hallway. "Never mind," I heard her angrily mumble as the distance between us increased.

Sighing, I left my guard post and sprinted after her. "Roxanne!" I quietly called out, trying not to wake my neighbors.

To my disappointment, Roxanne didn't turn around. Finally, I caught up to her, planting myself in her path so she couldn't enter the stairwell.

"What?" she hissed.

"I'm sorry. I'm just tired...you know how grumpy I get when I'm tired."

"Well, you shouldn't have stayed up so late then."

"You're right," I quickly admitted, whether I agreed with her or not.

She didn't respond, her eyes staring at the wall.

"I'm sorry, Roxy. Forgive me?"

Her eyes briefly caught mine, searching for an expression to match my words.

"Of course, but don't be a jerk."

"You know how hard that is for me," I laughed, holding my arms open to her.

She gravitated toward me and my arms enclosed her warm body. I rested my chin on her head, closing my eyes to appreciate the moment.

Pulling out of my grasp, Roxanne ended our short-lived intimacy sooner than I had wished. "Can we talk?" she asked again, her face completely void of expression.

My eyes flashed back down the hall toward my room. I debated silently about leaving Regan in there by herself. I didn't trust my roommate with much, but I figured he could handle a strange female. He was probably passed out somewhere else and wouldn't be waking for another half-day anyway. I decided to go with my best judgment: appease Roxanne.

I nodded, grabbing her hand and leading her down the stairs away from my hallway and into the lounge area on the main floor. It was too early in the morning to be disturbed by other people up and about. Whatever Roxanne needed to talk about, we had the necessary privacy.

Sitting across from her in a chair, I watched her settle down into the loveseat. I waited for her to speak. The less conversation I initiated, the better.

Elbow propped against the armrest, she rested her chin in the palm of her hand, staring blankly out the window. She was as still as a statue.

Finally, she sighed, hesitant to speak, "I don't know how to say this..."

I gulped. "What do you mean?"

"Tyler, for one minute can you pretend I'm just any other girl on campus? Can you pretend that we've just met and you don't have feelings for me?"

I had no idea where this conversation was going, but I was fairly sure it didn't have anything to do with Regan. To refrain from expressing my obvious feelings, I concentrated on breathing evenly. If only Roxanne knew what I had put myself through last night just to save myself for her. Would she even care?

I lost focus quickly. "Roxanne, you're *not* just any other girl..."

She rolled her eyes. "I don't know if I can do this..."

"No, please," I begged. Any extra time with Roxanne was appreciated, even if I had to pretend I wasn't madly in love with her. "Go ahead," I encouraged.

"Okay..." she began, taking a deep breath. She continued, "I'm going on a date tonight."

I watched her lips move, but I was sure I had heard her wrong.

"W-what?" I asked, hoping for some clarity.

"Tyler, I'm going on a date," she restated, firmly.

There was no misconstruing the information she just presented to me; no misunderstanding there. Her position was clear. The blood drained from my face and I was unsure if I was going to vomit. I wanted to be invisible.

"Tyler," her tone was laced with warning. The way a mother would warn her son before he plunged into a puddle of mud.

Knowing she would not receive a response, she continued, her voice now sad, "Tyler, I need my best friend. I can't talk to anyone else."

Anger immediately sparked inside of me. "You have a million friends, go talk to them."

"Don't be that way."

Why shouldn't I be that way?

Folding my arms across my chest, I peered out the same window she had just a few minutes earlier. I thought I was going to be able to give my mind a rest, instead thoughts raced around, making my head hurt. My heart was racing, too. Maybe I should hold my breath so that I would just pass out and forget this ever happened. I would much rather be in a coma right now than listen to this heart-breaking news.

In my periphery, I caught a glimpse of Roxanne leaning across the small space that enclosed us. "Tyler." Her hand rested gently on my arm.

I closed my eyes only briefly, opening them to realize they were wet. Why was I such a baby?

"No, please don't cry," her voice was apologetic.

I shook my head, blinking away the moisture. *Get over it!* I yelled at myself.

"Is that all you wanted to tell me?" I hoped she was done subjecting me to torture.

She grew quieter. "Well, I wanted to ask your opinion."

I glared at her. "I don't have an opinion."

"Yes, you do," she corrected.

"You're right, I do have an opinion. But it's biased, and why would you even expect me to condone this behavior?"

"*Condone this behavior?* You act like I'm sleeping around or something!"

"Well, how do I know?" I just couldn't keep my mouth shut long enough.

Covering her face with her hands, she leaned on her knees for support. Roxanne began nervously fidgeting her foot.

I immediately felt guilty. "Roxanne, I'm sorry, I didn't mean that."

Lifting her head up to meet my gaze, she responded quicker than I expected, "You're lucky I already knew that."

"I'm not a fool. You're beautiful, you're smart... you're great, period. Guys are bound to be interested. What I don't get is *why* you have to rub it in my face?"

"Tyler," her voice broke, "I'm not rubbing it in your face! I just need someone to talk to."

"I'm sorry," I reiterated. "I just can't discuss this kind of topic with you."

She nodded slowly, proving she finally understood. "I guess I understand."

I pointed my finger at her. Trying to lighten the mood a little, I said, "Be aware, if any guy hurts you, I will end up in prison."

A weak smile appeared across her lips. "I promise I'll visit."

"Bring me cake?"

"Yes, with real butter and everything."

"Sounds amazing," I rubbed my stomach.

She stared at me with pleading eyes. "I'm sorry."

I shook my head, because that's the only thing I could do. Shrugging lightly, but feeling a heavy weight on my shoulders at the same time, I said, "Don't worry about it."

After a short period of silence, Roxanne asked, "So, why did you drink last night?" Her tone was filled with mere curiosity, not judgmental at all.

I sighed, more loudly than I meant to. She stared at me, now concerned.

"Tyler, what's going on? How much did you drink last night? What happened?"

Uh-oh. I could feel my heart start to quicken its beat, pounding in my chest. There was a distinct lump in my throat. How was I going to tell her?

"Roxanne, bad things have happened lately...I thought the alcohol would help ease the situation...."

Her face scrunched together, worry laced around her eyes. "Tyler..."

"Roxanne, my parents are getting a divorce."

29

ROXANNE

I felt like a huge weight had been lifted off of my shoulders.

Although Tyler wasn't thrilled to learn about my relationship with Luke, at least he knew and I wouldn't have to feel like I was hiding anything from him. Unfortunately, that didn't necessarily make our friendship any easier, but I needed Tyler to know the truth. I didn't want him living in a dream world that would someday end in our marriage to each other. He meant too much to me; I didn't want to break his heart.

Tyler was a fantastic guy and a very loyal friend. When I pictured us as being more intimate, which I had to admit I thought about more than occasionally, a strange feeling overcame me. Something didn't feel right. I knew Tyler had had feelings for me, for years now. But I thought his feelings would change once being introduced to the masses of other available women on campus. I was so very wrong. It seemed that he had made up his mind about me and that was that. He would wait, wait for me to go through as many guys as it would take. He believed someday I would finally understand what I was searching for in a soul mate, and there he would be.

To his dismay, Tyler would be waiting an infinite amount of time. Although I didn't want to share him, I also knew that he could find a girl who would be everything he needed. That girl was not me.

The devastating news of Tyler's parents' divorce was lingering in my head. My mind raced with the possible consequences of the decision.

I knew there was nothing I could do to defuse the situation. Instead, I tried to concentrate on the current matters of my life.

Tonight, I was going on a date, though I specifically told Luke that I didn't date.

Luke disagreed. Instead, he rephrased his question.

"Fine then. Will you go on an un-date with me?"

Now he was just being obnoxious. I was out of excuses, so I said yes. If he was telling me it wasn't a date, then what excuse did I have?

I couldn't deny that I liked him, but I was nervous. I didn't know what I was doing. As much as the title "un-date" meant to me, I realized I was being stubborn. We wouldn't call it a date, but I knew it would be inferred. There was nothing I could do about that.

Even with my hesitation, the "un-date" went much better than I could have ever imagined it. If anyone other than Luke had asked me, I would have said no. Luke was different than the other guys I knew, extremely different. His mysteriousness strangely attracted me. I couldn't figure him out. He had a certain ambiguity about him.

I was surprised at how much fun I had with him. He was the only guy, beside Tyler, that I had ever spent time with alone. Before meeting Luke, I had made a rule for myself: don't expect anything. That way, you could never be disappointed.

If I *had* set certain expectations—although I didn't—Luke would have exceeded all of them. He was amazing company. We had natural conversation. I wrung my hands a few times in my lap trying to calm my nerves, but I felt that I succeeded in masking my tension.

Luke picked me up in one of his many cars. This one was a red Audi.

"Nice car," I muttered, sinking into the leather seat.

A grin was plastered to Luke's face. "Thanks, it's one of my favorites."

"Can you please tell me how you have so many cars?"

"Aren't you dying to know?" His face was unchanged, watching me from the corner of his eye.

I nodded. "Yes, yes I am."

He smirked at my curiosity. "Well, that's for me to know and you to find out."

"*Humph.*"

Luke laughed at me. I really enjoyed his laugh—a very playful, sincere laugh.

Our date started out exactly the opposite of what I wanted. We went to dinner. It was not my first choice of things to do, but he didn't ask my opinion. I pictured the worst: awkward staring, while simultaneously trying to seem interested. My worries were groundless; conversation during dinner was free flowing and easy, fairly superficial in nature.

"What do you want to do now?" Luke asked, revving up his Audi after finishing dinner.

"Isn't it your job to decide?" I probed.

"Who said I had a certain *job*?"

I shrugged, chagrined. I was so new to the dating scene that it seemed I didn't know my left from my right.

He must have noticed the tinge of pink in my cheeks. "Don't worry Roxanne, I already have it all figured out."

When I peeked up at him, Luke gave me a warm smile. He was always prepared.

Luke drove around the city of Gainesville like he owned the place. Maybe he *did* own the place. I still hadn't figured out how he owned so many cars, or where he put them all. For all I knew, Luke could be ridiculously rich. He never gave me the answers I looked for, and I knew there was a reason for that. Would he think I would like him less?

Eventually, Luke pulled the Audi onto a small landing surrounded by greenery, overlooking the city. I looked at him suspiciously.

"Are we...*parking*?" I asked, unable to hold back a laugh.

He pursed his lips together, eyebrows pulled down. "What? Of course we're *parking*." The last word flowed off his tongue in the same tone as I had spoken it.

I realized immediately Luke had no idea what I was talking about. His ignorance humbled me.

I chuckled, more to myself. "Never mind."

"I don't like how I don't understand your American jargon."

I shrugged, feeling a bit sad by his words. "It's no big deal. You'll be around long enough to get it eventually."

He shook his head, a solemn look on his face. I couldn't understand what his expression meant. He pulled open his door and slammed it shut. I followed, curious as to his plans.

"What's wrong?" I asked, watching Luke hop up onto the hood of his car. Leaning against the windshield, he clasped his hands behind his head.

Looking only upward, he said, "Tell me about your past."

My face scrunched in irritation. Besides the fact that he didn't answer my question, he was looking for information I did not want to give up.

Folding my arms across my chest, I commanded, "Answer my question."

As I stood waiting for him to respond, a wave of peace spread across his naturally tan face.

His chest rose and sank, a quiet sigh escaping his mouth. "Nothing, Roxanne. Nothing is wrong. I am absolutely perfect."

He was right; he *was* absolutely perfect. I hated it.

"Sure?" I wondered out loud.

He nodded, patting the unoccupied place on the windshield next to him.

"I don't want to scratch your car."

Surprisingly, he chortled. "You won't, I promise. Now get up here."

When he held out his hand for support, I grabbed it and carefully lunged up onto the hood. As I leaned my head back, I gasped in awe. The stars above, forming numerous constellations, shone down on us with extravagant beauty and glory.

Worried, Luke asked, "What?"

I pointed up. "They're...beautiful."

I wasn't able to take my eyes from the sky, but I could sense he was smiling.

"I thought you might enjoy this."

I grinned, continuing to stare up into the vast universe. "It's been awhile since I've really stargazed."

Luke's face was smug. "I might have guessed that."

Peeling my eyes from the sky, I turned to stare at him. "You're amazing."

His eyes softened, though he didn't respond.

I returned my focus to the lights above. Inhaling deeply, I sighed loudly.

We both gazed at the stars appreciatively, pointing out certain constellations when spotted. After a period of silence, Luke mumbled, "So, I answered your question."

I considered this. "Well, not truthfully. But, yes, I guess you did."

"Now answer mine."

I rolled my eyes, knowing I wouldn't be able to escape the issue easily.

"Why do you want to know?" My eyes avoided his, as I tried to distract myself by finding the stars that formed the Big Dipper.

"Roxanne," he placed his hand on my forearm, "I want to know everything about you."

Goosebumps prickled the spot he touched, though the night was warm.

"There's not much to know."

He snorted, "I disagree."

"How can you disagree if you don't know?"

"Because I do know."

Quickly, I found his eyes, trying to decipher the meaning behind his words.

I cautiously asked, "What do you mean..."

Before I could finish my question, Luke clarified, "I mean, I don't *know*, but I *know*."

I was bewildered.

"I'm not making sense."

"You're right." I sighed again.

"I don't know how to talk around you."

Flabbergasted, I stared at him. I didn't believe what he was saying. That was not true at all. "Yes, you do," I corrected.

He took a lasting look at the sky before he met my eyes again. "Please tell me about your past."

I bit my lip, unsure of what to say. I hated everything about the past. I especially didn't want to relive it now.

Luke gently placed his hand on my arm, grasping only slightly. "Please?"

Nervously, I laughed, "What do you want to know? There's not much." I repeated, hoping he would leave the subject alone.

"What about your family?" Right, of course he wanted to know about my family.

"What about them?" I said stiffly. I longed to curl up into a ball.

Not paying attention to his body position, I was a bit startled when I felt Luke's hand on my cheek, pulling my head toward him.

His warm brown eyes pierced through mine. "You can tell me."

I couldn't stop the tear that trickled down my cheek, dripping onto the red paint underneath me.

I appraised his face for expression. He didn't seem surprised by my emotion. How much *did* he already know about me? Or was I that easy to read?

"Tell me about your parents."

There it was, the question of the night. A quiet sob unwillingly broke out from my throat.

Softly, Luke called my name, "Roxanne..." His fingers traced up and down my arm, which was more comforting than I expected.

Again, silence filled the space between us. "My dad is dead. Has been for almost five years now."

He breathed evenly, so close to me that it was calming. I expected him to apologize like all the others, venture to persuade me that everything happens for a reason and bad things happen to good people. Instead, he said nothing.

Another sob escaped, against my will.

Pulling me close, Luke's arms wrapped around me. I rested there as I tried to pull myself together.

"I bet your dad was a great man."

I whispered, "He was."

"I bet he cared a lot about you and your sister."

I nodded, my chin digging into his shoulder. "He did."

One of his hands started rubbing my back. I closed my eyes, thoroughly enjoying the touch of his palm, but feeling uncomfortable at the same time.

"He loved you so much, Roxanne." His words were firm.

I nodded, another sob erupting. "I know," I choked.

"Does your dad have anything to do with your relationship with your sister? Didn't you used to be close?"

Luke was a stealthy interrogator, sneaking in questions nonchalantly.

Pulling away from his shoulder, I used my arm as a pillow to lie on my side against the Audi. I wiped my tears away with the back of my hand. Luke held my elbow, as if to keep me from falling over. Did I seem that unstable right now?

As much as I wanted to keep the deep, dark secrets of my past to myself, I also felt the need to share all my thoughts with Luke. He was a very good listener.

"I couldn't pull my life together after he left us. I tried! My sister mourned, but not for long. I would wake up every day and see her smile, but I couldn't. She would hang out with her friends and carry on, but I couldn't. I couldn't be myself. My dad was such a part of my life..."

"Was he close with your sister?" he gently prodded.

"Not like with me. He taught me everything. My sister was, is, closer to my mother." My breathing slowed, allowing me to keep from erupting in more tears.

"Are you jealous of your sister?" Luke's eyes begged me to be honest.

"No," I said, fiercely.

He didn't believe me. I stubbornly did not want to admit that I envied her coping mechanisms. "Really? Not even a little bit?"

My eyes looked down through the windshield into the car. I traced the outline of the steering wheel with my index finger.

"You don't have to answer me, but I'll take that as a yes."

I sniffed, continuing to trace the dashboard.

Luke's eyes dropped to the hand that held my arm. Hesitantly, he asked, "Do you feel like you've moved on?"

I hesitated to answer. I was so vulnerable at the moment. How could I have let it go this far? It was wrong of me to get so personal with Luke.

"Roxanne," Luke urged.

I shook my head, unable to look into his eyes.

"Roxanne," he repeated, a sense of warning in his tone.

Again, I shook of my head. I wasn't budging.

"Everyone dies. Death isn't so bad."

I flicked my eyes quickly to his. How could death not be bad? Death was a horrible thing. Death was the end, the very end.

"How can you say that?" I said, disgusted. Luke couldn't possibly understand my feelings.

He shrugged lightly. "I've had to deal with death, also."

My face smoothed, relaxing a little. Maybe I was wrong; maybe he did understand.

Quietly and with empathy, I asked, "Who died?"

He wagged his head. "I don't want to talk about it right now."

"But I told you..." How unfair. Could he not trust me like I trusted him?

"I'll tell you later." He patted my arm. "I promise."

Nodding, I sighed.

After small bouts of conversation on the hood of his Audi, staring at the stars above, we headed back to my dorm.

We approached my door and I was certain that the date was over; I felt exhausted. Intent on saying goodnight, I waited for him to initiate the next move. I didn't want to repeat the same scene that had happened on my bed earlier in the week. I would not be humiliated again.

Luke was not moving. He leaned against the wall, watching me shift nervously back and forth between my feet. Suddenly, he smiled.

"What are you doing?" he asked.

My eyebrows pulled together. "What do you mean?"

"We're not done here, are we?"

Was Luke asking for a kiss? I was confused.

"Go get changed," he instructed.

"For what?" I was wearing jeans, a decent shirt, and sandals.

"And grab your soccer ball." He winked to urge me on.

Grinning, I nodded and unlocked my door. Though I felt fatigued by the emotional outburst on the car, I couldn't resist feeling elated that the un-date was not over. After the intense conversation we had, a little soccer would lighten the mood.

"I'll wait out here," he pointed to the spot where he stood right outside my door. I walked inside my room and closing the door behind me.

After I had changed into a pair of shorts and an old t-shirt, along with running shoes, I grabbed my soccer ball and headed back out into the hallway. Luke flashed his beaming smile as I greeted him.

"Ready?" he asked, excitement building in his voice.

"For what?"

"Just say yes."

"Then, ask me again."

He looked at me, perplexed. "Okay...are you ready?"

"I was born ready!" I skipped down the hallway, tempting him to race me.

As soon as I turned my head, he was right beside me. "You're so fast," I complimented him, shoving the door open to the stairwell.

He shrugged, flying down the stairs quicker than I could.

At the bottom of the stairs, my breathing heavy, Luke placed his hand on my shoulder. "Don't wear yourself out yet. The night is young."

I eyed him curiously, still wondering what was next on the agenda for the night.

Luke pushed open the exit door to my dorm and headed outside, while I tried to catch up.

"Where are we going?" I asked, staring at his profile in the darkness.

He shook his head, unwilling to answer.

"Fine, I give up."

"Thank you," he responded. "You don't always have to know what's going on. Just trust me." He slowly emphasized his last three words. I laughed to myself about the irony of his phrase. Four months ago I wouldn't have trusted him. Now, I couldn't convince myself not to.

When we arrived to our destination—the recreational turf field tucked within the outdoor track adjacent to the student gym—I was excited. The bright lights glistened off the fake grass.

I noticed quickly that there was no one around. "Where is everyone?" Most nights this field was occupied by intramural football or soccer games.

"Guess there must be something better going on."

"That's your opinion," I offered, smiling.

We stepped onto the turf and headed toward the middle of the vast, open space. Before reaching it, Luke furtively stole the ball out from under my arm, throwing it on the ground and dribbling it between his feet.

"You might not be too bad," I commented.

"I've only played a bit."

I felt smug, sure that I could take him on. "How long?"

"Oh, fifteen years."

My eyes widened. "Why didn't you tell me you played?" I couldn't believe we had talked about so many things, yet never broached the subject of his underlying soccer skills.

I watched as he swiftly moved the ball around the surrounding area. He really *was* good. Feeling competitive, I sprinted after him, trying to steal the ball back.

"I don't think so!" Luke yelled. I circled him, looking for a chance to strike. He quickly moved around me without hesitation.

I had to stop to catch my breath. Resting my hands on my knees, I watched him bounce the ball continuously off his head, showing off. I shook my head, laughing at his confidence.

He paused to address my distress, a twinkle in his eye, "I thought you played collegiate soccer?"

In response to his question, I ran, hurtling myself at him, laughing at the same time. I took him down quickly with my body weight. It helped that he wasn't expecting my aggressiveness.

As soon as he was down on the ground, I sprang up and hooked the ball with my foot, sprinting away from him. I knew he would follow soon after.

I played with the ball for a while. When I realized he wasn't following, I scanned the field for him. Standing stoutly, arms folded across his chest, he wagged his head in defeat. I could only grin in response.

"I wish these lights weren't so bright!" he called from across the field.

As if at his beckoning, all of the stadium lights shut off. The night was darker than I remembered. I waited for my eyes to adjust to the black, searching around for any sight of Luke. I couldn't see his figure anywhere.

In my fretting, I neglected to listen for footsteps from behind. Crashing into me, two arms picked me up and swung me lightly around. Goosebumps covered my arms. My breath was taken away by the impact.

Sucking in some air, I caught my breath again. "Hey!" I shouted at him, immersed in laughter and surprise.

We tumbled to the ground for the second time, cries of glee filling the air. Still competing for the ball, Luke and I leaped to our feet, scouring the area for it. Spotting it rolling away, I lunged forward. Before I could reach it, Luke had caught up. Instead of kicking the ball out of my foot grasp, he picked me up and threw me over his shoulder.

The blood from my body rushed into my face. "You're crazy!" I laughed.

He carried me around the field a bit, kicking the ball around by himself.

"See, I can play soccer even with you on my back."

"Funny!" I called out in discomfort.

Soon after, he pulled me back into his arms, my legs dangling free. I held on tightly to his neck, trying to orient myself in space. Placing me gently on the ground, he held me close to his body. Even in the dark, I could see the spark in his eyes.

Before I could fully analyze the situation, Luke's lips were on mine. Automatically, I wrapped my hand around his neck, pulling his head closer to mine. His lips were cool, as well as his breath, reminding me of spearmint, so refreshing. I felt like this was what I had been waiting for the last eighteen years.

When he managed to break away, his expression was soft, a slight smile that reached up to his eyes.

His voice was quiet, but I could hear perfectly, "So that's what it feels like."

STAGE FOUR

DEPRESSION

30

LUKE

The countdown was ticking on and I was full of ignorance.

Frustratingly, I was not given specific information about the incident. How was I supposed to do my job—and do it successfully—if I was uninformed? The day could be tomorrow, maybe next week, possibly next year. There was no way for me to be prepared. There would be no warning sign.

When I was given the news of the countdown, I was struck with an unusual sadness. I couldn't stop thinking about what it meant to my relationship with Roxanne. My heart ached. I was brought into this world for one purpose and one purpose only. I had a very specific goal and I was not to falter. I had a job to do and I could never forget that.

I was deeply falling for Roxanne, which was quite obvious. Hurting her feelings was not a part of my job description, although neither was falling in love with her. I had been watching her for so long from afar, even before we had actually met. I knew everything about her. I felt like a creep, like a stalker, but I had to move past those thoughts. Following her was an instruction I had to follow. I had not intended to do more than what was necessary to keep her safe. I couldn't resist.

I was afraid of the future. Honestly, I was afraid of the present, also. What if I couldn't do it? Complete my job? What would happen to me? What if I lost Roxanne forever? I had no idea what I was saying....

31

TYLER

I felt like my life was crashing down on me.

I wanted Roxanne to love me. Yet, she had found someone else.

I wanted to be a part of a picture-perfect family. Rather, my family had turned dysfunctional overnight.

School was my escape. With all the troubles surrounding me, at least I could turn to studying to provide time away from reality. I would study chemical molecules and power equations all day long if it meant not thinking about the people closest to me.

In my angst, I was trying to avoid Regan. Immediately following my meeting with Roxanne about her date and my parent conflicts, I reentered my dorm room to find Regan rousing from sleep. Of course, she was confused.

Holding her head, her blonde hair a mess, she warily looked at me and said, "What happened?"

I wasn't in a very cheerful mood. "Would you believe me if I told you I found you passed out on the ground outside my dorm?"

She considered my proposal. "I might."

"No, that story would be too understandable. Okay, let's see. We were at the bar. You got drunk. I foolishly invited you back here, presuming to do who-knows-what. Before we could manage to mess up each other's lives, you passed out. And now, here you are."

She nodded her head slowly, taking in the information. "Sounds like something we would do."

I cleared my throat. "We?"

"Hey now, you took advantage of my incapacity to make sound judgment calls."

I laughed. "You sound so much more intelligent when you're hung over."

"That was mean," she commented, sliding off my bed. "So, where were you?"

"What's it to you?"

Regan folded her arms across her chest. "What's with you?"

I shook my head. "Not in a good mood."

She responded quickly, "Well, you know why?"

"Don't say it..."

"You know I'm right."

I sighed. "You're right. My dopamine levels are managed solely by my sexual desire." Although I wasn't sure she knew what dopamine was, I hoped she understood I was being sarcastic.

"Funny," she smirked, checking her appearance in the small mirror outside my closet.

"Well," I started, glancing around the room, searching for the appropriate words for the occasion.

"Well," she mocked. "Maybe next time."

My eyes widened. "Regan, we agreed..."

Her face narrowed. "No, *you* agreed, and yet *you* were the one to quickly forget *your* agreement."

I shook my head, which was beginning to throb. "Whatever."

"Tyler, you asked me here. Don't forget that."

She walked toward the door. My anxiety increased, a large lump rising in my stomach. "You won't tell Roxanne, will you?" I gulped.

"She would never believe me."

"But you won't?" I needed a straightforward answer, even if Regan couldn't be trusted.

After pausing for a moment, she replied, "No, I won't tattle this time. *This* time."

Without another word, I watched as Regan opened the door and walked out into the hall, shutting the door behind her. Plopping onto my bed, I sprawled out on the covers. I sighed loudly, relieved I wouldn't have to deal with the consequences of my actions. As much as I loathed the platonic relationship between Roxanne and I, I knew I couldn't drop my standards.

I checked the clock. It was ten. Surely Colt would be awake by now.

I dialed his number and waited. It rang and rang and rang. No answer.

I tried again, without answer.

I really wanted to talk to him. I decided to try one more time.

This time, it only took one ring. "Hello?" murmured the groggy voice on the other end.

"Hey."

"Man, it's like...early in the morning...what do you want?"

I imagined Colt always acted like that after a long night, so I was forgiving. "You okay?"

"Sure, sure. More importantly, how are *you?*"

"You don't even know. Regan passed out on me last night—which was a blessing; Roxanne decided to visit this morning—great timing—and she tells me she's dating someone—just what I needed to hear; and I told her about my parents. It's been a crazy last twelve hours."

"Sounds like it. Well, I haven't reached my ten hours of sleep yet. Call you later." *Click.*

He probably wouldn't even remember our conversation when we spoke next.

I lay in my bed, suddenly feeling tired. Drifting in and out of light sleep, I thought intermittently of the night before. How stupid I was, inviting a girl back here. Inviting *Regan* back here. That was very stupid, indeed. I turned on my side. When I became uncomfortable, I turned on my stomach, then again onto my back. I did this for two hours.

After a couple hours of unsuccessful sleep, I decided I was hungry enough to eat. Campus food wasn't sufficiently tempting, so I considered my other options. I recalled passing some places to eat downtown, so I decided to try my luck there. Showering quickly, I threw on clean clothes that didn't smell of alcohol. I half-heartedly fixed my hair, not caring to impress anyone.

Although the downtown area was not particularly close, I felt like taking a long walk would be good for me. The main street was comprised of the most popular shops, bars, and eateries, while the grid of surrounding streets housed a variety of eccentric and less-popular businesses. With my hands in my pockets, I perused the numerous options of places to eat, glancing back and forth, up and down the main street. My eyes were fixed on a pizza place a block up when my ears caught the sound of a girl singing. I traveled a few feet further up the street, letting my ears guide me in curiosity. The crescendo of music was enthralling and somewhat liberating. I wouldn't stop until I found the source.

After another few steps forward, it was clear where and to whom the voice belonged. A chalkboard sign placed on the sidewalk outside the small café read: Caroline Tucker, today's featured artist. I stepped into the establishment, which had a very warm atmosphere. It housed a number of petite round tables and a small stage at the front. On the stage sat a girl with beautiful wavy blonde hair, a guitar in her lap. Her eyes were closed, entranced in her art.

I took a seat at the back of the café, trying to blend in with the dispersed crowd. I listened to the girl for a long while before I considered eating anything. Although I wasn't paying particular attention to her lyrics, her voice and melody were addictive. The sound was a smooth mixture of country and blues. She played the guitar as if she had been playing since she was born. The strings moved softly under her delicate hands. Though I had never been very fond of this type of music, nothing could break my attention from this gorgeous women and her glorious sound.

After consuming a sandwich absentmindedly, I pondered my next move. Unexpectedly, I came up with a brilliant idea; I would get that girl's phone number. Though I felt down on my luck, I had to admit I really had nothing to lose. My heart was already smashed; what more could another girl do?

Waiting patiently, almost another hour, I ran through the plan in my head. I really was interested in getting to know her, so I couldn't just plunge into it. It was rather obvious that I was not experienced in the girl department, seeing as I had devoted all my love to one girl for my entire life.

I was about to order another sandwich when it was apparent she was done playing. Sucking in a deep breath, I exhaled slowly. Admittedly, I was nervous.

The girl was packing up her guitar on the side of the stage. I guessed now was as good as any other time. Slowly, I picked myself up out of my chair and headed toward her. Multiple times I considered turning around and walking right out of the door. Forcing my feet to move forward, I kept thinking, *nothing to lose, nothing to lose.*

Once I approached her, my words ran dry. I had practiced the conversation in my head about one hundred times in the past hour, yet I couldn't even manage to greet her with a head nod.

The girl was bent down at her guitar case. Noticing my presence, she turned toward me and smiled. What a wonderful smile, so refreshing.

"Hey there," she spoke, every syllable laden with a heavy southern accent. Could she get any better?

I was able to return the smile, but I only nodded in response. Confused, the girl returned to the task at hand.

"You were great," I drove out of my throat.

She smiled at me again. "Why, thank you. I'm glad you liked it."

Stupidly, I blurted out the first thing that came to mind, "You had me at hello."

The girl laughed, to my surprise. "Seems like someone watches *Jerry McGuire* a bit too much."

"Well—," I started, trying to give an excuse.

Interrupting me, she said, "No, it's great. I love that movie."

I laughed a little too, chagrined.

Here's your chance, I told myself. "I was wondering if I could buy you something to eat?"

At my suggestion, her perfect little nose scrunched up, a smile still on her face. "Oh, I'm sorry. I'm not interested."

Wow, I thought, *she couldn't have been more straightforward*.

"Well, maybe something to drink, then?" I couldn't help but test the waters.

She shook her head. "Sorry."

My shoulders slouched down; I was more distraught than I had imagined. I nodded at her and said, "Maybe next time."

She grinned, responding with, "Yes, next time."

32

ROXANNE

I only had one thing on my mind. His name was Luke.

I had decided that I needed to take a long drive and sort out my thoughts.

Heading out to the nearest parking garage, which sat nestled in between Tyler's dorm and my own, I tried to remember where I had parked. A small, metered parking lot sat in front of the garage, free only in the evening and on the weekends. I typically parked on the third floor of the five-story building if it was available. Since it was Saturday, I could be parked any number of places. I stopped in my tracks, trying desperately to recall the events of the past few days. Tapping my foot impatiently, I scanned the outside lot. My Nissan Xterra was not difficult to identify by its bright yellow color.

A drop of water hit my head. Looking toward the gloomy sky as the culprit, I shook my head in irritation. Another drop hit my arm, cold, giving me chills. I jogged into the opening of the parking garage, still contemplating where I had left my car.

"Lost?" someone asked from a short distance away.

The voice was so familiar by now I didn't need to see the face to know to whom it belonged. I spun around and faced the one person I was trying to get out of my head. "Hey," I said, smiling.

"What are you doing?" Luke asked, sounding very uninterested.

"Looking for my stupid car. I can't remember where I parked."
I grabbed his hand, radiating with warmth, and gripped it tight. I
appreciated the safety I felt with him.

He smiled at my assertiveness. "I think I saw it."

My eyebrows rose. "Really?" I shouldn't have been surprised.

"Yeah, fourth floor. Come on," he suggested, leading me
toward the staircase.

"Where did you come from?" I asked, suddenly wondering why
he just showed up out of nowhere.

A grin spread across his face, his white teeth flashing at me.
"See, when a man and woman love each other..."

"Ha, ha, you're so funny," I sarcastically commented, punching
him lightly in the arm.

Then Luke answered, "I actually just parked. I was coming to
find you."

"Oh, really?" I was surprised, even though Luke always showed
up unexpectedly.

"Of course, what else would I have going on?" He winked at
me.

"That's very true. Without me, you really have no life."

We topped the fourth flight of stairs. "You are so right. Where
were you headed, anyway?"

Absentmindedly, my eyes searched the rows for any sight of
yellow. Without allowing me to check any other rows, Luke pulled me
toward the opposite side of the garage. A car passed us, Luke stepping
on the outside to shield me protectively. I smiled softly at him, but he
didn't notice. He was always so careful.

"I just wanted to drive," I admitted, apprehensively.

"Sounds nice," he said, rubbing my back gently. His hands
traced up and down my spine, tickling a bit. I laughed, wiggling away
from him.

"I still don't see my car."

"Hang on, it's here somewhere."

Then, I saw it. Actually, I saw two of them. Two yellow Xterras, parked right next to each other. The cars looked identical, not one defining feature apparent.

I pulled my car key out of my purse and hit the unlock button. A flash of light shone from the first car's front lights, clarifying its ownership.

"Hop in," I told him, motioning toward the passenger's side door.

"Why don't we take my car?" he suggested, nodding toward the other Xterra.

Moving around toward the rear of my car, I gaped at him. "You're kidding me."

He laughed, amused by the expression on my face. "Get in." He took out his own car key and unlocked the doors, the same familiar lights flashing before my eyes.

"You're impossible," I declared, opening the passenger door.

Proudly, he said, "I try. Where would you like to go?"

"I don't care. Surprise me." The interior of his car looked just like mine, except there were no personal objects in sight. It reminded me of a new car, unused, unlived in.

"This rain is annoying," he commented, outlining the trail made from a drop of water on the windshield.

I nodded, "Yes, it is."

I leaned my head back as Luke drove to the mystery location, listening to the patter of the rain on the windows and the road water splash up against the bottom of the car. His hand reached over, covering mine. I couldn't imagine being anywhere else with anyone else at this very moment, inside the twin Xterra, the peaceful assurance of our breath the only sound floating through the air.

Luke pulled onto the highway, heading south toward Ocala.

"Where are you taking me?" I asked, curious.

"You'll see. Just lean back and enjoy the ride."

I did as told, reclining the seat back as far as it would go and closing my eyes.

Roused awake at the halting of the car less than an hour later, I groggily opened my eyes and examined our destination. The sun was bright and shining directly into my face, causing me to shift my gaze. We were parked in a gravel lot alongside many other cars. It took only a minute before I recognized my surroundings. The small trailhead sat to our right; runners, walkers, and bikers passing by it every few seconds. It was a gorgeous Florida Saturday morning in October, the perfect time to exercise.

We stepped out of the car, shutting the doors behind us. A St. Francis Trailhead sign welcomed us. Although I was naturally excited to be at the trail, I was confused about what we would be doing. Neither of us was dressed to do any sort of exercise, other than walk.

"So, what do you think?" Luke said, pleased with himself.

"I'm not sure. What are we doing here?" The gravel dust covered our shoes as we walked toward the opening to the trail.

"I thought we could reminisce."

"About...?"

He quietly laughed, "About the first time we met. How does that sound?"

I patted his arm. "Sounds good." Smiling, I thought, *I could have a good time with you anywhere.*

"Me too," he said.

My eyebrows furrowed. "What?"

He shook his head, chuckling. "Oh, nothing."

We walked down the trail, hand in hand, chatting about the change in weather from Gainesville to Ocala, the black squirrels that didn't hesitate to say hello, the variety of people passing by. It was nice just to walk for once, to really take in the environment and the sun. It felt so warm on my skin and I was thankful the bad weather didn't follow us south. It felt natural to be with Luke; I could easily be myself around him.

A bridge was approaching. I had run over this bridge more times than I could count, but I had never truly stopped to enjoy it. Luke walked to the edge of the bridge and peered down. I followed.

"These creeks are so beautiful," he said.

Nodding in agreement, I said, "Yeah. I typically don't stop to check out the scenery."

"You should, you know. Stop every once and awhile."

I latched onto his arm, linking us together. "That's why I have you."

The blue stream toppled over the rocks stuck in the earth floor, continuing to flow on its own schedule. Small fish of multiple colors traveled with the tide, stopping briefly every now and then. Watching the water, just like on the windshield, was entrancing. My mind had started to wander when Luke brought me back to reality.

"What are you thinking about?" he asked, leaning his body against the wooden railing.

I mimicked his actions, resting my elbows on top of the ledge, setting my chin down on my arm. "Being here, with you. It's so peaceful."

Luke didn't respond for a while, which slightly worried me, but I decided it was nothing. Sometimes he was unnaturally quiet, which was normal for him.

"Promise me something?" he barely breathed, bending close to me. His nose brushed my hair.

I turned my head so I could see his face. "Sure. Anything. As long as it doesn't involve skinny dipping."

He laughed at my pitiful joke but quickly became serious again. "Promise me..."

"Anything..." I reassured him.

He grew closer, his lips touching my ear. "We'll always be together, even if only in our dreams."

I lifted my head, taken aback by the overwhelming sadness laced in his voice. As I replayed his words in my head, I was lost in the meaning.

Sensing his vulnerability, I wrapped my arms around his neck and hugged him close. In response to his statement, I nodded, my chin tapping his shoulder. He squeezed me tenderly in his muscular arms, raising me off of the ground.

He repeated, "Even if only in our dreams."

33

REGAN

If I was going to the gym, I was going to be noticed.

Opening the entrance door to the school's student fitness center, I couldn't resist grinning at the responses I was getting. I was sporting a bright pink sports bra and short, black spandex running shorts. Was I here to run? Of course not. Was I here to turn heads? Yes!

I continued through the corridor, presenting my student identification to the worker, and headed on toward the main workout area. The large, multilevel gym was sectioned off into various areas, including treadmills, weight machines, fitness classes, and basketball and volleyball courts. Although I wasn't planning on exerting too much effort—sweating was not my thing—I figured walking on a treadmill wouldn't hurt anything. Plus, I would be able to watch all the hot guys running by me.

The treadmill room consisted of four long rows of machines with televisions bolted to the walls at the front for entertainment. It was fairly busy today, but thankfully I didn't have to wait in line. I scanned the room, trying to determine the best spot for viewing the most guys at one time. As I considered my options, I spotted a tall, finely sculpted, tan guy removing his shirt. I knew that was a sign for where I should park myself.

Making sure my hair was perfectly in place, I approached the empty treadmill adjacent to the guy. I stepped up onto the belt, pressed START, and with the straightest, most confident posture I could muster, I began walking. Forcing my attention to the television screen for the moment, I deliberated when I should make eye contact with my fellow exerciser. *Oh, just do it,* I convinced myself.

With a smirk on my face, I slightly turned to my left to catch an innocent glimpse of the guy.

"Luke!" I snapped, slapping his shoulder lightly. I should have known it would be him by that dumb hat he wore, always turned around backwards. The image of his face reminded me of our last encounter, specifically him leaving me for my sister. My eyes narrowed in frustration with him.

Acknowledging me with a small smile, he nodded his head, "Regan." He was briskly running, though I couldn't see any sweat. The tracker on the machine indicated he was finishing his fifth mile. My mouth dropped only slightly.

"I'm still mad at you," I remarked.

He didn't turn his head. "Sorry," he responded flatly. Luke was not budging.

My lips formed a pout. I waited for him to react but after a short while, I gave up. My need to talk overpowered my temper.

"Looks like you're in good shape," I offered, staring at the workout statistics on his treadmill's display.

"It takes hard work," he responded, barely enthused.

"I can tell," I agreed. I resisted the temptation to grab his muscular arm.

Luke must have felt my eyes continuously on him. While still running, he grabbed his white shirt that was strung over the machine and slithered back into it.

My eyebrows furrowed at his actions. He turned to me and explained, "It's getting cold in here, don't you think?"

On the contrary, the temperature was definitely increasing. Even with my very mild walking pace, I was beginning to feel perspiration on my forehead and neck. "Sure," I remarked, rolling my eyes.

Out of the corner of my eye, I saw another female mount the empty treadmill next to Luke. Turning to look at the girl out of curiosity, I immediately became riveted with annoyance.

"Roxanne, what are *you* doing here?" I asked, irritated.

Her eyes widened at the sight of me. Was it just my presence or was it my presence near Luke?

"Regan, it is natural for someone who likes to exercise to go to the gym. *You're* the one that doesn't belong here."

"Whatever. I can be here if I want."

She continued, "And goodness, Regan, *who* works out in that anyway?" I realized she was pointing at my outfit. "This is not the beach."

My face grew taut. "You're just jealous that you don't look like this."

Laughing cockily, Roxanne refuted, "Reality check, Regan. I look *exactly* like that. And do you see me wearing skimpy shorts, running around in my sports bra? No."

"It's my choice if I want to show off my body, thank you."

Barely audible, Roxanne said, "Yeah, and you're showing off my body, too."

"What was that?" I asked, my mouth forming a grin.

"Nothing. Do what you want."

Luke was quiet throughout our bantering, turning his head back and forth between us. Slowing his pace down to a walk, he placed a hand on Roxanne's shoulder.

"There's no reason to get upset," he whispered to her, pulling her closer to him.

I could see a glimpse of a smile on her face, which made me want to vomit.

Luke released her and pointing to the treadmill, said brightly, "Wanna race?"

Roxanne's face smoothed and she nodded. Before starting the machine, she turned back again to me and said, "You could have picked any treadmill."

"You're right," I retorted.

At that, Roxanne started walking, which quickly turned into a run without effort.

Luke mimicked her actions and began to explain, "Alright, when you hit one-quarter mile, we'll race to two miles."

"What do I get when I win?" she playfully questioned.

"*Whoever* wins..." he grinned, "Well, we'll decide the prize later." I saw him wink at her. Gross.

"You guys make me sick," I cursed under my breath.

"What was that?" Roxanne asked me, loudly.

"Nothing," I confirmed.

"That's what I thought."

Luke interrupted, "Okay, Rox, I hope you're ready to lose..." Glancing at the tracker on his machine, I could see that one-quarter mile was soon approaching. I was rooting for Luke, simply because the opponent was my sister.

"Ready...set...go!" he exclaimed, increasing his speed.

I had never seen any two people run so fast. Luke was clearly not struggling as much as Roxanne; she was trying desperately to keep up. He kept punching the button up...and up...and up....I stared in amazement as they were each running at 11 miles per hour, then 12 miles per hour, then 13....

Roxanne's heavy breathing kept me from focusing on the television. Her face was bright red and dismayed, obviously pushing her limit of maximal exertion. Luke, on the other hand, looked undisturbed—no sweat, no distress. His hand reached up to increase the speed once more.

I watched in horror as Roxanne's body tumbled off of the treadmill, the belt continuing to turn fast. Realizing what had happened, Luke jumped off his machine and knelt by her side. In fact, every person around us, including a gym employee, surrounded Roxanne as she lay on the floor.

Her eyes were open and she was breathing, though it was extremely labored. She put a hand over her face, trying to catch her short breath. Roxanne's other hand was clenching her chest.

Luke's face expressed deep concern, "Roxanne...Roxanne, are you okay?"

She was unable to answer, probably due to her inability to take in enough air to form a word. The employee knelt down on Roxanne's other side and took her heart rate.

"It's 200...that's not good," the employee announced.

I heard someone in the crowd say, "That's, like, her maximum heart rate."

"I'm calling 911," the employee stated, hurriedly pulling out her phone.

Luke shook his head, "She'll be okay."

The employee proceeded to dial.

Luke took the phone from the girl's hand and hung it up. He repeated, "She'll be okay."

I chewed on my cheek, watching Luke's interaction with the employee. How did he know? Roxanne did not look good.

Roxanne shook her head, agreeing with Luke, her face still covered.

His eyes drifted to my sister. "I'm so sorry," Luke apologized to her, his forehead wrinkled, "This is all my fault." Closing his eyes, he burrowed his face into his arm.

Roxanne weakly placed her hand on his arm, trying to comfort him.

Luke looked up at the employee and the bystanders and said "I better take her back to her dorm."

"Are you sure we shouldn't call?" the nervous girl asked Luke again.

He nodded, assuring her. "She just needs to rest."

Everyone looked anxious, not wanting to believe Luke. I couldn't blame them.

Roxanne removed her hand from her face and stared at the ceiling. Her breathing had finally calmed down. She slide her hand into Luke's and softly said, "Help me up."

Luke asked her, "What happened?"

Roxanne spoke slowly, "I think I tripped..."

"What am I going to do with you? First the trail, then the mall, now the gym..." Luke joked playfully.

Weakly, she said, "I believe you're the common factor in all those cases."

Smiling, Luke carefully pulled her to her feet. He supported her with his neck under her shoulder. He searched the crowd swiftly and locked his eyes with mine. I mouthed, "Will she be okay?"

He nodded, then turned and headed out of the large room with my sister.

34

TYLER

When Roxanne called saying she was sick, I knew exactly what to do.

Canned chicken noodle soup and crackers in hand, I trudged across campus toward Roxanne's dorm. I thought I would try to get her mind off of not feeling well. She didn't know I was coming though—thankfully she liked surprises. I wasn't quite sure what was wrong with her, but it didn't matter. Even though we weren't speaking as much anymore since our conversation about dating, there was really nothing I would rather do than attempt to make my best friend feel better.

As I passed by groups of college students, whether simply enjoying the last bit of summer sun studying or consumed in music, I reflected on the first few months of my college experience. I had met some pretty awesome characters and school was actually a breeze. Unannounced, my best friend had only become more beautiful since August. Whether my overwhelming jealousy was triggered in the wake of all the attractive guys lingering about, I wasn't sure. I knew she would attract attention from guys when we moved from Ocala to Gainesville, but I had no perception of how much attention she would actually receive.

Although I wasn't able to spend as much time with her as I wanted due to my increasing amounts of homework or her long soccer practices, I decided our friendship was as good as ever. Roxanne was always unrelentingly honest with me, despite the subject. She would always be my best friend, no matter the distance between us or whether others were standing in the way.

I approached her dorm and glowered at the stairs. Entering through the double doors, I sulked toward the stairwell. I absolutely hated climbing the four flights of stairs every time I wanted to see her. For Roxanne, it was great exercise. For me, it was a heart attack waiting to happen. The student fitness center had still not intrigued me enough to work out, even though I promised myself repetitively I would check it out every time I walked past it on my way to class. The resulting weakness and poor endurance were definitely taking their toll on me, even at my age.

Out of breath, I took a quick rest break at the top of the fourth flight. I didn't want to look tired when I finally got to see her, but she would probably be able to guess my problem by the beads of sweat on my forehead. Once my heart rate slowed, I gathered my breath and straightened my posture to look a bit taller. I strutted idiotically to her room, the fourth door on the right. Pausing, I stared appreciatively at the soccer décor that illuminated the brown wooden door. There were tons of pictures of her and her teammates, at practice and hanging out around campus. In the top corner, I smiled at a photograph of the two of us. It was taken soon after her eighteenth birthday earlier in the semester. Smirking, I was insanely relieved that this was the only co-ed picture displayed. Although she told me she was dating, somehow I knew she wasn't seriously involved. Roxanne was waiting for me. She just needed time to consciously recognize this.

Inhaling deeply, I brought my fist up to knock. Before my hand touched the door, I heard a familiar voice down at the other end of the hallway. I turned my head and almost fainted. There she was, with him. Roxanne was entwined in Luke's arms, playfully brushing his hair with her fingers. As much as I hated to admit it, she looked painfully happy. In fact, the way her eyes sparkled reminded me of someone else. Then it struck me. When her soft gaze caught his and her mouth curled into a bashful smile, I knew it was exactly the way I looked when I stared at her. I immediately felt nauseous.

Quietly I watched them from afar, flirting back and forth. I couldn't hear their conversation, which was probably for the best. Hand in hand, Luke gently pushed Roxanne up against the wall, his face inches from her nose. My blood was beginning to boil under my skin as I watched my worst nightmare unfold before my eyes. It all happened in slow motion for me. He leaned his body toward her, the distance between them closing. I gulped, because I knew what was coming. My fists tightened, my head shaking side to side. Time slowed even more as their lips met. I wanted to be hallucinating, but I knew it was all too true.

Anxiously, I had to decide what my next move would be. Should I leave quietly? Should I punch the door? Should I pretend like it never happened? I honestly had no idea what the best course of action was, but I needed to make up my mind fast.

Looking down at the can of soup in my hand, I could feel my breathing quicken again. She was supposed to be sick, the little liar. Roxanne's expressions were far from that of a sick person. She looked as if she were on cloud nine.

I had to keep my composure. After a minute of stressful thinking, I realized what I needed to do. Casually confronting her seemed to be the most appropriate choice.

Without really making the decision to do it, I began walking toward them. There was about two hundred feet between us. I was bound to come into her periphery soon enough. That's when I would speak.

As I approached them, while they were still in their own world, my feet started to drag. The extra noise just made it that much more dramatic. My eyes never left her face. Quickening my pace minutely, I realized that maybe I didn't want to get to her quicker. Between decreasing and increasing my speed, I came within fifty feet sooner than I could comprehend.

I watched as her brilliantly lit face broke his trance. I was definitely sweating now. She turned her face slightly to catch the distraction coming down the hall. Her eyes were easy to read as they met mine—busted. Dropping her hands down to her side, she frowned. Although she was no longer locked into his gaze, Luke continued to stare at her.

"Tyler," she mumbled, shock in her tone.

At the sound of my name, Luke's head whipped around. To my dismay, a grin broke out across his face.

I waited to answer, knowing my voice would be shaky. Finally, barely audible, I carefully spoke, "Roxanne, what's going on? I thought you were sick."

She cleared her throat, clearly embarrassed.

"Tyler, I am sick," she declared. I had to admit that she didn't look very good up close. The color in her face was a dusky pale and she didn't look as put together as she normally did.

I tried not to waver. "You certainly don't *seem* sick."

She glanced from Luke back to me, preparing to defend. "I know what this looks like."

"Really?" I asked, becoming annoyed. "What does it look like to you?"

She didn't answer. My anger only grew.

"You know what it looks like to me?" I probed her.

"I know," she answered with a soft voice. "Tyler, I told you..."

As we stared at each other, I knew neither of us wanted to acknowledge what was really happening here. She didn't want to break my heart. I wanted to stay in denial.

Changing the subject, I lifted the soup up, "Here, this is for you."

"Thank you, Tyler," Roxanne said awkwardly, taking the can and crackers from my hand.

All three of us stood in silence. I was staring at Roxanne, Roxanne was looking back and forth at Luke and me, and Luke was staring at her. The tension in the air was becoming more than I could handle.

I was the first to break the stillness. "Alright, well..." I began.

Roxanne interrupted, "No, please stay."

"Why?" I asked, very curious as to why anyone in my position would want to.

Glancing between Luke and me again, she continued, "We should all watch a movie or something. All I know is that I need to sit down, I'm not feeling so well."

I couldn't believe what she was suggesting. I was in no mood to be civil. My eyes were locked into her eyes. If she could read me, she would know exactly what I was thinking.

Moving her lips, without speaking, she mouthed, "I'm sorry."

The only movement I could make came from my head. It was a slight nod. It was a nod to acknowledge her voice but not to accept her apology. She should realize that.

Without another word, I turned my back to her, never making eye contact with the enemy. I forced myself to keep walking. One foot after the other. *Don't look back*, I urged myself.

Her desperate words rang in my ear with each new step taken. *I'm sorry.*

She wasn't as sorry as I was.

35

ROXANNE

I decided I had better call Tyler to try and explain.

"What?" he answered on the fourth ring, clearly not in the mood to talk.

"Tyler..." I mumbled.

"*What?*" Tyler repeated, annoyed.

"It wasn't what it seemed."

He cleared his throat, preparing for battle. "How can you say that, Roxanne? You told me you were sick. When I think of someone being sick, I think of sleep and feeling miserable and watching a lot of television. I saw none of those things. You were obviously feeling well enough to make out in the hall. C'mon, now...what was I supposed to think?"

I knew what he was saying was true, but I had my own argument to give. "Tyler, I know this may seem like an excuse, but I only told you I was sick, I didn't tell you how I felt. You don't even know the details."

Understandingly, he replied, "You're right."

I sighed in relief.

He continued, "It *does* sound like an excuse."

Groaning in frustration, I tapped the phone against my jaw, not quite sure how to make the situation right.

Details were key here. "Tyler, I fell off the treadmill at the gym."

Laughter flooded the phone piece. I rolled my eyes.

"I'm being serious. Don't be a jerk."

Another laugh came through. "Roxanne, that's the funniest thing I've heard all week!"

"Tyler," I growled.

"Okay, okay. Why did you fall off? Too many hot guys around?"

"*No*," I said, "I guess I tripped."

Tyler paused. "You guess?"

"I don't know, it all happened so fast."

"For some strange reason, I don't believe you."

Now I was becoming irritated. "Why is that?"

"Roxanne, you have been running since before you could walk. How is it that you become uncoordinated now, after all this time?"

"I don't know the answer. I just know that I was running fast and there I was, on the floor."

"Okay..."

"My point is, that I wasn't *sick* per se, but more I just needed to rest."

Tyler paused. "So why didn't you just tell me that?"

"I wasn't feeling well! You asked how I was, and I told you. I'm sorry."

There was another long pause before he spoke again. "I'm still mad at you."

"You have no right to be angry."

Tyler's voice became louder and louder as he talked. "Yes, I do. I took the time out of my day to come visit you to keep you company and I find you all over Luke! Of all guys!" He made a disgruntled noise to show his disgust.

"Get over it," I said, without thinking.

"Right. I'll just *get over it* and pretend like it never happened. And then everything will be fine and we'll just continue to be best friends. Right."

"Tyler—" I started.

"No, forget it."

Click. And he was gone, off the phone and temporarily out of my life.

36

LUKE

I could see the way he looked at her.

I envied that look; the way he felt about her. He was so *true* to her. I, on the other hand, was not true to her. She didn't know the real me...my real purpose in life. She couldn't know. It would ruin everything. The truth would only make my job more difficult. She would never believe me, anyway.

I felt terrible for hurting Tyler's feelings but I couldn't help how I felt about Roxanne.

Tyler would hate me forever. Since he had met her, he was bound and determined to make Roxanne his girlfriend. I bet if she told him she wanted to get married, he would drop everything he was doing and take her away. She was *all* he wanted. I took that away from him.

I was a horrible person.

But I had no other option, the way I saw it. I had to do whatever it took, because I knew what was at stake. I *had* to be with Roxanne. Tyler would never understand, even if I had the chance to explain it. He would hate me forever, but he might thank me someday.

37

ROXANNE

It had been a whole month without him.

Tyler was angry with me, I knew. He felt betrayed. I agreed his feelings were legitimate. I definitely wouldn't be receiving Best Friend of the Year Award anytime soon.

Making the choice between Tyler and Luke was not something I had ever planned on. I wanted my relationship with Luke to progress, but at what cost? Would it cost my friendship with Tyler? I couldn't bear the thought.

Between classes, soccer, girl friends, and spending time with Luke, Tyler didn't really fit into the schedule. It was all my fault.

The last soccer game of the season was at the end of the week. Florida's weather was changing to a chiller pattern. Finals were only one month away, with Christmas soon after.

Reminiscing on the past four months, I recognized I had grown up a lot this semester. I had conquered my fears of intimacy and gained self-confidence. Luke had taught me a lot about myself. I had nothing to lose in trusting him.

Except Tyler.

38

TYLER

I hadn't spoken to Roxanne in a few months.

I laid in my extra-small bed on a Friday night like a loser.

Even my deadbeat roommate was out. He was probably drunk by now, though it was still early.

I had my reasons for staying in, of course.

I *was* a loser. It was obvious that Roxanne didn't want me; she had never wanted me and she never would. She picked *him* over me. She was a liar and I was a fool for believing her. She should have just been honest and told me from the beginning that it *was* me and it *wasn't* her. I wasn't good enough for her. I thought no one was but, boy, was I wrong.

I stared at the ceiling. I had been staring for an hour now.

Surprisingly, I didn't cry the last time. No, I was far too used to her rejections. I finally took it like a man.

I wanted to kill Luke. The threat was literal. Anger was not something that typically ran through my blood, though now it had been lingering for months. I had found that if something was provoking enough, even the most deep-down emotions could come rushing through. I was brooding.

What would my next step be? I didn't know. I wasn't even sure life was worth living anymore. She was all I wanted in life. Everything I needed.

The hallway was so quiet that it was almost sickening. I knew the noise would eventually accumulate, but I would probably be asleep by then.

Startled by the sound, I stared at my ringing cell phone on my desk. *Who would be calling me?* I wasn't anyone important. Unwilling to move, I readjusted my focus back to the ceiling. I was starting to like it; it was steady and unchanging. It was something I could count on. The only thing I could count on. The ringing stopped. I sighed in relief. My head began to throb.

After a minute passed of blank staring, my cell phone rang again. The sound of my ring tone was beginning to annoy me. I let out a huff and got up to silence the cause of my headache. Curiously, I checked the caller ID. It was Colt.

Colt was the only one that knew about what happened. He was the only one I could trust. I picked up the phone and debated about answering. I guessed it couldn't hurt.

Flipping open the cover, I muttered, "Hey."

"Tyler, you okay?" the voice on the other end spoke.

"Nope," I honestly answered.

There was a moment of silence. "Why don't you come out tonight? It sounds like you need a drink."

I didn't need a drink. I needed a keg. "I'm okay."

"No, man. You haven't been okay since September. You definitely need to come out. My friends are having this Christmas party. It's going to be *wild*. Everyone is dressing up in retro Christmas sweaters—it promises to be awesome. Plus, a lot of hot girls."

I groaned away from the phone. "Colt, the last thing I need is another girl. I have enough girl problems as is."

He quickly replied, "You have *one* girl problem because you have feelings for her. You don't have to have feelings for *these* girls." The tone of his voice implied something I wasn't sure I was ready for.

"Come on, Colt. You know that's not me. And it's not you, either." I at least had to stay true to my morals.

I heard a chuckle on the other line. "Alright, alright. It's not, you're right. It was just a suggestion, though."

"I appreciate it," I said.

"Anyway, please come out. Have fun with the guys. You need to take your mind off her," he offered. The thought of it sounded good. But was it possible?

I hesitated, "I don't know."

"Get off your butt and get dressed. I'm coming for you."
Click.

Before I could argue, Colt had hung up. I knew him well enough to know that he would be here within minutes. He was serious about having fun. Fun was his middle name.

Scratching my head, I strolled to my closet and searched for something decent to wear. Didn't he say something about a Christmas sweater? I had nothing of the sort. I wasn't *that much* of a loser.

My cell phone rang out again. It was Colt again.

"What's up?" I asked.

"I forgot to tell you—I'm bringing you a sweater."

"Oh, goody," I remarked, sarcastically.

"See you soon." *Click.*

I changed out of my sweatpants into a pair of jeans and pulled on tennis shoes. I had no one to impress.

Before I could think of what to do next, there was a knock on my door. Opening it, I grumbled at Colt and the smirk he wore. He held up the most hideous sweater I had ever seen. There was a Santa and reindeer, topped off with some ornaments and snow. I actually laughed, mostly in disbelief.

"I'm not wearing that. I already feel like a loser, I don't need to look like one, too." I trudged back to my closet to mull over something decent to wear.

Colt stalked in, closing the door behind him. "No, you're wearing this. It's supposed to be funny."

I shook my head. "Are you trying to embarrass me? Is this some kind of fraternity prank?"

"Dude, don't insult me like that. I'm not in a fraternity. Look," Colt opened his jacket to show off his own Christmas sweater. It was almost as bad as the one he brought for me.

Grudgingly, I grabbed the dreadful sweater and pulled it on over my head. "If I look like a freak, it's your head. Got it?"

He grinned. "Whatever you say. You look stunning, by the way." It was hard to believe that he was actually making fun of me when he wore something just as ridiculous.

"Watch it," I warned. Finding my keys, I grabbed my phone and wallet and shoved them in my back pocket. "Okay, let's go."

Without moving, Colt grabbed me and held me at arm's length. "Where are you going?"

I rolled my eyes. "I thought we were going to this party."

"Well, duh. But you need to brush your teeth and put on some cologne or something. And do something with your hair." He pushed me back into the room.

I glared at him. Did I really have bad breath? "I didn't know you were so metro-sexual." Seizing my toothbrush and paste, along with my deodorant and cologne, I left the room. I trucked down the desolate hall to the community bathroom, relieved that no one in my dorm would see my attire. After cleaning up and fixing my hair, I headed back to my room.

Entering my room, I asked Colt, "Do I meet your standards?"

He shrugged. "I mean, I wouldn't bring you home to meet mom or anything, but yeah, you're presentable."

"Good, now let's go."

When we arrived at the house, I was surprised at the number of cars that lined the street. "Isn't it pretty early, still?"

Colt shook his head. "Tyler, it's been a long week for *everyone*."

We walked up to the front door. I grabbed Colt's shoulder and pointed at my sweater. "You promise this is a theme party?"

Colt guffawed at me. "I promise!"

Without knocking, Colt opened the door and my ears were immediately flooded with booming music. Colt held fast to his promise—every guy there was dressed in a tacky Christmas sweater. I couldn't help but laugh at the sight. The girls' attires were drastically different. There were coats with fur, boots with fur, and more clothing than I expected. They were classic snow bunnies, which was an odd sight for central Florida in December.

Stepping into the crowded living area, a few guys approached us and Colt shouted, "I'm here—now the party can start!" Beers were being handed out left and right. One was shoved into my hand; I didn't reject it.

Colt quickly introduced me to his friends. "Tyler, this is Reggie and Mac." Reggie and Mac looked like football players—built large and definitely not to be messed with. They both greeted me with nods and another can of beer. I hadn't even given a thought to the first can in my hand. Before I could object, Colt began to loudly sing along with the background music, a rap song. Throwing his hands up, he acted out the lyrics. He hurried off to chat with some other people he knew. I stood there facing the two humongous guys.

"So, what year are you guys?" I asked each of them.

Reggie answered. "Oh, four plus," he smiled, "But who's counting anyway?"

"I was thinking of being a student for life, actually," Mac contributed.

I managed a laugh so that my discomfort wasn't quite so obvious.

"You?" Reggie asked.

"I'm a sophomore," I said. "But who's counting?" I repeated, with a smirk. I didn't want to embarrass myself by admitting I was a freshman.

Mac nodded, "Right, right."

Apparently, the song rumbling through the house had changed. I only noticed because Colt was back, singing louder than before. He really was the life of the party.

Suddenly, everyone around us began singing along with the familiar song. Colt nudged me to join in but I still wasn't feeling like myself. I just shook my head, smiling slightly. I knew he would understand.

After the song ended, conversations broke out around us. Socializing didn't sound appealing, so I headed away from the group unnoticed. I parked myself down on a large couch in the living room. I seemed to be the only one sitting by myself. I honestly didn't care. The cans of beer were cold in my hands. Setting one down on the coffee table in front of me, I popped open the one left in my hand and took a sip. The liquid cooled my throat and left a significant aftertaste.

As he pranced through the house, Colt's voice echoed through the rooms in song. He was crazy. It only added to the respect I had for him. His class schedule was ridiculous, but Colt didn't let it get to him. I couldn't imagine myself as outgoing as him or even as happy. Although he was up to his ears in notes, homework, and textbooks, he didn't seem to have a care in the world. In contrast, I felt like all the cares of my world were crashing down on me all in one big heap.

As the night dragged on, the empty cans of beer in front of me began to multiply. Colt kept my supply coming without question. My tolerance for alcohol was not great. It was bitterly amusing to see that the impairment of my judgment matched that of the people around me. I watched as everybody became less cognizant with each downed drink. The introverted girls who were very quiet to begin with were now throwing themselves at the guys standing close. Modest guys were racing through the house naked. I could only feel lucky that my drunken state was depression, instead of lack of all inhibition.

With a pretty girl on his arm, Colt strolled back toward me. "Tyler!" he yelled obnoxiously, although he was only feet away. I noticed the unopened cans of beer in his hand, one of which was undoubtedly for me.

"Hey," I replied, rather sluggishly. I hadn't heard myself speak in a few hours. Listening to my voice, it sounded like my ears were plugged. My head was beginning to spin, my vision blurring.

"Ty, man, you look horrible!" Colt reminded me, throwing the beer into my lap.

"Thanks, thanks for the self-esteem boost," I said. I just wanted to drown in self-pity.

He pointed behind him. "Hey, there's this girl I want you to meet—"

Before he could continue, I stopped him, "Colt, I don't want to meet any girls, okay? Girls couldn't care less about us," I looked at the girl clinging to him, "Sorry, but it's true."

"Ah, c'mon. Let me go get her..." Colt turned with his friend and walked away, disregarding my opinion.

I sighed. I was not in the mood to mingle. Leaning my head against the back of the couch, I stared at the ceiling. I missed the ceiling in my dorm room. At least there I could have been completely unbothered.

"Hey!" Colt's annoying voice called out again. I could hear his hurried footsteps approaching. My head fell back down to an unbelievable sight.

I straightened up, my senses coming back to me. Blinking, I made sure I was seeing clearly. Was the alcohol making me hallucinate?

Standing next to Colt was the most magnificent girl I had ever seen. She had long, wavy blonde hair with bright green eyes highlighted by big eyelashes. Her smile was wide and innocent. The light reflected off her lip gloss, accenting her perfect lips. Her body had all the right curves. I wasn't sure if I would be able to speak.

"Ty!" Colt shouted, slapping my knee as he came within reach. "This is my good friend Caroline."

"Caroline," I repeated, standing, a sense of déjà vu coming over me. I practically lost my balance in the transition from sit to stand. Catching myself, I held out my hand to her.

She laughed. "Tyler," she responded back. Her voice was angelic, with a thick southern accent. In fact, I was sure she was an angel. She was absolutely adorable. She placed her hand in mine softly.

Colt looked back and forth between us, awkwardly. "Well, alright. I'm going to go attend to my female friend. You two have fun." And with that, he was trotting back in the direction he came.

Caroline stared at me. I sank back into the couch, keeping my eyes on her. I thought if for one second I would take my eyes off her, she would disappear. Timidly, I patted the space on the couch next to me.

She smiled and took the offer. I popped open the beer. I had no idea what number this was; I couldn't focus my eyes long enough to count the empty ones on the coffee table. Did I look like an alcoholic?

"Nice sweater," she said, pointing at my shirt.

"Th-thanks," I responded. I brought the can to my lips. This time, I was not drinking to mask the pain I felt. I was drinking because I was nervous.

Swiftly, Caroline pulled the beer away. "You really don't need this, you know."

As if I had never considered this on my own, I nodded. In reality, I knew this all along.

She turned her whole body to face me, propping her elbow on the back of the couch and leaning her chin into her hand. She stared curiously into my eyes.

I tried to focus on her face, though it was hard with the alcohol buzzing through my eyeballs. "You look awfully familiar."

This intrigued her. "I do, do I?"

"Yes, but I don't know why..." I pondered this for a minute. And then, a memory of a beautiful blonde girl playing the guitar surfaced. "You rejected me in that cafe," I remembered out loud, a playful smile on my face.

Suddenly, she grinned, as if recalling the same memory. "Small world."

I nodded, "Sure is."

There was a moment of awkward silence. I tried to recover. Stumbling over my words, I started, "S-So, do you go to school at the U?"

"No, I go to Sante Fe Community College. I'll be transferring here once I get done with my general education classes."

"Good," I said, but then quickly corrected myself, "I mean, it's g-good you're getting those classes done there first. Save some money."

She giggled. "Right. So where are you from?"

"I'm from Ocala," I responded, elated that she was interested in me.

She scrunched her face together. "Is that in Florida?" she asked.

"Oh, yeah. It's less than an hour south of here. I'm guessing you're not from here?"

"No...I'm from Georgia." That certainly explained the cute accent.

I smiled, sincerely this time. "Ah, so you're a Georgia peach? I like that."

Her cheeks reddened, clearly embarrassed. "Well, thank you."

"So, how do you know Colt?" I asked, turning my own body to match her position on the couch.

"Through mutual friends. He's such a great guy," she said.

I eyed her suspiciously. Maybe she had feelings for him.

She shook her head. "No, no, no...nothing like that. I know what you're thinking."

"Oh, do you?" I said, playfully.

"Yes, you think I like Colt," Caroline suggested.

"Who doesn't? I mean, I sort of have feelings for him, too." I grinned, so she would know I was joking.

"You don't know how many guys have told me those very words," she laughed.

"I know. Colt's kind of a big deal." As much as I admired Colt, I wanted to change the subject away from him.

"So what do you want to major in when you come to UF?" After proposing my question, I suddenly realized that I was very thirsty. I also really had to pee. Without waiting for her answer, I stood up. My balance seemed fairly steady this time.

Caroline looked up at me, confused. "What do you need?" she asked, concerned.

I looked around. "I'm really thirsty," I paused, but decided to finish the sentence anyway, "And I really have to go to the bathroom." Spotting what had to be the bathroom, I stepped forward. I swayed unsteadily. My balance was more impaired than I thought.

Swiftly, Caroline stood up and caught me. "Whoa, Tyler. How about I help you to the bathroom and get you some water?"

There was nothing I wanted more than her arm around me. "Oh, no, I got it," I replied stubbornly, waving her away. I stepped again and almost fell.

Pulling my arm over her shoulder, Caroline led me to the bathroom. "You don't need me to come in there with you, do you?" She made a face.

I shook my head. "Unless you want to, of course." I weakly smiled.

"I'm going to have to pass this time," she told me.

"Alright, your loss." I gave her a parting smile as I pushed open the bathroom door. Clinging onto the walls for stability, I watched her hurry into the kitchen and I closed the door.

When I finished, I opened the door and found her standing there, water in hand. "You're the best," I told her.

She took me by the arm and helped me back to the couch. I was glad she was there. When she handed me the glass of water, I thanked her.

"So what were we talking about?" I asked, taking a large drink from the glass.

"You were asking me what I was going to major in," she confirmed.

I put the glass down on the coffee table next to all the empty cans. Slapping my knee, I turned back to her. "That's right!" I exclaimed. "So, are you going to answer?"

She thought quietly for a minute. "Religious studies."

Surprised, my eyes opened widely. "Wow, religious studies? No wonder you're not drunk." I admired her morals.

"Some people don't have to get drunk to have a good time," Caroline replied, shyly looking down.

Defensively, I told her, "I'm not trying to have a good time."

Her eyes locked into mine, concerned. "Then what *are* you doing?"

In any other situation, I would never have told a complete stranger my problems, especially such a beautiful stranger. But this was not a normal situation. I firmly believed the beer was talking for me. "I'm trying to forget about the girl that broke my heart into a million pieces. I'm trying to forget that my life depended on her, revolved around her. I'm trying to forget about all the time I wasted on her. Is that okay with you?" I knew I sounded rude, but I couldn't help it.

Caroline continued to stare at her feet. Hesitantly, she said, "I'm, I'm sorry."

I sighed. "Don't apologize. You didn't do anything wrong. I just didn't know what else to do." Unexpectedly, I began to feel queasy. I grabbed my stomach.

Caroline put her hand on my shoulder. "Are you okay?"

I slumped over a little. "I," I started, "I don't...feel so good..."

Quickly, Caroline grabbed my hands and brought me to my feet. The motion did not agree with my stomach. "Oh," I moaned.

"C'mon," she pulled me toward the bathroom. The door was closed, so she banged her fist on it. The door opened and a girl and guy stared crudely at us.

"What do you want?" the guy asked Caroline.

She glared at him. "He needs the bathroom," she said, nodding toward me.

"So do I," the guy replied, attempting to close the door on us.

Caroline stopped the door mid-swing and pulled me inside. "Do you want him to puke on you?"

I must have looked convincing because the guy and girl quickly left without arguing any further.   Before I could thank Caroline, I curled over, leaning on the sink for extra support. I heard the sound of the door closing behind us. Caroline lifted the toilet seat, pulled the hand towel down from the rack on the wall, and draped the front of the toilet rim with it. I silently thanked God for her.

We spent hours in that bathroom. I was sure the sun would be rising soon. I felt ashamed. The smell was probably horrible, but Caroline stayed with me. She stroked my head as I lay in her lap on the floor next to the toilet. I told her to leave, but she refused. "I'm not going anywhere," she told me.

Eventually, we both fell asleep. She leaned her head back against the bathroom wall and I snuggled against her lap. A knock on the door startled us. "Come in," Caroline called, after awakening abruptly.

I heard the door creak open. I rolled over and instantly recognized the face peeking through the crack.

"Hey, I was wondering what happened to you!" Colt shouted.

"I've been in here for hours and this is the first time you've thought about me?" I asked, feeling a bit irritated.

"I thought you two, you know..." Colt shifted his eyes between Caroline and I.

Caroline quickly spoke, "No, I've been in here making sure Tyler was okay."

Colt shrugged, "Alright, alright. *Are* you okay, Tyler?"

"Yes, now. Thanks for asking," I smirked at him.

Colt apologized, "Look, I'm sorry. I wasn't in my right mind to know what was going on. Good thing for Caroline, here."

I looked up at her and smiled. "Yeah, good thing for Caroline."

"Want me to take you home?" Colt offered.

"No way! You're probably still drunk." There was no way I was getting in a car with him. I really didn't trust his driving sober, either.

Caroline interjected, "I'll take him home."

"Okay, okay. Call me later, man." Colt left the door open as he disappeared from sight.

Getting on my hands and knees, I inhaled deeply. I still felt sick, but not in the same way. I was still very drunk. I grabbed onto the sink for support, pulling myself to my feet. Dreading the sight, I looked into the mirror at myself. I groaned. I turned the cold water on and splashed my face thoroughly. It only made me feel slightly better. Turning to look at Caroline standing next to me, I said sadly, "I'm a mess."

She nodded. "Yes, you are. But that's okay. Let's get you home."

Caroline carried me by the arm to her car. My eyes became wide; I stumbled in astonishment. "*This* is your car?"

The sleek car that stood before us was a Ferrari 458 Italia Spider, the latest edition. The moonlight reflected off the polished paint job. In the dark it was hard to make out the specific color, but it had the distinct tint of orange rust. It was well equipped with the best amenities. The only bad thing about the car was that it was a foreign model.

She smiled slightly at me. "Yes, this is *my* car. What's it to you?"

"It's just that... well, it's not the best you could have gotten," I lied through my teeth.

"Oh, and why is that?" Caroline asked, unlocking my door and helping me in.

"Because it's not American made." I gave her a smirk as I strapped the seatbelt around me.

"For being wasted, you sure are political."

I followed her with my eyes as she shut my door and walked around to the driver's side. As she started the ignition, I listed to the car purr like a cat. I rested my head back against the seat, closed my eyes, and spouted off directions to my dorm.

I felt Caroline's hand on my shoulder. "You just rest, Mr. President."

Nodding in agreement, I waited until the car came to a complete stop before I opened my eyes.

The day was only starting to break as we walked into my dorm. By my request, we took the elevator to the second floor. At my door, I put my hands nervously into my jacket and stared at my feet. "Thanks again," I whispered to her. I was grateful for the solace she provided.

She placed her hand on my arm. "It was nothing."

I looked into her eyes. "Will I remember all of this?"

Caroline quietly laughed. "I don't know why you would want to."

I rephrased, "I mean, will I remember you?"

"Only if you want to," she softly answered.

"Does this count as a first date?" I asked, my eyes brightening.

"I hope not," Caroline replied, the side of her mouth curling into a half-smile.

"Want to come in?" I asked hopeful, pointing behind me.

She shook her head playfully. "Alright, Romeo. Why don't you get some sleep and call me if you need anything. My number is in your phone."

I took my phone out of my pocket and stared at it. "Wow, that was easier than I expected." I tried to smile widely, but I still felt really sick.

"I hope you feel better," Caroline said, walking toward the stairwell.

"Thanks." I opened my door slowly, continuing to watch Caroline as she entered the stairwell and trotted down the stairs. Not surprisingly, my roommate wasn't in his bed. I rarely saw him on the weekends. I was glad for the solitude. The only person I wanted to be around was Caroline.

I looked down the empty hallway and thought about my crazy night. Maybe getting over Roxanne wouldn't be so difficult after all.

39

ROXANNE

I was happier than I had felt in a very long time.

The only mail I ever received at school typically came from my mother – cards and care packages. So, when I opened my mailbox in the morning to find a folded piece of parchment, with my name inscribed on the outside in slick letters, I was more than surprised. My first assumption was that it was from Tyler. I had no real basis for my guess, maybe it was an inner longing from my subconscious to hear from him. I hadn't seen or heard from him in months. I couldn't imagine why he would send me anything through the mail when he could call, text, or e-mail.

As I unfolded the parchment, a thin piece of tan paper fell swiftly to the ground. I bent down to pick it up, quickly recognizing the small print and organization of the text. It was a page from the Bible. My brows furrowed, opening the delicate paper and glancing back to the parchment. This letter was definitely not from Tyler.

The ink was crisp, written with a fine point pen. The script resembled the writing on the front. I read the words slowly:

My dearest Roxanne,

As I read this passage day after day,

I think of nothing but you.

*I don't know if you understand
the intensity of my feelings, but you will.
I can't stop thinking about you.
And if we are ever to separate,
know that we will meet again.
For my feelings are eternal
and my love is everlasting.*

Lucio

Before I could fully grasp what he was saying through his letter, I shifted my eyes back to the torn Bible page. My eyes swelled with tears as I read the 13th chapter of 1 Corinthians. I traced the last sentence of the passage with my finger, a tear streaming down my cheek. I repeated the words aloud: "Now these three remain: faith, hope, and love. But the greatest of these is love."

How many times had a heard these verses at weddings? Too many to count, yet, the words pierced my soul as if it were the very first time. I had no idea that Luke felt this way. Our time together had been so short. Smiling, I wiped my tears away with the palm of my hand.

With every step I took back to my dorm room, I reread the words, etching them into my memory. I absentmindedly bumped into someone headed down the stairs, my mind clearly not focused on anything but Luke.

Allison wasn't in the room when I returned, for which I was thankful. I sat down at my desk, leaned back, and glanced thoughtfully back at the passage that Luke had given me. Each time I recited it in my mind, it was new to me. I liked the feeling.

When a knock sounded abruptly on my door, I was slightly startled, not expecting any company. I walked to the door, the letter still in my hand, my eyes glued to the words.

As the door swung open, I was still staring at the letter. "Yeah?" I was expecting it was one of the girls in my hall.

"Well, aren't we rude today?" the male voice responded.

Instantly I looked at the handsome boy that stood in my doorway. Without much thought, I threw my arms around him in a tight hug.

"Nice to see you, too," he laughed, startled by my behavior.

Releasing my grasp, I grabbed his hand and ushered him into the room, shutting the door behind me. I held up the letter that was clutched beneath my fingers.

"Can't you be sent to Hell for something like this?" I teased.

Confusion struck his perfect face. "For telling the girl of my dreams how I feel about her?"

I laughed, shaking my head. "No, ripping a page out of the Bible!"

He grinned, his shoulders relaxing. "Oh, I asked for permission, don't worry."

I shook my head, smiling.

Luke started walking toward me, cornering me with a sly smirk on his mouth. "So, I'm guessing you liked the letter?"

He moved closer, his breath growing nearer.

I gulped and bit my lip. "Yes, all except one part."

He waited for me to continue. Finally, I spoke, "The goodbye part."

Luke shook his head in confusion. "Goodbye part?"

"When you talk about separating. It clearly says *Goodbye Roxanne*," I said half-heartedly, with a hint of sarcasm in my eyes.

Grasping my shoulders, Luke gently shook me. "Roxanne, I'm not going *anywhere*. I was just trying to...oh, heck, I just want you to know that I love you."

Luke spoke so casually that the moment was almost surreal. Those three words registered in my head with such delay that it felt like time had slowed. I felt a lump stuck in my throat. I couldn't manage to speak, though there was so much to be said.

He waited expectantly.

And he continued to wait, the prominent features in his face slowly dropped in disappointment.

Finally, I barely breathed out, "You love me?"

Luke was clearly getting annoyed, a look he didn't wear well or often. "Yeah, you didn't know that?"

"How was I supposed to know?" I snapped back.

"Here." He grabbed my hand and placed it gently on his chest, above his heart. "Can you feel the beat?"

I nodded solemnly.

I watched him close his eyes, a peaceful look emerging on his face. "You can tell in the rhythm."

Carefully, I admitted, "I can't tell the difference."

Luke's eyes popped open, startling me. "If it was in your heart, you would know."

I let my hand fall away from his body and back down to my side. Luke had answered the question before it was asked. I never understood how he could do that. Although I knew I hadn't yet come to love him, I wasn't rightfully about to admit it. I wanted to believe that I did love him. I cared about him very much, more than I could even imagine. But something was missing; something very strong was holding me back. Was it the sad picture of my best friend lurking in the back of my mind? Or the feelings of despair that surfaced when thinking about my dead father? I couldn't decide in all the confusion of the emotions that were racing through my mind at that very moment.

He broke the awkward silence. "It's okay, you know."

The tears came back; my face scrunched to try and hide the pain I felt for him. "No..."

Pulling me into a hug, I could feel his breath on my hair, "No, really, you are enough for me. You wouldn't have to say any words at all. You're enough."

Tears streamed constantly down my cheeks as I soaked in what he was saying. I didn't deserve him.

After a few minutes of his comforting hold, Luke stepped back and took the letter that was still in my hand. "Let's put this away. I didn't realize it was going to wreak such havoc. I won't be writing *you* any more letters any time soon."

I recognized the glint of sarcasm in his voice and his eyes. My mouth formed a small smile in response, to let him know that I was okay.

Walking over to my desk, he pulled open a drawer and stuffed the folded piece of paper toward the back. He turned to glance at me with a slight grin on his face and inquired, "You do *like* me, though, right? Because if you don't...I need to know."

I laughed lightly. "Of course. Who wouldn't like you?"

"Mmm, I can think of at least one person. But you know, all is fair in love and war."

Before I could comment, Luke pulled me into a kiss. The feeling of his lips on mine was distinctly different from the way I felt when Tyler had kissed me at the lake. I knew that much was true. I searched for that feeling—the difference in feelings that Luke had mentioned. I didn't know what I was looking for, but there was a chance that I might be searching for a long time.

40

ROXANNE

After not seeing Tyler in months, I hadn't expected to run into him with a girl wrapped around his arm.

"Tyler?" I choked, shocked at his presence. A beautiful girl with blonde wavy hair and blue eyes was standing next to him, clearly not just a friend. A wave of jealousy immediately crashed over me, though I knew it wasn't justified.

"Caroline?" Luke asked from beside me, right after I spoke. He was referring to the girl by Tyler's side. Now I was really confused.

Luke and I were taking a stroll around campus, a hobby that we liked to do on the weekends. We had only recently made it a habit after the Christmas break. On this day, we brought a Frisbee to throw around though it was a bit chilly and windy for such an activity. I wasn't paying any attention as I sprinted for the overthrown disc that had been carried by a gust of wind and bumped right into Tyler.

I stared at Luke's face. His facial expressions read concern as his eyes focused on this Caroline girl. How did they know each other? I had never seen her before. Another wave of jealousy hit me hard.

Tyler glanced back and forth between Caroline and Luke, obviously disgruntled. I knew Tyler did not like Luke. I was sure that Tyler felt threatened by his presence, especially now, when Luke seemed to know his girlfriend.

"How do you two know each other?" Tyler looked to Caroline, his eyes trying to stay soft for her.

She smiled a brilliant smile. "Tyler, this is my friend Luke," she pointed to Luke standing next to me. This was news to me. Luke had never mentioned her. She continued, gesturing to Luke, "It's been a while, hasn't it?"

Luke paused briefly, and then spoke, "Yes, it has. Good to see you, again. How do you two know each other?"

Tyler and Caroline locked eyes, grinning intently. "We met through a friend," Caroline answered.

"Good for you," Luke said to Tyler. It sounded half-pretentious, half-sincere.

The smile faded from Tyler's face. He was noticeably offended by Luke's words.

Through his teeth, Tyler responded, "Yes, I'm very happy."

I watched as Caroline gingerly squeezed Tyler's arm to comfort him. "Tyler, how do you know Luke?" She glanced momentarily at Luke with words in her eyes that I didn't understand.

I sensed fire rising in Tyler's eyes as he thought of an answer. His gaze shifted between Luke and me. Eventually, his face softened, preparing himself to answer appropriately.

"Caroline," he said slowly, "This is Roxanne and Luke is her boyfriend."

Recognition registered on Caroline's face immediately. She held out her hand kindly. "Nice to meet you, Roxanne."

"Same here," I cordially replied. I couldn't decide if she was genuine.

Caroline politely asked, "So, how long have you two been dating?"

Tyler quickly looked at Caroline as if she had spoken a forbidden language. He unwillingly turned toward Luke and me for an answer.

I smiled at Luke and he answered, "About eight months."

My eyes widened, knowing this answer was far from the truth. I had only met Luke eight months ago, at the beginning of my last summer at home. We had only begun dating in October. The specific details wouldn't matter if we weren't talking to Tyler. Tyler would know the difference. He would feel betrayed, as if I had been hiding Luke all along. He would never forgive me.

"Is that so?" Tyler commented, very unenthused.

Luke took the opportunity to pull me closer to his side. "Yep." The tension in the air between Tyler and Luke was palpable.

I tried to take the focus off of our relationship. "What about you two?" Of course, I didn't actually care to know the answer, but felt it was an appropriate segue.

Before Caroline could speak, Tyler quickly answered, "Two months, one week, and five days." Turning to his girlfriend, he smiled; I hadn't seen him smile like that in a very long time. Although I knew what his intentions were with his answer, I could see a distinct sparkle in his eye when he looked at her. I should be happy for him. Instead, I wanted to scream.

Without thinking, I said, "*Wow*, looks like *someone's* counting." I knew I should have just kept my mouth shut.

Tyler and Caroline shot me serious looks.

"Well," Luke started, "Seems we'll be going now." And suddenly, Luke was tugging on my arm.

Caroline spoke hurriedly, "Wait. Roxanne, can I speak with you? Just for a moment."

What was I supposed to say? "Sure, I guess..."

She took my elbow and led me away from the guys, out of hearing range. I was curious as to what this was about.

"Roxanne, I just have to say...*thank you*."

I stared at her, not quite understanding. "For...?"

In her sweet southern accent, she said, "Thank you for helping Tyler move on with his life. If you hadn't been so honest about your relationship with Luke, he might still be hanging around your dorm room, pondering ways to get you to become his girlfriend. You did me a huge favor, and you didn't even know me! So I must say, thank you."

My mouth hung slightly gapped, digesting her speech. Was she really saying what I thought she was saying?

She didn't let me respond. Instead, she lightly squeezed my elbow and pranced back over to Tyler's side. Luke looked at me curiously.

We began walking in the opposite direction, away from our awkward encounter. Glancing briefly over my shoulder, I caught Tyler doing the same. This time, his face was somewhat sad. He was a mystery to me; I didn't know him anymore.

Once I had a moment to think about what she said, I turned to Luke. "She *thanked* me! Can you believe her?"

"Thank you?" he asked. "For what?"

"That was my question exactly! She thanked me for giving up Tyler so she could have him."

"Why is that a bad thing?" Luke asked, his voice hinting disappointment.

"She acted like I had control of him! Like...like...I was playing games to keep him around."

"Why didn't you just tell him about us?"

I stopped, realizing that Luke had stopped walking a few steps back. His face had a gloomy look. He was concerned. I didn't know how to explain.

"I did. Sort of." I knew that answer wouldn't suffice. "Well, when you first asked me on a date."

"So you told him about me?" A beam of light from his eyes glistened in hope.

My eyes floated to the ground. "Not exactly..."

"Not exactly? So, he didn't know about me."

I felt the urge to cry, but had to control myself. "I didn't want to hurt his feelings."

"That day, when he saw us after your episode at the gym...he had no clue?"

"Tyler is my friend."

"He had no clue." Luke was making a statement, not a question.

I tried to justify my insensitivity. "He has never had a clue!"

"Give the guy a break! He's wanted you for practically his whole lifetime and you didn't have the courage to come out and say 'Hey, I have a boyfriend'? It's not his fault; it's on you this time. Tyler thought he still had a chance with you. You were the one responsible for telling him that you were taken. It's not his fault..."

Luke had never rebuked me before. I was too hurt to decide if I deserved it or not. Childishly, I left him, standing there expectantly, and walked away. I couldn't handle two rejections at the same time, especially from my two favorite people, regardless of the circumstances. How could Luke stick up for Tyler? Luke was supposed to support *me*.

My arms folded across my chest as I drug my feet back toward my dorm. I didn't know what I was going to do when I got there, but I knew I probably wouldn't be there long. The more I considered Luke's argument, the more tears penetrated my eyes. Maybe Luke was right. He always was.

Suddenly, I felt a tap on my shoulder. I turned and found Luke, gazing at me apologetically. "I'm sorry," he breathed, pulling me into a hug.

I couldn't formulate any words.

He put me at an arm's distance away, still holding onto me. "I just think you could have spared him some feelings. But I understand. He's your friend. You care about him. But sometimes, you need to care about me more." Luke smiled, obviously joking, but I knew there was truth in what he was saying.

I nodded, comforted by his understanding. "You're right."

"I'm always right," he affirmed smugly, putting his arm around my shoulder.

I rolled my eyes. As we began walking back to my dorm, all I could think about was how absolutely right he was.

41

LUKE

"What in God's name are you doing here?" I asked her as I wrung my hands together nervously.

I was pacing the room uncontrollably. Her arrival had severely affected my mental concentration.

"Why do you have to be so literal all the time?" she asked, smiling. This was not a laughing matter.

"Caroline, I'm serious."

"Sit down already. You're making *me* nervous."

"I can't. I don't know. I can't control it."

"It's because you're freaking out. Just breathe."

"I can't breathe with you here."

"I don't understand. What's so bad about me being here?"

I glared at her. "You're here to mess everything up."

She rose from her seated position. "No, Luke, quite the contrary. I'm here to make sure *you* don't mess everything up."

I wrinkled my forehead in concern. "What do you mean?"

Caroline stepped close to me, and spoke somberly, "Don't you see what you've done?"

My eyes didn't flicker from her face. I didn't blink. "I don't know what you're speaking of."

Looking at her feet briefly, she resumed her gaze. "Luke, you've fallen in love with her."

"No, I haven't," I lied hastily.

"It's wrong to lie. Especially to me."

I nodded slightly. She was right.

"You had one simple task, Luke," she held up one finger.

Shaking my head, I disagreed, "Not simple. Not simple at all."

Caroline sighed, "It could have been."

"How? How?" I challenged her.

"Easily. You could have simply been at the right place at the right time. You didn't have to become *a part* of her."

I dwelled on her choice of the word *a part*. Roxanne was more than just a part of me; she was everything to me.

"It wouldn't have worked."

"You could have made it work."

I shook my head.

She gently took my shoulders. "You have to break it off."

I closed my eyes. I feared she would say that.

"You *have* to."

Biting my lip, I held back tears. Opening my eyes, my vision blurred. I blinked a few times, helping my tears disappear.

"No, I can't. I won't!"

Her jaw was tight. "This won't end well."

"It doesn't have to end."

"Ha!" she let out, clearly amused by my naiveties.

"I know," I admitted. "I can't stay here forever."

"I know you love her, but you have to return with me someday. I have a feeling that day is coming sooner than you expect."

"How do you know?" I asked, curious.

"Luke, I was sent here to protect you from yourself. I can only try and help the situation. You must ultimately make the final decision."

I was fully aware she was avoiding my question, though I nodded in acknowledgment.

After a short period of silence, I asked, "Can I ask you something?"

She shrugged, "Sure."

"Why Tyler? You couldn't have picked anyone else?"

Caroline giggled. I frowned.

"Aw, he's cute, Luke! I like him."

"But *why*?" I prodded.

"Luke, you know as well as I do that Tyler needs to be taken out of the equation temporarily. His protection is also necessary. He must stay alive for Roxanne."

My head hung sadly. I didn't want to leave Roxanne. I didn't want Tyler to have her. I wanted her to myself.

Caroline wrapped her tiny arms around my body, embracing me gently. Whispering softly into my ear, she said, "You can't always get what you want."

42

ROXANNE

February in Florida typically held temperatures of around seventy degrees.

Although I couldn't say the exact number, the weather outside was far from that warm. The rushing wind against my dorm window distracted me from studying for a test I had at the end of the week. The pelting hail made me appreciate the comfort of my small, suffocating space. I watched as the raindrops trickled down the pane in diagonals.

Allison was studying quietly at her desk. "Isn't this weather crazy?" I asked her. I hadn't heard her voice for a while.

"Hm?" she answered, without turning around to acknowledge me.

"The weather. It's weird."

Quickly and monotone, she replied, "Oh, yeah. I guess so."

I folded my arms across my chest and gazed outside again. The sky swirled with clouds of dark and light gray. A cold chill passed through the room and I shivered. Something just didn't feel right.

Leaning my head against the wall adjacent to the window, I sighed, sinking into a daydream. In the past, my family had always joked with my sister that she should be a meteorologist instead of a journalist, since the weather in Ocala changed so little. Regan would always smirk at us and then join in the laughter. The only experience I had with bad weather occurred when I was six years old. A small tornado rolled through innocent Ocala, selectively hitting one or two houses on the outskirt of town. All the residents of the city were thrown into panic, but the tornado came and went very quickly. The weather had cleared by the time anyone had initiated disaster plans.

Central Florida, where Ocala was located, didn't suffer from the passing hurricanes that so severely hit the west and east coastlines of the state. The aftermath of the treacherous water whirlwinds many miles away would cause merely a downpour in our city. Ocala was relatively unaffected by the destructive storms that changed the lives of so many others on the coast.

My daydream was disrupted by a loud *ping* on the window. Focusing my eyes outside, I realized what was happening. "Allison, it's hailing!"

"Hm," she mumbled again, clearly unconcerned.

"Allison, maybe it doesn't hail in Miami, but it *definitely* doesn't hail in Gainesville!"

"Unless it cancels my test tomorrow, I don't care."

Before I came to college, I considered myself pretty studious. Then I met Allison, and my study habits were blown away by her consistent dedication. It could be so annoying.

I turned my attention back outside, where I spotted a poor, unsuspecting student running from the pelting ice. After only minutes, the hail was accumulating on the grass surrounding our dorm, white speckles amongst the brownish-green. Eventually, a white sheet would cover every inch of the ground.

"Good thing my car is parked in the parking garage," I said out loud, more to myself than my uninterested roommate.

Allison didn't make a peep.

Smiling, I continued, "I hope Regan's car is outside."

I heard a stifled laugh come from Allison. Without removing her eyes from her textbook, she commented, "But then it would be your mom's problem, wouldn't it?"

I nodded. "True."

Suddenly, a loud *whoosh* sounded outside the window, startling both of us. I grabbed my chest, breathing hard now.

"This weather is crazy," I repeated. Grabbing the remote from my desk, I turned on the television to the weather channel.

"...Strong winds of up to 50 miles per hour and large golf-ball-sized hail are expected throughout the day. The National Weather Service advises everyone to stay inside..." the meteorologist announced, with an undertone of caution.

I continued to listen. "The current severe weather warning will remain in effect until 10:00 pm tonight. As you can see here on the radar, the storm is surrounding the entire Gainesville area and the cities northwest of the region. The storm appears slow moving. Again, the severe weather advisory will last until 10:00 pm tonight..."

Flipping off the television, I replaced the remote on my desk.

Without instigation, Allison said, "Maybe soccer practice will be cancelled."

I laughed, "Yeah...right...there isn't anything that would stop coach from having practice, not even 50 mile-an-hour winds and golf-ball-sized hail."

She turned around in her seat and pointed at me, "True."

For the next couple hours, I tried to concentrate on reading for class but wasn't very successful. The strong winds and hail continued to distract me from studying. I wasn't looking forward to making the upcoming trek from my dorm to the sports complex for practice.

Curious as to any change in the weather, I turned the television back on.

"You better not be watching some full-of-crap reality show..." Allison muttered.

I rolled my eyes. The screen showed the radar for the area. There was a lot of red.

"...The current weather condition has been changed to a tornado warning. Rotational activity has been detected near the Gainesville metro area. The tornados in the area are projected to contain 80 to 110 mile-per-hour winds, with damage to roofs, mobile homes, and moving cars likely. The National Weather Service advises residents to find shelter underground as soon as possible..."

As soon as the meteorologist finished his last sentence, a loud siren started blaring. Allison and I exchanged looks.

"I think practice is cancelled," I proclaimed.

Someone started shouting in the hallway outside our door. "Everyone out of your rooms, NOW!"

Quickly, Allison and I slipped on our shoes. Opening our door, we were greeted by herds of people running down the hall. I started to panic. My legs were frozen, stuck in the doorway watching all the commotion. Allison gripped my hand and led me toward the shouting voice, directing people downstairs to the basement of the building.

My mind was spinning with anxiety and hypothetical situations. Allison and I followed the stream of people down the stairs and into the large open basement area, with washers and dryers lining the outskirts of the walls. As more and more people trickled into the space, the area started to make me feel claustrophobic. Allison was still holding my hand; I squeezed it tighter. I felt my other hand squeeze my cell phone tighter and I had a sinking feeling. I needed to get a hold of Luke, but I couldn't. I accidentally left my cell phone in our dorm room.

The vision of Tyler popped into my head, sitting in the basement of his own dorm. A mixture of feelings ranging from worry to anger filled my chest. A sudden urgency came down on me, making my heart pound. I needed to find Tyler. As my heart raced, I stood, searching around me. After multiple attempts at connecting with him on the phone, I shoved it in my back pocket. I grabbed my face and closed my eyes, unsure of what to do.

"I need to find him," I told Allison.

"Luke?" she asked.

Shaking my head, I said, "Tyler."

Allison instinctively grabbed my hand and formed a stiff grasp. "Oh no, you don't. Tyler will be fine."

I shook my head, unbelieving. Slithering out of her grip, I tried to run across the basement to the other entrance to the laundry room, which intercepted an underground hallway that eventually connected to Tyler's dorm. My speed was less than acceptable, with the masses of people interrupting my route. I was beginning to panic.

The room temperature was climbing from the body heat of so many people. Many noises filled the air, from shouting school personnel to ringing cell phones to students fretting about the impending destruction the storm would cause. I tried to focus on maneuvering through the crowd. Finally, I found a path with less resistance. I picked up speed and eventually made it out of the laundry room and into the tunnel that led to Tyler's dorm.

A distant voice filled my head, calling my name, "Roxanne! Roxanne!"

Before I could turn my head to evaluate the scene, I was wrapped in the arms of Luke.

"Roxanne!" Luke yelled, although he was standing right beside me.

I started to cry at the image of his face, the warmth of his body, the comfort of his touch.

"Roxanne, we have to go!" he frantically shouted over the voices of those around us. Luke's voice was normally so cool and calm, so the change made me my concern increase.

I studied the scene in the basement, chaos unraveling.

I didn't want to tell him about my angst for Tyler, but I couldn't contain my emotions. "Luke," I shook my head, "we have to find Tyler!" The anxiety on my face couldn't be masked.

He took my jaw in his hand, not forcefully but intently, and slowly said, "No, we need to leave, now. He'll be fine." His deep brown eyes were trying to tell me something he couldn't physically say out loud. He was trying to convince me.

"You don't know that! I need to go." I struggled under his hold.

He gripped my jaw a little tighter. "Please."

I whipped my head out of his grasp. "But Tyler!"

Luke grabbed my shoulders. "Roxanne, you are going to have to trust me. I'm begging you to trust me."

I anxiously glanced around.

His voice grew intense. "Roxanne, do you trust me?"

With reluctance, I nodded. Luke peered around the crowd, then turn his eyes back to mine. "We need to go. Now." He grabbed me around the waist. Entering the laundry area again, I could hear Allison yelling my name but I couldn't find her face amongst all the people.

Finally, she came barreling up to us, grabbing my wrist. "What's going on?"

I looked solemnly at her. "Allison, I have to go..."

She shook her head. "Are you crazy? I really don't think—"

Luke reached out and lightly touched her arm. "Allison, everything will be okay."

A strange sensation came over me just then. Although Luke sounded sure of himself, I didn't believe his words to Allison. Everything would surely *not* be okay.

Hesitantly, Allison removed her hand. Her eyes were pleading with me.

I mouthed, "Sorry."

At my parting words to my roommate, Luke whisked me toward the exit out of the basement.

I expected someone to stop us, since it was definitely against code to let students outside during a tornado warming. No one yelled at us, no one even seemed to notice, except for Allison. I waved to her as the door to the basement shut behind us. Leaving her was something I didn't want to do, but I knew I had to follow Luke.

"Where are we going?" I let out through heavy breaths as we raced up the stairs to the main entrance.

Luke didn't answer. I shook his arm through my grasp on his hand. Still, he didn't disclose anything.

We continued on our path for the exit outside. When we reached the double doors, I stopped. The dark gray skies had turned into a swirl of purples and greens, an astounding sight. The high winds were throwing small debris around the dorm, the trees practically blowing horizontally. I was amazed and yet terrified at the same time. There was no way I was going outside.

Luke had kept walking when I had stopped. Feeling my resistance, he turned toward me, his face full of anger I had never experienced from him before. The fierceness in his face accentuated his strong jaw and high cheekbones.

"What are you doing?" he asked, harshly.

I stared at my feet, scared of the Luke that stood before me. "I can't go out there."

He yanked on my arm, urging me to come forward. "Yes, you can."

Shaking my head, I kept my eyes down at the ground.

He lowered his height so our eyes were at the same level. His voice was careful and intense, "Please don't make me carry you."

I wanted to trust him but I was torn between love and intuition.

He added, "Please don't make this harder than it has to be." Without waiting for my answer, Luke grabbed my elbow and lunged toward the door. It was apparent I didn't have a choice in the matter. I wouldn't be able to fight his grip.

Outside, the wind whipped my hair around my face. I could feel pieces of the earth hitting my uncovered skin. The air was filled with rain, ice, and a strange mixture of warm and cold. I tried to wrap my arms around me to preserve the warmth, but Luke was pulling so fast and hard on my arm that I couldn't manage to do anything except try and keep up with his pace.

"I'm parked right over there," Luke shouted over the wind, pointing to a small parking lot outside the dorm. He pulled harder on my arm and it began to ache.

Throwing the door open to an unfamiliar vehicle, he practically shoved me inside. As soon as the door shut behind me, I burst into tears. I didn't know what I was getting myself into.

Luke jumped inside the idling silver Hummer and threw the SUV into drive. Although I was crying, he didn't pay any attention to me. He was quiet as we drove away from the dorm and eventually off campus. Every so often, he would divert his eyes to the sky and peer out all the windows to check on the weather.

Nervously, I jumped when the wind tugged the vehicle around the road.

Breaking the silence, he announced, "The winds are going to get stronger. More funnel clouds will make ground contact. We have to get out of the area."

Suppressing my sobs, I wiped my nose on my hand. "How do you know that?" I asked, doubtful.

His eyes focused straight ahead. "I just do."

"Oh, okay," I replied, sarcastically. Erratically, I started laughing out of unbelief. How did I get myself into this predicament?

"What's so funny?" Luke asked, surprise and caution in his voice.

"You know what's funny? It's funny that I'm not safe in that basement and instead here with you." I wanted to continue but a lump emerged in my throat and prevented any further talk.

With a wag of his head, he dejectedly said, "I promise you won't regret trusting me."

"Where are you taking me?" I mumbled through the lump.

"North."

I shouldn't have been surprised, but I was. "What's north?"

"Better weather. Please put on your seatbelt." He touched his own belt.

I timidly obeyed, gingerly grabbing the buckle and slipping it across my chest.

"What about Tyler?" At the sound of his name, a sob erupted from my throat. I left him. I traded in my friendship with Tyler for a relationship with Luke. I bit down hard on my lip.

Luke sighed. "I told you, he's fine."

"You don't know that!" I huffed.

"Roxanne, please calm down."

"I left him." I folded my arms across my chest, upset with myself for being so trusting.

Luke didn't respond. I searched his face for any sense of expression. Although he was stern, almost statue-like, there was a hint of pain soaking through. He was fighting his emotions.

"How could you let me leave him?" I muttered under my breath.

"Because, for the millionth time, he'll be fine! Now, it'd do us both some good for you to stop mentioning his name." He took off his hat and ran his hand through his hair in exasperation.

I watched the tortured sky as we turned onto the highway and headed North toward Valdosta, Georgia. In the distance, I recognized small tunnels forming, reaching down to touch the ground. It was horrific – the reality of it all. I felt like I was watching a movie and I was the main character, none of it real. The wind brought reality back to me, whipping the large vehicle sideways a bit on the road. A shriek escaped my throat, alarmed by the sudden shake.

The highway was relatively clear of traffic, a rare occasion for the typically congested area. I leaned my head against the cold window, closing my eyes and praying to God for a miracle. Luke had asked me to put my faith in him, but I wondered if I had made a mistake. In the eight months of his existence in my life, I had became close to a guy who I could completely open myself up to, someone I could rely on for anything, and more importantly, someone I could imagine myself with in the future. The attention Luke gave me – similar yet very different from Tyler's attention—made me feel like I was somebody, that I was wanted.

Tyler and I had always held a strong bond. When I looked at Tyler, he reminded me of my father. He reminded me of my past, which I was constantly trying to avoid. I always had felt too emotionally unstable to be his girlfriend. I sighed at the thought, because we weren't even really friends anymore. How could so much change in such a short amount of time?

The short drive to Valdosta, a mere hundred miles, lasted forever in my mind. There was little conversation between Luke and I, which I preferred. The more I considered my predicament, the more I regretted how I felt.

I didn't know what awaited me in Valdosta. What would we do? How long would we be there?

The sign, "Valdosta Welcomes You," brought on a typhoon of emotions—angst and joy simultaneously. I was relieved to be away from the storm but feared for Tyler.

Easing off the highway, I sat upright in the seat. There was a stoplight approaching. I glanced around the surrounding area and realized the vicinity was deserted, which sent chills up my spine.

"Luke, I want to go home," I admitted, shrunken with worry.

He shook his head. "We can't. I'm sorry."

In a moment of hysteria, I snapped. I swiftly yanked on the door, imagining myself lunging out of the car. Dread exploded in my chest when I realized that the doors were locked. Not only locked, but practically bolted shut. Frantically, I lurched across an unsuspecting Luke and grabbed at his door. I was screaming and yelling out of delirium.

Suddenly, though my screaming didn't quit, I was in a state of immobility. Luke had his large hands gripped around my shoulders. Thrashing about, I tried to escape. He was so strong that I knew I would be likely to give up before he would feel even the slightest fatigue.

"Roxanne, stop!" he bellowed, his sharp voice vibrating my eardrums.

"No! Let me go!" I continued to struggle.

"Roxanne!" Luke yelled, releasing me.

I scrambled into the back seat, diving for the door handles. My hand grasped the cool metal, but before I could manage to pull, I felt Luke climbing on top of me.

I was terrified. As I started to shake, Luke wrapped his arms around me and pulled me into a close embrace. I feverishly sobbed. He gently stroked my hair and calmly whispered, "If you really love me, you will rely on me to protect you. Have faith in me."

He left me laying supine in the back seat, resting quietly. Occupying the driver's seat again, he put the car into drive and made a right turn onto the barren street. Staring out through the window, I could see gray clouds lingering above the city. The wind there was only subtle, not rushing like in Gainesville. I predicted a downpour in the near future.

Tears streamed down my cheek, my imminent future unknown. I tried to sob, but my muffled cries only annoyed me. With effort, I turned my whole body to face away from the front of the car, my nose inches from the seat. I didn't want to see my surroundings anymore; I didn't want to make up things in my head based on what I saw outside. I would suffer alone.

I tried to drown out his voice with my thoughts, but his words were unmistakable, "Now the winds are 136-165 miles an hour...incredible..."

The radio was off. He didn't own a cell phone. How he knew the weather forecast, I didn't know. Luke did not cease to amaze me.

My head was throbbing. I wished I could sleep to stop the pain.

Minutes later, I felt the SUV slowing again. Flipping back over from my side to my back, I was able to maneuver enough to peek out the window. Luke was pulling into the parking lot of a motel. My eyebrows furrowed.

"Don't go anywhere," he pleaded, getting out of the car.

He returned shortly, a room key in hand. Pulling the car around closer to the room, he shut the driver's door as he stepped out. I sat up as Luke moved around the car to the door. The door opened and I peered up at him forlornly.

His eyes were soft, eyes that I recognized. "Don't be scared," he whispered.

I closed my eyes, whimpering softly. He didn't understand. How could he? He had no reason to be scared. Before I could open them, I was being thrust over his shoulder and carried into the motel room with ease.

He laid me gently on the bed then returned to the door to close it, locking it behind him. Two beds furnished the room, along with old wooden dressers and tacky lamps. The wallpaper was clearly manufactured in the seventies, with tiny pink flowers crawling up the blue background. The room smelled musty, probably laden with rotting mold.

Luke sat purposefully on the bed across from mine. He stared at me with an unreadable expression.

Slowly, he moved across the space that separated us and I stiffened. "Don't be scared," he repeated, the softness returning to his face. He sat beside me. Leaning his elbow on his knee, he rested his chin in the palm of his hand. He stared at the wall. There was no conversation.

After minutes of quiet, he said, "This is for your wellbeing."

I followed his body movements closely as he stood and walked across the room. He motioned toward the small television sitting on a small desk. Turning on the power, he pushed the channel button on the television until he found the national news.

"This was all for your wellbeing," Luke repeated, touching the dusty screen with his index finger.

My eyes shifted to the screen. The flashing words in big letters caught my attention immediately: *"University of Florida Destroyed By Tornado."* I watched as horrific pictures of campus from a helicopter view popped onto the screen. Automatically, I covered my mouth with my hand, pained by the sight of my school. Every scene displayed seemed to be more disastrous than the previous one. Eventually, a building I barely recognized was shown—Tyler's dorm. It was torn apart by the tornado, looking more like a honeycomb than anything else. Debris from the building lay covering the surrounding grass. A flood of thoughts entered my already tired mind.

I thought of Tyler, my best friend. A loud sob erupted from my mouth, tears streaming down my face. Allison's face came to view, as well as my twin sister's. Were they safe?

"...Fifty students were killed, hundreds injured..." I heard the anchor say. I gulped, praying to God in silent incoherence.

Before I knew it, Luke was back next to me, rubbing my back comfortingly. As my gaze stayed fixed on the television images, my heart began racing and I started to panic again.

"Roxanne, can I get you something?" he asked.

"Water," I answered solemnly.

Luke headed toward the small bathroom. I quickly assessed his movements. As soon as he was out of sight, I swiftly leaped off the bed, grabbed the car keys sitting next to the television, and raced out of the motel room. Without looking behind me, I hurriedly unlocked the door and dove into the driver's seat of the car and lurched the gear into reverse. I slammed on the accelerator and was jolted forward. Changing gears, I drove speedily out of the parking lot.

I raced forward, leaving the motel in my wake. The street was still relatively abandoned. In the distance, I recognized a large gas station sign. I needed a phone.

In the rearview mirror, I caught a glimpse of Luke trailing behind me on foot. He was incredibly fast. I tried to focus on the goal of reaching the gas station.

As the small parking lot grew closer and closer, I spotted a group of men standing around their cars, bickering back and forth. Their appearance—with bandanas wrapped around their heads, hats turned sideways, baggy pants, tattooed arms—threw me off.

Once I approached the parking lot at full speed, I heard the bantering of the group grow louder, even with my window closed. Through a quick scan of the lot, I briefly caught a glimpse of one guy pushing another guy away. Frantically, I parked the car outside the doors of the building and scurried out, waiting for the automatic sensor to let me inside. When the doors didn't budge, I started banging on the glass. I peered inside, where there wasn't a person to be found. I continued to bang, glancing intermittently over my shoulder for any sight of Luke.

One of the group members yelled an obscenity at me, though I wasn't paying enough attention to make out the words. There had to be a payphone close by, I was counting on it. If I could only call Tyler to make sure he was safe.

The shouting from the group continued, though now it wasn't directed at me, but rather back at each other. Dashing toward the right side of the building, my hope instantly deflated at the absence of a payphone. I pivoted back in the other direction to search the left side. Moving this way put me much closer to the hostile gang, but I had to take my chances.

The events that ensued as I picked up the phone happened in slow motion before my eyes. It was if I was watching a movie of my life, with the speed significantly reduced. All at the same time, multiple things occurred. The increasingly aggressive quarrels from the nearby group filling my ears; the sight of Luke swiftly advancing, with an unforgettable look of fear on his face; the sound of a bullet firing into the air, then another shot.

"Roxanne, no!" Luke called out, suddenly so near to me that he could have been whispering.

As I turned toward the commotion, Luke flung himself in front of me, in a protective stance. In an instant, he slid to the ground, a small dime-sized hole piercing his shirt below his right shoulder. The group was scattering now, unlikely to take responsibility for the horrific crime.

My body fell onto his, sobs tangled with cries of his name fleeing from my mouth. His eyes were closed, his body so still he could have been asleep.

"Luke! Luke!" I repeatedly yelled, shaking him.

When he didn't respond, I shouted hysterically. Luke had saved my life by giving up his own. I cried. I cried so much my head was pounding beneath my temples.

I threw my head back, closing my eyes. A mixture of crying and shouting, I screamed, "Help... someone help..."

Luke's chest stirred beneath my trembling hand. I almost fainted when I saw his eyes open, narrow slits peering up into my wet face.

"What happened...?" he groaned.

"You've been shot..." I ran my index finger over the bullet outline in his shirt. Though his skin and shirt should have been soaked with blood from the bullet, there wasn't any red visible. I inspected the rest of his body, the ground, and found nothing. Not one droplet of blood.

My eyes widened. "But, how...?" I mouthed, unsure if I had made a sound.

He shook his head, still on the ground. "I'm fine."

Sitting up slowly, holding his right shoulder, Luke took a couple deep breaths in and out. I examined his back, looking for the exit wound. His shirt was clean, other than small specs of asphalt from the parking lot.

Finally, he stood. I could feel the color in my face drain. He really did look fine, a little shaken, but fine nonetheless. He dusted his pants off and said, "We really need to talk."

43

LUKE

I had a lot of explaining to do.

After I miraculously emerged from the dead, which was quite impossible since I was technically already dead, Roxanne and I quickly fled the gas station parking lot so we wouldn't be questioned if the authorities arrived. We sat on the floor of the motel room, our backs to the wall, as I tried to educate Roxanne on my purpose. She listened, ever so carefully, as my story unfolded.

I was trying to find the right words, my face tortured with the task of explaining myself.

"Roxanne, I was brought here...I was given the job..." I paused momentarily, then continued, "Look, I have been following you for a long time now. Even before meeting you on the trail. I know you better than you know yourself. I came here, into your life, for one purpose and one purpose only."

She was trying to digest this new information, a pained expression on her face.

I finished, "My purpose in your life is to be your...to be your...guardian angel, of sorts."

"My guardian angel?" she said slowly, asking as if she hadn't heard me correctly.

"Yes," I confirmed. "To protect you."

"Protect me from...today?" she asked.

"I guess so. I was put here to save your life, today, that is. See, we will all die someday, obviously, but we don't know when that is.

Certain angels have been appointed the duty of saving specific humans from death before their actual time is up. It happens all the time. Every time a human is saved from dying, it's because of an angel. When humans finally die, that is their chosen time. Every time *a miracle* is performed, you can thank an angel."

"A real angel..." Roxanne said, in a trance. She lightly brushed my forehead with her fingers, as if to make sure I was actually real.

I softly grabbed her wrists and cupped her hands around my chin, our hands forming a blanket together. "I'm real."

Unexpectedly, she pulled her hands away, a wary look crossing her face.

"No," she started, "You're not real."

I nodded. I could see where the conversation was going.

"Well, I'm physically real, but only for a short time. But I can be real as long as you want in here, " I touched below her left collarbone. I slid my hand into her hair and let my fingers travel down through the soft brown strands until my hand reached her shoulder.

Roxanne removed my hand. "No, you're not real at all."

Her head fell towards her lap, her face covered with her hands. She sobbed quietly.

I didn't understand. "Why are you so sad?"

Gazing up at me with her beautiful hazel eyes, I saw for the first time what real hurt looked like. I had hurt her, not physically, but emotionally.

"I loved you," she admitted for the first time. Oh, how I longed to hear her says those words. Yet, simultaneously, I wished she had never said them. It only made the situation harder.

I grabbed her hand, bringing it to my lips and kissing it. "You don't have to stop."

Tears rolled down her pink cheeks. Her head shook ever so slightly. "How can you say that?" she asked, her face pained.

She was right. How could I say that? I *wasn't* real, not real enough for her. She needed lasting physical companionship.

"I guess I can't," I confessed. She couldn't love me. No, it wasn't fair to her.

Awkward silence filled the space between us. I would wait for her to speak. I listened to her even breathing, in and out. The smell of her hair was so strong. I watched every small move she made. My senses were so alive; I tried very hard to control them so I could focus on her needs.

After believing she might have fallen asleep, right there against the wall, she sighed.

"I kept my promise," I told her.

"Promise?" Roxanne asked.

I nodded. "Tyler's safe."

Her eyes closed, an expression of relief falling over her face.

I added, "But you wouldn't have been if I had let you go." The muted news on the television continued to flash pictures of the destroyed campus.

Another heavy sigh escaped her mouth.

She didn't speak. My mouth turned down into a frown. I wanted to cheer her up.

"Wanna hear something cool?" I offered her.

Roxanne's eyes slowly opened to stare at me, her face lacking expression.

"I can pretty much dream up anything I want, and there it is."

Her eyebrows furrowed. "The cars?" she affirmed.

I nodded and a frail smile appeared on her lips.

"I knew something was strange about all the mysterious cars."

I laughed, "Yes, something strange. You were wrong. I didn't steal any of them. They don't even have VIN numbers, they technically don't exist."

"So crazy..." she said, sighing. "You know, I thought you were stalking me at first."

"Yeah, sorry about that," I chuckled. "I knew that blind date thing was really out on a limb, but I had to continue to run into you. All in the plan, you know. A part of the job."

"Was falling in love with me a part of the job?"

Her question took me by surprise. I knew the subject made her upset easily. "No, in fact, I wasn't supposed to get this close."

"What happened? I thought you had rules."

I smiled at her. "Love doesn't follow rules."

Weakly, she returned my smile with one of her own.

Changing the subject, I persisted on with my special talents, "I can appear and disappear." I was hoping she would ask me to demonstrate.

"Can I see?"

Grinning, I instantly disappeared from her sight and reappeared outside the motel door. I knocked three times, pleased with myself. I loved finally getting the opportunity to show off.

She opened the door with wide eyes. "Wow," she muttered.

"Pretty cool, huh?"

Shutting the door behind us, Roxanne walked over to the bed and sat down. "Oh...yes...I'm sorry, it's just so weird. This is just a lot for me. I'm trying to adjust it all in my head."

I sat next to her, troubled by the thought of causing her any more pain. Placing my hand on her knee, I bent my head down to meet her eyes. "I'm *so* sorry it had to be this way. I know you didn't want to leave Tyler. I thought the storm was going to take you. And then when I realized the tornado had subsided, I was fearful. Fearful of what else could happen, but I couldn't figure it out." Then, he recited, "*No one knows about that day or hour, not even the angels in heaven, nor the Son, but only the Father...*"

"I wanted to trust you." She was staring toward her lap, her voice filled with pain.

"You did trust me. If you hadn't, you might be dead," I tried to assure her.

Roxanne glanced up at me, not smiling but not frowning either. "You did what you had to do."

I was devastated. "Maybe there was a better way..." I could recall my last conversation with Caroline.

Her hand patted my forearm. "Maybe not. You did what you thought was best."

"I'm sorry," I said again, repeating the words over and over again in my head.

We moved back over to the wall, leaning our bodies heavily against it. Roxanne rested her head against my knee. It was so natural. I was elated at the feeling of her touch. I couldn't get enough of it.

I placed my hand on top of her head. Leaning my head against the wall, I sighed and closed my eyes. What was I to do next? I had no idea.

Beneath my hand, Roxanne lifted her head and the next thing I knew, her lips were pressed against mine. There was nothing better than the taste of her soft lips.

Although I wished it to last, I pulled away. It was only fair. I knew what had to be done eventually.

She didn't seem to mind. Wrapping her arms around my bent legs, Roxanne graciously peered up at me, her head resting sideways on my knees.

"You know everything, don't you?" she quietly asked.

I nodded. "Yes."

"That's interesting," she commented, nonchalantly.

"Why interesting?" I asked.

"Do you know what I'm thinking about right now?" she squeezed her eyes shut.

I laughed. "You think I have a nice body."

Her eyes popped open, a grin on her lips. "No!"

I paused, and then finished, "Okay, you wish I would get rid of this hat." I placed my hand on my head, feeling the curves of my favorite baseball cap. I would *not* be getting rid of it.

She nodded. "You're amazing."

"You know, I once was plain and normal just like you."

Her eyes grew soft. "I'm sure you were never plain, or normal. And I'm a little offended by you calling me that."

I shook my head lightly. "It was a compliment. I wish I was normal sometimes."

"Why?" she asked, her eyes filled with bewilderment.

I put it rather simply, "I'm temporary."

Roxanne's beautifully lit face fell flat. Reality was beginning to sink in.

I pushed my index finger into her nose. "You, my dear, are permanent."

"Not forever," she corrected.

"Okay, I guess *you're* right," I said.

She managed to smile. I was thankful for that.

She rested her head back against my knees. We both closed our eyes and rested.

"So, I have another question."

My eyes flew open. "Let me have it," I said, thankful for her immense interest in me, even after all that had happened.

"How did you get the job as my guardian angel? Does that mean we have a connection somehow?" she probed, hope laced in her sweet voice.

I chuckled just then, visions of years past flooding my head. Shaking my head, I answered, "You have no idea."

44

LUKE

I could recall the day it happened as if it were yesterday.

Firstly, I reminded Roxanne of the first time I laid eyes on her, years ago. She was on a trip with her family in Venice. They were eating in a café when I met her gaze. She was the most beautiful American girl I had ever seen. I prayed that I would see her again but I never actually expected that to happen.

Then, I told her the story of the second time I saw her.

I sat on the floor of Gate 13 with my back against a wall, taking in my surroundings. I desperately wanted to close my eyes and nap, but I had a lot on my mind. I stared down at the book in my hand – a gift from my cousin — about America. As the minutes passed by, the people began to file into the gate, each seat being filled almost synchronously. I didn't mind the floor. I shouldn't have had to wait much longer...

My flight to Rome was boarding in approximately fifteen minutes. I was flying home, back to my family—my Alexandra, Sophie, Joseph, Julius, Priscilla, Mamma, and Babbo—after a short visit with a friend in a suburb of New York City. I couldn't deny the homesickness I felt. I had never traveled for so long or so far away from my family. I was the oldest of my siblings and expected to care for them when Babbo was away at work. Even though no one would admit the inconvenience of my absence, I knew my parents would be happy to have me back to help around the house.

I forced myself to stop thinking. It would only make the anxiety worse. Flying was not something I looked forward to. I needed to distract myself. Maybe I would put the book to use.

A family of four approached the boarding line where I sat. I couldn't help but admire the two young daughters of the family. Each seemed uniquely different, but both were beautiful. One girl had light brown hair which loosely hugged around her shoulders and glowing hazel eyes. She was very tan and slender. When she smiled, her face lit up the area, and I sensed I had seen her smile before. Her sister stood next to her, with straight blonde hair which fell down the sides of her cheeks and reached her mid-back. Unlike the brunette, the blonde wore a mask of makeup, falsely accenting her brilliant blue eyes. I was positive she didn't need it at all. My eyes fluttered between their faces. It was obvious they were twins.

"Now, Roxanne, Regan, you two need to make sure your mom stays sane. She will need help around the house for a while until I get back from Paris." The father had a hand on both of his daughters' shoulders as he spoke. The expression he carried was one of slight regret.

The brunette quickly rebuked him with a chuckle, "Oh, dad. Like you help mom out that much when you *are* home." Her words forced a smile onto her father's saddened face. Her mother's eyes gleamed.

The father shook his head playfully. "Alright, alright, kiddo. That's enough. Now come here and give your old dad a hug." His smile appeared strained as he motioned for his daughters to come closer. His family closed in and embraced him.

After hugging, his wife grabbed his face in her hands. "Make sure you call as soon as you land. I'll miss you. Terribly."

"Don't worry. I will call as soon as I can. The time will fly by while I'm gone. You won't even know I'm gone." As soon as he spoke the words, he knew it was a lie. He *would* be missed. And he would miss his family.

A voice came over the intercom: *Flight 2539 to Rome, Italy, is now boarding at Gate 13. Please gather all belongings and stand in line.*

The time had come. I followed the intercom's instructions and gathered my belongings. There wasn't much to gather, for all I had was a backpack. I didn't own a lot in Italy.

On standing, I gazed back at the family I was watching. The father was waving a goodbye as he headed into the hallway leading to the plane, his wife and daughters watched with hands linked gloomily at their sides. I was not the only one that hated being away from family.

The mother abruptly turned to face her daughters. "I guess it's back to Ocala, Florida. New York has suddenly left a bad taste in my mouth." In agreement, the girls followed their mother's lead out of Gate 13.

I followed the crowd through the long tunnel into the plane. Searching my boarding pass for a seat number, I spotted the number-letter combination and spoke under my breath, "14D." My eyes scanned the rows as I passed each one until I reached row 14. Seat D was the aisle. As I threw my backpack into the overhead bin, I was aware that I recognized my neighbor sitting in 14E. It was the father of the family from Florida.

His eyes rose to meet mine as I plopped into the aisle seat; they were kind and welcoming. Although I knew he was distressed about his current situation, he managed to smile at me. I was pleasantly surprised, smiling in return.

The man shot his hand out toward me and mumbled, "Hello, son. What's your name?"

I took his hand and shook it. My spoken English was not impressive, but understandable. "My name is Lucio, sir."

He slighted a chuckle and responded, "No need to call me *sir*, it makes me sound old."

I hesitantly laughed back. "Okay." My small English vocabulary limited my responses greatly.

"Where are you from, Lucio? Did I say that right?" He was very friendly.

A female flight attendant spoke into the speaker: *Please fasten your seatbelts. As demonstrated, the exits are in the front, the middle, and the back of the aircraft...*

The instructions continued for a few minutes before I was able to answer his questions. The plane began moving and, with a look of anxiety rising on my face, I fastened my belt tighter. My neighbor laughed again.

"Don't like flying? Me neither. If it were possible to drive across the Atlantic, I would!" He folded his hands together and sat them in his lap. He seemed to be reacting casually to the flying situation. I didn't believe him.

"I'm from Italy," I remembered, "and yes, you said my name correctly. Thank you for your concern." My mother made sure I perfected my politeness before I came to the United States. "May I ask your name?"

"The name's Dan. Dan Clarke."

The airplane began moving on the runway only minutes later. Eventually, we were off the ground and ascending into the deep blue sky. I tried to steady my breathing as my ears became filled with an uncomfortable pressure.

Dan reached across the seat between us, offering one small stick in his hand. "Gum?"

I nodded, taking the stick from him and popping it into my mouth. If nothing else, it would take my mind off the pain that was created on either side of my head.

Once in the air, the pain was assuaged; my ears popped as the pressure stabilized. I leaned my head back against the seat and sighed.

"Don't fly much, do you?" Dan asked me, a goofy smile on his face.

I shook my head.

"Where you headed, son?" he continued to question.

"Home. To Italy." If I kept my sentences short, I could lessen the English errors I spoke.

"Nice. I'm headed to Paris for a business meeting. I really enjoy the traveling but can't stand to be away from my family. I bet your family will be glad to see you." Dan leaned down between his legs and pulled out a magazine entitled *International Business*, opening it up to a bookmarked page.

"I assume so," I answered, studying the front page.

Keeping his eyes locked on the paper in front of him, Dan asked, "You have a big family?"

"Yes, sir. There are six of us."

"Wow," Dan exclaimed, gazing up at me from his reading material. He noticed my interest and held out the magazine for me to take. "You can take a look, if you'd like."

I nodded, meekly smiling. I took the magazine from his hand and flipped through the pages, unable to understand most of it. The pictures were interesting, though.

Dan must have had many magazines in his sack because he casually pulled out another one and began reading it.

One half hour passed, the two of us reading about international affairs and the array of business policies flooding the global market, according to him. Again, I found the graphics very informative, especially to someone who knew the basic principles of English and not much more than that. Dan peered over at me, intently examining my reactions to the articles. He laughed out loud, catching my attention.

"Do you understand any of it?" he bluntly questioned.

Feebly, I shook my head. "Not really."

Laughing again, he said, "Me neither."

"That's funny," I told him, unsure what he meant.

"How old are you, Lucio?"

"I'm eighteen, sir."

"Just call me Dan."

"Dan," I nodded.

"Too bad. I have two fourteen-year-old girls. Eighteen is bit old for them. But you seem like a nice kid. I can't get over the boys they went to school with. I'm putting them into private school. Well, I guess there are a *couple* decent boys..."

I stared at him, trying to follow the conversation.

"I'm rambling, aren't I?"

"Rambling?" I repeated.

"Sorry... I have a problem with talking sometimes. I just want the best for my girls, that's all."

"Of course," I commented.

"You're a good kid, I can tell."

"Thank you," then I added, "Dan."

"There you go. No *sir* for me." His wide smile was contagious, reaching from his cheeks up to his dark eyes.

The flight would take approximately nine hours in length. I had brought plenty of Italian music to pass the time, as well as schoolwork. My winter vacation was ending as soon as I returned home. I enjoyed school well enough, so it didn't bother me as much as it bothered my siblings.

Although I had planned on completing a large amount of homework, the soothing sway of the plane, as well as the business magazine, put me to sleep within two hours of the departure from New York.

I was suddenly awoken with a jerk of my seat. In my hazy awakening, I couldn't determine reality from dreaming. Until I heard the nervous shouting of the passengers around me, I hadn't quite realized the seriousness of the situation. The overhead lights began to flicker. My heart rate quickened.

A voice came over the speaker: "*Please remain seated and stay calm. We are currently passing through some heavy rain. Turbulence is expected. Again, please stay seated with your seatbelt fastened.*"

Nervously, I cinched my already-tight lap belt. I peered over to Dan. Sweat was beading around his upper forehead, though he looked relatively calm.

"Nothing to worry about, son," he assured me. His voice did not shake at all.

I nodded, trying hard to believe him.

The plane slightly rocked at first, then gradually increased over the next several minutes. I was beginning to feel sick.

Dan was very observant. As an attendant quickly passed by, Dan called out, "Can we get a bag over here? The boy looks terrible."

My own sweat was beginning to show on my face and the nausea continued. I tried to close my eyes, hoping that would help.

Unexpectedly, I felt a plastic bag being laid in my lap. I gripped it tightly, not wanting to dare open my eyes to look at it. I would trust it would be there if I needed it.

I could feel it coming...at the same time, I could hear people crying out in the background...uh, oh...

Opening my bag, I vomited once and it was over.

Around me, it seemed the worst was just beginning.

People were on their cell phones, the flight attendants urging them to stop. They were frantically calling loved ones, fear laden in their voices.

I didn't understand. I thought the pilot made it clear that this would be temporary.

Suddenly, a hand on my arm. I turned to find Dan's smiling face, though not quite as cheerful as before.

"It's okay, son."

As soon as he spoke, the cabin went completely dark. The sound of the wind was extremely loud against the windows of the plane. Rain pelted the pane. I tried to see outside through the small window, but could only see water and dark clouds.

Closing my eyes again, I began saying a prayer in Italian. I must have been speaking out loud, because Dan reached over and grabbed my hand. His whisper came out clearly, "Ask Him to take care of my girls."

I never woke up from my prayer.

45

ROXANNE

I realized I was holding my breath only once I began gasping for air.

"Roxanne, are you okay?" Luke's voice was soft, caring.

I tasted the salt from my tears, which had poured continuously down my cheeks since the moment he mentioned my father.

"Roxanne?" Luke probed, concern flushing his golden face. His warm hand grazed my cold forearm.

Closing my eyes, I tried to understand all the events that had taken place in the past twelve hours. The recent memories of being in my dorm's basement during a rare Florida tornado; the anxiety of Luke rescuing me; the look of his unfamiliar, stern face; my escape from him; the bullet piercing his chest; and ultimately, his death—his apparent death. My mind fluttered many years back, to the day of my father's departing flight, the final flight. It was all too much for me to bear.

Slightly gripping me, he urged, "Please just say something."

My eyelids opened, but I still saw darkness. "I have to go."

Immediately he bellowed, a hint of anger in his tone. "Go where?"

Just then, I stood up. Without much further thought, without much further care, I opened the hotel room door and proceeded outside. I couldn't turn to look back at him. I didn't give a second thought to the person I was leaving behind in that musty, old room.

My legs were carrying me away, far from the reality of all that I had endured.

At the hotel desk, the attendant phoned a cab for me. Rather quickly, I was in the backseat of that yellow sedan, hoping desperately that I was only living a nightmare and soon I would awake back in my dorm room and the sun would be out and Tyler would be waiting at my door. In the blink of an eye, I was dropped off at the nearest Greyhound bus stop. Had any time even passed since stooping inside that smoke-scented cab? I felt as though time was eluding me, that seconds and minutes were no longer real.

The bus ride would not stop in Gainesville; I needed to go home. I would arrive back at my house in Ocala, drag my feet to my bed, and sleep. Sleep. And when I would wake, I would know that none of this was real.

STAGE FIVE

ACCEPTANCE

46

ROXANNE

The sun was very bright in my eyes as I ran up the hill.

I was all but squinting to make sure I wouldn't trip on any unsuspecting deviation in the asphalt. It was a glorious spring day in April, the bright array of tulips blooming out from the ground, making their seasonal appearance. Small dogs chained in front yards yipped at me as I passed by their houses. It made me shake my head and laugh.

In the distance I could make out the community softball field full of people playing a pick-up game. Yes, it was definitely the season of laughter, fun, and sun. I had been waiting all winter long for it to arrive.

I smiled at the players as I moved from the asphalt onto the sidewalk. The sidewalks in my neighborhood were not regular and smooth but rather sporadic. The areas that did have sidewalks proved to be very unsafe—cracks and holes galore. I recalled memories of the numerous times I had tripped, quickly searched for any laughing onlookers, and picked up my pace to leave the scene unseen.

Normally, running was the time I speculated on the various situations in my life. Right now, I had many things to think about. Thinking always made running seamless, while at the same time, always making thinking so clear. The two activities paralleled each other flawlessly.

Today was different. I didn't want to think. I had plenty of harmless things to daydream about—turning the ripe old age of twenty-five, coaching the girl's soccer team at my old high school, my mom's new romance, my sister's hit career as a anchorwoman—but there was only one thing on my mind: Luke.

Speaking the name in my head was forbidden. The last time I had seen him...well, that was the day I walked away from him at the motel, six long years ago. He never came running after me. I didn't blame him for that. What good would it have done? There really was no point in even believing he had once existed. I still questioned his presence in my life so many years ago.

Forget him, I warned myself. Déjà vu suddenly struck me. My mind, against my will, traced back through history and put my thoughts back on the St. Francis trail. I was running in the early morning, darkness surrounding me. An annoying stranger greeted me. He wouldn't leave me alone. He didn't leave me alone for months. I didn't want him to leave me alone. Then, just as quickly as he came into my life, he left. Not only did he leave no trace behind, he physically couldn't. *He wasn't even real.*

Shaking my head, I grunted. *Stop it*, I urged myself.

Unrelentingly, I couldn't get his face out of my mind. Trying to push his image away, I started to wallow in self-pity. Would I ever love again? Would I be able to be happy for my friends that were getting married this summer? Would I always be bitter when it came to men? Would I always be bitter when it came to God? Those questions had been on my mind for years.

I thought it infuriatingly ironic that the one guy I could let myself love wasn't even a real person. He was just a ghost...he was dead yet he was the most alive *thing* I knew. God was destining me to eternal misery by bringing Luke in and then out of my life. If I couldn't see myself with anyone before Luke, I definitely couldn't see myself with anyone after him. He was my everything, yet not really anything at all.

I recognized one of my neighbors playing basketball with a bunch of guys next to the tiny softball field. Smiling, I nodded.

He called out, "Hey Rox! Wanna play?" He passed the ball back and forth between his hands, even under his legs. Show-off.

"No thanks," I yelled back. "I hate basketball!"

He laughed, shaking his head. "Did I finally find a sport that Roxanne Clarke can't play?" he gawked. All of his friends were staring at me.

"I suck," I affirmed.

"I could show you," he suggested, winking. An eruption of cackling and grunting sounded from all the guys. Apparently they thought this casual exchange was funny.

"Maybe some other time," I laughed, jokingly. I really did hate basketball. There was no guy who could make me play. Almost.

When the group of guys was out of sight, I sighed. Sure, my neighbor was a cute, nice guy who had a decent job and enjoyed being active, but that was it for him. My mom thought we would be perfect together. In fact, my mom tried to set me up a lot. There was no doubt she had been talking to the guy behind my back.

I ran for another mile, trying to stifle all thoughts of any guys. Just then, when I had cleared my head of any male remnants, one unexpected face popped into view.

I hadn't seen Tyler in over five years, except for the occasional crossed path on campus, which was really depressing. I had no idea what he was doing with his life or where he was living. My mom purposefully did not give me any information about the situation, knowing that it would upset me. The truth was that I really did miss him, regardless of the reason we weren't currently in contact. Although we hadn't stayed in touch, he would always be my brother, my best friend, and my soul mate.

I knew our lack of communication was my fault. I chose Luke over him and I would never forgive myself for that. In the end, I didn't have either of them. After the tornado, I tried helplessly to get a hold of him, but he had finally given up on me. I wanted to hate how ignorant and selfish he was but I couldn't blame him. He let my love for someone else split our friendship. The very person he despised happened to be a physical impossibility. If Tyler had only known...and yet, he will never know. I wouldn't be able to tell him the truth—if you could call it that. He would think I was psychotic and he would undoubtedly have me admitted to the local mental hospital. It didn't matter, anyway; he had banned me from his life forever, I suspected. I deserved it.

My focus on Tyler almost caused me to miss the youth soccer game happening to my right, in a grassy green field behind an elementary school. Young kids, both boys and girls, were running everywhere, scattering after soccer balls and racing each other. Although the practice appeared organized from a distance, chaos reeked out to the close bystanders. I slowed to a stop, realizing that there was only one coach for the thirty or so kids. The man leading the group, blowing his whistle obnoxiously, looked frayed. He was so clearly *not* in charge of the herd of children.

Jogging across the fifty feet of greenery, I called out when I came within hearing distance, "Need some help?"

The man turned toward me, peering at me through sunglasses. Though I couldn't see his eyes, his expression spoke relief. He probably could care less who I was, as long as I could help.

Removing his sunglasses, he smiled widely. "You'd be saving my life."

I laughed softly, peeking around him at the kids running from one end of the field to the other. "Looks like you have a handful," I nodded behind him.

When I finally stood next to him, I could see he had brilliant blue eyes. He wore a goatee, a very appropriate look for him. A Florida Gators baseball hat covered any length of hair he managed to have. His face proved he had a few years on me, but he was definitely attractive.

"More like two hands full," he brought up his open hands to display, still grinning sheepishly. It was clear he was the kind of guy that did not eagerly ask for help.

"You think I could have a try?" I asked, pointing around the field.

He chuckled, obviously finding me unworthy. "Go for it."

I rolled my eyes. This guy had no idea who he was messing with.

"Alright," I smiled and stepped toward the gang of kids. Turning back, I said, "I'm Roxanne, by the way."

He nodded at me, "Steve. And good luck."

To get the attention of the kids, I whistled through my teeth, a sharp, piercing sound. Suddenly, all eyes were on me.

"Call me Coach Roxanne," I began, picking up cones from the ground. "So, here's what we're going to do..."

After easily organizing the children into four teams, I set up the cones for drills. The kids seemed enthusiastic enough to me about having a plan for practice. I instructed them on some basic skills, watered down for their age level. Once I demonstrated what I wanted and answered their questions, I let them try the drills on their own. Taking my place back next to Steve, I folded my arms across my chest and smiled at the kids.

He was speechless, so I spoke first. "Piece of cake."

"Coach Roxanne: Who are you and where did you come from?" Steve finally mumbled, clearly shocked.

My smile widened in pride and I held out my hand. "Roxanne Clarke, head coach for the girls varsity soccer team at the high school."

Steve's face registered the connection. Shaking my hand firmly, he admitted, "I knew I recognized you from somewhere."

I crooked my neck curiously at him.

"I've been to a few games up at the school. You know, trying to get tips." He tried not to smile.

"I see. Well, I hope you didn't get your teaching style from me."

"Yeah... about that..." Steve rubbed his neck shyly, embarrassed at his coaching tactics.

"I guess it was all about perfect timing," I commented.

"Perfect timing," he agreed.

"So do you coach them normally or are you just a sub?" I joked.

"Ha ha, very funny. I actually do have *some* coaching skill. Well, at least I thought I did. Maybe I was deceiving myself. This is your first gig coaching, right?"

"Yeah. The last coach, who had coached me, decided to move away at the last minute and contacted me. She knew I had played college ball and asked if I was interested. God couldn't have planned it better...it was exactly what I wanted to do."

He nodded, a peaceful expression across his face. "It's funny how God opens doors for you, but only after he closes so many."

His comment stopped my breathing. I inhaled deeply, a whiff of freshly cut grass stimulating my nostrils.

"Yeah," was the only word I could manage. I peered up at his face to smile a little, noticing his hat again.

Pointing up at the Gator hat, I asked, "Alumni?"

Grinning, he responded, "Yeah, graduated about...well...a while ago. How about you?"

I quickly realized that Steve was *much* older than I.

"Two years ago," I said.

"Aw, you're just a baby."

My smile went flat, the expression draining from my face. Shortly after recognizing my sour reaction, his cheeks turned a shade of red and kept his eyes on the ground. His comment wasn't meant to hurt my feelings, but it embarrassed me. I wasn't a baby; I was an adult, with an adult job.

Trying to quickly recover from his accidental insult, Steve asked casually, "So, you run often?"

I turned my attention to the kids, whose excitement was dwindling. After yelling out to switch drills, I looked back to Steve. "Every day," I answered.

"Wow, that's dedication. I'm not much of a runner anymore..." his voice trailed off.

Before I could ask him to finish his thought, a young boy hurdled toward us, a bright smile on his face. "Dad!" he screamed out, lunging toward Steve and wrapping his short arms around Steve's leg. My eyes widened. I immediately, yet casually, searched for a wedding ring on his left hand. There was no jewelry to be found. I sighed only slightly.

Steve gave a brief smile to me and turned his attention to his son. "Hey, why aren't you out there with the rest of the kids?"

The little boy had the most beautiful blue eyes, clearly inherited. "I want to know if Coach Roxanne can coach us *every practice!*"

I tried to stifle a laugh, but my attempt failed.

Steve gave me a jokingly annoyed look. Looking back to his son, he pointed back toward the others and said, "Jordan, go!"

The little guy named Jordan smiled wide and trotted back to his friends, waving at me with his departure.

"So," I hesitated, "you have a son."

"Is that a question or a statement?" Steve glanced at me curiously.

"Well, unless that kid calls every guy *dad*, he's definitely your offspring."

He nodded, serious. "Yes, Jordan is mine. I wouldn't be coaching if he weren't on the team."

"So the truth comes out," I laughed.

"Whoops," he shrugged, grinning.

A sudden moment of silence filled the air. "He's cute," I stated, trying to dismiss any awkwardness.

"Just like his daddy, right?" Steve winked in my direction.

Without making eye contact, I said, "I bet his mom is gorgeous."

"Are you saying he gets his good looks from his *mom*?" There was a distinct accusatory tone to his voice.

Faintly, I smiled. *I bet she is gorgeous, with my luck.*

"Although his mom was a looker, he definitely takes after me."

Was? I thought.

"Are you divorced?" I couldn't stop myself from asking.

He shook his head. Steve was flirting with me and he was married!

As if realizing I was having a conflicting moment, he swiftly said, "Jordan's mom died a couple years ago in a car accident."

I gulped. I was so insensitive. "I'm so sorry," I offered.

"No reason to be. She's in a better place." He smiled a pure, sincere smile.

"Yeah," I agreed, half-heartedly. I was feeling very guilty for thinking such bad thoughts about a man I hardly knew, after he experienced the awful death of his wife.

"Hey," Steve touched my arm, "it's really okay."

I liked the way his arm felt on mine. Returning his smile, I felt oddly at peace with his reassurance.

An unexpected urge came over me. I needed to leave. There was somewhere I needed to go, somewhere I needed to be.

I glanced down at my watch, pretending to realize it was later than expected. "Well, I better head out. It's getting late."

Steve looked disappointed. "So soon?"

"Yeah, sorry. You'll be fine with the kids." I knew he was disappointed about my leaving the kids, but he wouldn't admit it.

"Coach Roxanne, thanks for all your help."

"Coach Steve, it's been fun."

Without thinking, I turned around and started to jog away. Abruptly, Steve called out my name. Stopping and facing him, I cocked my head to the side.

He walked toward me, rubbing the palms of his hands on his shorts. It seemed he was nervous.

"I know we just met, and you haven't even seen my best soccer skills, but I was wondering...can I get your number?" His older face momentarily appeared young, a sense of vulnerability evident.

I smiled, very obliged at his forwardness.

"Sure," I replied. After giving him the information, he tipped his hat at me and replaced his sunglasses back over his eyes. "Very nice to meet you."

I nodded back, my cheeks undoubtedly pink, "Same to you."

Still focused on my new destination, I turned quickly and jogged back to the sidewalk. Steve seemed like a nice guy, even if he was older. Maybe guys weren't all bad after all.

As the field grew further and further away, I gave Steve and his kids one last parting look. Of course, he was staring. I waved and he returned the gesture.

The sun was slowly setting on the horizon, so I picked up my pace. I needed to reach my destination, preferably before sunset. The place was approximately three miles away, which would only take me about twenty minutes. The more I concentrated on getting there, the faster I wanted to run.

The time seemed to pass by quickly with my mind racing around in so many different directions. I contemplated my meeting with Steve and his adorable son, Jordan. Could I even bring myself to date someone again, especially someone with a family? I completely understood Steve's situation, having lived with grief myself for eleven years. I was only able to move past my lingering mourning because of...

The corners of my mouth turned down into a frown. Luke had helped me feel some closure, which I had longed for a very long time. But Luke wasn't real. He made me feel real things, but he wasn't real. He would never be real, no matter how many days and nights I would pray to God to bring him back to me. I had already tried that tactic. Prayers were not always answered so easily.

I saw a familiar turn in the road. My destination was around the corner. I sighed in relief. The yearning inside me was overwhelming.

The ring of barred fence around the place was representative of its limitations. Emotions could be set free within the wrought-iron gates, but required an awful masking on leaving. It was not culturally acceptable to be depressed all the time. People died every day. People moved on. How was it so easy?

I slowed to a walk as I approached the entrance to the Ocala Cemetery. Placing my hand on the hinged gate, I sucked in as much air as I could manage. Sweat dripped down my forehead onto my shirt. Licking my lips, I tasted the bitter salt that comprised my sweat. Oddly, I liked the familiarity of its taste.

My eyes scanned the graveyard for others. I didn't spot anyone, for which I was glad. In my times of bereavement, I preferred to be alone. Although I was very good at masking my emotions to others, when I was visiting my father, I couldn't be sure what would happen. It was best for it to be just us.

Stepping into the gated area, I followed the path to where it led to my father's tombstone. I was upset with myself that I didn't have anything to give to him on this visit. I imagined he wouldn't care though.

My feet automatically moved toward his plot, ten down from the aisle. Fresh flowers, a mixture of beautiful colors, lay adjacent to his headstone. Smiling, I thought of my mother.

I carefully knelt on the ground and sat cross-legged, facing his name. DANIEL RUTHERFORD CLARKE. MORE THAN A MAN, FATHER, HUSBAND. Tears welled up in my eyes, a short laugh erupting at the saying under his name. He was most certainly the best man I knew. If only he were here....

My eyes shut, remembering the good memories I had with my father, dating back to when I was a young girl. Although he had always wanted a boy, he was happy that we enjoyed similar activities. He taught me sports, fishing, and how to get dirty. My happiness lingered only momentarily. As if the wind blew them, my peaceful thoughts of childhood were swept away, replaced with a deep longing. I felt a huge hole in my heart, dreadfully missing my father. I needed him more than ever, which never seemed to stop being the case.

I read his headstone five times. A sob erupted from my chest, followed by many more quiet ones. I dropped my face into my hands, shaking my head. "Dad..." my voice broke through the wailing. Although I was unable to say more than that, so much of what I wanted to say festered in my head.

When I was able to catch my breath, I pleaded with him, "Dad, I can't be this way anymore. Your life should be celebrated, not grieved. I'm done grieving, dad. I'm done with this..." My fist hit the ground next to me.

Leaning my elbow against my knee, I covered my eyes with my hand. I tried to breathe evenly. I wanted him to be here so badly, but I couldn't let that disrupt my life, like it had in the past.

"I can't let this affect my life anymore...it's nothing personal, you understand. I want to smile when I think of you, not cry. I want to know you're keeping an eye on me and that you're rooting for my success. That's all I want...why can't God just give that to me?"

Sighing, I let my chin rest in my palm. I traced out his name with my finger, letting the remaining tears stream down my cheek, eventually dropping onto my legs.

Whispering now, I said, "I miss you so much..."

I closed my eyes, allowing the setting sun to envelop my skin and the breeze to take me away. All I could hear was birds chirping in the trees lingering above me.

"Roxanne?"

I gasped, startled by the voice of another person behind me. Turning to meet the stranger, my mouth dropped.

Tyler stood there, watching me from the trunk of a nearby tree. My hand instinctively reached for the soccer ball necklace that rested at the base of my throat.

Quickly standing, I brushed off the dirt from my legs. Suddenly, I felt very self-conscious. The feeling was foreign to me.

"You don't recognize me?" he asked, stepping forward toward me.

My throat unlocked and I was able to speak. "You haven't changed at all." His appearance seemed the same, though he appeared slightly taller.

"You look..." he paused, contemplating the right word. "Awesome."

I tried to smile, but found it hard. I was still shocked by his unexpected visit.

He frowned. "I guess you're not very excited to see me."

I shook my head. I wanted him to understand how thrilled I was to see him, but at the same time all the pain and suffering he had caused nearly knocked me off my feet.

"What?" Tyler asked, creeping closer.

The tears came back, but I tried desperately to conceal them. I bit my lip to concentrate.

"Roxanne, please talk to me."

Tyler stood less than a foot from me. The smell of his sweet cologne instantly drew me in. Staring up at him, I took in his handsome features. His skin was a golden brown, tan from the sun. His short blonde hair was styled perfectly in place. Through his shirt, I could see muscle definition from his chest. He had been working out, which was surprising and impressive. I was wrong about my initial impression; he didn't look the same, he looked *better*.

Crashing down on me like a downpour of rain, another hole ripped open in my heart. This hole had Tyler's name on it. I quickly threw my arms around him, clinging tight. His wonderful smell was comforting.

Returning the greeting, Tyler wrapped his arms around my back and shoulders. His grip was strong, the newly formed muscles flexing against my skin.

"Tyler," I whispered into his neck.

"Roxanne," he mumbled, stroking my hair.

"Why did you leave me?"

Abruptly, he pulled away. Instantly, I wished I had kept my mouth shut.

He was confused. "What?"

I gulped. *What did I say?*

"Where have you been?" I asked, rephrasing my question.

He didn't waver. "That was not the question you asked me."

"I asked you...why you left me..." I really didn't see the shame in the question, but felt suddenly embarrassed for wondering.

He shook his head. "Are you kidding me? I didn't leave you. You left me."

"You must have a bad memory—" I insisted.

Tyler interrupted, "Wow, wow." His body language spoke louder than his words. He seemed to close down, shocked with disbelief.

I really didn't want to argue, especially at my father's grave.

"What are you doing here?" I rashly responded.

He glanced down at the grave behind me. "I came to pay my respects."

Angrily, I said, "He doesn't need your respect."

I thought Tyler would turn around and walk right back out of my life as quickly as he came. When he stood his ground, I realized he had changed more than his appearance.

"Now hold on here. What's gotten into you? We haven't seen each other for years and you respond to me *like this*. Can't we be civil?"

Tyler's maturity surprised me. It was a very attractive quality.

I nodded. He was right, of course. But I was still upset with him.

Holding out his hand, he waved his head away from the gravesite, gesturing for me to follow. I hesitated, glancing back and forth between him and the headstone. I wasn't sure I was ready to say goodbye for the evening.

"Roxanne," he reassured me.

Kissing the tips of my fingers, I pressed them against the headstone. "Love you," I told my father. "I'll be back soon."

I didn't take Tyler's hand, but instead let him place his hand on my back. I wasn't quite equipped to jump back into the old relationship we had just yet.

"Do you drink coffee? Can I take you out for coffee?" A hopeful expression lit his face.

I took another parting look back behind us. Turning back to Tyler's face, I nodded. "Sure, I drink coffee now."

"Looks like some things have changed," he lightly joked.

"Yeah," I agreed, dully.

"Did you run here?" Pointing to my clothing, I knew he already knew the answer.

"You didn't need to ask that," I informed him.

"Guess *that* hasn't changed."

"Never."

We approached a small sedan and I laughed. "Is this what you're driving these days?"

He gave me a weary look. "You kidding? This is my mom's car. You must have lost your memory."

He drove us to a local coffee shop, one that I occasionally visited. This particular place was a longtime favorite of my sister's in high school.

"I always liked this place," he commented, more to himself than to me.

"And I always hated this place." I didn't have to explain my remark because Tyler knew how I had felt about my sister.

"Speaking of...how is your sister?" He seemed genuinely interested, which struck me as unusual.

Taking seats inside, we ordered drinks and continued our conversation.

"She's doing exceptionally well. I'm so proud of her. She's working at the news station as the lead anchor. But you probably already knew that."

He raised one of his eyebrows. "Why would you assume that I knew that?"

"Come on, now. Even though we haven't spoken in years doesn't mean our mothers haven't."

He nodded in consent. "That's awfully true."

Once our drinks arrived, the conversation seemed strained.

"So, we need to have a little talk," Tyler declared following a long period of staring into his coffee cup.

This amused me. "A little talk?" I repeated.

"Yes, a talk. Of little magnitude."

I laughed quietly at his sense of humor and demeanor.

Grabbing my left hand, Tyler inspected it thoroughly.

"No ring," he announced.

"Way to state the obvious. And you would know if I was married. Remember, our mothers."

"Good point," he concurred.

I nodded my head. The boy was confusing me with his pointless banter.

"What happened to Luke?"

And there it was, the inevitable question. Did I really expect him to not bring it up? Of course not; but so soon? We had only reunited fifteen minutes ago!

After a short period of silence, I muttered, "Long story."

Leaning closer across the table, Tyler sternly said, "I have time." He didn't seem distraught about my damaged love life at all. It appeared to enthrall him.

"I don't."

Cocking his head to the side, he asked, "You don't?"

I clarified, "I will *never* have the time to tell you the story."

Slowly nodding, he said, "Okay...I get it. Bad breakup. End of story."

Tyler was starting to irritate me with his new attitude. "We didn't *break up*."

My words caught his attention. "What?"

I was kicking myself for opening up my mouth because now I would have to either make something up or dance around the subject. "It was a...mutual...ending." The statement wasn't true at all, but I didn't know what else to say. *Hey, Tyler, you know that guy I chose over you? Yeah, he was an angel. No, a real angel. Sent to save my life. Yeah, it sounds crazy...*I could picture the scene now.

"Oh, I get it."

Quickly changing the subject, I added, "What about that Caroline girl?"

"Amazing in bed, but dumb as a rock," he said, nonchalantly.

My eyes widened. I must have looked shocked, because his eyes brightened.

Laughing to himself, he threw his head back. "Yeah, right. Roxanne, you know me better than that. She broke it off. I guess I wasn't good enough for her."

Relief flooded through me. I sighed quietly, simultaneously shaking my head in disagreement. "Now, Tyler, that isn't true."

His eyes narrowed. "How can *you* say that?"

"You deserve the best," I reiterated.

He didn't respond, only shaking his head.

I watched him sip his coffee, wondering what he would bring up next.

He watched me watching him, his eyes searching for answers to questions he wasn't asking out loud.

"So, tell me, what are you up to these days?"

I was thankful for a lighter topic. Smiling crookedly, I said, "I bet you already know the answer to that question, too."

"Well, dang it, Roxanne, it's really hard to catch up when my mother is the town's gossip queen. How's coaching going for you?"

I smiled. "It's great. I love it. It's what I always imagined it to be. We have a tournament coming up. The girls have practiced so hard. I think they're ready for it."

He returned the smile, sipping his coffee.

"What?" I asked, curious as to what he was thinking.

"I love the way you talk about your job. You must really be happy."

I sipped my own coffee. "I am."

"I'm so happy for you. I wish I could see them play." His bright smile remained.

"So, what have you been you up to these past couple years?"

"You probably know the answer to that..." he assumed.

Chagrined, I wagged my head. "Sorry...my mom doesn't talk about you."

"Ouch. You hate me that much? That's pretty harsh."

"Don't take it personally. You *have* been ignoring me for the last few years."

His face fell flat. "Now, wait just a minute. After the disaster, I called you multiple times every day. You wouldn't speak to me. You didn't come back to school. Your mother had to inform me that you were safe. I was so worried about you! And on top of that, for me to ignore you, that would imply that you were actively trying to get a hold of me. Is that true?"

Heat rose to my cheeks. "Yes!"

"Okay, well, I was still upset at your abandonment."

"C'mon. Abandonment? Really?" I gave him a knowing look, feeling that his terminology was a bit exaggerated.

"Okay, maybe 'abandonment' is overkill. Anyway, let's change the subject. To answer your question, I live in St. Louis now. I'm working at an engineering company there."

I was astonished at his news. Living in Missouri? I never pictured Tyler moving so far away from home. Then again, I never pictured him moving without me in tow, either.

Realizing I hadn't reacted, I said, "That's great, Tyler. Do you like it?"

"I love it. St. Louis isn't bad, either. The weather sucks, but you get used to it."

I sipped my coffee, considering both of our lives and how separate they were. We both had good jobs. We were both settled. We were both happy, without each other. The concept seemed unfamiliar. Tyler had been so much a part of my life for so long. For him to succeed without me meant he didn't need me. He never needed me.

"What's wrong?" Tyler asked, noticing my despair.

I tried to look happy. "Oh nothing, I'm just surprised at how things turned out for us."

He agreed, "Yeah, I know."

"You look great," I told him, completely off subject.

He grinned, displaying his perfect white teeth. "Thanks. I finally conquered my fear of the gym when I moved and now I hit the gym about every day."

"That's great."

Suddenly becoming shy, Tyler fumbled with his fingers on the table. "You look great, too."

"Tyler, I'm drenched in sweat. I do not look great."

Staring at his hands, he countered, "Roxanne, you always look great. You would look great after running a marathon for goodness sake."

I smiled thoughtfully, "Thank you."

"You're welcome," he firmly said. "So, ever been to Missouri?"

I laughed. "Why would I *ever* go there?"

"Hey now...they have great...cows...there...and rivers, yeah, lots of big rivers." He was grinning.

"Wow, cows. And rivers. Sounds like a good time. Why would I want to miss that?"

"So, it's settled then. You're coming out to see me this summer. How does that sound?" His eyes were glowing with excitement.

Shaking my head slightly, I said, "I don't know..."

"Oh, why not? What could beat a vacation to good ol' Missouri?"

I could think of a thousand things. "How about a beach?"

"We have a beach! Granted, it surrounds a lake, but regardless, there's sand."

I didn't like how he used *we*, signifying that Missouri was his home now. No more Florida. Sadness formed within my heart.

"I guess I could swing a short visit to the Midwest."

"Yes, you *have* to *experience* the great Midwest."

I giggled, "You're crazy, you know that?"

"We're all a bit crazy, aren't we?"

He was right, more than he knew. "I guess a bit." I studied the back of my hand while I daydreamed in my head for a minute. Then I asked, "So, when do you head back?"

"Actually, I head out tomorrow." There was a distinct sorrow in his voice.

"Oh," I responded, with a tone matching his. I hadn't seen my best friend in years, yet he was leaving so soon?

"Are you sad?" With his words, he reached across the little café table and placed his hand gently on top of mine.

I shrugged. "Well, yeah, I guess so."

"You guess?"

Shaking my head, I corrected, "No, no, that's not what I meant. It's just...all of this is so surprising and I feel like my life just got settled down and...well... here you are."

"Our reunion disrupts your settling?" One of his eyebrows was raised in curiosity, searching for the underlying meaning to my words.

"Well, in a way. Life is, well, a bit more interesting now."

He smiled at that. "I'll take that as a compliment."

"You're welcome."

Sliding his hand away from mine, back to his coffee cup, Tyler stared at me admiringly. I was very accustomed to that look of his and had been somewhat immune to it in the past. Now, I found myself blushing.

His eyes shifted to my neck. "Is that what I think it is?" he asked, studying the soccer ball necklace he gave me for my 18th birthday. One corner of his lips was turned up into a grin. I could tell he was pleased with the realization.

I smiled and affirmed, "Yes, it is." I touched the cool metal with my fingertip.

"I had always wondered if you really liked it." Tyler responded, his eyes appreciative. "Now, I know."

We sipped our coffees quietly, making small, lackluster conversation.

Eventually, I asked, "What time do you leave tomorrow?"

Slowly, allowing me to take in his answer, he said, "Six in the morning."

"Wow," I remarked, trying to disguise my obvious disappointment.

"I know. I wish we had more time together."

I paused for a moment before I spoke. "Why did you wait?"

He sighed, disturbed by the question. "Wait for what?"

"Wait until the day before you left to find me?"

Tyler's smile faded and his eyes fluttered away from mine. "Roxanne..." he sighed again.

"What?" I asked, confused.

"I didn't *try* to find you. It was purely by accident."

My jaw dropped slightly, in disappointment, in embarrassment. I stiffened my face to fight back the hurt. "I thought..." mumbled from my mouth.

Reaching his hands back across the table, he held mine tightly. "But I'm so glad I did. You must understand, I was under the impression that you wanted nothing to do with me."

There was truth to his words. I made it very clear to my mom that Tyler's mother should know I was upset. He was trying to avoid me because of me.

"Hey, we'll see each other again. Very soon," he assured me.

"There's always that summer visit, right?" I offered, trying to sound cheery.

"Yes, summer. Too bad it's not closer."

"Oh, just a few months away," I breathed, "No sweat."

He smiled and repeated, "No sweat." Then Tyler scrunched his face together and added, "Well, no, that's a lie. There *is* sweat...in fact, lots of it."

I waved him off. "I live in sweat!"

Laughing, he said, "You're right. You do. You'll fit in quite nicely."

Suddenly, I blurted out, "I've missed you."

Tyler leaned closer to me over the table. "Words can't describe."

47

ROXANNE

I was pretty good with directions, but I had absolutely no idea where we were going.

This was my first time in St. Louis. In fact, this was my first time in the Midwestern part of the United States. Missouri was not my first choice of places to visit after graduation. Well, not in my top 25, really. St. Louis seemed right in the middle of nowhere. It seemed ironic that I found myself in the last place I expected to be.

Tyler was driving fast, faster than I thought was necessary. The windows were down, blowing my hair in every direction. It was a very warm day, probably 90 hot degrees. The humidity here was comforting. I almost felt at home, with the exception of the beach and the palm trees. I watched the many cars fly by us on the highway with Tyler swerving in and out of the traffic. I gripped my seat for comfort.

"Do you really have to go 85 miles an hour? Isn't the speed limit 65 here?" I asked, trying to keep my hair out of my face.

He laughed, without looking at me. I was glad he was keeping his eyes on the road. "Roxy, no one follows the speed limit here. In order to stay safe, you have to drive fast. I'm just following traffic."

He was right. No one drove 65 miles per hour on this highway. It seemed like traffic laws were not enforced here. I wasn't sure I could get used to that. My anxiety would get the best of me. Good thing I wasn't staying long.

After driving for a while, Tyler spoke. "Hey, there's our exit." Pulling into the off-ramp lane, I relaxed at the slowing speed. My hair was beginning to tame also. The tall buildings in the horizon caught my attention and I squealed. The sight of downtown St. Louis excited me. I knew St. Louis was very populated, but the idea of Missouri brought pictures of cows and grasslands into mind. I always enjoyed big city life. It was really all I knew. Ocala, Florida, was small but it wasn't like Missouri. It wasn't so bare.

"Oh, wow," I mumbled, in awe. I couldn't take my eyes off this new place.

"Just wait," Tyler promised, a smile breaking through his voice.

He turned at a few stoplights and my mouth dropped at the first large building that came into view. I recognized it immediately: Busch Stadium, Home of the Cardinals. My eyes grew wide with amazement and I stared as we passed by the gigantic arena. Even though I had watched so many games played here on television, I felt like I had never seen it before. It was so much better than on television.

Tyler reached across the cab and patted my leg. "I thought you would enjoy seeing this."

"Tyler," I began, my eyes still glued, "it's awesome. I wish it was baseball season so we could go to a game!"

His hand did not move from my leg. "I know, but the Cardinals aren't going anywhere. There's always time."

"I'll have to come back so we can go to a game. That would be so much fun." The thought of attending a Cardinals game with Tyler made me smile.

"Tons of fun, except for the fact that I don't like baseball," he chuckled.

Astounded, I turned to face him. His hand quickly retracted back to his own lap. "You still don't like baseball? And you live in St. Louis? I can't believe it."

He shrugged. "I know. I'm a horrible St. Louisan. The city'll probably kick me out eventually. But on the up side, I do drink a lot of beer, so that makes up for it."

"How?" I wondered out loud.

He grinned. "St. Louis is also home to Anheuser Busch."

"I'm not sure that makes up for not being a Cardinals fan," I laughed. I gazed around at all the different buildings that we passed as we headed south, further into the downtown area. "Where are we going?" I asked. Tyler had not told me.

"You'll see," he firmly said. The ride was quiet while I continued to admire the scenery.

Only minutes had passed when Tyler spoke again. "Alright, now close your eyes."

I glared at him. "Ah, do I have to?" My lips formed a pout.

My expression didn't faze him. "Yes, you have to. Now do it."

Unwillingly, I shut my eyelids. The brightness of the day didn't disappear through the shield. Wondering what Tyler was planning, I peeked sideways at him. "Can I look now?"

Swiftly, he covered my eyes with his hand. "Stop that! I'll tell you when," Tyler commanded, keeping his hand plastered over my vision.

When we pulled to a stop, I heard Tyler put the truck into park and turn off the ignition. He lifted his hand from my eyes. I realized that the bright sun was not there anymore, even with my lids shut. "Now?" I asked.

"Sure," he responded, opening his door.

My eyes popped open. I frowned. "We're in a parking garage?"

I heard him cackle as he slammed his door shut. I watched as he moved around the truck to my door. Opening it, his bright eyes met mine. "Very good."

Confused, I hopped out and onto the shaded cement. There were few cars around. Tyler grabbed my hand momentarily and pulled me into a direction that led to sunshine. "Come on," he prompted.

337

Following his lead, I was light on my feet in anticipation. "I can't wait to see what's going on," I told him.

He didn't respond but he did look at the ground, smiling to himself.

When the light was only feet away, he dropped my hand. We walked quietly out of the garage and I was blinded. The intense light of the sun pierced my vision, willing me to shut my eyes. Cautiously opening my lids slowly, I peered at the monument that sat standing there, much taller than the tallest building, gleaming down at the surrounding downtown area. It was magnificent.

"The Arch," I announced.

"Correct again," Tyler added. He gestured for me to follow him and then put his hands into his jean pockets.

Walking behind his steps, my eyes followed the Arch from its start to its end. The sunlight reflected off certain tiles in a beautiful way. I was never much into history, but I felt the history of St. Louis in a very real way right now.

"Is that Illinois?" I asked, pointing across the Mississippi river.

He nodded, "Yup."

Tyler led me around the Arch's left base, facing the river. He turned, walking into the middle of the area, right in between the two bases. Stopping abruptly, I stumbled into him, and he faced me. He surprised me, I was sure it read on my face. I could only smile at him.

"This," Tyler stared, looking up and using his arms to gesture toward the bend directly above us, "Is the Gateway to the West."

Awkwardly staring at him, I agreed, "Yes, yes it is."

With a sparkle in his eyes, Tyler continued, "You know what else it is?"

I made a funny face. "What's that?"

"The Gateway to my Heart." Tyler reached into his pocket and pulled out a shiny ring. I gasped. Frozen, I watched as he eased down onto one knee and held the ring out to me.

"Roxanne, I told myself that if you ever came back into my life, I would not let you leave again. After twenty years, my feelings have never changed for you. You are the same person I have always loved. With that said, you have rejected me around 53 times, but really, who's counting? I'm asking you to seriously consider my proposal before you reject me this time. And if you do decide to reject me, I will accept your wishes and I won't bother you again. Please…"

I glanced down at the beautiful ring, his hand shaking slightly beneath it. He was sweating.

He finished, "Roxanne Olivia Clarke, will you give me everything I have ever dreamed of by marrying me?"

Visions of my life flashed simultaneously through my head. Pictures of Tyler and I as children, as teenagers, as college freshmen. Thoughts of my father flooded into my mind, especially the way he considered Tyler as his own son. He would have wanted this for us. My stomach cramped. I tried not to think of the only person I had ever loved. He was not here, asking for my hand. He abandoned me. He was gone. Tyler was sitting here, asking me to love him unconditionally, just as he had all these years. I didn't understand how he could love someone that had hurt him so badly. Tyler wanted to forgive me. He didn't care about the past.

My mouth opened slightly. For a second, I thought I wouldn't be able to speak. He waited patiently for my answer, longing in his eyes. He would wait forever for my voice.

I began moving my head, up and down. Unannounced, tears trickled down my cheeks. "Yes," I breathed. "Yes, I will marry you," I spoke more loudly.

Slipping the diamond ring over my trembling finger, Tyler stood, grabbing both my hands in his own. He beamed at me. "I won't disappoint you."

Picking me up from the ground, he squeezed me tightly. I wrapped my arms around my new fiancée. Leaning in close to his ear,

I whispered, "I know." I truly believed him. He had never disappointed me.

He set me down on my feet, his eyes never leaving my face. For the first time in too long, I felt like I was actually making a good decision. Glancing around, I noticed that bystanders were watching us. Each person smiled, aware of what just happened. I was elated at the feeling. I was getting married!

48

TYLER

"Yes," she said, barely loud enough for my ears. "Yes, I will marry you."

My heart sang. I wanted to cry for joy. Sustaining my moment of internal bliss, my wobbly hand slid the diamond ring over her left ring finger, and I took both her hands in my own.

"I won't disappoint you," I promised her.

I picked Roxanne up off her feet and swung her in a circle, like a little girl. She was *my* girl. Hugging her so tightly, I was not sure I could let go. When she wrapped her arms around my neck, I finally felt like the world was spinning in the right direction. For so long my life had been incomplete, but that was all changing now.

She leaned in toward my ear and gently spoke, "I know." Her trust in me was something I treasured and would never falter in delivering to her. She knew that.

My world was now complete.

Now it included Roxanne.

49

REGAN

I slowly, slowly opened my eyes. My vision was fuzzy, as well as my mind.

The room around me was a starch white, with dim light shining from above. Small beams of sunlight shined through the partially closed plastic curtains. I had no idea where I was.

Suddenly, there was warmth on my right hand. Hazily, I swung my head to acknowledge the source. There, I saw a slightly blurry view of my twin sister, sitting sadly next to my bed, her head hanging down, eyes on the ground.

I blinked away the blurriness. "Roxanne," I barely spoke. My throat was very sore.

Quickly, she jerked her head up at the sound of my hoarse voice. Relief flooded her tired expression.

"Regan," she sighed.

"Roxanne, where am I?"

She bit her lip, nervously. I knew something was terribly wrong.

Extremely calm, my sister said, "Regan, you're in the hospital."

"I am?" *I was*? I thought.

I watched her head nod up and down.

Resting my head back against the uncomfortable pillow, I closed my eyes and breathed a heavy sigh.

Without opening my eyes, I asked reluctantly, "What happened?"

"Sweetie, you were hit by a car."

A car? I don't remember anything...

Another thought briefly crossed my mind. My sister has *never* called me sweetie. Things must really be bad.

"How? What?" I couldn't form coherent questions.

"You were riding your bike across Broadview and a car ran the light..."

I gulped, tears forming in the corner of my closed eyes. "How did I survive?"

A short silence, then Roxanne spoke, "I don't know. What I want to know is why in the world were you exercising? You know how bad that is for you."

Noting the sarcasm in her voice, I opened my eyes and forced a smile.

"I'll remember that next time."

She rubbed my hand gently, so gently as if not to hurt me.

Another question came to mind. "How long have I been in the hospital?"

"A few days..."

"And this is the first time I've been awake?"

Roxanne started patting my hand. I took that as a yes.

Her shaky voice pierced the stiffness in the hospital room. "Regan, I was so scared."

"When you heard about the accident?" I assumed.

"No, when I saw you."

"What do you mean?" I asked, confused.

"Regan, I saw the accident happen."

I sighed again. "You did?"

There was another pat on my hand. I realized that she might be on the verge of tears, unable to speak.

"Roxanne, it's okay. I'm okay."

I felt a strong grip. "You're not okay!" she muffled through sobs.

With all the conversation, I hadn't taken a look at my body. My mangled body. Apparently, both of my legs were broken, and were now casted. My left arm was also broken and splinted. The areas of my body I could see were bruised. As I reached over my chest with my right hand, I felt a small plastic tube escaping from beneath my left armpit where my ribs sat.

"Roxanne, what is this tube?" A hint of panic streaked my tone.

"That's a chest tube. Your lung collapsed, but the doctors say it's re-inflating. They say it should be back to normal in a few days."

"Why aren't I in pain? I look like I would be in pain."

Roxanne pointed to a tall pole next to my bed, a small box anchored to it. "Morphine," she confirmed.

"Morphine," I repeated. I wondered when it would wear off and how bad the pain would be.

"You won't feel anything," my sister said, reading my mind.

"Are you sure?" I asked, scared of the pain.

"Yes."

"Where's mom?" I suddenly wondered.

"She's at work. She needed a break. This has been extremely hard on her."

Hard on her? I thought. *How about hard on me?* I tried shaking off my arrogant thoughts. I blamed it on the morphine.

I lay there and she sat there, in silence for a little while. It was nice to have her company for once. Memories of our childhood and then our adolescence flooded my mind. Wasn't death supposed to unite a family? Instead, it broke ours apart. Roxanne and I should have been there for each other, for the long haul ahead of us. No, instead we had hated each other, wishing awful things. I could truthfully say I would have never wished this on her. Would she have wished this on me? I would like to think not, but I had only recently begun to really know her.

"Regan," Roxanne quietly said, "I have some news for you."

I wasn't sure I could handle any more news. My accident and current state was enough for a lifetime.

"Is it good news?" I needed to rightly prepare myself.

A weak smile appeared across her lips. "Yes."

I nodded. "I think I can handle good news right now."

Roxanne gingerly placed her left hand on my forearm. The light from the window glistened off of the large diamond ring that was sitting nicely on her ring finger. It didn't take long before this registered with me.

Surprised, I gripped her hand and pulled it closer, "You're engaged?"

Without a word, she nodded. For being newly engaged, Roxanne didn't look as I pictured she might. I would describe her as only partially happy.

"To who?" I asked, still examining her gorgeous ring.

"Guess," she probed, less than enthused.

"Who? *Tyler?*" I joked.

Roxanne held her weak smile. Slowly, realization sank in. I was joking, but she was not.

"You're marrying *Tyler?*" I couldn't disguise the disgust in my voice.

Her eyes turned dark. "What's wrong with that?" She was offended.

I rested my head back, unsure of what to say, unsure of how to explain, where to begin.

"Regan!" she screeched.

I briefly closed my eyes, sighed, and then opened them again. Roxanne's face was turning a slight shade of pink, whether out of embarrassment or anger, I couldn't tell.

"Roxanne, don't marry him."

"Well, why not?"

"First of all, you don't love him," I reminded her.

"And secondly?" she added, annoyed.

"Can we address the first reason?"

Leaning back in her visitor chair, she folded her arms across her chest and turned her head away from me.

"You don't love him, do you?"

Roxanne mumbled, "I love him."

"No, you don't."

Fiercely, she countered, "You don't even really know me! How would you know who I love?"

"Although we weren't friends for half of our lives, I'm not stupid. As much as you don't want to admit it right now, you don't love him, you never have, and you never will. Roxanne, you cannot force yourself to love someone!" My throat was starting to really burn.

She huffed. There was no rebuttal, just disgruntled noise. I was right, and she knew it.

"How long have you been dating?" I asked.

"You're just jealous," she barely muttered under her breath.

My eyes widened. Raising my voice, though it hurt, I said, "Excuse me?"

"You heard me." She still wouldn't look me in the eye.

"Well, I guess that brings me to my next point."

My statement piqued her interest, not in a positive way.

"There is another reason you shouldn't marry him..."

"Yeah, you're jealous. I can see that now."

I cleared my burning throat. "Roxanne, you don't really know Tyler."

"What do you mean? Tyler is my best friend."

I nodded. "Yes, yes, of course he was. But you never really *knew* him."

She was starting to really get angry.

I hesitantly added, "Not like I knew him."

Her eyebrows furrowed at me. At that moment, I thought I might die right there in the hospital bed. Fortunately, I unfroze my tongue and continued.

"Roxanne, please calm down. You need to hear this."

She paused in her movements, as if getting ready to pounce. I silently prayed.

"Roxanne, Tyler and I...you need to know that...we sort of...had a *thing*."

Only her lips moved. "A *thing*?"

I carefully nodded. "Nothing serious...just fun, you know. You wouldn't...so I..."

"How long?" she said through grinding teeth.

I was afraid to speak, but I was more afraid of what would happen if I didn't. "Off and on for years, I guess."

"When did it start?"

I slightly shrugged, which sent a surge of pain through my left arm.

"When!" she insisted.

"Probably since we were fourteen...after dad died...it was nothing, Roxanne."

"If it were nothing, you wouldn't be bringing it up now, now would you?"

She had a point. "I wanted you to know."

The skin on her face loosened measurably. "Oh, how *nice* of you. All these years, stealing my best friend away from me when I'm not looking to do who-knows-what! I don't even want to know!"

"Roxanne—"

"No, I do want to know. What did you do to him?"

I shook my head. I knew she didn't really want to know the details.

"What did you do to him?"

"You mean, what did he do to me?"

347

She quickly reached across the bed and I closed my eyes. I was fear-stricken. Nothing happened, though. Cautiously I peeked at her. She was facing out of the half-open window.

"Roxanne, we never...you know...like I said, nothing serious. Why do you think I'm telling you all this? Because after all these years, he hasn't been honest with you."

Without facing me, she said, "Neither have you."

"But I had an excuse. Why do you think I did it? Because I *liked* him? No! It was to get back at you. Believe me, I planned on using this against you for my own benefit. Instead, I'm trying to save you from making a huge mistake!"

Roxanne was quiet for a very long time. Eventually she sat down. I was going to wait for her to speak before I said anything else. She needed time. This was big news.

I closed my eyes, waiting.

After awhile, I felt a hand on mine. Upon opening my eyes, I realized it was not my sister, but instead my mother. Roxanne had left the room. I honestly wondered if I would ever see her again.

50

TYLER

I lay wide-awake, though it was almost two in the morning.

I couldn't manage to sleep with Roxanne next to me, crying out Luke's name every ten minutes. Many late nights and early mornings I would stare at our bedroom ceiling, wanting to cry but knowing I couldn't. I didn't want Roxanne to know that I heard her, because I'm not sure she even knew it herself.

Turning onto my side, away from her and toward the window, I quietly sighed. Her nightmares had been plaguing me for weeks. After the engagement, she decided to stay in St. Louis at my apartment for the summer. I was excited for her to move in, but now I regretted the decision. I loved Roxanne, but night after night, a small piece of me was dying.

Sometimes I would remove myself and sleep for a few hours in the living room, silently returning to bed before dawn. Sometimes I would put a pillow over my ears to drown out the noise. Sometimes I wanted to put the pillow over my face.

Roxanne hadn't told me the story about what happened between her and Luke. I couldn't imagine it being that terrible. As much as I didn't want to admit it, he seemed decent enough. She wasn't the kind of girl to stay in a bad situation. She was smarter than that. Had he cheated on her? Or worse, abused her? I shuddered at the thought. Against my hopes, there was also a chance she was stricken with grief about losing him, no matter what actually happened. The thought made me very sad.

Roxanne's happiness was constantly on my mind. I traveled to work each and every day with her in my thoughts. She appeared content enough here, but not truly happy. I tried to communicate with her about any apprehensions, but she didn't mention anything in particular. I tried to convince myself that she was just adjusting to her new home and the idea of getting married. Of course, my introduction back into her life was fairly fast and with the proposal came many new changes.

We had decided that it was best for me to move back to Central Florida, where it would be easier for me to obtain a job than her moving to Missouri. Additionally, she was extremely happy with her position as head soccer coach at her old high school. I didn't want to take that away from her.

I closed my eyes as I heard her mumble his name, again. *When would it stop?* I thought. I wasn't sure how long I could handle the torture.

Many nights, like this one, I thought about whether Roxanne made the right choice in saying yes to marrying me. I undoubtedly loved her and wanted to make her my wife, but she had been less than enthusiastic about the wedding since her temporary move to the Midwest. Was marrying me just an attempt at being normal for her? I wouldn't ask her, for the fear that my theories were in fact right. I just got her back and I didn't want to lose her.

Though, I had to be realistic. Living in an unsatisfying marriage would not end well. I honestly didn't know what to do.

I was trying to be everything Roxanne wanted. But, truthfully, I couldn't say whether that was enough. Maybe I would never live up to her standards. I would never be Luke, if that was what she desired.

Closing my eyes, I concentrated on clearing my mind. Hopefully the groaning would halt.

I awoke with a start, hitting the alarm clock. Thankfully, I had been able to fall back asleep. Rolling onto my back, I realized Roxanne was not next to me. Getting up, I turned on the bedroom light. I trudged over to the closet and recognized her missing running shoes.

I pulled work clothes out of my side of the closet. In my dresser drawer, I searched for dress socks, but found only one. Since Roxanne did the laundry, I assumed the sock might have ended up in her drawer. Rummaging through her undergarments, I regrettably did not find the missing sock, but did find something else.

My eyebrows furrowed as I stared at the folded letter with her name on it.

Slowly unfolding the paper, I began reading.

My heart sunk as I read the words on the page.

Out loud, I mumbled,

My dearest Roxanne,

As I read this passage day after day,

I think of nothing but you.

I don't know if you understand

the intensity of my feelings, but you will.

I can't stop thinking about you.

And if we are ever to separate,

know that we will meet again.

For my feelings are eternal

and my love is everlasting.

Lucio

My fingers pressed over the scribbled writing, trying desperately to understand why my fiancée would be holding onto this letter.

It was obvious she was clutching something. She was clinging to memories of Luke.

Suddenly, I heard the front door open and shut. "Tyler? You up?" Roxanne called from the kitchen.

I quietly shoved the letter into my pocket. Heading into the kitchen, I tried to mask my underlying anger. The letter's words continuously ran through my mind.

Roxanne opened the refrigerator. I stood across the kitchen from her, leaning against the counter. Rubbing my forehead, I contemplated what to do.

"How'd you sleep?" she asked, cheerily.

"Not well at all," I said, trying to keep my voice steady.

"Oh," she responded, continuing to search for food.

"How'd you sleep?" I asked her, warily, curious as to her answer.

She shrugged, without turning around. "Fine, I guess."

"Well, we both know that's not true."

Roxanne turned to face me. "What do you mean?"

"Are you cheating on me?" I asked, stern and serious.

She laughed. "Are you kidding?"

I shook my head. Out of my pocket, I pulled the letter. Handing it to her, I could see the shock on her face.

"Luke," I offered.

"Tyler," she began, grudgingly taking the letter from my hand, "Luke is...Luke is gone. I'm not cheating on you."

I glared at her. "Roxanne, infidelity isn't only physical."

She stared at the letter beneath her fingers, appearing speechless.

"Well?" I asked, "Do you have anything to say?"

Slowly, her head shook side to side. I wanted to scream.

"Nothing?" I sharply probed. "Nothing at all?"

Roxanne lifted her eyes to meet mine. They were filled with sorrow. I wanted to scream even more.

"You have a voice, now speak!" I shouted.

Meekly, she mumbled, "I...I...don't know what to tell you. It's not what it seems."

"If it's not what it seems, then what is it?"

After a long pause, "You're right. I shouldn't have this." And with that, she ripped the letter up—though obviously with hesitation—and threw it in the trashcan. Her actions did not retract any of the anger I felt.

"Well, that's great, Roxanne. But why did you have it in the first place? It's painfully obvious you still have feelings for the guy." There were so many more questions I had mustered inside, but I wasn't sure it was the right time.

Aggressively, she answered, "Tyler, I don't know! I don't know anything, anymore."

"What are you saying?"

"I'm saying I don't know!"

"Roxanne, your options are simple. You either want to be with me or you don't." My heart moved into my throat with my last words. I wanted her to choose me.

"I do want to be with you," she replied hastily.

"Really? Because I don't want to be jerked around. I've waited close to 20 years for you. My heart is vulnerable to you. You hold the power, right now. I will try to make this work as best I can. But I want to know you're in it 120%."

Silence filled the space between us. I hated the silence. She wasn't proving her case of her love for me with silence. Deafening silence.

Lowering her eyes and her voice, she started mumbling again. I only caught one muttered word. "Whatever."

"Whatever!" I yelled. "What is your problem?"

When she lifted her eyes, hatred pulsed through. "How can you say you have been waiting for me for 20 years when you have been fondling my sister since our freshman year of high school!"

I gulped. *How did she know?* I wasn't expecting this turn of events.

"Who told you that?" I asked, trying to appear unconcerned.

"Who do you think?"

"And you believe everything she says?"

"Maybe not normally, but she was practically lying on her death bed in the hospital. Why would she choose to tell me that of all things?"

I rolled my eyes. "Roxanne, she has a few broken bones and a bruised lung. Give it a rest."

"No, I won't give it a rest! She's my sister. My *twin* sister." She folded her arms across her chest in opposition.

"So, she gets in an accident and now you two are best buddies again. And now you believe some bull she's feeding you about me."

"Sometimes it takes a life-changing event for a person to really appreciate family. And right now, I'd believe her over anything you say."

I sighed loudly, clearly irritated. "Fine, believe everything she says. I don't care." I stomped back into the bedroom, threw a mismatched sock onto my bare foot, grabbed my suit jacket and slipped into my shoes.

As I headed back into the living room, shoving my arms into my jacket, I said to her, "We'll discuss this later."

"Yeah, right," she said absently in my general direction as I motioned toward the door.

"I'm serious." The last glimpse I got of my fiancée was one of her staring into the trashcan. It took all the strength I could gather to keeping walking out of the apartment. Instead, I slammed the door so hard I heard a picture fall off the wall and shatter on the ground. I didn't care.

Work was extremely taxing. Not because of the actual workload, but because I couldn't focus. All I could think about was Roxanne. I knew I was wrong. I shouldn't have lied to her about what Regan had told her. Of course it was my fault.

I tried phoning Roxanne throughout the day, but as expected, she didn't answer. I knew I wasn't her favorite person right now, and I could accept that. I should never have gotten involved with Regan. The temptation was too strong to overcome...but I should have done it anyway.

I had convinced myself that Roxanne and I would work our problems out. We were even now, the way I saw it. She had messed up by keeping the letter and I had messed up with Regan. Yes, we were even now. Surely that would make our transition to peace smoother.

As soon as the clock struck five, I was out the door and into my car. What an unproductive day, in every aspect of my life. Pulling into the apartment complex, I realized Roxanne's SUV was nowhere in sight. The absence didn't settle well with me.

I opened the door to our apartment. "Roxanne?"

No answer.

"Honey?" I tried again, to no avail.

I spotted an irregularity in the living room. On the coffee table sat an open book. As I approached, the text looked more familiar. It was the Bible. Picking up the leather-bound book with my hands, I stared at the pages, 1 Corinthians. Oddly, a page had been ripped out. I didn't have much time or care to decipher what it meant, so I closed the book and set it back down on the table.

Tossing my jacket over the couch, I trudged into the kitchen. My eye spotted a white sheet of paper on the counter. Curiously, I picked it up.

It read: "Just be honest. If we can't be honest with each other, then what can we be? I need time to think. I've taken my things. I'm staying in a hotel until I can fly back to FL. I'm sorry. —R"

I slumped to the kitchen floor, sobbing loudly into my hands.

It took me several minutes to pull myself together. Without much thought, I rose from the ground and pulled open the top cabinet above my head. Grabbing two large bottles of alcohol, I considered retrieving a glass but decided that would be pointless.

An hour later, two empty bottles sat ironically on the coffee table next to the Bible. In a drunken stupor, I decided that I wasn't going to let Roxanne leave that easily. Absentmindedly, I ambled loosely to the bathroom to splash some water on my face. My wet reflection in the mirror slightly startled me, but I didn't care.

Heading back into the living room toward the front door, I grabbed my car keys and slammed the door shut behind me, not remembering if I locked it and not caring.

I couldn't think clearly enough to formulate any kind of plan or mode of action, but I was desperate. I would go to every hotel in the surrounding area and win her back. She was the love of my life. I couldn't let her go! I would do whatever she wanted. I couldn't lose her.

Driving sloppily down the road, I hazily tried to think where some of the hotels were. Grabbing my phone from the passenger seat, I began dialing Roxanne's number, praying she would answer. As I dialed the last number in the sequence, I accidentally dropped it down below my feet. Cursing, I struggled to grab it but couldn't find it. Peering my head down into the darkened space beneath my legs, I spotted the phone. Before I could bring my eyes back to the road, a loud crashing sound filled the air. My body was jerked around, my head hitting the steering wheel. I felt the truck ease backward; smoke was pouring out from the front of my hood.

I stumbled out of the truck, unsure of what had just unfolded. My head was throbbing, blood dripping from my nose. As I focused my vision, I recognized the bright yellow Xterra wrapped around the front of my truck. The driver was slumped over the steering wheel, as still as a statue.

Distantly, I could hear her moaning his name. I thought of her strained voice as I stared absentmindedly at the bland walls.

"Please rise," the officer announced.

We rose.

Behind me, my mother. My only support now.

The large man in black appeared from a side door. He sat down. We all sat down.

"The verdict," the man in black said sternly, turning to face the jury panel of my peers.

I stood then, awaiting my fate.

A woman representing the jury stood.

"We, the jury, unanimously find Tyler Christopher Hansen *guilty* of first-degree manslaughter of Roxanne Olivia Clarke and driving while intoxicated..."

I couldn't listen to the rest. It didn't matter anymore.

I pleaded guilty. Her death was inadvertently my fault. If I had just been honest with her, told her the truth; she would be alive right now. If I hadn't gotten drunk and tried to get her to take me back; she would be alive right now. If I had just shoved that dumb letter back into that drawer; she would be alive right now.

As the man in grey led me away, I heard my mother sob loudly, screaming. On the other side of the aisle, I found Regan. Her sister was dead because of me. Although she had a hand in Roxanne's death, I didn't blame her. I was the murderer.

Next to her, her mother Rebecca and my father. Rebecca and my *father*. Why weren't my parents sitting together, supporting me side by side? My father couldn't have a criminal for a son. He would support Roxanne's family and mourn with them. He wouldn't mourn for me.

My world was winding down around me.

With each step I took, I recounted the events that led to that very moment.

I found Roxanne's hidden letter from Luke, which made me furious. Then, when I learned that Regan had told Roxanne about our past together, I knew nothing good would come of it. I didn't know how long she had known about the secret. Roxanne would be upset with me after finding out, I knew. The one and only person I ever loved and would ever love would feel betrayed. And then, the accident...

My life was over. It had begun with Roxanne and it would end with her. I was no one without my best friend.

51

TYLER

A loud *thump* woke me up.

With my eyes wide and heart pounding, I stared around, realizing I was still in my apartment. Two empty bottles of liquor sat on the coffee table in front of me. I pushed them onto the floor. Drool was slathered across my hand as well as the pillow I curled up to. The picture I broke earlier was still shattered on the ground.

Sitting upright, I let my head fall into my hands and quietly sobbed at the nightmares that flooded my thoughts. The idea of losing Roxanne crushed me. I knew as soon as I could talk with her, I would make the situation right. I would be completely honest about my relationship with Regan. I didn't care about Luke anymore, I just wanted Roxanne to trust me.

A strange rap at the door startled me. I peered toward the noise, wondering who would be at the door and considered not moving.

Then, another sound. The sound of a voice. Standing, I walked to the door, unlashed the lock, and opened it. To my surprise, Roxanne was sitting on the welcome mat with her legs crossed.

"Roxanne?" I asked, overwhelmed at the sight of her.

She peeked up at me, tears strolling down her face. I helped her to her feet and pulled her into a tight embrace. I couldn't stop my own tears from flowing. We quietly wept together in our doorway.

Holding her face at an arm's length, I smiled, "I've never been so happy to see you. I was sure I had lost you."

I grabbed her hand and led her into the apartment, shutting the door behind us. Turning, I stopped suddenly and knelt onto one knee. Her hand was nestled in mine. I closed my eyes briefly.

When I opened them, I recognized the most beautiful girl I had ever laid eyes on. More tears trickled down my cheek. Taking a deep breath, I let out an exhausted sigh. "I will do whatever it takes to keep you happy. I will honestly answer any question you have for me. I will tell you anything and everything you want to know. I will go wherever you want to go."

I paused to stifle a whimper. Finally, I squeezed her hand and added, "But I can't lose you."

Roxanne smiled, kneeling beside me. "I'll tell you everything. I want for us to be honest with each other. I don't want to lose you, either."

52

ROXANNE

As Tyler held me close, I recalled the drive I took trying to keep my mind off of him.

Tyler had plagued my thoughts but Luke had plagued my heart.

In the passenger seat sat one single page from the Bible that Tyler owned. I glanced at it every few seconds.

I had found out that my new fiancée had been somewhat unfaithful in the past, with my own twin sister. Yes, it was true we weren't dating at the time, but I called it unfaithful because he never told me. We were best friends and I never knew he was messing around with my sister. That must say something about my attentiveness. How did I not notice? Was it my fault?

In addition, Tyler caught me with the letter Luke had given me so many years ago. It was the only physical proof of his existence. Nightmares of the last day I saw Luke, as well as about my father's plane accident, inundated my sleep most nights.

Daily, I tried to force my thoughts away from Luke, but I didn't have the will power. In my head, I would constantly retrace my short history with him, the stages of our time together. Initially, I denied Luke's good intentions toward me. Then, anger followed as he kept inserting himself into my private life. Eventually, I was bargaining my relationship with Tyler for my relationship with Luke. Once I found out Luke's purpose in my life, and recognized the reality of the situation, I dove into a deep depression. Though it took years, ultimately I was able to find solace and accept that he was gone and wasn't coming back. I accepted that I needed to move on with my life. My newfound acceptance held for quite some time, until Tyler proposed.

Since my sister's confession, I had seriously doubted my commitment to Tyler. I didn't know if I loved Tyler. I knew I wanted to love him. Well, before I found out his secret. What if there were more? More secrets? Could I handle it? I wasn't sure I was really handling the one secret I knew about. And now I was seriously regretting being intimate with him. I had just assumed that was my life's course and believed I had to accept it. Maybe I was wrong.

How could Tyler truly love me and want me as his wife if he wasn't going to be honest with me? Would he have kept quiet through our whole marriage? Would I have found out on his deathbed? On my own? I couldn't help but ask myself the same questions with regard to Luke.

Maybe I was overreacting, but it was hard to convince myself that I was. To another person, Tyler's actions might be forgivable. But Tyler was my *best friend*. I had hated my sister and he knew that. He could have chosen to date anyone, be with and do anything with anyone, but why *my sister*? Did he not know this would kill me? Apparently he thought I would never know.

How could I trust and be with someone who once told me he loved me, yet behind my back was kissing and fondling my sister? My evil sister!

Yes, she would do this to me. But not my *best friend*. Not *Tyler*.

Then, I had a slight epiphany. Maybe Tyler was right. What if Regan was lying? What if Tyler never did any of the things she claimed he did? Why would I trust my sister over my best friend and fiancée? I couldn't trust her, even if she was broken at the moment. I couldn't trust her, even if she were dying.

I tried to block out any thoughts. I didn't know what to do. Who to trust? Abruptly, I had an overwhelming yearning for Luke and his soothing touch. This frustrated me, in addition to all the anger I had built up over Tyler. I just wanted to go home.

My SUV was approaching a stop sign. Suddenly, only one emotion gripped me. I missed Tyler. I missed who we used to be, before all the drama that college brought. Tyler had messed up, yes, but so had I. Our partnership severely lacked communication, but this could be fixed. Our love was worth fixing.

Slamming on the brakes, I made a quick u-turn and headed back toward the apartment.

In that moment, I decided I was finally done running.

EPILOGUE

LUKE

She was happy.

Her happiness was all that mattered to me. I knew Tyler would take good care of her.

Unfortunately, I couldn't warn her of what was coming.

Soon enough, Tyler would need a guardian angel of his own.

Though earth and moon were gone,
And suns and universes ceased to be,
And Thou wert left alone,
Every existence would exist in Thee.
There is not room for Death,
Nor atom that his might could render void:
Thou - Thou art Being and Breath,
And what Thou art may never be destroyed.

Emily Bronte
No Coward Soul is Mine

The Stages of Grief were originally developed by Elisabeth Kübler-Ross and are outlined in her book, *On Death and Dying*[1]. According to her website[2], the stages comprise a "model," an experience that is not liner but rather a framework of an individual's emotional journey in an attempt to reach acceptance. These very stages helped map the emotional journey Roxanne took after the death of her father.

[1]Kübler-Ross, E. *On Death and Dying*. Macmillan. New York. 1969.

[2]Five Stages of Grief. EKR Foundation. http://www.ekrfoundation.org/five-stages-of-grief/

Acknowledgments

All the glory and praise I give to my Father God. Without Him, nothing would be possible.

Thanks to Andi, my wonderful husband and best friend for letting me continuously chase my dreams.

Thanks to my beautiful mother for always believing in me and showing unconditional love in my times of most need. And to my brothers, Mike and Andy, for your love and annoyance throughout the years.

To all of my nieces and nephews, I hope I can help you chase your dreams some day, too.

Thanks to all my good friends that have supported me in this endeavor and to those that read my book when it was just words on many 8.5 x 11 inch papers in a 3-ring binder with sticky notes EVERYWHERE with your editorial comments. I can't begin to express how much it meant to me.

Thanks to my editor, Marta Ferguson, who helped put on the finishing touches to make Stages what you see before you.

A big thanks to my fury children, Rocky and Zena, who have spent many an hour cuddled up at my feet while I pecked away at my laptop.

And lastly, thanks to all the musical artists who helped inspire each and every chapter, including: Dashboard Confessional, Evanescence, Pink, Ting Tings, David Archuleta, Colbie Caillat, Jet, All-American Rejects, Rihanna, Jimmy Eat World, Madonna, Rooney, Gabriella Cilmi, Matchbox 20, Dave Matthews Band, Cyndi Lauper, Alesana, Paramore, Mat Kearney, The Script, Metro Station, White Tie Affair, Parachute, Keane, Blue October, Nickelback, The Calling, The Rolling Stones, U2, Adele, FlyLeaf, Judy Garland, NeedToBreathe, Rob Thomas, and Linkin Park.